THE UNRAVELING

THE UNRAVELING

QUINTIN VARGAS

ISBN: 9781733702843

CAST OF CHARACTERS

ABRAHAM EPSTEIN: cardiologist living in Skokie, IL and Miró's father

ALESSANDRO: Corsican bodyguard and valet for Rodrigo

ANGELO CALABRESE: retired FBI/CIA agent, former college roommate of Ram Edmunds

BRUCE JONES: Chicago real estate agent

CHICHO: Corsican driver employed at Rodrigo's safe house

DAVID MATTEL: American expatriate living in Mazatlán

DIEGO MONTEMAYOR: botanist, biochemist, and European drug lord

DONALD WRIGHT: American expatriate living in Mazatlán

DR. IVO WU: Expert plastic surgeon

EDUARDO SÁNCHEZ: Chief Inspector of Las Palmas PD, Canary Islands

EMILY FARNSWORTH: administrative assistant of Dr. Nate Shelley (from Chicago)

ESTEVAN CHENGFU: former business associate of Rodrigo Díaz and now his consiglieri

EUGENE & DORIS KEMPBALL: grandparents of Max Kempball living in Three Rivers, TX

FEDERICO: Corsican chef and sommelier employed by Rodrigo

GABRIEL PICARD: Deputy Secretary General of Interpol and friend of Inspector Sánchez

HORACE (ROSIE) ROSENBERG: Chicago Tribune reporter

ISABELLA: Corsican attendant employed by Rodrigo

JACOBY HOMELY: Deputy Director of the FBI

LIONEL FINN: Evanston PD detective

LUCAS WILLIAMS: driver employed by Rodrigo Díaz

MALCOLM BORTONI: Canadian expatriate living in Mazatlán

MARK YUEJONG: Nanotechnology guru

MAXIMILLIAN (MAX) KEMPBALL: PI from Austin, TX and Miró's half-brother

MINERVA (MINNIE) EPSTEIN-SHELLEY: Miró's thirteen-year-old daughter (Nate's stepdaughter)

MIRIAM EPSTEIN: retired pediatrician from Skokie, IL and Miró's mother

MIROSLAVA (MIRÓ) EPSTEIN-SHELLEY: university professor and wife of Nate Shelley

NATHANIEL (NATE) SHELLEY: psychoanalyst and amateur sleuth living in Evanston, IL

OLIVIA KEMPBALL: deceased mother of Max Kempball

PEDRO AND MACARIO ROSALES: Twins from Chicago involved with drug cartels

RAM EDMUNDS: Special FBI Agent in charge of Chicago field office

RODDY & EUNICE BLOOMINGTON: British expatriates living in Mazatlán

RODRIGO DÍAZ: emergent drug lord living in Mazatlán, MX

RUDOLPH VON STEINER: portrait artist, WWII war hero, and friend of Max's grandfather

SPENCER PENROSE: British expatriate living in Mazatlán

TÍO DANTE: former friend and executive vice president of Diego Montemayor's empire

PART ONE

PART ONE

CHAPTER 1

MAX

Evanston, IL · September 22, 2019

NATE REFUSED TO BELIEVE the phone call. Hesitant to call the police, he called me, his wife's half-brother, instead.

"What did the caller say? Exact words," I said.

"It was brief, four sentences... I've been over the words... studied them... a dozen times.' Robot-like, Nate recited them: "'Hello, my friend. Your wife Miró is being held at the Orrington Hotel, near the Northwestern University campus.' Some coughing, then, 'She's in room #125 with a man who's armed. He's a killer.'"

"And this dude, he didn't demand money, you're sure? No threats?"

"No, Max, he simply ended the call. Nothing else."

"And the voice, can you describe it?"

"Aging male voice, raspy—maybe a smoker's cough. Slightly accented. English is probably his second language."

. . .

Maximillian Kempball, that's my name. I'm a private investigator from Austin, Texas. Right now, though, I'm in the Chicago North Shore area. My sister, who lives in Evanston with her family, disappeared. Just like that: bam, Miró disappeared. A rising star university professor, happily married, and a loving mother. Why would she simply walk out of her office and not come back? I'm not saying that I know Miró well. In fact, I know diddly about her. But people who know her consider her a 'responsible professional'. To her secretary—executive assistant, whatever—the whole thing was unusual. The way she left her university office on Tuesday afternoon at exactly 4:30 PM without giving instructions. Nothing about where she'd be or when she'd be back.

When my brother-in-law received the 'call from hell' (that's how Nate referred to it), I'd been in Chicagoland for three days. I'd been staying with my dad and his wife, Miriam. In this short time, I'd come to realize that Nate is a straight-up loving husband and stepfather. He doesn't trust the police with his family's safety, though.

When he called me instead of the police, Nate sounded frightened. I told him I'd drive him to the Orrington Hotel, where Miró was being held. The chill outside brought on by a sudden drizzle caused me to grab a sweater on the way out. Before heading out to Nate's, though, I stopped at a coffee shop close to the university campus.

As I drove up to Nate and Miró's home in Evanston, I heard Nate call out to his stepdaughter, "Tell your grandparents we'll be back soon, Minnie." Golden leaves were raining on Nate's front porch, and the fresh smell of pine cones invigorated my senses. He stepped out the doorway and immediately stuffed his hands in his coat pockets. I could tell he felt the chill blowing in from the lake. The heavy mist, which activated my rental's wipers, soaked the pine needles on the two firs of the picket-fenced front yard. Nate zipped up his blue windbreaker. Per Nate, Minnie's grandparents had arrived five minutes earlier, just in time to keep their thirteen-year-old granddaughter company.

"Okay, Nate, hop in. I called the cops, and they're on their way. They may be there already. Sit tight and tell me again. What exactly did the caller say?"

"Look—regarding his exact words—I'm certain." Nate bit his lip.

"I know y'all—shrinks—are precise about what you hear. I don't mean to doubt you. Just making sure."

"What baffles me is why he'd call? You think it's a trap for me... us?"

"Doubtful. This dude, he guessed you'd call the police... Besides, even perps can behave honorably."

Though I'd been told it was too early in the fall for wearing wool, I pulled up my winter sweater collar. The distraction caused me to slow down. I came to a full stop at a traffic light, and almost spilled my steaming Starbucks drink. "This traffic is unbelievable. Is it always like this?"

A driver in the next lane leaned on his horn. I must've swerved onto his lane.

Nate didn't answer. He seemed deep in thought. So, I shut up and let him think.

· · ·

Just three days ago, I was in my Austin apartment, A/C cranked up, when I got the call from my old man. It was the morning after my half-sister disappeared. He seemed beside himself. He practically begged me to find Miró. I remember protesting, "Dad, I hardly know Miró. And, her husband, Nate, I've never met him. Not even sure he's interested in meeting me."

"Exactly. So why should you consider this different from any other case? I can be a client who's hired you to find a sister you hardly know. Besides, you won't have any lodging or travel expenses. I'll handle that."

I flew to Chicago later that day.

That's how I got involved. From the beginning, it felt wrong. Miró had disappeared, and no one had heard from her. Not her husband, her daughter, no one.

· · ·

We continued driving on the slick streets in complete silence. Minutes later, Nate muttered something about the police getting to the Orrington Hotel before us. He said he was worried about Miró's safety.

I turned to reassure my passenger, "Miró's fine. You'll see." I took another sip of my Starbucks. The robust taste of the Gold Coast brew warmed my bones.

"Just keep your eyes on the traffic. I'd like to get there alive, Max."

Approaching the corner of Elgin Road and Orrington, we spotted five patrol cars blocking a large section of the hotel's front entrance. The bright lights of the first responders' vehicles illuminated the fine rain, which seemed to be getting heavier. Their flashing blue and red lights announced to gawkers that an Evanston PD investigation was in progress. An ambulance was also at the scene.

Numerous snoopers used umbrellas. They stopped, seemingly paralyzed in eager anticipation. A young woman pushing a twin baby stroller zipped its plastic cover to witness the scene. She tightened her hoodie around her face. A middle-aged man wearing a raincoat and a fedora also stood in the crowd. Though it was overcast, he sported sunglasses. Two smiling dudes without umbrellas were dressed in black, light jackets, racing shorts, and hoodies. They held on to their bikes and stood in the middle of the small crowd. Probably Middle Eastern or Hispanic, they both snickered as our car slowed to a stop. The bikers, they captured the scene on their cell phones. I noticed other curious onlookers also video recording the activity. Some people, regardless of their ethnicity, act like jerks when they're at a crime scene.

In my best impersonation of a NASCAR driver pausing at the pit, I applied my brakes and in a fluid motion raced out of the car. I jogged to where Finn, Nate's 'favorite detective', was standing. Two joggers in purple and white jogging sweats almost tripped me as I rushed into the hotel entrance. As much as I enjoy the brisk autumn smells of pine cones, it felt good to get indoors and out of the cold. Finn saw me and waved us into the open corridor of the hotel. Several policemen and emergency medical personnel rushed about the hallway. Finn led us to the room identified by the caller... room 125.

Scrambling behind me, Nate's face lit up when he saw Miró... alive. Ramming past the moving uniforms, he froze when he spotted Miró sitting on an armless chair by a king-sized bed. The room was larger than the average guest room. It was decorated in what I assumed were the nearby university colors, purple and white. The art on the wall displayed sketches of university buildings and campus scenes.

Though a luggage rack was by the side of the bed, no suitcases were visible. A large yellow umbrella leaned against the far corner of the room. The only item on the dresser was what appeared to be an Apple cell phone charger.

Miró was answering police questions, but she looked dazed and unsteady. Her large, caramel-colored eyes, they darted around the room. Startled to see Nate, she jumped and rushed to him. Sobbing, she said, "Oh, Nate, thank God you're here!" Her exact words. Then, she threw her arms around him.

On the far side of the bed lay a stranger, and he appeared to be dead. He, like Miró, was fully dressed in day clothes.

Mechanically, Nate's arms reached for Miró. She buried her face in Nate's cradling embrace. Wiping her face with the back of her hand, she added, "I knew you'd come."

As Nate started to pull away, Miró clasped his wet elbows and drew him closer. She tried to nuzzle again, but stopped. Miró examined Nate's face as she dusted off an invisible speck of dust from his windbreaker. I noticed a distant look on Nate's face, and perhaps Miró also saw it. Though he held his clinch, Nate remained quiet. He was still looking at the stranger lying on the bed.

Miró paused to escape the awkward moment, and I noticed she whispered to Nate with an inquisitive look in my direction. I don't think she recognized me. Nate turned to me, and addressing Miró, he stated, "Your brother Max from Austin joined us to help find you, my love. He's been very helpful."

As the coroner removed the body from the bed, Detective Finn picked up the yellow umbrella and put it back against the far wall. I noticed he was not wearing an investigator's blue gloves. He walked over to Nate and Miró and interrupted the embrace. When he attempted to remove my sister from the scene, Nate squared his shoulders and glared at Finn. The detective acknowledged the look, and explained that—with Nate's permission—he'd be leading Miró to an adjoining room where he could continue his interrogation. On his way, he turned to Nate and asked, "Is this the first time?"

"First time for what exactly, Detective?"

Finn responded with a pause and an expression of sympathy—more like pity. "You know... the first time she's been gone... for days?" He had a half-grin on his face.

Miró removed her arm from Finn's grip. "What is that supposed to mean, Detective?"

Even in her unkempt condition, my sister's beauty was unmistakable, evident to everyone in the room. Her wild, chestnut hair gave her a disheveled look, almost sultry and seductive. It was that kind of careless, unplanned attitude worn by women who are confident about their physical appearance. Nate, on the other hand, carried himself differently. Though also unconcerned about his appearance, the dude's plain looks could've used some attention to detail.

Barely within hearing distance, the other police officers were now standing around drinking coffee provided by the hotel manager. The aroma of freshly brewed French roast filled the room. They smirked and waited for Nate's reply. By now, Nate had probably lost his concentration. The distant look in his eyes was gone. He deflected and quickly responded, "I won't dignify your interrogation with a response, Detective."

My hunch is that Nate understood their reactions. Hard-boiled cops—and PIs like me—see it every day. Cheating spouses who get caught in compromising situations frequently play the victims.

It was more than a hunch; Nate could certainly understand the cops' reactions. In the last few days, I'd detected a couple of 'tells' in Nate. Like poor poker players who change their behavior when they get a bad hand, Nate bit his lower lip when he felt uncertain or threatened. Also, his right eye twitched twice in quick succession and, often, his knees appeared to buckle during stressful situations. If my observations were accurate, Nate was failing the emotional test badly. He was playing into the hands of the cynical cops around him. His legs turned to jelly. Fortunately, he clung to Miró and removed her from Finn's side. He asked for a few seconds with his wife and forced her to sit next to him on the bed. It showed everyone in the room firm support for Miró.

I'm not the expert, but my guess is that Nate simply thought of nothing else to do. The renowned psychoanalyst was probably humiliated, scared, and thinking he was cuckolded. More than likely feeling impotent, Nate regarded the smirks on the cops' faces as entirely justified.

"I came as quickly as I could," Nate said, trying to recover. "Max and I are here with you, my love. Everything will be fine. Are you hurt?"

"No, no. I'm perfectly fine. I love you for being here," Miró said.

CHAPTER TWO

MAX WONDERED HOW HE'D ended up working this case. He was 'out of his element'. He didn't know the Midwest, the people, the culture, and least of all, the half-sister he'd met only once or twice. Not until he graduated from high school did he even learn he had a sibling. His mom had said that Max's father was a surgeon of some kind, living in South Texas. This estranged father was married and had a daughter younger than Max, by three or four years. That half-sister was now missing.

"Abraham is not a bad guy," Olivia Kempball, Max's mom, had said back then. "He was just not ready for a family. Neither was I, for that matter. Anyway," she said, "he wants to attend your high school graduation." That was more than two decades ago, and now Max was in the Chicago metropolitan area trying to find this virtual stranger, his sister, Professor Miró Epstein-Shelley.

Earlier that fateful Sunday morning when Miró was found, she woke up not knowing where she was. When Nate and Max arrived, the police and hotel manager were in Miró's room. EMS personnel were also there. Miró had no idea, no memory of the previous few days. In a rush, the hotel manager accommodated Detective Finn's request for an adjoining room.

The slightly rotund and authoritative detective had taken the hotel manager aside to demand full cooperation. "I want absolute privacy to interrogate my 'suspect' in a separate room," Finn had told the Orrington Hotel's general manager. When Finn shuffled back in for Miró, in a surge of magnanimity, he informed Nate and Max they could wait there while he completed his interrogation in the adjacent room.

Curiously, Finn referred to the 'scene of the crime' and repeated the phrase several times. To Nate and Max, it was unclear if the detective considered Miró's kidnapping or the death of the stranger as 'the crime'.

Meanwhile, Max and Nate speculated that Finn and his men might be uncertain about the cause of death. Perhaps, the coroner would need to perform an autopsy on the dead man before determining cause of death. And, since Miró was the only other person in the room, Finn might be ensuring that Miró could be cleared of any implications or suspicions.

"Of course, the coroner might decide the man died of natural causes," Nate said. "Surely, the detective must also consider that, right?"

"Or, the man could've died of an overdose, a self-inflicted wound, or some other cause," Max added.

Both men second-guessed each other for the next few moments.

"Of course," Nate said, "none of those indications appear to be the case right now." Nate seemed to be asking a question, rather than making a statement.

"That's exactly right," Max said.

The next few minutes were uneventful. Max jotted down some questions he'd like to ask Miró. And, Nate fidgeted, changing positions in his seat, searching on his iPhone's internet for updates on the developing story which was being covered by a couple of Chicago news reporters. Cameras were still rolling. Oddly, the rain outside had ceased as abruptly as it began.

Finn took his time interrogating Miró. He walked out of the adjoining room a couple of times to retrieve several cups of coffee. Nate, on the other hand, appreciated having a few moments away from the stares of Finn's men, who were dismissed by Finn until further notice.

After several minutes, Finn left the 'interrogation room', as he called it. He stated, "My men have collected all forensic evidence and taken proper procedures to ensure there will be no further tampering. However, refrain from touching anything unnecessarily."

"We haven't moved, Detective. Don't worry, no tampering going on," Nate said.

"Nonetheless, I thought I should warn you about the importance of a tightly managed investigation. Rest assured that my men and I will find the answers we need. This case will soon be resolved." Without another word, Finn returned to his interrogation room.

After Finn's lengthy interview, Max demanded a few minutes with Miró. Reluctantly, Finn gave him 'just five minutes'. Max wasted no time. But before taking his phone and notebook, Max removed his wool sweater. With trusted phone-recorder in hand, he began questioning his half-sister.

Miró was still groggy, but she was trying to cooperate. "Like I told Finn, Max, I woke up lying on my side, and the first thing I saw was my cell phone on the nightstand lit up with unread texts—countless ones. And I was in this unfamiliar bed. I was afraid to move. Without turning over, I reached to the opposite side of the bed, and felt a body—I knew it was the man I'd met at Café Ba-Ba-Reeba."

"The what again?" Max asked.

"It's a popular restaurant in Lincoln Park," Miró said.

Max still did not have his bearings in Chicagoland. Lincoln Park could have been anywhere in the vast area, but he took notes carefully and recorded every word. His research would follow.

"Okay. Now, you said that without turning over, you reached to the opposite side of the bed and knew it was the same dude who kidnapped you. How?"

"From what I could recognize. I felt his silk shirt and this huge metal belt buckle. I'd noticed it when I joined him at the restaurant."

"And this dude, you met him there because… ?"

"He threatened to take Minnie if I didn't do as he said. That's why I left my office in a hurry."

"Go on."

"I jumped out of bed and saw him staring blankly at the ceiling. It was still early with twilight coming in from the windows," Miró said.

"Were the drapes drawn?"

"Yes, almost completely as the police found them this morning... He wasn't moving. I turned away. While I stood there on my side of the bed, I reached across and used my phone to nudge him. I was so horrified... I think I had my eyes closed. Nothing... he was stiff, dead. I froze. I couldn't think of anything to do... Max, why am I being interrogated like this?"

Max explained, "The police probably believe you killed him, Miró."

Max was tempted to add that he thought Finn was a jerk and an inept investigator, but he held his tongue. *En boca cerrada, no entran moscas* was a saying he had just learned from his old man, Abraham. Roughly translated, it meant, 'A closed mouth gathers no flies.'

"That's ridiculous. I'm the victim here, remember? I was kidnapped!"

Max asked, "Could he have spiked your drink, or did you inhale anything? Please try to remember. It'll be crucial."

"Probably," Miró said. "At the restaurant, he was sitting at a table when I came in."

"Already there when you joined him at the restaurant," Max took notes.

"Yes. He ordered a Bellini for me, which I refused to drink. He didn't talk much, and I bombarded him with questions. I was upset and told him to stay away from my family. His only reaction was to grin and reassure me that Minnie would be fine—if I followed instructions."

"This dude, had you met him before?"

"I'm certain I had not," Miró said. "I would've remembered him."

"Why do you say that?"

"Because he had this sinister grin and a persistent cough. I must admit, though, he was not offensive in his actions nor his speech. Not ill-spoken, or anything... Oh, and he also had some gold teeth. His smile reminded me of that evil character in the old 007 movies."

"Sinister. Anything else?"

"Well, he was tall, fit, quite muscular, in his fifties, maybe? Could've been a former athlete. Like I said, he expressed himself quite well, with an extensive vocabulary. He was probably as tall as you, Max, but at least thirty pounds heavier. He was built like a professional wrestler."

Though his biological father was not a short man, Max Kempball had inherited his height from his maternal grandfather and that side of the family. At 5'11", Abraham was the tallest in his family. However, all Kempball males measured more than six feet. In fact, Max had reached his full height at seventeen when he was listed as 6'3" in his high school basketball roster.

Max's notes indicated the perp was over six feet tall.

"An accent?"

"Yes, a slight one. Obviously, Spanish was his first language, and it was impeccable. And his English was fluid."

In underlined letters, Max noted in his pad that the perp was probably Hispanic, but tall. He used three exclamation marks at the end of his sentence.

"Okay, walk me through your initial meeting with him."

"Like I said, I dominated the first ten minutes of the conversation. A waitperson came by twice to ask for our order, and I sent her away. He said very little, but he was polite... to prying ears, a perfect gentleman. Even reassured me about Minnie and the rest of our family. He knew all about Nate, my dad, and my mom. Then he excused himself to use the men's room."

"Hold on. You're saying he left you alone at the table?"

"Yes, he did. But when he came back to the table, he approached me from behind and gently cupped a hand over my face. Before losing consciousness, I remember the server who had waited on us helping this man walk me to a strange car. Everything is blank after that. Then, I wake up in this strange hotel room with a man in my bed... a dead one at that."

Though Max could see that Miró was tired, he pressed on. "You said earlier when you tried to move him, he was unresponsive and that you didn't know what to do."

"Yes, Max."

"Then what?"

"Then, I tried to call Nate, but the call went to voicemail."

"I know Finn probably asked, but I need to be clear. How were you dressed? Did you have clothes on?"

"Yes! Yes. I was wearing what I have on right now... the same clothes I had on at work—on Tuesday... what was it, Tuesday or Wednesday?"

"You left work Tuesday afternoon."

Max's notes stated: 'Same clothes she was wearing Tuesday, black slacks, white silk shirt, and smart auburn jacket'. The jacket was the only item of clothing still hanging in the adjacent room's closet.

Silence from Miró.

"And you're certain you've never seen him before? Previously I asked, but I've been hired by... by Dad... to help."

"Max, I understand. Nate mentioned how much you've done. He told me you've been far better than the local authorities."

Max smiled, but he still insisted, "Anything else you can remember?"

"That's about it, but I'm curious to know what you think happened to me."

"I think that a form of strychnine powder was used to partially paralyze you. This powder form has been turning up in our country, after first reappearing in Europe."

"I'm familiar with it," Miró said. "Isn't it commonly used as a date-rape drug?"

"Not often, 'cause it's still expensive. Strychnine was first used as a pesticide, and it can be deadly. It must've been a variation of the drug. Lab results, they'll indicate exactly what you had in your system. The drug obviously incapacitated your muscles within seconds. I'm sure you were unable to walk. You probably had no control of your limbs, nor your speech."

"Hmm." Squinting, Miró became pensive and appeared distracted. Miró's eyes were the color of her hair and jacket. The gold flecks circling her irises glistened because her eyes were tearing.

Max continued, "The thing is that the effects of the drug—if it's been modified by pharmacists—normally are short-lived and last for a few hours. But you were unconscious for several days."

"Mm hmm..." Miró again squinted. "So, do you think that I was raped or somehow molested while I was..."

"That doesn't seem to be the case, but again, we must wait on the medical and lab results. Miró, the reason I need to know details is that... something doesn't fit."

"For instance?"

"Well, the dead man on the bed—I know he was wearing clothes like the ones worn by the dude at the restaurant, but... I'm unsure it's the same person that abducted you."

"What?"

"Finn told me that you described the person at the restaurant being approximately 6'2", olive complexion, and straight black hair. I know that may describe the corpse found in your bed."

"Well, then, what 'doesn't fit', Max?"

"You said that the man who kidnapped you was in his fifties. From what I saw, the man the coroner took away, he's older."

"I'm terrible at judging ages," Miró said. "I could've been mistaken about his age."

"In addition, although I don't think it was the cause of death, I bet the dead man will also show strychnine in his system. Lab results will let us know."

"That's strange," Miró said. "Why do you believe that?"

"I noticed some powder residue on the corpse's nostrils," said Max.

"Hmm." It didn't seem that Miró could fathom the complications.

"Talking to Nate, he's convinced there's a connection with the perps in the Canary Islands. He told me about your spending time in a Spanish jail during your stay there."

"The nightmare three years ago?"

"Yes."

While Finn gathered his men, Nate and Max sat with Miró. Nate could see the darkness take control of Miró. Following her session with Max, a dread that didn't fit the self-assured, university professor that he'd come to know came upon her. Nate didn't know what went through her mind, but her facial expression, her posture, her eyes in particular— which darted from side to side—showed raw fear, all the same signals Nate had seen in many patients. Her shoulders drooped. And her normally steady, even conversation became a stammering and disjointed account of previous events.

Miró repeated to Finn and Max that she'd received mysterious email communications and photo attachments. She explained that a telephone call warned her not to contact the authorities nor share a single thing with anyone. But, most importantly, she described how fearful she was for Minnie's safety.

"But not once," Miró told Nate, "did they mention any connection to the Canary Islands."

. . .

With thumbs locked on his suspenders, Finn sauntered back into the room, two uniforms in tow. He announced that he didn't have any updates from the coroner, so he couldn't 'ascertain' the cause of death. He went on to say that he had some 'ideas'.

"Would you mind sharing those ideas, Detective?" Nate asked.

"I can tell you this, I will not be making any arrests... today," Finn said. Again, he smirked with half his face.

"Well, that's very useful to know," said Max as he stood up to leave.

The detective cleared his throat loudly. Although he did not detain Miró, with as much authority as he could muster, Finn announced he'd like to interrogate her further at the station house about the death of her 'bed partner'.

Nate's face visibly reddened. "You make one more slanderous statement about my wife, Detective, and I will have you in court before you complete this investigation." Miró and Max instinctively reached for Nate and led him toward the door. "You have no basis for detaining her, and you know it, Finn." Nate had his final say before being shuffled out the door by Miró.

"Furthermore," said Max as he led Nate to the door, "since you have not determined cause of death here, Finn, you can only *ascertain* a woman's disappearance. That happens to be Miró Epstein-Shelley."

"As soon as we hear from the coroner," Finn said, "you'll be hearing from us, cowboy."

. . .

As Max escorted Nate and Miró out to his rental car, which was surprisingly still parked at the hotel's main entrance, most of the crowd had dispersed. The young woman with the twins was now at the curb boarding an old yellow Volvo; she and the babies sat in the back seat. The bikers in black hoodies had disappeared, and the man wearing the fedora was hailing a taxicab by the side of the hotel.

Although the rain had dissipated, a cool breeze blowing in from the northeast and fast-moving dark clouds suggested the possibility of oncoming storms. Nate hurried around the rental Cherokee SUV to open the front passenger door for Miró to get in. He almost bumped into the same joggers wearing purple and white sweat suits. They were headed back the way they came.

CHAPTER 3

Mazatlán, MX · Late September, 2019

AZATLÁN IS A HIDDEN treasure in the western coast of Mexico. A beach resort town, it is bordered by a mountain range on the east and the Pacific coast on the west. Like other charming spots throughout the world, it was the colonial architecture that first attracted many foreign travelers and writers, who decided to move in and begin their own burgeoning communities. Of course, the ideal weather conditions also contributed to the appeal, beckoning vacationers to return to the friendly environment during the entire year, and many of them chose to stay. It gave the town a reputation for being a jewel to be discovered by retirees needing a place to spend their retirement funds.

Throughout the last several decades, many such micro-communities in Mazatlán have come and gone. Some have passed on, and others continue to thrive with new arrivals from colder climates. As most of these fraternities do, the repatriated arrivals in Mazatlán formed small groups of people with shared interests who preferred to spend time together. They tended to be sociable, friendly, and not entirely exclusive. It was not unheard of for original Mazatlán locals to join the inner circles, although it tended to be uncommon.

The most important aspect for the survival of such micro-communities is the need to be informed. That is the purpose for inner circles. Insiders must know the goings-on of the larger community. And, when questionable issues arise, it is the responsibility of these self-appointed civic leaders to demystify such enigmas.

The arrival of the Airbus A380 in the newly constructed private landing strip by a large compound on the eastern outskirts of Mazatlán deepened an emerging mystery for all in the retirement community. Early most mornings, the locals, both originals and repatriated ones, gathered in the coffee shops and bars where they enjoyed their pastries and cappuccinos. After a round or two at the Marina Mazatlán golf course, they later congregated at some local bars to continue their speculations. Each member of the clique had his theory regarding the most recent arrival living in that palatial and obscenely extravagant hacienda.

The most popular town gossip, Spencer Penrose, who'd spent thirty years working for British Airways, said that rumors back home had anonymously confirmed that the recent addition to their established community of retirees was a wealthy investor from the French Riviera. Chatting with Roddy Bloomington at Rico's Café, over a simple breakfast of pastries and coffee, they'd decided that the 'detached' stranger was either a rich investor or banker.

"Donald mentioned that the compound is surrounded by sixteen-foot walls and miles of barbed wire," Penrose said.

Donald Wright, who'd served in Vietnam, was one of the few who'd met their neighbor living at the western edge of Lookout Mountain. Twice he'd driven his jeep to the hacienda, but he was unable to even have a glimpse of the mystery man.

"Through sheer serendipity," Wright said, "shortly after he arrived in Mazatlán, the stranger, accompanied by a beautiful young brunette, wandered down to the commercial district for a quick drink at Edgar's Bar and later stopped at the tobacco shop in search of Cuban cigars. There, I met our neighbor. He acknowledged my welcome and even shook my hand."

Wright then, pausing for effect, lamented that the close-mouthed enigma of a neighbor 'refused to disclose his name'. Drinking margaritas at Edgar's Bar with Penrose, Bloomington joined them in formulating scenarios involving the stranger's past, his country of origin, and the secrets he certainly kept.

Roddy Bloomington, a novelist and world traveler, described him as 'cryptic' and 'enigmatic' and 'inscrutable'. The three recognized that though most repatriates had their own secret pasts, the Mediterranean-looking mystery man concealed his identity with unusual intrigue and guardedness.

Although none of the men had visited the inside of the picturesque hacienda at the edge of the mountains, Malcolm Bortoni, the real estate agent who made the sale, informed them that the purchaser was a trust in the name of some executor in Geneva.

"The hacienda," Bortoni said, "not only has every convenience imaginable, but it is being renovated as we speak." He went on to say that all negotiations were made through the beautiful brunette, who also failed to share her own name. She, however, had verbally slipped once and referred to her boss as 'Rodrigo'.

The three men continued to debate good-naturedly the potential identity and origin of the neighbor, but they all agreed that their small community of retirees had become a much more fascinating place since the arrival of the mysterious stranger.

. . .

In time, they began to call him 'Rodrigo' as the brunette had called him once. And, for convenience, they also concluded that he must be either Italian or French. Lanky, olive complected, and with an obviously Roman profile, the stranger continued to baffle the growing circle of repatriates who added juicy bits of information to every discussion they had at their meetings. Whether over coffee or margaritas, each had a hypothesis to hone.

The debates revolved around the frequent use of the Airbus and the arrivals of smaller private planes at all hours of day or night. Some reported the arrival and departure of groups of children, mostly young girls of preteen and early teenage years. This fueled new speculations that their neighbor might oversee a large charity for orphans.

Whatever the case, the stranger's private runways seemed to have more traffic than the local airport. Having an opposite effect, the frequent sightings of armed guards at the gated entrances to the hacienda generated less-generous rumors and speculations about the nature of Rodrigo's undercover work.

David Mattel, who owned a fleet of helicopters for tourist sightseeing, was a helpful informer for the quizzical circle of retirees. He'd served as a chopper pilot in Nam and now enjoyed his semi-retirement tremendously. He reported to the group of gossips that often, in his flights over the compound, he would observe Rodrigo's daily routine. The man habitually included an early morning regimen of tai chi. Later in the day, he spent his time growing an assortment of plants and testing what appeared to be flamethrowers—"You know, like the World War II weapons". He also apparently had a large collection of animals from the surrounding mountain range 'all in cages'.

"One day during a particularly low flight pattern," Mattel said, "I waved at him, and immediately his armed guards shot several times in my direction."

"You mean he actually tried to shoot you down?" Spencer Penrose asked, horrified.

"No, I believe they were merely warning shots, but that's the last time I attempt something like that," the amiable Mattel said.

Early on a late September morning, one of Rodrigo's assistants who made the shopping runs at the deli and fruit markets, bumped into Mrs. Roddy Bloomington, a chatty and friendly woman, who directly asked Rodrigo's assistant about his boss.

"What sort of business is he in?" the plump lady asked, holding her wide-brimmed hat to keep it from being blown away by the early sea breeze. "And, where, pray tell me, is he from?" As she stood there, the taciturn assistant turned and walked away.

"This absolutely boorish and unbelievably rude man completely ignored me—without a word, he simply left me standing there... without saying a word... me, with a smile on my face and an extended hand which had greeted him." Eunice Bloomington had never encountered "such a vile human being," she said. "I believe he was of Chinese extraction."

Eunice Bloomington did not realize at the time that Rodrigo's assistant had been born mute. Although he was blessed with the gift of hearing, the rest of his siblings had been born deaf and mute.

CHAPTER 4

MAX

L IKE I SAID, MY old man called the morning after
Miró's disappearance. "Your sister's in danger."
That's all he said. "Your sister's in danger."

He seldom called me. My old man and I had grown
apart. When he moved to Chicago with his wife, Miriam,
we lost touch. I suppose it was mostly my fault. At first, he
and Miriam were busy with the move. Her starting her new
practice in Chicago, and all. Plus, he started teaching at
Northwestern. At first we spoke every couple of weeks. Then,
hardly ever. Only around Christmas, maybe. And birthdays,
his and mine.

He tried. I tried. For maybe fifteen years we tried. For
a brief time, my biological dad and I got to know each other.
First time I went to visit after his move, he picked me up
at O'Hare. We talked all the way to his home in Skokie.
Interrupted each other and laughed a lot. Then, we got home
and the conversation got spotty, as if we'd run out of things
to say.

Don't get me wrong. It had nothing to do with my stepmom. Miriam, she's cool. We get along fine. It's just that Abraham and I have grown apart. Don't have much in common. Thing is, I grew up thinking I was an orphan. My mom told me from early on that my father had suffered from a terminal condition when she met him. And, that he'd died soon after I was born. Later—much later—maybe when I turned seventeen, she told me the truth. That the terminal malady was lust. And, that my old man was alive. She admitted that during their first year in college they'd fallen in lust and conceived me. It was terminal, she said, "It'll get him sooner or later. But," and this one got me by the short hairs, "it'll get you too if you let it. Never, ever, mistake it for the real thing." So I've remained a bachelor, afraid to make the same mistake.

. . .

The first couple of days in Chicagoland, I felt like I was in over my head. Nothing fit. Not me, not the string of events, not even the way that Nate suspected some international thugs getting involved. What did I know about international crime?

The next few days, I realized that the local cops were even less prepared than me. After my dad and Nate reported Miró missing, the cops just sat on the case. They were clueless. The investigating detectives got involved *after* I flew into Chicago. Three whole days after Miró was reported missing, detectives took a serious interest.

My dad helped me find my footing. We reviewed the details of the Iberian nightmare that took place in the Canary Islands. He explained why Nate had reason to suspect them. Nonetheless, Dad reassured me about my own skills and the years of experience I'd had dealing with common criminals.

"People are people, Max. Whether good or bad, whether Midwesterners or Europeans, we all share common faults. Criminals, like law-abiding citizens, make mistakes."

"I don't feel like I'm in my element, that's all, Dad."

"That's why I love to read Conan Doyle," he said. "His medical expertise helped him write those fascinating exploits of his fictitious Holmes. He and his sidekick, Dr. Watson, always solved their cases by identifying the mistakes. Those oversights will get you."

"You're right, Dad," I said,

"In most respects, your job is no different from mine," Abraham said. "Where then, do we start?"

"At the beginning," I said.

"You got it, Max. We must begin with what we know."

"Thanks, Dad, I'll take it from here," I said. I rushed upstairs, and began taking notes. I wrote hurriedly, and I made several drafts. The substance of my reflections led to a clarity of mind, unlike any I'd had since arriving in Chicago.

Miró left work late afternoon on a Tuesday. That night she didn't return. No calls. No texts. No communication. When she failed to come home that evening, Abraham and Miró's hubby, Nate, contacted the authorities, but it was obvious the cops weren't interested. Any adult gone for less than forty-eight hours is not considered 'missing', not by them, that is. Most cases involving absent spouses, they assume to be the result of 'marital discord'.

When a uniformed cop showed up at Nate's home that first night, he went through a standard questioning. Disinterested, he merely went through the motions to file a report on a married woman who'd left home. His questions for Nate consisted of, "Were you arguing? Has she been upset? When was your last fight? Has she left the house for extended periods before?" This cop, he proceeded to ask Minerva, my thirteen-year-old niece, "Do your mom and stepdad fight a lot?" Per my niece, the policeman seemed 'bored out of his mind'.

So, my old man, Abraham, he wakes up the following morning—on Wednesday—and convinces me to fly to Chicago. Immediately after arriving, I made some calls. Local hospitals. The morgue. Checked out eateries and coffee shops around my sister's university campus. Came up blank. Even secured campus security videos. Miró had walked to her university parking space and driven out of the parking garage in a hurry. But getting the city to hand over traffic footage without a warrant was, of course, impossible. Local cops, unfortunately, had failed to check traffic videos and security cameras.

On Friday, the Chicagoland minions of the law finally showed interest. Well, curiosity, more than interest. They returned to Nate's home for a second visit. Nate answered the doorbell and received Chicago's finest at the door. That's when we all met Finn for the first time.

"You realize that in missing cases the first forty-eight hours are crucial?" Though I was in the study, I could hear the loud, nasal voice of the officer in charge, Lionel Finn. "After that, chances of locating a missing person—alive, that is—are dismal to bleak." Finn, this detective in charge, oozed 'prodigious tact', as a friend back home is fond of saying.

When Abraham and Nate told Finn that his own department had ignored the case until the forty-eight-hour period had elapsed, he just shrugged. Shaking his head, he grinned and mumbled, "Yeah, leave it to the bureaucrats." Per Nate, he was oblivious to the irony.

"Where's the hired cowboy sleuth?" Finn asked them. Dad had explained to him that they'd employed a PI from Texas. "He's in the study," Nate said.

I heard Finn shuffling into the hallway. "So, Mr. Investigator from Texas, have you solved this disappearance?" Finn ambled in, fixing his baggy pants which framed his belly. He had a stupid grin on his face. A small guy, he was forty pounds overweight, and I already disliked him. I stood up from behind the desk, towered over him, and extended my hand to shake his.

"I'm Max Kempball, and I was hired by Drs. Epstein and Shelley."

"Whoa, whoa... how many doctors are we dealing with here? Isn't the missing woman also a doctor? How many others are there?" Finn asked. He had stepped back three feet, feeling awkward looking up at me. He ambled around the study, reading and fingering the various diplomas hanging on the wall.

"Well, there's Dr. Abraham Epstein, a cardiac surgeon and father of the missing person. And, the husband is Dr. Nate Shelley, a psychiatrist. The missing person is Dr. Miroslava Epstein-Shelley, a PhD and university professor." I didn't add that she was my half-sister.

"Sheesh… quite a distinguished bunch. So, have you found anything?" Finn pretended to examine the world globe standing in the corner. He rotated the globe and left it spinning as he walked away.

"Just looking through the two desktops. Nothing jumps out," I lied.

"Well," big grin, "I'll be the judge of that." Prince of a guy, that Finn.

I'd discovered a deleted email in Miró's hard drive. It read, 'I know Minerva's schedule.' My niece is Miró's only child. The email went on to name her school, the time she boards the school bus, her teachers' names… even names of her best friends. Attached to the message were four photographs of Minnie chatting with her friends at school, returning home, and visiting with her friends at the local coffee bar. I tried to trace the email sender, but the return address was scrambled. It was done professionally. In fact, my digital search for the sender took me on a time-wasting trek throughout Europe, to South America, to Mexico, then to California. Whoever sent the email was a pro who knew how to cover his digital tracks.

CHAPTER 5

Mazatlán, MX · Early October, 2019

ODRIGO'S LAST VENTURE INTO the Mazatlán central district was filled with unpleasantness. Like previous times, everywhere he went he inspired double-takes, whispered mutterings, and inquisitive looks. A few locals offered courteous smiles and feigned indifference, but Estevan Chengfu, his bodyguard, informed him that as soon as he turned his back, the gawkers consulted each other about their latest sightings. Some individuals even followed him through a few cobblestoned alleys and furtively took photographs with their iPhones.

Although satisfied that no law enforcement agency was involved, Rodrigo was annoyed, rather than worried, by the imprudent behavior of the locals. The law enforcement officials he'd already paid off. It was the local busybodies that convinced him he could no longer saunter into a tobacco shop or business establishment without being assaulted by prying eyes and nosy scandalmongers.

Convalescing and following his personal physician's advice, Rodrigo took his constitutional walks at home. However, he enjoyed the sea breezes of the Mazatlán tourist district occasionally, especially when he could stroll barefoot on the beach. His gait was still stiff and tentative. If he attempted more than a two-mile walk, he would suffer pain and soreness in every muscle and every joint of his reconstituted limbs. Indeed, his recovery from the surgeries three months' prior had been slower than he anticipated.

Disgusted by the insufferable tittle tattlers, Rodrigo drew his iPhone from the deep pockets of his linen pants and dialed. Still barefoot with his pants rolled up, he stood a mere fifteen feet from the surf. Lucas Williams, one of his drivers, answered his call immediately.

The voice was vaguely familiar. *Of course it is*, Rodrigo reminded himself. *It's my only driver with an Australian accent.*

"Oi, boss, what can I do for you?"

"Come get us immediately, Lucas. I can't stand this place anymore." Rodrigo severed the connection.

The Carretera Internacional, the principal road going northeast from the central district, seemed to stretch for an eternity. But soon the vulgar marketplaces and shops of Mazatlán fell away and a bit of greenery appeared by the side of the road. An occasional home by the side of the road displayed colorful wisterias and bougainvillea, which brightened Rodrigo's spirits. As they approached his compound, the countryside seemed to change into a background groomed for a family portrait. He remembered several photographs of his deceased wife, frames which he proudly displayed in his European home. The memory brought a smile to his face.

Rodrigo caught Lucas, the driver, eyeing him warily in his mirror. He was probably assessing Rodrigo's mood in order to tell the rest of the staff upon arrival what to expect. When he looked at Estevan, his confidante and bodyguard, he was gazing out the window at the passing countryside.

Upon reflection, Rodrigo realized that he needed to count his blessings. Estevan had been a recent addition to his personnel. So far, he'd been impressed with his abilities and his perceptive business acumen. Although Rodrigo had met Estevan in Central America—or, was it Colombia—he learned that Estevan was born in Xinjiang, China.

When he first met Estevan, he'd entrusted him with shipping to Shanghai a valuable cargo of 'assorted goods' that Rodrigo could not specifically describe. Estevan and his father had been discreet, respectful of his privacy, and prompt in their delivery. They picked up the shipment in Lisbon, and Rodrigo's clients received their merchandise before the deadline.

Curiously, Estevan's obvious limitation of being mute had not affected the management of his father's business interests in Latin America. A polyglot, Estevan at an early age took over the international side of his father's enterprise. Although few Latinos in his line of business could interpret sign language, Estevan traveled with his own assistant wherever he went. His capable assistant—a young woman of impeccable manners, educational upbringing, and proficient in the interpretation of sign language—conducted all his business communications seamlessly and efficiently.

Obviously, Estevan had earned Rodrigo's confidence. He was trustworthy. Shortly after moving his operations to North America, Rodrigo's life had been threatened by business competitors, who feared his encroachment into 'their hemisphere's territory'. The threats were carried out on multiple occasions, nearly succeeding each time. Since Rodrigo had recently undergone several surgeries, his rivals took advantage of his weakened state. Twice he was attacked in a Mexico City private hospital, which he'd leased for himself.

Estevan, visiting his ailing friend and colleague during that fateful second attempt on Rodrigo's life, took on five ruthless assailants, who belonged to the Zetas cartel and had received American special forces training. Although two of Rodrigo's own bodyguards were killed, Estevan was unscathed, and he valiantly saved his associate's life.

Rodrigo hired Estevan on the spot. When he made the offer, Rodrigo paid dearly not only to hire Estevan, but to buy out the shipping company. To this day, although his father still ran the company in his own name, Estevan Chengfu oversaw the operation and reported to Rodrigo on the business' financial progress.

When Rodrigo asked his bodyguard where he'd learned to fight like that, Estevan responded with a written note.

'From my father who was considered a warrior.'

Rodrigo inquired in which specific war he'd served. Estevan proudly responded with another scribbled note, 'His battles were legendary. He ran the CID (Central Investigation Department) and was Mao Zedong's closest associate.'

"You mean the secret police and intelligence agency?" Rodrigo asked.

With a smile, Estevan simply nodded.

Rodrigo had earlier learned from others that after Mao's death, Estevan's father had collaborated with the Greek shipping magnate Aristotle Onassis to bring into China secret cargo in violation of the trade embargo imposed by the West.

Like his other siblings, Estevan had mastered several forms of martial arts. His father had taught all his children tai chi, not only as a defensive form of martial arts, but also for its health and meditation benefits.

CHAPTER 6

MAX

Skokie, IL · Monday, October 7,
fifteen days after Miró was found.

I'VE BEEN STAYING AT Miriam's and Dad's home. They try to make me feel welcome. Though I'm uncomfortable talking about his relationship with Mom, Abraham speaks freely and fondly of her. From our conversations, I've learned that Dad loved her 'absolutely and with conviction', as he put it. In fact, he was prepared to 'do the responsible thing' when he learned she was pregnant. Of course, knowing Mom, she wouldn't have that nonsense. My mother, when she discovered I was on the way, she cut off communication with Dad.

"I didn't want to force Abraham into marriage," Mom said many years ago. "I was as much to blame as he was. We had casual sex, and you were my wonderful consequence. Make no mistake about it, Max, you've been the greatest source of joy in my life."

So, she moved from Austin to her family's ranch back in Three Rivers, Texas. And Abraham did not hear from Mom until years later, after he had married Miriam. "Max, when I discovered she was back in Austin, Miriam and I traveled to meet with your mom. She was a different person, a staunch feminist with a chip on her shoulder."

"To the last, she had strong opinions, and she spoke her mind," I said. "When she passed two years ago, her last words to me were, 'Never mistake lust for love'."

"She told us—Miriam and me—that she didn't need our concern, our gifts, nor our communication."

"On numerous occasions," Miriam said, "Abrám sent your mom funds for your education, Max. Each time, she sent our money back."

"'I'd like to be part of my son's life,' your dad told her. 'And, we'd like to provide for his education.'"

Per Abraham, Mom simply smiled and said, "No, thanks. I'm perfectly able to provide for my boy."

"For years, I kept on trying, Max, even after we had Miró."

"She never told me, Dad. She said you'd died after I was born."

"Later," Abraham said, "much later, I found out what she'd told you. But, to her credit, Olivia had a change of heart. As you know, she let me attend your high school graduation ceremony."

Miriam quickly added, "I've never seen Abrám so thrilled, Max. He took hundreds of photographs, and he spoke of nothing else for weeks. He bragged about your scholarship to the University of Texas to anyone who'd listen."

"Your old man loves you, son," admitted a sheepish Abraham.

As I approach middle age, I've discovered I'm much like my old man. He's single-minded, stubborn, and a little too obsessive about certain things. He's an idealist or a romantic, and Mom accused me of the same. My appetite is monumental at times, but I'm blessed by a good metabolism. So is my dad.

I believe Mom's cynicism affected her spirituality. An avowed atheist, she often pointed out, "Why would a good God permit so much suffering in this world?" Somehow, it didn't rub off on me. Mom considered me her 'insufferable' idealist.

Despite such an upbringing, I became a born-again believer a few years ago. When I moved in with Dad and Miriam, I wondered if my Christian beliefs would clash with their Jewish faith. Rather than a wedge for our fragile relationship, I discovered that my faith forged a bond with them.

Though Miriam and Abraham are more orthodox than most of my Jewish acquaintances, my Christian faith is not an issue around them. When Abraham and Miriam pray, there's much in common. In fact, I tell my dad that the only difference in our beliefs is a matter of timing. While I believe that the Messiah has come, he's still waiting for Him. No deal breaker there.

During these few days, I have also gotten to know Nate. Strictly from a PI's perspective, the dude is a fine man, extremely bright and loving. He is thoughtful and considerate, sometimes to an extreme. He is a devoted husband and father. Obviously, he's an accomplished and successful psychoanalyst—a celebrity of sorts. He regularly publishes articles in major medical journals. And, for two years he's been the president of the World Psychiatric Association, which is a pretty big deal in his profession. Surprisingly, he's also somewhat tentative and overly cautious, but in a funny kind of way, he seems disgusted by his indecisiveness.

Oddly, I've come to know Abraham and Nate better than Miró. My sister has been distracted by her abduction and later by the police suspecting her of murder. For the next two weeks, Finn continued to visit Miró and Nate, supposedly to seek further clarification of her 'disappearance', as he preferred to call it.

Though we continued to pressure for a more aggressive investigation regarding the kidnapping and the identity of the dead man in Miró's hotel room, the local investigation slowed down to a crawl... no, more of a stagnation.

Contrary to her family's advice, Miró returned to her university office to regroup and 'seek a semblance of normalcy'. She returned to her office to discover that her colleagues did not know how to react to her return. All of them expressed relief and were welcoming, but they politely refrained from asking for details. The Tribune had splashed details of her disappearance, but the newspaper only sketchily reported on the male victim discovered at the hotel in Miró's hotel room. Rumors abounded.

Meanwhile, Finn and his men still refuse to share information about the stranger's mysterious death at the Orrington Hotel. When asked about the coroner's report, Finn says results were 'inconclusive'.

"What does that mean, Finn?" I continually ask.

"That, exactly, cowboy. Not even the Feds can figure it out."

"Let me get this straight, Finn," I said when I visited his office. "I saw you taking fingerprints of the dead man before he was taken from the Orrington Hotel. You mentioned twice that dental examinations took place, both locally and by the dental examiner sent by the Feds. You even said that DNA samples were being taken because of the challenges they were facing. Considering the vast information, surely there must be some clue about his identity."

"Look, Max, I'm giving you everything I know. Now, let me do my job."

I called several colleagues back home to pick their brains. I came up blank, since no one picked up. I left voicemails and asked for call-backs. Although I was frustrated, I knew Nate and Miró were even more so. I dropped by to see Rosie, my reporter friend at the Chicago Tribune. A receptionist at the entrance to the reporters' pit told me he was out, but that he'd reach out to me upon return.

She leaned across her desk and whispered, "I'll tell you in confidence, Mr. Kempball, that Mr. Rosenfeld mentioned something about an 'important update' he had for you."

I left the Tribune offices hopeful for some good news. Arriving mid-afternoon at my upstairs 'home office' in Skokie, I transcribed my voice recordings-to-self so I could organize my thoughts. Without a single lead, I felt stymied. Useless.

Abraham arrived home unusually early, minutes after 6 PM. He followed his ritual of changing into his 'comfies', as he called them. He then walked into the living room, where I waited. I told him I needed to pick his brain.

"Go ahead."

"Finn cannot ID the dead man yet. Worse, he still does not have cause of death. Now, I know many consider the state of Texas as being backward, ignorant, and somewhat country. I regularly pick up on that. Listening to network news outlets, snide remarks frequently suggest it. However, I've never experienced anything like this back in Austin. Once law enforcement gets a coroner's report, some definitive statements can be made to the public."

"Son, do you know which evidence was collected on the spot?"

"Yes, Dad. In fact, Finn himself took fingerprints. He claims a thorough dental examination was made and matched with state and national data. Today, he stated that DNA samples are being examined from organ tissues taken during the autopsy."

"And...?"

"Zero, zilch, nada," I said.

Dad retrieved his leather journal. "Max, I know we're desperate for information, especially given Finn's veiled accusations against Miró. But we must remember that DNA results can take up to eight weeks."

"Okay, so what about the fingerprints, the dental records? Usually, that's all it takes."

"Yes, unless our national database cannot come up with a match," Abraham said. "If an individual has not been fingerprinted in the past, fingerprints will be useless. A match will be nonexistent. Same thing with dental records."

"Dad, what are the odds that a fifty-year-old in this country would not have had dental work, or even had a dental cleaning? And, I think this dude was older than that."

"Granted, son. You must admit, though, it's possible."

"Okay, Dad, I agree it's possible. The National Crime Information Center, however, they file X-rays, dental records, everything. Every time you get a cleaning, Forensic Odontology requires a code to be filed with the government. They may not file the entire X-ray, but the actual X-ray can be recovered by use of the code. And that code will trace your identity. Isn't that true?"

"Not to burst your bubble," Dad said, "but recently the reliability of dental records is now questioned. Bite mark comparisons are doubtful. Almost sixty-five percent are false identifications, and forensic odontologists are being taken to task."

"I didn't know that, Dad. So, reliability of these data is out the window?"

"I'm afraid so."

CHAPTER 7

Evanston, IL · October 18, 2019

NATE CANCELED ALL HIS appointments and called a family meeting at his home to discuss strategy. Miriam Epstein, however, volunteered to pick up her granddaughter after school since Miró chose to bury herself in her university duties. Max and Abraham joined Nate in his home office. Because it had become apparent that they could not expect cooperation from the Evanston PD, Nate suggested they take the investigation into their own hands. He further acknowledged that his behavior might have contributed to the adversarial relationship with the local authorities.

"To be clear," Nate said, "Max and I believe that Finn, the detective in charge, is not only convinced of foul play in the death of the kidnapper, but he's hinting that Miró is responsible for the 'murder'. No longer is the initial crime of kidnapping his central concern. Now, he's focused on the kidnapper's death."

Abraham got up from his easy chair to take his black leather journal from the mantel. Pen in hand, he told Nate,

"Yes, Max has explained most of it. I agree that to clear Miró of this suspicion, we must take aggressive steps."

"I'm glad you agree."

"Do you believe that we're reliving the Iberian fiasco here in our own country?"

"It feels that way."

"What we need is the lawyer you found in Spain—this high-priced dude, what's his name—Lacrosse, Lacroe?" Max asked.

"His name is Carlos Lacroa," Nate said. "Yes, we could use his skills and his team of investigators… no offense intended, Max."

"Of course not. None taken. In a case like this one, I can use as much help as I can get. I'd gladly move out of the way, if I thought it would help."

"This will take a team effort," Abraham said. "And, both Max and I are up to the challenge, Nate. And, if I can add, the ladies in our family, including Minnie, can also be enormous help."

"As far as next steps are concerned," Nate said, "I believe that you, Max, must communicate with the authorities in the Canary Islands. More specifically, I want you to pick the brain of Chief Inspector Sánchez of the Las Palmas police force. I'll pay for your trip."

"Remind me again. You're referring to the investigator, this ol' dude that cracked the case when you and Miró were suspected of murder. Am I right?"

"That's right."

"Didn't I hear from the Tribune reporter that he was also related to a drug trafficker?" Max asked.

"Not exactly. His goddaughter was married to the drug lord. The chief inspector was related through his goddaughter's marriage."

"Ahem… could I chime in?" Abraham asked. "I may not be trained in law enforcement or police investigations, but it seems to me that you, Nate, are convinced that this involves the same criminals responsible for our problems in the Canaries three years ago. Far be it from me to dispute the matter, but there's no evidence that there's a connection."

"I agree with Dad," said Max. "First, the authorities still don't know the cause of death. And, secondly, they can't even ID the dead man."

"So, you two don't agree there's a connection?" Nate asked.

There was a long pause. "Maybe if you explain to us the reasons why you see a connection," said Max.

"Miró and I have discussed this. Max, you said the kidnapper used a powdery substance—perhaps strychnine."

"I did mention that to Miró," said Max. "At the time, I didn't know that the perps in the Canary Islands had used that same drug to kidnap Minnie. But, let's be clear, I was just guessing. Finn and his men have not even confirmed the presence of drugs… in either Miró's test results nor those of the deceased man."

"That's the frustrating part," Nate said. "Not even the press can get the local cops to share test results. Rosenfeld, the Tribune reporter, is convinced there's a cover-up."

Abraham interjected, "Again, I underscore the fact that I'm no Sherlock Holmes, but I'm certain you have additional impressions, Nate. What else tells you that the mob from the Canaries is involved?"

"The M.O. is so similar," Nate said. "The mysterious phone calls, the sophisticated use of technology to not only make contact, but also to cover their tracks... to remove evidence. Even the planting of individuals in high places to conceal evidence."

"I know the behavior of the local police, and the medical examiner's office, is incredibly incompetent and slow, but can we be convinced that there is a cover-up, as the Tribune reporter seems to think?" Abraham asked.

"Dad, I'm with Rosenberg—and with Nate—on this one," Max said.

"Uh, do you mean Rosenfeld?" Nate asked.

"Yeah, sorry. I call him 'Rosie'. For the life of me, I can't seem to get his name straight. He doesn't seem to mind; in fact, he seems to like it. He refers to me as 'Mad Max'."

Nate smiled.

"I shared this with Dad, Nate. I've never seen anything like it. I'm not saying cops back in Texas are the most competent, but taking four weeks to identify a dead man is extreme. And, per Finn, not even the federal medical examiners can determine cause of death. Something's wrong here." Max raked his longish hair with his left hand, and he typed on his laptop's keyboard using his right forefinger.

"Strategizing with Miró," Nate said, "we've wondered whether to speak to the state's Attorney General or to continue working with the press, and, perhaps involve a wider net of journalists. By that I mean, going to TV news outlets and risk antagonizing the local authorities even more."

"We're obviously here to help," Abraham said. "What I'm saying is let's not jump to conclusions."

"Are you saying we should simply wait for Finn and his men... till when?" Nate asked.

"As your father-in-law, I believe that I can also help you analyze this whole approach. But from my vantage point, we can only be certain of three things. Miró was kidnapped. We have her back safe and healthy, thank God. And, the man found at her side died."

"True. At this point, the rest is unknown," Max said.

"Not knowing the cause of death scares us," Nate said. "If the coroner comes back and declares foul play, what then? Miró cannot sleep knowing that this suspicion of murder is looming over her."

"I totally understand," Abraham said.

Nate continued. "Also, I remind you, Max, that you commented that the man the coroner took away was much older than the person Miró described as her kidnapper." Nate rose from his swivel armchair, "That, too, is frightful. Could it mean others are involved in this?"

"Nate, I was merely going on Miró's description of the kidnapper," Max said. "Remember, while at the restaurant, she was conscious for only a few minutes. She may not have had enough time to have a clear memory of the man's features."

"She remembers a man with some gold teeth," Nate said. "Did you notice gold teeth, Max?"

"I couldn't examine him, Nate. You remember how Finn refused to let us 'contaminate' forensic evidence?" Max asked.

"Wait, you two. No one told me about this dental peculiarity." Abraham also rose from his seat. He walked about, and he pointed with the journal in his hand, "That's your trump card. We force them to give us one little detail. If a forensic odontology exam was conducted, we don't even need a match of bite marks. We simply ask if the dead man had any gold teeth."

"Better still," Nate said. "We go to Rosenfeld and allow the press to ask the question. We'll apply pressure indirectly."

"I like it," Max said. "Rosie will call me later today, and I can share that piece of information. I don't think he's aware of Miró's description of the kidnapper."

Skokie, IL · October 23, 2019

Max answered the call from Horace Rosenfeld, the Chicago Tribune reporter, as he was coming downstairs to join Miriam and Abraham for dinner.

"Hello Mad Max, I heard you came by to see me. I was out digging for information on your case."

"Hey, Rosie, you called at a bad time. We're about to start dinner in a few minutes…"

Overhearing Max's conversation, Miriam flailed her arms, trying to get Max's attention.

"Hold on, Rosie. My stepmom is wanting to talk to you…"

"Mr. Rosenfeld, don't listen to Max," Miriam said. "You're not far from us. And, since I know you haven't had dinner, I'll slow-heat our plates and set an extra place for you. All I ask is that you bring your appetite. Nothing fancy, we're just having leftovers."

"Dr. Epstein, how gracious. I would never refuse an offer like that. I'll be right over," Rosenfeld said.

"Soon after we returned from the Canary Islands, Mr. Rosenfeld used to come by for dinner occasionally, Max. He came by to interview us several times while he was writing a series for the Tribune. Since he'd show up at dinnertime, we'd ask him to join us for dinner," Miriam said.

"Yeah," Abraham said, "He stretched out the series of articles just to enjoy Miriam's cooking. The poor kid would wolf everything down, and return to his desk to work for the greater part of the night."

Abraham served three wine glasses to kill time before Rosenfeld showed up. Within ten minutes, he rang the doorbell. Apologizing profusely, the young reporter sat down at the dinner table and shared his breaking news.

"Believe it or not," Rosenfeld said, breathlessly. "I think there's progress being made on Miró's case. The Feds claim that fingerprint evidence collected at the scene—at the Orrington Hotel—is getting them closer to an identification of the 'victim', as Finn continues to call him."

"Rosie, I can't understand it. I spoke to Finn today, and he didn't say a thing about that," Max said.

"I'm telling you, Max, I found it hard to believe, but when I spoke to a contact at the FBI headquarters in DC, in the strictest confidence, she shared with me the good news. Whether Finn knows about it is a different matter."

"I hate to interrupt," Miriam said, "but I'm serving dinner while we continue. Abrám, given the circumstances, will you permit us to discuss 'business' at the dinner table?"

"Absolutely. I doubt if I'll participate in the discussion, since I can't wait to start on that Tuscan chicken you prepared," Abraham said.

"Remember, everyone, that we're having leftovers," Miriam said.

"Those aromas are unbelievable," said Rosenfeld.

Abraham said grace, and immediately served the pinot noir.

Not waiting for the wine, Rosenfeld took his first bite. "Dr. Epstein, I have never tasted a better chicken dish in my life. I would gladly give up red meat if I could have this every day!"

"My Miriam is the best chef I know," Abraham said, in full agreement.

"And the pinot, is it French?" Rosenfeld asked.

"Californian, actually. Do you like it?"

"Abraham is always good at pairing his wines," Miriam said.

"Back to the breaking news," Max said. "What else does your source know?"

"It seems," Rosenfeld said, "that our locals were unable to match fingerprints to any database. But somehow, the Feds, in collaboration with international law enforcement, came up with a match."

"So," Max asked, "the fingerprint samples that Finn took of the dead man matched a known database?"

"Not sure. When I pressed my source, she said the fingerprints were found *in the hotel room.* Regardless," Rosenfeld said, "in tomorrow's early edition my findings will be printed, and it'll force Finn and his men to formulate a public response."

Miriam Epstein added, "Mr. Rosenfeld, does your source also have access to dental records of the deceased? Even if no matches can be found on international databases, whether gold teeth were present in those exams could be of great importance."

"What do you mean, Dr. Epstein?"

"My wife is referring to Miró telling Detective Finn that her abductor had gold teeth. That simple fact could be helpful, in the absence of any specific matches." Abraham paused, then asked, "Had Finn shared that with you, Mr. Rosenfeld?"

"Oddly, no," Rosenfeld said. "But you can be certain, that also will be in tomorrow's article."

October 24, 2019

As promised, the early edition of the newspaper included several blunt criticisms of local law enforcement, especially the inability to identify the corpse found during the 'celebrated case of Professor Miró Epstein-Shelley's kidnapping'. The article went on to question the medical examiner's uncertainty related to cause of death. 'Going into the sixth week of dithering, the local police, as well as the medical examiner's office, cannot determine cause of death. Either the perpetrator of that sordid kidnapping died of natural causes, or he didn't.'

Rosenfeld had called Finn after leaving the Epstein residence, and he reported 'on-the-record comments from local officials'. The article went on to quote the investigator in charge of the investigation, 'Our medical examiner is being very deliberate in determining cause of death. After all, this is an important case.'

Without veiling his criticism, Rosenfeld stated, 'Unless the police department is concealing evidence to the contrary, certainly medical science can determine that simple fact.'

In the Sunday edition of the newspaper, two letters to the editor called for 'justice to be done'. One went on to speculate how the law enforcement agencies were again protecting the powerful and 'those who constantly lined the pockets' of those unfairly appointed to top positions.

Early on Monday, October 28, the Police Commissioner, along with Detective Lionel Finn, held a news conference to clarify the 'difficult investigation' and to address serious allegations made by the media and 'other local critics'.

During the news conference, the Police Commissioner admitted that the investigators in charge of the 'complex case' were indeed attempting to protect individuals... private citizens who were innocent of any wrongdoing.

"Because we were afraid the media might misinterpret evidence that could implicate the victim of this crime—namely, Professor Miró Epstein-Shelley—we delayed the reporting of important facts," Police Commissioner W. Edward White said. "Without divulging police procedure, we intended to trap guilty parties, hoping they would come forth with details that only we, in a very small circle of investigators, knew. Unfortunately, because of the media's intrusion in this case, our police efforts have been compromised."

The Commissioner responded to questions, but quickly asked the 'detective in charge of the case' to address the questions of multiple journalists.

Finn did his best to respond to questions, but it was clear that he could add little to the information already published by Horace Rosenfeld. He admitted that the dead man's 'antemortem records of any sort—fingerprints or dental—were not found in any domestic databases.'

Rosenfeld then asked, "Are you saying that you still do not know the identity of the deceased, Detective Finn?"

"When international databases were consulted, federal officials found a match. However, we have not received that information from our colleagues in Washington DC," Finn said.

"Can we assume that your colleagues in Washington DC were at least able to determine cause of death?" Rosenfeld asked.

Detective Finn cleared his throat, "I believe they have made that determination, yes."

A reporter from the local CNBS asked, "And…?"

Again, Finn cleared his throat, "The FBI headquarters in Washington DC will be holding a similar news conference later today. They will provide details." With that, Finn and the Police Commissioner left the podium.

The gaggle of reporters left behind looked at each other, wondering if the 'press conference' had been a waste of everyone's time.

"Relax, we all know what damage control looks like," Horace Rosenfeld said. "Let's see what the Feds reveal later today."

Rather than hosting a news conference, the Deputy Director of the FBI, Jacoby Homely, held a prime-time interview with the TV news anchor, Jim Limer, who introduced him as perhaps the most brilliant law enforcement personality living today.

"Director Homely, can you shed light on a kidnapping case that has been baffling law enforcement officials throughout our country? Of course," Limer said, "I'm speaking of the academic from Chicago who was found in bed with her own lifeless kidnapper by her side."

"Jim, although this is still an ongoing investigation, I can reveal to the public that a break in the 'Chicago mystery' has occurred. An international criminal may have been identified as the kidnapper of a prominent university official at Northwestern University. In addition, the Washington DC headquarters can say with certainty that the international criminal perished of natural causes, since a cardiac arrest was determined as the cause of death."

Suppressing a gasp, Limer went on, "Well, that is indeed a break in the case. I know the public has been waiting for answers, and, as usual, we have our intelligence community coming forth with answers. Will you be able to share the identification of this international fugitive found dead in a Chicago hotel?"

"As soon as I'm able, Jim. As you know, this is an ongoing investigation, and in our country of laws we are diligent about protecting the rights of others, even violators of our laws."

"Well, please be aware that you have an open invitation at CNBS. Please return to inform our audience, whenever possible." With that, the interview of Deputy Director Homely was over.

. . .

"Max, did you watch Limer's interview tonight?" It was Rosenfeld calling. Max was at his upstairs desk, having finished an early dinner.

"What a weasel, huh? Homely is so sanctimonious. You would think that Edgar Hoover had come back to life," Rosenfeld said.

"You think Finn will continue to stonewall?" Max asked.

"I can't see how. No one knows the identity of the perp, but we know he died of natural causes. There's no way that veil of suspicion over Miró can remain," Rosenfeld said. "That's one good thing that came out of Limer's interview."

Late that night, the reporter received a call from Detective Lionel Finn. "Rosenfeld, I'm ready to make a statement. However, I want you to print exactly what I say— no commentary, no snide remarks, no innuendoes."

"You've got my word, Detective."

"Okay, here goes, and I want you to print every word I say. 'Today, the investigative team of the Evanston Police Department can proudly say that, after protecting the reputation of Professor Miroslava Epstein-Shelley, we have concluded that the dead man found at the Orrington Hotel in Evanston died of natural causes. To be specific, the deceased died of a heart attack. We unequivocally proclaim to the public—and, specifically, the media—that any veil of suspicion regarding Professor Epstein-Shelley be lifted.' Now, Rosenfeld, read it back to me."

Horace Rosenfeld chuckled and repeated Finn's statement verbatim. "Off the record, Detective, if I can remind you, no published article has implicated the professor. I'm uncertain why you would make such a statement."

"Well, Rosenfeld, you know the rumors that have been flying around," Finn said.

"No, I don't know. If rumors were flying, they certainly did not come from the media."

The following morning, the Chicago Tribune published Detective Finn's statement.

CHAPTER 8

Mountain Compound in Mazatlán, MX ·
Late October, 2019

THE MYSTERIOUS NEW OWNER of the compound had swept in scarcely weeks before. Already he had instilled fear in most of his men. Emerging on the international scene overnight, it seemed, the man known as 'Rodrigo' was dreaded rather than respected. Most of his men in Mexico and the U.S. secretly referred to him as 'El Gachupín', a derogatory term for Spaniards.

The expansive compound, now commandeered by Rodrigo, was formerly owned by El Chato Gómez. American journalists had called El Chato the biggest cartel kingpin in the world. Gómez had never named it, but Rodrigo immediately marked the compound with his imprimatur for his North American headquarters—'La Hacienda de Rodrigo'.

El Chato Gómez was still a legend. After numerous escapes from American and Mexican federal prisons, Gómez had been convicted in the U.S. on several counts of murder, kidnapping, drug and human trafficking. Thanks to the testimony of two of Gómez's lieutenants, U.S. federal officials had brought him to justice. Now, the two cartel lieutenants of El Chato worked for Rodrigo.

The European had swiftly muscled in. He had not only taken over El Chato's drug cartel, but he had also consolidated El Chato's fiefdom with his own vast trafficking enterprise in Europe. Few people underground knew how Rodrigo had gained total control of the largest drug cartel in the world. They did know, however, that most of Rodrigo's principal competitors had mysteriously disappeared. Leaders of the well-known Zetas, Beltrán-Leyva, and the Gulf cartels went missing, and Rodrigo had appropriated Mexico at a most convenient time. Few were willing to question his authority, and those who did vanished.

Rodrigo was an early riser. His personal valet Estevan Chengfu would prepare his morning coffee, always two cups of Blue Mountain coffee from Jamaica. By seven, he enjoyed a full breakfast also prepared by Estevan. Little known to others, he spent forty-five minutes perfecting his tai chi in the compound's gardens. Estevan, a tai chi master, or *Taijiquan* trainer, guided Rodrigo.

During the day, Rodrigo amused himself by indulging his ravenous appetite for learning. Recently, his newest passion was pyrotechnics. Immediately after moving into the mountain compound, he had replaced all but one of El Chato's chimneys and barbecue grills with bioethanol fireplaces. Rodrigo did preserve the enormous central wood-burning fireplace in the central patio. He demanded that it be left intact. The rest were transformed, because per Rodrigo, 'the use of bioethanol fuel protects the environment. It burns cleanly and quietly, plus it produces a beautifully rich, dancing flame.'

Rodrigo spent hours studying his new ethanol fireplaces. The remote gadgets that controlled the bio-flames enthralled him even more. He scribed meticulous notes as he disassembled and reassembled each one. On his second week at the compound, he summoned two of his European associates, who helped him use the remote controls to propel the ethanol fires from the fireplaces to targets that Rodrigo had placed eight feet away. Initially, he torched inanimate objects for his targets. His obsession grew, and within days after arriving at the compound he had asked Estevan to secure wildlife, small animals and rodents that roamed the compound. One by one, he would first scorch, then sear, then reignite them to cremate each one to ashen remains. Every experiment pleased him incrementally. On the second week of experimentation, he added photographs to his already voluminous note-taking.

When the man known as Rodrigo filled his second three-inch notebook, he asked Estevan to secure bigger wildlife—stray dogs, wild cats, and coyotes. "Cage them, Estevan, and keep them in the motor barn or near the stables."

Estevan signed, *'How many new cages should we buy?'* The mute valet had managed his condition from birth. Rodrigo had learned enough sign language to understand Estevan's simple questions.

"Get fifty... for now," the boss said.

"Also, email our nanotechnology guru, what's his name Yuekong, Yulong...? Tell him I need him here immediately."

Estevan patiently wrote in his ever-present notepad, 'His name is Mark Yuejong.'

"That's him. Get him here," Rodrigo said.

Forty-eight hours later, Dr. Yuejong, the renowned biomedical nanotechnologist, was sitting with Rodrigo in his living room, enjoying a glass of Albariño. He complained to his boss, "My work revolves around IoMT, which entails data sharing, storage, and analysis, boss. I'm not a weapons expert."

"Mark, I pay you enough to pursue your research interests. Now, humor me," Rodrigo said. "I'm interested in developing what I've already perfected into a more practical and portable toy."

The scientist shook his head, perplexed.

"Presently, I can direct with accuracy a bio-flame, even control it remotely, up to eight feet. I simply want that same effect directed from my wrist to a target that is farther. I just need a tiny remote."

"Boss," the pleading scientist said, "my expertise may not help you in this project."

"If you need help from another colleague, get him. But I want this done... soon. If you fail me, you can kiss your research funds goodbye." Rodrigo rose from his seat and walked away.

"Boss, can you give me a week?"

Without turning to face Dr. Yuejong, Rodrigo said, "You've got a week; just get it done."

. . .

Pedro and Macario Rosales had never met Rodrigo, their new boss. They'd not even talked to him directly. Electronic communication with their boss had been transmitted through their contact, only known as Estevan. Following Rodrigo's orders, the Rosales twins flew from Chicago Midway to LAX. Upon arrival in Los Angeles, they received further instructions from Estevan to fly to Mazatlán in Mexico, where neither twin had been. Their tickets were awaiting them at the American Airlines counter. Landing in Mazatlán, Pedro Rosales read the text instructing the twins to retrieve their luggage, where they would be picked up and transported to La Hacienda de Rodrigo. The hacienda was located on the side of Lookout Mountain, the highest point on the Sierra Madre mountain range.

The twins had been repeatedly told that their boss preferred the title 'boss' or 'patrón', but the twins knew that behind his back other fellow members of Rodrigo's organization in the U.S. and Mexico called him 'El Gachupín'. Rodrigo was the new kid on the block and rumors abounded. The underworld, and the Rosales twins, only knew that this mysterious figure had taken over El Chato Gómez's drug cartel and added it to his own European empire. Like the rest of them, the Rosales twins were eager to learn more.

Pedro Rosales remembered using the term 'El Gachupín' with a mid-level member of Rodrigo's organization, and he was quickly warned by the frightened Brit, "Mate, if you value your life, don't ever use that term around him. Boss, patrón, jefe, but never gachupín."

When the driver of the black Suburban picked them up at the Mazatlán airport, it appeared to the twins that another fellow employee from Great Britain was picking them up. Pedro asked, "How many of you Brits are employed by Rodrigo?"

"I'm an Aussie, mate. Can't you tell the difference?"

Pedro looked at his twin brother, and chuckled, "You all sound the same to us."

"Oi, mate, only bogans mistake us," the driver said. "By the way, my name is Lucas."

The twins looked at each other and shrugged shoulders.

The drive from the airport to the central district of Mazatlán impressed the twins. Lush tropical plants and palm trees reminded the twins of their family vacation in Hawaii. Both families with their children had flown to Oahu and toured the islands for ten glorious days. It had been a trip to remember.

Macario asked his brother, "Does it remind you of Hawaii?"

"Yeah, bro, my kids still talk about it. Next time, I think we should bring them here."

Lucas stopped at a local restaurant and treated the twins to a hearty lunch. "This arvo, I'll drive you to meet with the boss. But first, you need to learn to follow protocol. First, when you enter do not shake hands, stand at least eight feet away from him, and wear these facial coverings. Unless he invites you closer, stay eight feet away. And thirdly, address him as sir, boss, or patrón."

"You're kidding, right?" Pedro Rosales asked. "My brother and I worked for the biggest kingpin in the world, and he never demanded all that stuff. He was just El Chato."

"The boss rarely kids around, mate."

. . .

Estevan opened the massive door to the compound. He wore white linen pants and a loose linen white-on-white guayabera that had subtle embroidery of pineapples and pomegranates. He also wore woven leather sandals that seemed to provide cloud-like support and silent footsteps. Estevan did not utter a word. Silently, he walked away, leading the twins to the open galería. He appeared to glide rather than step into the expansive, colorfully decorated central gardens.

The hacienda was an impressive fortress with massive pillars, black wrought-iron door hinges, and Saltillo tiled floors. Shiny blue Oaxacan mosaics and marble slabs adorned some accent walls, like Diego Rivera murals.

The galería itself was an airy loggia, with a red-tiled roof supported by massive dark acacia beams. The white stuccoed walls contrasted with the explosion of reds from the numerous hanging bougainvillea and the large blooming hibiscus in flower pots throughout the garden. Despite the lateness of the season, two enormous jacaranda trees were in full bloom, adorning the garden in their majestic purple flowers. Yellow esperanzas punctuated the corners of each eight-foot wall that permitted only the view of the distant mountain range. The mountains encircled the compound and the Mazatlán bay below.

Walking alongside Estevan, Pedro felt underdressed. He was fond of wearing denim shorts, even late into the fall. A worn Che Guevara T-shirt and a black Chicago White Sox baseball hat completed his outfit. Given the coastal Mexican heat, he'd chosen his more relaxed attire, not thinking his business meeting with the boss would be formal. As for Macario, he wore his usual workout gear, loose nylon pants, a matching hooded windbreaker, and white Adidas sneakers.

. . .

Rodrigo was also dressed in linen. He was facing away from the patio entrance and gloated over a gigantic fire in the central fireplace. The boss looked like a man used to giving orders only once. Indeed, he was unaccustomed to revisiting matters a second time. Rodrigo grinned as he received the Rosales twins. Without rising from his swivel patio stool, he put his Cuban cigar down.

"I finally get to meet you, my good friends from the United States. Not much good comes out of your country, but I admit you've impressed me. Let's see, you must be Pedro. You two look exactly alike, but you, the one wearing shorts... I'll call you 'Half Pants'."

Rodrigo took a puff, pausing as he exhaled, "I'm confused, don't I pay you enough?" the patrón asked.

"Yeah... yes, of course," Pedro said. "Why do you ask?"

"I've made you such a rich man, Pedro, and you can't afford the rest of the pants?"

He turned his scrutiny to Macario. He got up from his deeply cushioned patio stool, gazed into Macario's eyes, and walked around him, studying him from every angle.

Macario stood perfectly still and did not utter a word. He did not flinch, nor did he fidget. He held Rodrigo's stare.

"You're the quiet one," the boss said. "I'll call you Mudo."

. . .

Pedro Rosales' testimony in court had secured the conviction of El Chato Gómez—his former employer. Although Pedro was given lifelong protective custody, Rodrigo had 'rescued' him from his Arizona safe house, which had been provided by grateful U.S. Feds.

"So, how are we going to begin our relationship, my little Half Pants... with good news or bad news? What can you tell me about your assignment's demise? Were you able to accomplish your job?"

An embarrassed silence and two solemn faces—downcast and focused on their navels—displeased Rodrigo.

"Give me the good news! Sit down and tell your papi how you got rid of your assignment."

Changing the subject, Rodrigo asked, "Don't you remember how I first reached out to you?"

"Of course. How can I forget?" answered Pedro Half-Pants. "You asked me if I could get a truckload of live sheep from Sinaloa to Chicago."

"And do you remember what you said?" Without waiting, the boss went on, "You answered, 'No problem, boss.' That's what I like to hear from my men—'No problem, boss'."

"I remember it well."

"You've impressed me because you have a 'can-do' attitude, Half-Pants. You moved two million American dollars' worth of coca with that shipment, and you never even asked what else was in the truck full of sheep."

"You said I had testicular fortitude. I'd never heard it put that way." Pedro grinned and turned to his twin brother. He grabbed his crotch proudly. Tilting his head back, he aimed his chin at his brother. Mudo turned away.

"Well, will you need a new pair? If you give me bad news, you will lose all the equipment you need to keep on living."

"Boss, you can trust me and my brother. We're well equipped." This time Pedro simply grinned.

"That's what I want to hear," Rodrigo said. He looked at Mudo, then he turned his gaze on Half-Pants. "Now, one more time, no need to fear me. Just tell me about your assignment's demise."

"What do you mean his 'demise', boss?" Pedro asked.

"Deceso... deceso, the Spanish word for the one who experienced his demise. Haven't you heard the word in your illiterate Chicago Spanish? It means 'death' or refers to your assignment's 'elimination'. Out with it. Is he, or is he not dead?"

The outspoken twin answered. "No sé… don't know, boss. We thought…"

Rodrigo stood and circled both brothers like a lion casing his prey.

Pedro Half-Pants did not smile. He looked at his flip-flops and remained standing about ten feet away from Rodrigo. Mudo sat at the far end of the loggia, on the tiled cover for the shelf where the firewood was stored. He looked away to the distant fountain where three armed men were standing sentinel, backs to the loggia.

The boss continued circling. He walked up to Pedro, nostrils flared, close enough for Half-Pants to feel the warmth of his exhaling, "Tell me that your target is dead." He then inserted middle and forefinger into Pedro Half-Pants' nostrils and pulled him to where his twin brother was sitting. He tossed Pedro down, and sat him next to Mudo on the sky-blue tiled bench. Before speaking, he rubbed his fingers dry on Mudo's shirttails. He called out to Estevan for hand sanitizer. "Now, both of you, tell me that he's dead."

"What we can tell you, boss, is that Chicago local officials and the U.S. Department of Justice announced last night that an unidentified man was found dead. It's all over the newspapers," Pedro Half-Pants said. "We think that we did such a good job that no one can trace the murder to us. They still don't know who it is."

Rodrigo raised his hands up in the air and pumped a fist above. He uttered some expletives in Spanish, unknown to the American-raised twins. He laughed loudly, and turned to the twins, gleefully rubbing their heads, "Now, that wasn't so hard, was it? This calls for a toast!"

"It's a little early for me, boss," Pedro Half-Pants said.

"How about you, Mudo?"

"For me too."

"Bola de maricones." Rodrigo called out to Estevan, "Bring us a bottle of anís."

"Anís will help your appetite, compañeros."

He put his arms around the twins, and led them to his outdoor *comedor*, or dining area. The bar, a large, elaborately carved acacia piece of furniture, stood at the corner of the dining area. Behind it, mirrored shelves with numerous spirits lit up the vast area with reflecting indirect lighting. Most of the bottles were unfamiliar to the twins. "If you don't care for anís, you can celebrate with a beer or anything else you like," their satisfied boss said.

"I'll have a Miller Lite," said Mudo.

"No light beer in these parts, Mudo. Have a man's brew." Rodrigo turned to Estevan and told him to bring Mudo and Half-Pants a couple of Estrellas.

Pedro Half-Pants spoke up first. "Boss, some federales in the U.S. think that our target was found in Chicago, but my brother and I have additional information."

Rodrigo took the bottle of anís and served himself a thimbleful. He waited for the twins to take the beers from

Estevan. Estevan left the two beers on the table and stood behind the twins. "That'll be all, Estevan."

"Salud, amor, y pesetas," Rodrigo said. He raised his glass and downed his drink. The twins obligingly tipped their bottles against their boss's glass and sucked on their longnecks. As the boss filled his glass again, Pedro continued.

"As you know, we have contacts at DOJ."

"Of course, I know that. Bien que me cuesta. I pay dearly for those relationships, my friends." The boss downed his second glass of anís.

"Other contacts... our contacts... think that the man found dead may not have been our assignment."

Disbelief all over his face, Rodrigo paused. His unspoken question prompted Mudo to add, "We think it may have been another one of your enemies."

"What do you mean, it wasn't him? Imbéciles! Son unos imbéciles. Como diablos?"

The man only known as Rodrigo went into a rampage filled with profanities, which he seldom used. "...Entonces a quien eliminaron?" He was furious. "Who did you kill instead?"

"We don't know," Pedro said. "And, it's possible our target has disappeared... for the time being." He continued, "I don't mean to say that we won't find our assignment. We just don't know where he is... right now."

Staring down at the polished mesquite table and slowly rubbing the grain of the wood with his fingertips, Rodrigo stated in a deliberate, hushed tone, "Why should I care if someone else was found dead?"

"Because it could have been someone more dangerous to our organization than our own target," Pedro Half-Pants said.

Still virtually whispering, Rodrigo said, "Odio cuentos largos. I told you I don't like long stories. So, tell me why I should care about all this."

"Because we think he was hot on our trail. We think it's the same federal agent that hunted down El Chato Gómez."

At this point, the boss stood up, clenching his right fist. The twins were at the table, averting his glare. Mudo rubbed his eyes, and Pedro peeled the label from his beer bottle.

"I've got the most powerful organization in the world, and you're bringing me horror stories about a lone ranger that is trying to fix the world?" screamed Rodrigo. "So, I'll ask the question again. Did your target die?"

"Though some in the U.S. think so, we're not sure," Pedro said.

Grabbing Pedro's beer bottle, Rodrigo swung down on the crown of Mudo's head, smashing the half-empty bottle. Using a powerful tennis backhand, he swung at Pedro, slashing his face with the broken shard in his hand. Rodrigo's crisp white guayabera was splattered with blood.

"Get out of my sight!"

Rodrigo marched into his den, and called out to Estevan, "Clean up this mess."

CHAPTER 9

MACARIO LEARNED FROM LUCAS Williams, the Aussie, that La Hacienda de Rodrigo employed its own physician, one of the many perks offered by their employer. Although the twins had intended to fly back home to Chicago, Lucas, the twins' only trusted contact at the compound, advised them to retreat to their quarters, until the boss cooled down. Though Lucas was only able to provide antiseptics and bandages, he retrieved the doctor within minutes of the fracas.

Two hours later, both twins were bandaged and sedated. Pedro got twelve stitches on his face. However, before leaving, the physician informed Pedro that he would probably live with a nasty scar on his cheek for the rest of his life.

Late that evening, Lucas knocked on the door to the suite occupied by the twins. He had a light dinner that had been sent by Estevan. "The rest of us get fed by a local cook employed by EG, but you boys get a meal from the boss's kitchen. How's that for a reception?"

The twins thanked Lucas, but they asked him to stick around.

Pedro told Lucas, "Dude, we have a million questions. Macario and I need to know, should we show our faces around the compound? Do we stay away from the boss? How long are we supposed to wait until we get word from him regarding further instructions? And, how do we repay Rodrigo for the towels we ruined while cleaning up our wounds?"

Hearing Pedro's last question, Lucas laughed, "Mate, the towels are the least of your worries. But whatever you do, unless you want to lose your employment—and your heads—do not return to Chicago until you've been dismissed by EG."

"Who's EG, Lucas?" Pedro asked. "That's the second time you mention 'EG'."

Forefinger placed vertically on his lips, and volume almost down to a whisper, Lucas said, "That's what most of us call him here at the compound. It stands for 'El Gachupín'... the only sign of rebellion we're brave enough to muster."

The twins laughed.

"EG will cool down. He's got a terrible temper, but he moves on. Word is around the compound that you blokes connected EG to the U.S. spooks, and..."

"The spooks?" Macario asked.

"Yeah, you know, the spies, the Feds involved with all kinds of espionage," Lucas said.

"Got it," Macario said.

"Anyway, word is that you blokes are too valuable for the boss to risk losing you to another cartel, or to other corporate competitors, as he calls them."

"Like I said, Lucas," Pedro said, "we have a million questions."

"It's simple. If EG has not dismissed you, count your blessings. Stay clear of his way, get to know the compound. If you haven't noticed, these are beautiful grounds, and the weather is perfect. I'll take you into town any time you want. Your monthly deposits from the corporation will continue to flow, so enjoy it while you can. By the way, the señoritas in town are much fun."

"We're both happily married," Macario said.

"As you wish, mates."

. . .

Two days later, barely after sunrise at 6:45, Estevan knocked on the twins' suite. He handed them a note in a piece of expensive stationery. The note read, 'Please join me for breakfast promptly at 0700 hours.' It was signed by Rodrigo. Pedro mentioned to Macario he'd never seen such fancy handwriting.

Although they rushed to make it on time, when the twins joined their boss, he was already seated having a glass of freshly squeezed orange juice. The twins wondered if their boss used the crystal daily.

"Beautiful crystal," Pedro said, hoping to open with innocuous small talk.

"It's Waterford, but the orange juice is even better. We get the oranges from Valencia," Rodrigo said. "I hope you got a good night's rest."

"Yes, we did, boss," Pedro said. "Our accommodations are better than any five-star hotel we've been to."

"That was fancy handwriting on your invitation," Macario said.

"Well, well, you do talk after all, Mudo... It's called calligraphy, and I use a brush," Rodrigo said.

"Wow," is all that Macario could say.

"Though my breakfast is usually hearty, I start out with fruit," Rodrigo said. "I move on from there to my eggs accompanied by smoked salmon. However, you just ask Estevan for your preferences."

In addition to coffee, the twins asked for bacon and egg omelets.

"And, how's your healing progressing, boys?"

"Just a small cut, boss," Pedro said, turning his face to hide the bandage from their host.

"As I remember it, Half-Pants, it was more than a small abrasion. Did our doctor take good care of you both?"

"No worries, boss. He took good care, and we're on the mend," Pedro said.

"A cut to the face like the one I inflicted on you may leave a nasty scar. I will send you to my personal plastic surgeon, and you will be as good as new. We can even improve your looks," Rodrigo said.

Pedro forced a big smile.

"Better still, since I have him on retainer, I'll bring him here." Rodrigo rose from his chair, and Pedro recoiled. "Relax, Half-Pants, I'm getting you some more bacon. You wolfed yours down."

Before the boss got to the large serving platter, Estevan rushed to his side and asked him to return to his seat.

"Let's keep them well fed, Estevan."

Estevan nodded.

CHAPTER 10

Evanston, IL · November 13, 2019,
eight weeks after Miró was found.

O<small>N BEHALF OF THE</small> Evanston PD and the entire Chicagoland law enforcement community, Detective Finn called the news editor of the Chicago Tribune to thank the newspaper for its responsible reporting on the Epstein-Shelley kidnapping case. He went on to say how the close cooperation of the media with law enforcement enabled the quick resolution of a difficult matter, which could easily involve crime of global proportions. When the news editor asked for clarification, Finn refused to give any further information. He insisted that the first item on his agenda was to notify the victim's family of the latest developments.

That evening, Detective Lionel Finn telephoned Nate Shelley's residence. He asked to speak to Dr. Shelley.

"This is Dr. Nathaniel Shelley, Detective Finn."

"I prefer to speak to Dr. Miró Epstein-Shelley," Finn said. "Is she home?"

"Although she's out, can I relay a message to her?" Nate asked.

"Only this, Dr. Shelley, I have more good news. I couldn't share much with your family earlier, since the Feds had taken over the investigation."

"You hadn't mentioned anything about federal agents being involved, Detective Finn."

"It was hush-hush, you get my drift? They imposed a gag order on us."

"I see," Nate said. "And, the good news?"

"First, some clarification. We pride ourselves in running a tight ship around here. We're not incompetent. I mean, it's one thing being unable to determine cause of death, but failing to identify a dead body... sheesh. We knew from the beginning. I just couldn't share details."

"Okay, so tell me who kidnapped my wife."

"We can safely say that the man found dead, with your wife—in the same bed—was the kidnapper. Turns out he was a known international criminal by the name of Theo, full spelling of T-E-O-D-O-S-I-O, last name, Dante. He was fifty-three years old at the time of his death. Apparently, to the underworld he was known as 'Tío'."

"I've heard the name before, Finn."

"Just thought you and your wife would like to know, Dr. Shelley. We'll be closing the file on this one soon."

"Hate to disappoint you, Finn, but, if indeed Tío Dante was involved, you and the Feds are merely scratching the surface." Disgusted, Nate had heard enough from Finn. He ended the call and dialed Max and his in-laws to inform them of the latest. He and Miró would have much to discuss when she got home.

. . .

That night Nate took Miró out to dinner. He texted her after her weekly evening seminar which was meant for doctoral students who were preparing for the dissertation phase of their studies. Miró was exhausted after a lengthy day of administrative work and a full evening of teaching.

"What's the occasion, lover boy? Are you treating me for dinner at the new romantic spot you discovered?" Miró teasingly asked.

"Not the new spot, but our favorite romantic go-to, Va Pensiero," Nate said.

"A late, relaxing dinner sounds ideal, Corazón. I'll meet you there."

Following dinner, Nate and Miró shared a light dessert of berries and cream. Nate carefully addressed the news he'd received from Finn. "It seems, my love, that we finally have conclusive results. Federal investigators informed Finn and the other local officials that our old nemesis from the Canary Islands, Tío Dante, was involved in your kidnapping. Better put, they're confirming not only that Tío kidnapped you, but also that the dead man was Tío himself."

"Wait, do the Feds claim he died of natural causes?"

"Yep, a heart attack."

"Well, I wouldn't say that I remember a specimen in perfect health… he did cough a lot, but my kidnapper seemed to be in good shape and robust enough to be around many more years. Natural causes, eh?"

"That's what federal medical examiners claim," Nate said.

"I know you tried to convince us to consider connections with the drug traffickers from the Canary Islands, and we ignored you," Miró said. "All along, your instincts were correct. I'm sorry."

"There's nothing for which you need to apologize. I suppose we're now aware of the challenge ahead," Nate said. "I just want you to have confidence in us as a family. We'll overcome this."

"We certainly can't depend on local law enforcement," Miró said. "Nate, do you think Max is up to the challenge?"

"Like your dad says, my love, it'll take a team effort. First thing we need to do is bring Max up to speed. Abraham and Miriam have already shared some of our experiences in the Canary Islands, but I don't think Max is aware of the magnitude of that criminal network."

Early the following morning, Nate called Abraham from his office. "Have you brought Max up to date on our Canary adventure?"

"Hi, Nate. I meant to talk to you today," Abraham said. "I've already learned about the latest news regarding the positive identification of the corpse. Rosenfeld called earlier. We should've listened to you, Nate. I think you suspected Tío from the start."

"No worries, Abraham. Miró and I were wondering last night how much Max knew about our problems three years ago. We don't think he understands completely."

"We've been so caught up in our challenges with Finn and his men that not much else seemed to matter. Of course, Miriam and I have described our nightmarish experiences, but I don't think that Max knows many details."

"We're thinking you could ask Max to read Rosenfeld's accounts of the way we narrowly escaped a murder trial in the Spanish court system. Didn't he win some kind of award for his series?"

"Yes, he did. Listen, you've got enough on your plate. We'll bring Max up to speed," Abraham said. "I kept every article, and I also saved the accounts published by the foreign newspapers."

· · ·

Abraham left his clinic at exactly 5 PM. Standing on the crowded Red Line train car to Wilmette, Abraham reread Rosenfeld's articles. Though he prided himself on being intuitive and observant, he noticed for the first time how impressed Rosenfeld had been with Tío Dante's business acumen.

Several articles also described Tío's expertise in explosives and the vast military experience that he obviously had acquired during the Gulf War. Tío had been one of the few Special Forces deployed by Spain to the Middle East. Serving primarily with U.N. forces, Tío Dante had enjoyed a stellar military career and distinguished himself in battle. He rose through the ranks and was promoted several times. Honorably discharged with a rank of colonel, he returned to Spain a decorated war hero.

Rosenfeld, of course, had not met any of the players in the Canary drug ring, but he conducted much research, studying military records, foreign newspapers, and Interpol papers. In an article, Rosenfeld highlighted the enormous success of E-LEVATE, the staff training business in Spain that served as a laundering operation for the illegal trafficking enterprise. 'The success of E-LEVATE,' Rosenfeld gushed, 'was due to the person who administered the operation, Tío Dante.'

Later that evening, Abraham shared with Max how, at the time, Horace Rosenfeld was a 'rookie young reporter'. He went on to comment that Rosenfeld had elaborated much on Tío Dante, although Tío was not the principal player in the 'Canary Islands imbroglio'.

"Yeah, you've mentioned that Tío was the drug lord's right-hand man, right?"

"Exactly. But, as I reread the articles on my way home, I noticed how impressed Rosenfeld was with Tío's accomplishments. As you know, the Tribune received some journalistic awards for the series. Rosenfeld's dad, by the way, was Harry, the editor of the Washington Post at one time."

"Yeah, Miriam talked about the articles," Max said. "Rosie certainly did his homework."

"I'd like for you to read them, because I promised Nate that I'd bring you up to speed," Abraham said. "You should also read the articles published by the major newspaper in Madrid, El Mundo. You can get them translated."

"Before reading the series, what do you think of inviting Nate and Miró to join us for a nightcap?" Max asked. "It would be great to get a verbal synopsis straight from the horses' mouths, so to speak."

"I'll call," Miriam said, "but since it's a week day, they may have already sent Minerva to bed. If so, I'll offer to babysit."

"May I remind you, my dear, that your granddaughter is no longer a baby. She turned thirteen already," Abraham said.

"You know exactly what I mean, Abrám. I prefer that Minnie not be left alone at home."

Nate and Miró arrived thirty minutes later, Minnie in tow, wearing her PJs. "Minnie has a big test tomorrow, and she preferred to study here," Miró said. "We'll have one drink, then head back home."

Before sitting, Nate asked, "Max, have Miriam and Abraham told you all about Diego and Yael Montemayor?"

"Stop right there, who the hell are Diego and Y'ahl Montemayor?" Max asked.

"Max," Miró said, "Her name was Yael—Y-A-E-L. She was Diego's wife. Died in a fire in the Canaries when Nate and I got married."

"Okay. Then Diego, he's the dude who was, or is, the drug lord. Right?" Max asked.

Although Nate and Miró attempted to describe to Max in detail what had occurred three years ago in the Canary Islands, Max seemed to lose interest.

Instead, Max asked them, "Can you just provide 'headlines' right now? Dad has armed me with numerous articles and other documents. Right now, help me with a synopsis."

Nate and Miró briefly summarized how on their trip to the Canary Islands, they had been accused of murdering one of Miró's former American students. Although they had been vindicated and released from jail, it was a lengthy and traumatic experience. Nate and Miró had confronted the real murderer, who died in a nightmarish fire. Her husband, Diego Montemayor, a suspected drug lord, promised to avenge his wife's death.

"Furthermore, in his quest to find the murderer, Nate bravely interviewed Diego Montemayor's executive vice president—the person who ran Diego's business," Miriam said. "Nate is too modest to take any credit, but he penetrated the ranks of a notorious drug ring, something Interpol itself had been unable to do."

"And, are you saying that the executive vice president was Tío Dante?" Max asked.

"One and the same," Nate said. "Two important details, Max, are that Tío Dante sported gold incisors and he wore a huge pewter belt buckle. It was his trademark."

"So, Miró, when you met your kidnapper at the restaurant, why didn't you recognize him?" Max asked.

"That's just it," Abraham said. "Miró never met Tío. Nate is the only one in the family that had a face-to-face meeting with him."

Nate then took the time to berate himself about not being able to place the voice earlier. "That phone call that I received telling me where I could find Miró came from Tío, Max. I don't know why I didn't make that connection immediately."

"I'm not the shrink here, Nate, but it's probably why subconsciously you knew Diego's goons were involved," Max said.

"It's definitely an indication that Diego Montemayor was involved," Nate said.

"But if he kidnapped me, why would Tío give you information where to find me?" Miró asked.

"That's what I can't figure out," Nate said.

Max had listened intently, but he suspected there was much more to the story. The description of the drug lord and his organization was brief but impactful. Something told Max that they were not simply facing a gang of thugs. It wasn't the mob, nor some isolated extortionists specializing in kidnapping and ransom tactics. What Nate and Miró briefly described, wide-eyed and terrified, was an international cartel—syndicate, whatever—that was deeply embedded in international business and political circles.

As if she had read Max's mind, Miró said, "If this is one of those cartels we read about, it's a conglomeration of cartels—a super-cartel, if you will—that controls all kinds of illegal trafficking. Drugs as well as human. Child enslavement, and cybercrime. If its reach is not worldwide, then it at least spans the Americas and Europe."

"Not that I doubt this," Max said, "but how do you know these things?"

Miró was already distracted and deep in thought. Her body was shaking. Nate was concerned she was descending into another catatonic episode. She didn't answer.

"I know you're both probably distracted, but how can you possibly have so many details?" Max asked.

Abraham responded, "A person high up in Interpol and his good friend, Chief Inspector Sánchez from the Canaries, solved the murders… the ones for which Nate and Miró were vindicated two years ago."

Nate added, "They shared their information with us, Max. You should establish contact with those two. At this point, though, we need to return home. I need to put my two lovelies to sleep."

PART TWO

CHAPTER 11

Skokie, IL · Friday, November 22, 2019,
nine weeks after Miró was found.

ITH A SMILE ON his face, Abraham drove into
his circular driveway and parked at the visitors'
entrance to his own home. Not anticipating the
first snow of the fall, he'd crammed garden tools and the
bulky snow blower, which needed a tune-up, in his normally
empty garage stall. He chided himself, *Abraham, that's what
you get for procrastinating.*

Opening the door to his Genesis 90, he turned up the
collar of his tweed jacket. A frigid wind from the east blew
through the tall blue firs. Their needles had a covering of
white, like wool. Meant to break the wintry air that blew in
from Lake Michigan, the trees instead created a wind tunnel
that redirected the chill to the front entryway. The thick, wet
flakes that covered the flat needles instantly turned his jacket
lapels and goatee completely white. He took short steps to
avoid slipping on a cap of black ice. The first virgin snow of
the season had packed less than half an inch on the ground.

It was enough to force Abraham to toe carefully up to the covered front porch. He stamped the snow off the leather soles of his Allen Edmonds.

Miriam met him at the door. She had her cell phone in one hand and a heavy, cotton throw in the other. She signaled to him to use the parson's bench at the foyer, so he could remove his dampened shoes. As she cradled the phone between shoulder and neck, she mouthed in silence, "I'll bring your slippers."

Abraham assumed that Miriam had Miró on the line, getting updates on the dead man's identity. He'd already heard from his son Max, who was fiercely consuming every relevant piece of information on Tío Dante and drug cartels in general.

Miriam returned with sheepskin slippers in hand. She handed him a wooden hanger for his sports jacket. Walking past the fireplace in the den, Abraham was tempted to warm his frozen toes by the hearth. *First things first*, said his inner voice—that ever-present companion of his that impelled him toward excellence in all matters. Abraham returned his tweed jacket to the furthest slot in his closet wardrobe. By the time he returned to the den, Miriam was there, his favorite cardigan sweater in hand and handing him a steaming mug of decaf hot tea with the other. They sat by the carved stone fireplace. The raging fire welcomed them both.

"That was our Miró on the phone," Miriam said. "That poor baby is beside herself. She's confused, and I sense she's still worried about Minnie's well-being."

"Slow down, my precious jewel. You still treat her like your baby. Miró is a grown woman, a very capable mother, and a strong, resilient individual. What's confusing her?"

"Simply that Finn and even federal officials have identified her kidnapper. The fact that he ended up dead—of a cardiac arrest—is mystifying to Miró. We must admit the whole mystery is beyond a simple explanation."

"Miriam, my darling, tell me one thing. Was it the local officials that provided positive identification?"

"No. Federal agents determined that."

"Ah, there we have it!" Abraham said. "Our federal government has access to more reliable testing and data. Since the matches didn't occur domestically, it required our Feds to give us an ID. We cannot continue to second-guess ourselves."

. . .

Far past the second cup of Earl Grey, Abraham sat on his easy chair, pretending to be unconcerned about Miró's predicament. The bleak scene beyond the wooden deck in his backyard was darkening. The thick, gray sheet of horizontal snow falling on his manicured lawn darkened his mood.

Abraham put in writing several thoughts, notes, and reminders in his leather journal. Though he understood Miró's—and Miriam's—concerns, he would offer reassurance and security to both. He would not give in to doubt and worry. In silence, Abraham weighed Miró's options. She had three choices. One, do nothing. Two, enlist the rest of the family to run a parallel investigation regarding the dead man's identity and cause of death. Three, enlist the help of Interpol, or some independent agencies of law enforcement, to uncover other truths. He acknowledged that the involvement of a dangerous criminal like Tío Dante did not bode well for his family.

Abraham brooded some more.

- Was it Tío Dante who kidnapped Miró?
- If so, why?
- Was the kidnapper the same person that was found dead at the Orrington Hotel?
- If the kidnapper was fifty-three years old, why did Max estimate the age of the dead man to be at least twenty years greater?
- Did the deceased die of natural causes?
- If he did, why couldn't local medical examiners make that simple determination?
- If he didn't die of natural causes, what was cause of death?
- Are Miró, Nate, and Minnie still in danger?

Abraham dozed off while considering his daughter's three choices for going forward.

. . .

A muffled ring awakened Abraham. He fumbled around the sides of his reclining easy chair. No cell phone in the crevices nor under his outstretched legs. Again, he chastised himself for the ample paunch which seemed to grow every fall. It made it difficult to lift his weight from his prone position. Trying every shirt and slacks pocket, he finally reached into the deep side pockets of his cotton cardigan and interrupted the annoying ring.

"Is this the distinguished Dr. Abraham Epstein?"

"Yes, this is Dr. Epstein. Who is this?"

Abraham had never heard the voice before. It was coarse and rugged and laced with guttural sounds, suggesting the presence of phlegm in the pulmonary cavity. Despite the grinding effect, the voice was not menacing. "I have important information to share with you, Dr. Epstein."

"Thank you, but could you identify yourself?"

"I'm afraid I cannot do that. However, you need to know that the dead man found in your daughter's hotel room was not Mr. Dante."

"How did you arrive at this conclusion, may I ask?"

"I have personal knowledge... and evidence. I happen to know that the dead man was a former federal official."

"And, how would you know such a thing?" Abraham's discomfort grew. He regretted using the edge in his voice and the harsh tone.

As if enjoying the control, the caller used an overtone that revealed a calm power in the exchange. He audibly chuckled and said, "Here's a bonus. You previously met this former federal official."

"I repeat my question; how would you know such a thing?" Abraham asked.

"I'm afraid that is all I can trust you with, Dr. Epstein."

Skokie, IL · Sunday, November 24, 2019

Abraham and Miriam hosted an early Sunday dinner for the family. Abraham promised Max that he would have the best paella that he'd ever had. "Miriam and Miró," Abraham said, "have perfected several Spanish recipes for Nate's sake. Since his visit to the Iberian Peninsula and the Canary Islands, he's become a lover of all things Spanish, principally the cuisine and wines."

"Funny, I would think that the problems y'all experienced in Spain—false accusations and incarcerations—would've soured your impression of Spain," Max said.

Abraham uncorked a bottle of Bermejo Seco. He served two goblets and offered one to Max.

"Much to the contrary, Spain has become very dear to our hearts, Max. I suppose we did have a bittersweet experience there. Despite their problems, remember that Nate and Miró chose the Canary Islands for their wedding.

They consider the greater part of their stay in Las Palmas their honeymoon, an especially romantic one."

"I'm intrigued," Max said.

"What you're drinking, Son, is Nate's favorite wine. It's a refreshing white wine more appropriate for summer sipping, but we're having it in honor of Nate's belated birthday. With all that's been going on, we didn't have a chance to celebrate last week."

"Not a wine drinker, Dad, but this one is interesting. It's not too dry, with a twist—a unique flavor that I've never tasted before."

"That's the volcanic aftertaste that fascinated Nate," Abraham said. "It's produced in Lanzarote, one of the islands in the Canarian archipelago."

Three insistent rings of the doorbell told them that the rest of the company had arrived. Minnie rushed in first and joined them in the den. Her grandmother followed her as Minnie shrugged out of her parka. Miriam took the heavy coat and stopped to complain to her husband.

"So, you two started without me, eh? How'd you like the Bermejo, Max?"

"Bermejo?" Minnie asked. "Isn't that my dad's favorite wine from Spain?"

"Yes, it is, Minnie. You've got a good memory," Miriam said.

"I tasted Bermejo three years ago, Uncle Max, but I thought it was a little bitter. I liked the cava better, though."

"It was just a taste, Max," Miriam said. "Please don't think we allow her to have alcohol of any kind."

"Well, Minnie Mouse, though I'm not a wine drinker, your stepdad's choice is quite crisp and…"

"Refreshing?" Miriam asked.

"Yeah, exactly," Max said.

Nate and Miró walked in, did a quick round of hugs and European double-kisses, and shuffled directly to the fireplace.

"The first snowfalls are always the best," Miró addressed Max. "A pristine white with a hush unlike any other silence on earth." With arms outstretched toward the raging fire, Miró added, "Let's enjoy it while we can."

"Mom, please tell Uncle Max to stop calling me 'Minnie Mouse'," said Minerva.

"I'm sorry. I promise to stop," Max said. "Besides, mice are cuter than you!"

"Uncle Max!"

"Honey," Nate said, "the best thing to do is to let Max know that he's failing to get your goat."

"Huh?"

"Your dad is telling you to ignore Max. Don't let him get the best of you. If he knows you're not bothered by it, he'll stop teasing." Miró put her arms around Minnie.

"Okay, Abraham, how about some of that Bermejo? Are you making me suffer?" Nate asked.

"Coming right up."

"Mom said she was preparing paella, Max. Do you like rice dishes, Big Brother?" Miró asked.

"In truth, I've never had it, Sis. But those aromas coming from the kitchen are great... Wait a minute, doesn't paella contain shellfish?"

"It's paella Valenciana, Max. Without the shellfish or rabbit. Completely kosher."

Over the next ninety minutes, the entire family offered celebratory toasts and 'over-the-hill' birthday wishes. In self-defense, Nate stated he'd never felt better in his life and that forty-seven was not 'that old'.

Although Abraham opened two bottles of his favorite Tempranillo, Bermejo remained the beverage of choice. Minnie enjoyed her ginger ale.

Max had two servings of paella and vowed to have it at least once a week. Though he compared it to the Mexican dish arroz con pollo, Max noted that the saffron gave the Spanish dish a totally different, and more 'exotic', flavor. After the dirty dishes had been picked up from the table, Abraham made an offer of sherry for his guests. Then, he abruptly led everyone into the den for what seemed to be a serious family discussion. Adults opted for coffee, and Minnie asked for chai tea. As they followed Abraham into the den, Nate and Miró arched their eyebrows and glanced at each other.

"Don't look so somber," Abraham said. "I tend to switch my concentration without warning, and it usually has an unwanted response in people. My patients sometimes complain."

"Dad," Miró said, "you're only making it worse. Get on with it."

"Okay, you're right... Friday night I received a call. I think it was the same voice you described earlier, Nate."

"You mean Tío's voice?" Nate asked.

"Tío is supposed to be dead, per the Feds," Max interrupted.

"Exactly," Abraham said. "That's what's troubling. I considered the possibility that someone could be impersonating Tío. I even thought that the drug lord, Diego—or his men—were setting a trap."

"Dad, get to the point." Miró was already fidgeting and looking for her mom to jump into the conversation. Only Miriam could prompt Abraham along during his long-winded diatribes.

"Okay, I know how you all accuse me of verbosity. So, I'll get to the point."

"Hear, hear!" Nate led everyone in a group toast. They all raised a cup in jest.

"The anonymous caller told me the dead man was not Tío Dante. I asked him how he knew, and he responded by saying only that the dead man was a former federal official..."

"How could he possibly know that?" Miró asked.

"Mi'jita, that's exactly what I asked. He merely said that he had 'personal knowledge and evidence'."

"Dad," Max said, "are you sure you're not putting words in this caller's mouth?"

"I wouldn't make up such a story. Of course, I'm certain."

"Assuming that the caller is telling the truth," Max said, "what does he want you to do with the information?"

"He didn't say. I suppose he just wanted me to know."

"Dad, that doesn't make any sense. He obviously wants you to do something about it." Max waved the suggestion away.

"That's not all. The caller also said that I'd met the dead man before."

"Do you remember ever treating a former federal agent?" Nate asked.

"I don't. However, I'll review my files when I return to work on Monday," Abraham said. "But if the caller is telling the truth… well, I could've met this former federal agent in other capacities."

"Dad," complained Miró, "I thought you said we should stop second-guessing the authorities. We already know who the kidnapper was. And the Feds told us he died of natural causes. Are they lying?"

Max nodded in agreement. "Like Miró says, the Feds are ready to close the case on this one. Of course, we may have our doubts, but the caller could have countless motivations— instilling fear in us, leading the authorities off their trail, all sorts of things."

Nate shook his head vigorously. "No, I can't buy it. What would a federal official be doing in Miró's room? Or, was the caller also saying that the Feds kidnapped Miró?"

"I'm not suggesting we should believe the caller, every-one. What I'm trying to explain is different altogether," Abraham said.

"Everyone, I'll jump in to defend Gramps," Minnie said. "I know I'm just a kid without experience, but give Gramps a chance to explain what he thinks. Stop interrupting him!"

"Thank you, Minnie," Abraham said. "Finally, someone comes to my defense. I'm trying to say that we cannot dismiss the caller's claim. What if Tío Dante is still alive? What if the federal officials got it wrong, and they erroneously identified the corpse?"

Nate put his arm around his stepdaughter. "You're right, Min. Let's give Abraham a chance to talk."

"Abrám, mi amor, speak your mind," Miriam said.

"Thank you. And thank you, Minnie," Abraham said. "If we at least consider the caller may be telling the truth, it will change the entire investigation. The focus of our questions will revolve around the Feds, and what they may be trying to protect."

"Dad, do you realize what you're saying?"

"Mom," Minnie said, "we agreed we'd give Gramps a chance to speak his mind. Chill, let's listen."

"You're right, Minnie," a contrite Miró said.

"The only thing that I can add," Abraham said, "is that I'll review my medical files. If I can identify a former patient who was also a federal official, of approximately the same age, we'll have a lead. We can then examine his origins, his medical condition, occupation, and his genealogical records."

"Here we go again," Nate said. "I knew it would come back to his love of genealogy... Oops, I know, I know, Minnie. I'll let Gramps finish."

Abraham smiled good-naturedly. "I agree, Nate. I can't wait to investigate a stranger's genealogy. However, I'll do even better. I'll approach it from two sources. I'm thinking I'll place another call to our colleagues, Sánchez and Picard, to find out more about Tío Dante and his associates. If I can get birth records, parental origins and such, we'll find possible connections between him and the phantom federal official."

"And, if we find no connections, Dad?" Miró asked.

"Then we'll know the anonymous caller is lying and setting a trap for us," answered Abraham.

CHAPTER 12

Mazatlán, MX · November 2019

SEVERAL WEEKS HAD PASSED since the Rosales twins' arrival at Rodrigo's hacienda. Mornings and evenings had gotten slightly cooler, although temperatures during the day still rose into the eighties. The twins had become accustomed to the pleasant weather conditions and to their new routines under Rodrigo's roof. Not only had Estevan kept Pedro and Macario Rosales well fed, but Pedro had undergone two facial reconstructive surgeries. Cheekbones and skin grafting had given Pedro a more chiseled profile, and he had grown a well-trimmed goatee that contrasted with his brother's clean-shaven look. Their boss suggested that Pedro Half-Pants looked more distinguished, more serious.

Thus, Pedro Half-Pants gave up his denim shorts and adopted a dressy-casual attire that suited his 'station in life' more appropriately. Rodrigo approved.

"Mudo, I need to fix your pock-marked face. After he's done with Pedro, I'll tell Dr. Ivo Wu to clean you up." The following week, Mudo went under the knife. Following the dermabrasion and other tiny surgeries, Macario's healing failed to inspire him to buy a new wardrobe. He insisted that his workout clothing was more comfortable and just fine, despite Rodrigo's less-than-subtle suggestions.

. . .

Rodrigo's staff at the compound wondered why the new American arrivals, who were considered peers, were receiving such favorable treatment.

"Mates, if you haven't noticed, EG has taken you under his wing. He's dedicating time to grooming you for something big," Lucas Williams said. "The rest of the staff is curious... and a little jealous."

"While we have you here," Macario asked, "can you explain to us why Rodrigo uses 'thirteen', 'fourteen', 'nineteen hours', but sometimes he just says 'eight', or 'ten hours'? We can't make heads or tails out of it. Why doesn't he use regular hours on the clock?"

"That's because he uses military time," Lucas explained. "It's also called astronomical time. Not that complicated, mate."

Lucas went on to provide answers to the twins' many questions. He first started by saying that the military employed a twenty-four-hour clock, in which a day runs from midnight to midnight. Thus, 1 PM becomes 'thirteen hundred hours', and 4 PM is 'twelve plus four, or sixteen hundred hours'.

"Got it," Macario said, "so, 11 PM, in Rodrigo's language, is twenty-three hundred hours."

"You're a quick learner, Macario," Lucas said.

"Hold on," Pedro Half-Pants said. "I still don't get it."

"Hey, bro, don't worry. I'll go over it with you. Like Lucas said, it's not complicated," Macario said.

"We just want to stay in his good graces, Lucas," Pedro said. "And, in the last few weeks, we've learned more about different weapons than ever. Our daily visits to the gym and the firing range makes us better."

"You do look more fit now than when you arrived. That's for certain," Lucas said. "That's what I like about you, mates. You're fair dinkum."

"We have no idea what that means," Macario said.

Lucas chuckled, "Oh, I'm just saying, mates, you're okay, you're genuine. You know, you're straight-up."

"Rodrigo's told us, more than once, that he wants us to be prepared for our next trip back home to Chicago," Pedro said. "But we still don't know what our next assignment will be."

Over the next few days, the twins followed a regimen imposed on them by Rodrigo. Usually, instructions came from Estevan, but occasionally Rodrigo himself would send notes in his distinctive penmanship. The twins were 'on-call' twenty-four hours a day.

Pedro and Macario Rosales grew accustomed to being summoned. Estevan normally delivered individual messages to them. Since the twins required 24/7 healthcare following their surgeries, Rodrigo granted them separate suites. Always in calligraphy, the invitations gave them a precise time and location in the compound where Rodrigo wanted to meet. The latest invitation read, 'Meet me at the firing range at 1600 hours.'

Arriving ten minutes before their meeting time, the twins were surprised that at 1605 the boss had not arrived. Seconds later, Rodrigo opened the metal door and said, "Out here. I meant *at* the firing range, not *in* the firing range. I want you out here."

The twins were surprised to see the boss wearing an asbestos suit and a glass mask.

"Do you see those coyotes thirty meters away?" Rodrigo asked. The creatures were caged and seemed paralyzed. He swung a bulky tank on his left shoulder and triggered a rifle-like flamethrower. The swish of the huge flame was immediately followed by a moment of faint whimpers. The caged coyotes were quickly charred to a crisp. A couple of surrounding trees and some brush below caught fire. Attendants close by quickly put out the flames. The howling laughter from Rodrigo compelled the twins to also chuckle nervously.

"Now, witness this." Rodrigo took off his asbestos gear and turned in the opposite direction. The same sentinels that had been standing guard when the twins arrived at the hacienda set two cages down. One held two jaguars and the other one a pair of goats. In a dramatic pose worthy of an illusionist, Rodrigo planted his feet, and with one outstretched arm held his left hand outward, fingers splayed pointing upward. An unexpected laser-like flame surgically scorched the animals, without burning the cages or even leaving a trace of a singe on the vegetation around the cages.

"Wow," exclaimed Mudo.

Though speechless at first, Pedro added, "How did you do that, boss? And, where'd the flame come from?"

"It's a brand-new weapon. I had it developed," Rodrigo said. "I use bioethanol; it's a clean fuel."

"What weapon? I didn't see a weapon," Pedro said.

"I'll show you, Half-Pants." Rodrigo came closer and showed the twins a band on his wrist. "See that small caiman crawling behind you?"

Out of a watch-like gadget inside his wrist, from a tiny aperture came the laser-like flame into the ground three feet away. Pedro leapt two feet in the air. The frying sound that comes when an insect is electrocuted by a zapper filament galvanized the air. The caiman disintegrated.

"That's what I like to see. That's the way my enemies will burn."

"Which ones, Rodrigo?"

"You'll know in due time. Now, which of the two flamethrowers would you prefer?"

"The second one, of course," Pedro said. "It also looks safer, for the user, that is."

"I'll say."

With a twin on either side, Rodrigo started his walk back to the hacienda. A meandering gravel path lined with tall Mexican fan palms marked the way to the back entrance of the hacienda that led to the galería. As they approached the gardens, the twins got a whiff of the wisteria's fragrance. "I've grown to appreciate you like my own kids," Rodrigo said. "You're like family."

"Thanks," Pedro said.

Mudo looked away.

"Boys, my contacts in Washington DC called me today about the announcement they just made."

Silence from the twins.

"You know to what I'm referring. The authorities announced that your assignment is dead. And, you boys were too modest to bring me the news."

Each twin stole a glance, asking each other what Rodrigo meant. The boss went on.

"That's the reason that I'm taking you into my confidence. In return, I want you to have more trust in me," Rodrigo said. "Perhaps it's been my fault, but I feel like there are too many secrets between us."

"I don't know what you mean," Pedro said.

"For instance, I don't know how you gained access to the FBI, CÍA, and the American federales. Tell me how that happened."

"Boss, you've got more influence than we do," Pedro said.

"Tell you what. If we talk about connections, you show me yours, and I'll show you mine," Rodrigo said. All three men laughed.

Mudo opened his mouth, but only to address his brother. "Tell him about Cal, Pedro."

"Who the devil is Cal?" Rodrigo asked.

"I think you know who we're talking about," Pedro said.

"No, I don't."

"Maybe this is a test, boss, but you know who Cal is. But, if you want, we'll play along," Pedro said.

"Look, tell me who this Cal is," the boss said. Mudo could tell that Rodrigo was losing his temper.

"Just play along, Pedro," Mudo said.

"Okay, this may be a long story."

"You know I detest long stories, Pedro. Spit it out. Who's Cal?"

"Well, he's responsible for my switching sides, from El Chato's organization to yours. Cal knew we were El Chato Gómez's lieutenants, and he warned us that it was time to get out. He told us El Chato was going down."

"Whoa! You two have been keeping things from me. This sounds like an important player that I know nothing about."

"C'mon, boss. You know Cal."

"You're wrong. I don't," Rodrigo said.

"Actually, you did know about back door connections with El Chato's cartel. But you told us, through Estevan, that you didn't want direct contact or specific names. Your orders."

"So, do I need to know now?"

"If you want us to tell you, yes."

"Go ahead."

"Tell him, Pedro," Mudo said.

"Boss, you probably know all this, but Cal is an old friend of the Rosales family. He grew up in my dad's hood. Cal and my dad worked together in Chicago. In fact, Cal introduced me and my brother to the world of smuggling. When we were kids, because our hands were small enough to reach into gas tanks of cars, he taught us to stash drugs."

"How small a kid? Seven, eight?"

"I was six when I first got paid for my first job."

"So why is this important to me?" the boss asked.

The twins hesitated again.

"Boss, you can probably tell better than anyone why it's so important," Pedro said.

"Look, I'm losing my patience. I enjoy solving puzzles, but we're talking in circles."

"I think I see what you're doing, boss. You want to know how much information we have. But you also need to trust us. We'd never give away any of your secrets."

A hearty laugh. "Just like you betrayed your old boss, El Chato?" Rodrigo asked.

"This is very different."

"Explain why," Rodrigo said.

. . .

"Obviously, our comfort levels with each other need to improve before proceeding to the next level," Rodrigo said.

"Let me address a more pressing issue. I believe you're ready to return to Chicago. I've got an assignment for you."

For the next two hours, Rodrigo explained his plan very carefully. "It would simply entail eliminating a driver on her way home."

"Why is this target so important, boss?"

"Do I have to spell everything out to you?" Rodrigo asked. "I want her dead, and that's all you need to know."

"Well, I thought your most important goal was a different one... the ones you told us about at the firing range."

"Let me spell it out. Do you play billiards, Half-Pants?"

"You mean pool? Yes, I do."

"So, you know what 'prepping' is, right?"

"Yes, you mean preparing the next shot by locating your cue ball into position?"

"Exactly, you anticipate your next shot by placing the cue ball into the exact position to execute the kill shot," Rodrigo said. "This is the same thing, Half-Pants. My ultimate wish is to see my enemies burn. To get to them, I need for you to execute your assignment."

"I get it," Mudo said. "Our assignment is just the 'prep shot'."

"Yes, now you get it."

. . .

"Your present target is the key to reach my ultimate wish," Rodrigo said.

"So, do we go after that ultimate wish—the end goal— or should we go for the prep shot?" Pedro Half-Pants asked.

Rodrigo rolled his eyes, then closed them and mumbled, "Dios mío, dime si tengo un par de idiotas en mis manos." Rodrigo walked away without answering Pedro Half-Pants' question. He had exceeded all he could stomach from the two simpletons.

Pedro Half-Pants turned to his twin brother, shrugged and asked, "What did I say?"

CHAPTER 13

Evanston, IL · November 24, 2019

Unconvinced, Nate and Miró returned home after learning of the anonymous call to Abraham. The mysterious caller claimed that Tío Dante was alive. Furthermore, at least to Abraham, the caller's voice sounded like the one Nate had described the day Miró was found.

"What if—as remote a possibility as it may sound—what if the caller is providing accurate information?" Nate asked. "As Abraham says, can we afford to simply ignore the call?"

"I agree," admitted Miró. "It's frightening to consider that our law enforcement—all the way to the top—is covering something up. But, at least, we should dig some more."

"Since you don't have a morning class, we can both cancel appointments tomorrow morning. It'll give us a chance to visit Finn," Nate said.

Monday morning, Nate and Miró ventured into the frigid, barren streets to quiz Finn about the identity of the

Orrington Hotel casualty. The pristine and immaculate virgin snow that had been as white as wool just weeks before had undergone a sad transformation. The stuff covering the lawns and treetops of suburban Chicago was now a dull gray. The cold winds whipped the leafless, skeletal limbs of deciduous trees and dotted the Evanston neighborhoods with a lifeless blanket. The approaching winter had transformed the idyllic North Shore pastoral settings into a wet and slushy landscape. Driving Miró's SUV, Nate followed the parallel ruts on their street, making sure they didn't disturb the ugly drifts of snow on either side of their Volvo, lest they add to the dark berms against the curbs already forming along major boulevards.

A courteous and amiable Detective Finn greeted them at the police station lobby. He quickly offered mugs of hot coffee and doughnuts to 'warm their insides'. Miró and Nate declined. They looked at each other, surprised by the warm reception offered by a normally surly investigator.

"We were hoping to discuss the latest information you shared with the press and our PI," Miró said. "We learned that you've finally identified the dead man."

"We'd love to take the credit, ma'am, but the Feds took over the investigation early in the process. They telephoned us with all their findings. The deceased was a Mr. T. Dante, a foreign national. I'm pretty sure he was a Spaniard."

"Detective Finn, when you say, 'the Feds', to whom are you referring?" Nate asked.

"Our primary contact is in the Department of Justice headquarters in Washington DC. Apparently, he's been tracking this Tío Dante for a long time—since the Clinton era, I believe. His name is Jacoby Homely."

Miró spoke up. "When Max asked to see the coroner's report on the dead man, you refused, Detective. Also, Tribune reporter Horace Rosenfeld asked for those files, and he says you stonewalled him. Why the secrecy?"

"There's no 'stonewalling', as you call it, Mrs. Shelley."

"I'll ask for the courtesy of using my wife's appropriate title, Dr. or Professor Epstein-Shelley, Detective," Nate said. "As for the reluctance to share what should be a public record, we're simply baffled."

"Listen, Dr. Epstein, you might have to take it up with DOJ. They've imposed a gag order, and we can't do anything about it. Maybe they have an ongoing investigation, who knows? If so, they've got bigger fish to fry. You know what I mean?"

To extend the length of the conversation, Nate accepted Finn's coffee offer.

"Of course, Dr. Shelley. I just brewed a fresh pot."

Nate tasted the weak brew and smiled agreeably. "Detective Finn, we'd like to offer information about the deceased you've identified. Miró and I had some unfortunate contact with Mr. Dante and a European cartel with which he was involved two years ago."

"I see," Finn said.

For the next several minutes Nate and Miró described their misadventures in the Canary Islands. Though polite, Finn was dismissive and unimpressed. He acknowledged their direct contact with Tío Dante in Las Palmas, calling this 'unfortunate experience in the Caribbean' completely irrelevant for his purposes.

Miró corrected Finn, explaining that the Canary Islands are not in the Caribbean but near the Western coast of Africa. Finn responded with an unsurprising, "Whatever".

"When you say that this information is irrelevant to your purposes, Detective, what do you mean?" Nate asked. "Doesn't it suggest to you that other powerful criminals may be involved?"

"Like I said, Dr. Shelley, the whole investigation—if there is a continuing investigation—is out of my hands." With that, Finn looked at his watch and pretended to be late for 'an important meeting.' Their visit with Finn was over.

November 29, 2019

Given Finn's disinterest in learning about Tío Dante, Nate and Miró returned to their workweek, hoping to tackle their tasks with more productive results. Nate stopped at Starbucks before attacking the work in his office. He checked his phone and realized an email from Dr. Beech, an old friend from the World Psychiatric Association, had landed in his inbox. The reality was that the communication had been dispatched by Macario Rosales, the more tech savvy of the twins that worked for Rodrigo. When Nate opened the email and checked the attachment, an old photo of the Canary Islands world conference appeared. By opening the attachment, Nate unleashed a sophisticated malware attack that instantly seized control of his phone's operating system. Within seconds, Nate's phone exported all his emails to Macario, as well as private messages, telephone metadata, and his entire internet browsing history. All this occurred without Nate's knowledge. Worse still, via the malware, his phone's camera and microphone provided a live feed of Nate's every move.

In addition, Macario and his twin brother now had access to all the private numbers in Nate's contact list, and even those numbers were compromised fully.

Nate ended his day, satisfied that he had accomplished some things at work, even if his meeting with Finn had flopped.

• • •

Late that week, Max invited himself to dinner at Nate's.

"I'll show up with a couple of pizzas, and we can chat for a while," Max said. "I'd like to compare notes with y'all— you and Miró, I mean. Dad seems to be on a roll, and I need help understanding him."

"We welcome the opportunity to get away from turkey dishes for a while. Thanksgiving dinner always does that to me," Nate said. "Deep dishes for you and me, thin crusts for Miró and Minnie."

"Dude, it's Friday. Minnie has a date viewing the latest movie with her grandparents, remember?"

Max showed up at 7:30 with a stack of pizza boxes from Lou Malnati's. Before placing the pizzas on the kitchen island, he took his last bite of the buffalo wings he'd bought on the side.

Miró could tell that Max was eager to get into his account of Abraham's latest musings. "Okay, Big Brother, you've had your first slice. Before you wolf down the rest of the pizza, I'll serve you another glass of chianti and…"

"I brought a six-pack of Negra Modelo, and I'll grab one of those instead," Max said. "I left them in the fridge." As he retrieved his beer, Max jumped right in, "Dad, he's now shaping a wild conspiracy that involves the NSA and other government agencies."

"What? Dad does have an imagination… and a tendency to fashion intricate scenarios," Miró said. "In his defense, though, I admit that his wild musings during the Canary Islands adventure led us to the killer."

"That part of the story I had not heard," Max said. He wondered, *Was it possible that Abraham was right? What were the odds?* "His imagination is going wild," Max said. "I mean, what are the odds that our own spies would attempt to kidnap you—or Minnie, for that matter?"

"Why on earth would the CIA or NSA do that?" Miró asked.

"What?" exclaimed Nate. "Can't you believe the Feds would harm our family?"

"Are you on Dad's side now, Nate? Are you serious?"

"Okay, my turn," Nate said. "Why didn't the authorities release to the press—or even to us—the dead man's autopsy report, his dental records, or other vital physical records?"

No response.

"Look, you two. From Miró's description of the dead man, it could have been a person other than Tío," Nate said. Now addressing Max, Nate went on to say, "Do you remember that you even told me that the corpse looked older?"

"Nate, the description of the man who kidnapped Miró fit Tío Dante's description," Max said.

"Not entirely. Something about the corpse made you think he was older," Nate said. "What was that?"

"Fair enough, Dad asked the same thing. I told him that the man's forearms and elbows had crepe-like skin."

"What was Abraham's response?"

"I must admit that his explanation made a lot of sense," Max said. "He explained that although a person's muscle tone could be excellent, the skin is always a giveaway. With age, the skin gets thinner... and crepe-like."

"Didn't that catch your attention?" Nate asked.

"I suppose it still seems far-fetched. Don't you agree?"

"Look, everyone, all of us have vacillated throughout this whole thing. From the start, nothing added up. What I suggest," Nate said, "is that we give Abraham an opportunity to state his case. It's not entirely fair to get his explanation through our filtered perspectives."

"I'll give Dad a call," Miró said, "and I'll ask him if he's willing to get in a call with us. We'll use speakerphone."

. . .

"Hey, you two, Dad is asking us to come over and give the three of them time to finish watching the movie. Minnie is into the movie, and she would not consider allowing her Gramps to skip such a great flick. What do you say?" Miró asked. "It's only a little past nine and Dad says the roads look decent."

They arrived at Abraham's home shortly before ten. As soon as they unloaded coats and mufflers, they shuffled to the living room, where Abraham and Miriam were waiting. Minnie was on a phone call with Calvin, one of the most serious contenders for her undivided attention.

Max opened the conversation with a confession of sorts. "Dad, I needed to compare notes with Nate and Miró. You know how I disagree with you about your most recent hypothesis."

"Son, don't apologize. You're getting paid to examine every viewpoint, even mine. I, too, fail to understand this whole thing," Abraham said.

"Dad, is there someone in particular that you suspect? When you talked to Max, were you thinking of a government employee, a staff member, or patient, whom you suspect?"

"No, Miró. Since my son is an investigator examining a death, a kidnapping, and possibly a murder, I'm considering all possibilities. I don't know any government goons that may be involved. If I had such a patient, I would not have a legal right to review publicly every detail of his file. However, if I did have any privileged files, I would be obligated to share them with various federal offices, even those without security clearance, in the name of national security."

"Hmm. Good to know," Miró said.

. . .

The following morning Nate called the local office of the FBI. He was surprised that the local "field office" worked Saturdays. The receptionist directed his call to the chief's personal secretary. Although Special Agent Ram Edmunds was unavailable, Laurie, the friendly assistant, assured Nate that Agent Edmunds promptly responded to all calls within twenty-four hours. Nate left his cellular phone number and the reason for his call.

After hearing the nature of Nate's call, Laurie quickly added, "If it concerns the Epstein-Shelley case, I'm certain he'll respond right away. For the last two days, Agent Edmunds has called for 'an all-hands-on-deck'. For him, this particular case seems to be of high priority."

Shortly after 1 PM, Nate received the call from Special Agent Edmunds. "Thank you for contacting our field office,

Dr. Shelley. I've been reviewing your wife's case, and, frankly, I have several concerns."

"As we do, Agent Edmunds," Nate said. "Of greatest concern is the amount of time it took to identify the cause of the kidnapper's death and even his identity."

"I can understand."

"I don't want to be indelicate," Nate said, "but we—our family—has reasons to believe that some procedural questions are warranted."

"Please clarify, Dr. Shelley," Edmunds said.

"Sorry for being so vague, Agent Edmunds. Of course, we were frustrated about the length of time it took to make such simple determinations as cause of death and identification of the deceased. However—and you may think we're out of line—we also question whether the identification of the corpse is accurate... and we believe we have information that may help you."

"And you believe the information that you can provide," asked Edmunds, "is information that our local police, as well as the personnel at the national headquarters of the FBI, simply overlooked?"

"As unlikely as it may sound, yes," Nate said.

Edmunds paused for a long while. He then asked Nate if he could put him on hold. After several moments, he returned to the line. "I've asked Laurie, my assistant, to adjust my schedule, Dr. Shelley. Could I ask you to come downtown to our field office for a brief meeting?"

Nate agreed and asked if he could bring Miró with him. Edmunds, of course, agreed.

By 4:15 PM the Shelleys were sitting in Edmunds' office. Laurie offered them refreshments, but only Nate agreed to have some mineral water. "Thank you for meeting with us, Agent Edmunds. We have been extremely frustrated about..."

Miró interrupted, "...about getting a runaround from law enforcement."

"I'm sorry to hear that. I cannot promise that I have any additional information, but I can assure you that I will disclose to you whatever is possible within the law."

"We'll get to the point. There are several reasons why we doubt the information that's been made public by the FBI headquarters and the local police administration, but I'll address the two most important points," Nate said. Enumerating with his forefinger, he stated his first point. "The day we found Miró after her kidnapping, I received an anonymous call telling me where I could find my wife."

"Please wait, Dr. Shelley," Edmunds said. "Nowhere in the various reports that I've read is that detail listed. All reports suggest that the local police were notified by your PI, Maximillian Kempball. Notes also indicate that you and Mr. Kempball arrived at the Orrington Hotel shortly after the police."

Miró agreed, "It is true that Max called the police. However, Nate called Max, rather than the police, because he was confused about receiving such a strange call."

"May I ask what you found strange, Dr. Shelley?" Edmunds asked, as he turned to Nate.

"The caller had a gruff, gravelly voice, and he told me my wife was at the hotel, being held by a killer. I suspected it was a trap of some kind," Nate said.

"Hmm."

"I should also add that, although I didn't recognize the voice at the time, it sounded much like Tío Dante's voice. And, as you know, your colleagues at the DC headquarters have identified Tío Dante as the deceased kidnapper."

"So, clarify for me, Dr. Shelley. How could you possibly identify Teodosio Dante's voice?" Ram Edmunds asked.

"When our family went through false accusations of murder in the Canary Islands three years ago, I met an unsavory character who was deeply involved with a drug lord. In fact, he served as the drug lord's right-hand man. His name was Teodosio Dante, though he was known as 'Tío' back then."

"Assuming it's the same person you met in the Canary Islands, you find it difficult to believe that he would've placed that call which informed you of your wife's whereabouts." Edmunds was asking a question.

"Think about it. What possible reason could the kidnapper have for leading me to Miró, his kidnapped victim?"

"Did the caller demand a ransom?"

"No."

"I realize it stretches the imagination, Dr. Shelley, but you must agree it would not be an impossibility... you said you had two important points."

Nate gestured with his second finger. "I believe the second matter could be definitive," Nate said. "Tío Dante, the presumed dead kidnapper, had two prominent gold incisors. If we can get a confirmation from the federal medical examiner that the deceased did indeed have the gold teeth, I—and the rest of our family—will be satisfied with the present findings. In other words, we'll accept the fact that the dead man was Tío Dante."

"Excellent. I believe that should not be difficult to obtain," said Agent Edmunds. "I know that several odontological exams were made. We should be able to get the actual X-rays."

CHAPTER 14

Chicago, IL · December 2, 2019

FTER THE WEEKEND MEETING at the Chicago field office, Miró returned to her normal schedule at the university. On her drive, she used her headphones to listen to one of her husband's favorite songs, *Here Comes the Sun*. A spring to her step that had disappeared returned. The smells of winter in the university offices seemed to improve the collective mood of the entire campus. Even the normally distracted faculty members appeared to smile more, and the flavored hot teas around campus, mixed with the pine cones in the occasional wreath, warmed the community with cheer.

As a tenured faculty member, her hours afforded the most flexibility, but she felt she'd abused her leave privileges. Thus, she asked Abraham, Miriam, and Max to take charge of Minnie's transportation to and from school. With volleyball practices and after-school activities, Minnie's schedule often required more coordination than the five adults could handle.

Nate also returned to his office on Monday in a more hopeful state. He wondered, however, if Ram Edmunds would truly investigate the various inconsistencies that he and Miró had presented. Or, like others in the law enforcement community, would Edmunds ignore their doubts and continue with business as usual?

After the lengthy layoff from his practice, which had lasted more than he'd anticipated, Nate tried to catch up with neglected patients and emails. He asked his executive assistant to reschedule patients and extend his consultation hours. Other important correspondence, related to the World Psychiatric Association, also demanded his immediate attention.

As he took his first sip of the wassail that his executive assistant had offered upon arrival, Nate found the short email that had arrived at 5:45 that morning. It brought on instantaneous nausea. Without time to even grab his wooden wastebasket, he vomited twice. His violent heaves could be heard from his assistant's office area. Fortunately, only one patient was waiting for his session. He was a new patient who curiously wore a fedora on a cold Chicago morning. Emily Farnsworth, Nate's executive assistant, deliberately kicked a small metal wastebasket to make a distracting noise, and she busily rustled some papers on her desk. More than likely, the patient in the waiting area could still hear the violent retching from within. Emily nervously got up from her desk and offered the new patient some coffee or any other desired beverage. The man thanked her, but refused her offer.

Ms. Farnsworth assumed her boss was feeling ill, and she hoped that her recipe for homemade wassail had not upset Nate's stomach. But she was embarrassed for him. The noise coming from his office quickly became more faint, as she heard the door to his private bathroom open and shut. Smiling, the new patient announced he was canceling his appointment. Shaking his head, he walked out.

Already behind in his practice because of his frequent need to attend to family matters, Nate felt ambushed by the menacing email. The words had assaulted his emotional and physical well-being. 'A severe form of distress' would have been his initial note if he were his own patient. His own personal therapist and mentor, Mike Stein, would probably ask him, "How did your reaction to the email make you feel, Nate?"

"Embarrassed, Mike. I was embarrassed. Somehow it made me feel weak as a man and incompetent as a psychoanalyst." The entire hypothetical dialogue played out in Nate's mind. What he would've withheld from his mentor was that in addition to the violent vomiting, he'd experienced momentary bladder incontinence. He'd peed on himself.

Totally humiliated, he barricaded himself in his office for the rest of the day and instructed Ms. Farnsworth to cancel the rest of his appointments. That afternoon at 5:30, he instructed her to go home and not to worry about locking up the office. He'd take care of that. Finally, at 6 PM, Nate took the Red Line to Evanston, certain that everyone on the train could smell the stale urine on his gray worsted wool pants. None of this would he later divulge to anyone.

. . .

Nate got home and changed immediately. Then, he drove directly to the nearby dry cleaners to deposit his slacks in the overnight slot.

Although he did not intend to share the embarrassing part with Miró, he thought of the best way to inform her about the email without alarming her. He decided to do it over dessert at their favorite restaurant.

Nate called Miró to suggest that his in-laws hold the regularly scheduled 'Friday night flick watching' on Monday night. And, that it be hosted at the Shelleys' own home in Evanston.

"Nate! That's a couple of hours away. They just hosted Minnie last Friday night. We need to give them an advanced notice for these things. You know how Mom goes all out to prepare a meal, dips, popcorn, et cetera."

"I know. I know I'm being inconsiderate, but after you hear the reason, you'll agree this situation merits a change in plans," Nate said.

"And, you know how Minnie enjoys her Friday night visits to her grandparents..."

Nate realized that though he'd spent a mini-fortune on fancy speakers and a larger flat-screen, he knew that Minnie preferred her Gramps' full media room—featuring the best home theater system. Abraham had invested big bucks on a Polk audio system, with massive sound from eleven speakers and 3.1 channels and a subwoofer, whatever that meant.

Plus, the theater-like reclining-easy-chair viewing was hard to match. "Nothing but the best for my granddaughter," Abraham had said, although Nate suspected Abraham enjoyed his toy just as much as Minnie.

Using a more conciliatory tone, Miró finished her thought. "But if you think it's that important, I'll go along. I'll even be the one to explain to my parents why there's been a change in plans."

"No need. I spoke to Abraham already."

Nate outlined his plans for them both to visit Va Pensiero for post-dinner desserts and drinks. He also mentioned that Max had offered to join the watch party.

"Then, we'll talk about an email that I received today." Nate bit his lower lip.

"What email, Nate?"

"Please don't think I'm being dramatic," Nate said, "but it'll be better if we can both dedicate full attention to this thing over dessert. It needs to happen away from home, where no one will be eavesdropping."

"Now you're scaring me."

"Just trust me. This can wait until we get to the restaurant. I'll explain the whole thing," Nate said as reassuringly as he could.

Though compliant, Miró was distracted during dinner at home. She and Nate explained to Minnie about the need to change plans for the evening, and Minnie accepted it better than they both anticipated.

The frozen salmon piccata that Norma—their three-day-a-week cook—had left for them was perfect. There was no fuss in the reheating and minimal clean-up. By 8:40 that evening, Nate and Miró were sitting at their favorite table at Va Pensiero. Though Nate was tempted to ask for a glass of wine, he decided a cappuccino was a better choice. He needed to stay focused and sharp.

"So, Sherlock, why aren't you wearing your surfer sleuth clothing?" Miró asked.

"My what?" Nate asked.

Miró grinned and responded, "That's what I call the persona that overtakes you when you get into sleuth mode: Surfer Sleuth."

"Okay, I remember. You're referring to the clothes I'd wear in the Canaries when I finally got proactive and took things into my own hands."

"Well, just remember that you did get help from Inspector Sánchez, Carlos Lacroa, and even Interpol," Miró said.

"True."

"Okay, out with it. The lingering question remains. What did this ominous email say?" Miró asked.

"'Minnie is next'; that's all it said."

A lengthy silence.

Then, Miró bombarded Nate. "Did you respond? Did you attempt to trace it? 'Next' for what? Did they explain it?" Nate failed to immediately address any of her questions. She was lost in the worst pit of the imagination.

When Nate did respond, he knew he was filling air space. Miró was not listening.

"Of course I tried to immediately respond to the email. 'Who is this?' I asked in an email. After several attempts, I called in the techies at the office. They couldn't help either. I then called Max to ask if I should report it to Finn or the Feds. His answer was: 'Don't expect anything from any of the cops, but have them in the loop. More importantly, if needed in the future, you can cite that you reported this threat.'"

Miró said, "I know we both need a clear head, but I'm asking for a Bellini, my love."

"Of course." Before Nate had a chance to summon their waiter, he was at Nate's side, asking what they'd like. The Bellini took less than ninety seconds to arrive.

Miró gulped it down and asked for another one. She reassured Nate with a stroke of her hand on his forearm, "Don't worry. I won't overdo it. But I do need this—now!"

Again, the Bellini arrived quickly.

"You know," Nate said, "when we brought up the Canarian crooks at the Orrington, you almost lost it. I don't want that again, love." Nate felt dishonest withholding his own vomiting episode at the office and his bladder incontinence.

"Nate, I'll be fine. This just caught me unprepared. I suppose going through my own kidnapping… and my second murder accusation… well, I assumed things were under control. My kidnapper is dead, or, at least, we think he is.

If someone else ends up dead, then I'll consider it the bad guys eliminating each other... but this..."

"Listen to me," Nate said, "we won't let this email overwhelm us. Last time in the Canaries, we almost allowed that lurking evil to defeat us. That's before we learned how powerful we can be when we fight back... together." Nate continued with a smile. "And... that was before we learned how awesome I can be when I wear those flowery beach shirts, which transform me into the 'surfer sleuth'."

Miró laughed. It was the first visceral levity Miró had shown all evening. "My love, do you mean the dude who tails criminals, rescues children, and protects families?"

Nate felt like such a fake. "That's right. About time I bring out that wardrobe."

They both remembered with fondness how each time Nate took the initiative to retaliate against the seasoned Canary Islands criminals, something good happened.

Although the concern did not disappear, Nate realized how powerfully his reassurance affected his wife. Though he felt totally fraudulent, his bravado seemed to help them both.

CHAPTER 15

That Monday night, as soon as they got home, Nate rushed upstairs to change. Miró, instead, joined the party in the den where Minnie, her uncle Max, and her grandparents were into their second tub of buttered popcorn and about to finish watching *Tolkien*.

"Mom," Minnie said, "you would enjoy the movie. It's all about how the author fell in love, had this sad love affair, then joined a group of friends who inspired him to write *The Hobbit, Lord of the Rings,* and all the other cool stuff. Oh, and how World War I affected all of them. We can watch again from the beginning, if you're interested."

Miró smiled at the rest of the party, "Maybe later this coming weekend, munchkin. It may be late to start a movie at this hour."

When Nate returned downstairs, he was wearing his yellow flowered beach shirt over a black Tee. Though he did not wear his shades, he did wear the Cubbies baseball cap. Completing the look of this alternate persona were his khakis and white sneakers.

"Ah, yes, my dear," Miró said. "I see you're back to the out-fit you wore when you rescued me from that fire at the hospital."

"Mom!" complained Minnie. "That's the outfit he used when he rescued me from those horrible kidnappers. The night of the fire, he was not wearing his 'beach sleuth' clothes."

Nate agreed. "My love, Minnie's right. I first wore this outfit the day I rescued her from Diego Montemayor's house."

"Okay. I stand corrected, but the term I use for your stepdad is 'surfer sleuth', not 'beach sleuth', Minnie."

"Whatever, Mom. I still think it's cool."

Max interjected, "Isn't the term for 'cool' now 'Gucci', Ms. Mouse?"

"Oh, Uncle Max, 'Gucci' is so yesterday!" With exaggerated disapproval, she reacted to Max's attempt. Then, after a slight pause, she admitted to her uncle she was impressed.

Bravely, Max asked, "Can someone explain to me what the beach fashions have to do with anything?"

Miriam rushed into the conversation, "It's somewhat complicated, but suffice it to say that Nate seems to take on a magical persona when he dons those clothes, Max."

"That's cool. So, are you intending to take over my job, Bro?" Max smiled as he stuffed his face with a handful of popcorn.

While Miró convinced Minnie it was time for her to turn in, Max and Nate discussed their plans to watch the Chiefs play the Patriots that coming weekend. "I'm betting on that kid from Kansas City to give the Patriots a whupping," Max said.

Nate apologized to Max for abruptly shifting the subject from the football viewing.

"Now that Miró is taking Minnie to bed, I'll briefly explain to you what I shared with Miró this evening."

He addressed several questions, but summarized it all by saying, "We're very concerned, Family, but I believe Miró is in dire need of all our support."

Friday, December 6, 2019

Preparing for the weekend full of football viewing, Max picked Abraham up at his downtown clinic to run some errands. As Max and Abraham drove into the circular entry, they noticed Nate's vehicle parked in front. "Hmm... what's Nate doing here at this hour?" As Max clicked the remote garage opener, Nate stormed out the front door.

"What the hell, Max?" Nate was screaming. "Why didn't you let Abraham take the train back from work?"

"Nate, calm down." Miró followed Nate out. Not once had she heard Nate use that tone—or volume. "Max left Minnie in good hands. It's not the first time that Mom picks her up."

"Not after receiving a death threat!"

Abraham retrieved his own bag and the wine they'd picked up at Sam's Liquor Store. He closed the trunk and in his measured tone, intervened, "Okay, mi'jita, tell me what happened..."

"We think Minnie's been taken, Dad." Now, releasing her first sob, Miró stammered, "We tried calling you, texting you..."

"What?" Max could not believe it. He'd been checking his cell phone every fifteen minutes. "We received nothing from you, Miró."

Nate interrupted, "Nor did you think of calling or checking, did you?"

"Nate, please." Miró was embracing her dad but walked over to Nate to soothe him. She gave Max an apologetic look.

"No, Nate's right. I deserve that. I should've known better." Max walked over to Nate and tried to apologize. Nate turned from him and walked into Abraham's house.

Max stood at the kitchen's granite island and checked his phone for missed messages. None. The rest walked into the den, with Abraham asking for details. Miró provided them. Nate continued to interrupt, stating that he needed to secure better professional protection.

"Dang," Max said from the kitchen. "I can't understand it." He slapped the hard surface and berated himself in silence. With tears in his eyes, he approached Nate to beg for forgiveness.

Again, Nate walked away.

"When was the last time you heard from Minnie?" Abraham scrutinized his daughter's countenance.

"This morning. She texted me from school before lunch period, as she normally does."

"And, your mom?" Miró could tell that her dad was holding his breath.

"We haven't heard from Mom either..."

"Since when?"

"Since she told me Max had asked her to pick up Minnie. That must've been between 8:30 and 9:00 this morning."

Hardly waiting for Miró to finish her response, Abraham immediately dialed Miriam's number. The call went directly to voicemail.

Max broke the painful silence, "I'm trying to track Minnie's phone, and Miriam's, via GPS. No luck. Someone's scrambled locations to link up with police dispatchers in Chicago."

Just then, Max got a call. It was Detective Finn.

"Hi, Tex. Finn here. You got any information for me?"

"I was hoping for some information from you, Officer Finn."

"As a detective, I can only tell you that we have an APB on a new model, black Suburban with slight front-end damage. Both Minnie and her grandmother were broadsided by this Suburban outside Ursuline Academy. CCTV images are clear up to a certain point."

"What do you mean, up to a certain point?"

"Somehow, images following the accident just disappeared."

"How the devil does a CCTV image just disappear, Finn?"

"Hey, I'm the messenger here. I'm telling you like it is."

"They were hit when, Finn? What time?"

"At exactly 4:13 PM."

"But school lets out at 3:30 PM," Max said. "That's more than a thirty-minute gap."

A pause from Finn, "I'm here merely to tell you what we know, Tex. I'm not justifying the perps' poor scheduling." That Finn. Always a charmer.

CHAPTER 16

S INCE FINN MENTIONED THE intersection of two roads behind Ursuline Academy, Max determined the next steps to be taken. He would ask Finn for available CCTV files showing the accident. "Nate, let's drive to the station house to look at the video files. I will need your help."

A few minutes later Max and Nate arrived at the police station. Finn was cooperative. The CCTV footage showed two vehicles—one a silver Lexus SUV, the other a late-model black Suburban that hit the passenger side of the Lexus broadside.

Although CCTV showed two females inside the Lexus, they remained in the vehicle throughout the recording. Two men, same height and built, presumably the drivers of the Suburban, wore the same black attire—jeans, black jackets, and black baseball hats. They both wore black hiking boots. The emblem on the caps was not legible, but Nate thought it said Sox. The men in black walked around to both vehicles, examining the damage.

Oddly, in the video the females remained seated in the Lexus without moving, and they seemed to look forward throughout. To a few passersby, the scene appeared to be the result of a simple fender-bender involving two vehicles. The men in black who were examining the damage waved at the passersby and smiled cordially, indicating all was in order. They both nodded in unison to bid onlookers on their way.

Next, the video showed a gray-haired man walking his Yorkie. Confronted by the Suburban driver, the man and his dog quickly departed. Picking up his pet, he hurriedly marched home.

The ensuing fifty seconds of the video, however, stood out. Though the two males looked in all directions and hesitated before making their next move, one trotted to the Suburban and held open the side door. The other one, baseball bat in hand, took the arm of the woman on the driver's side of the Lexus and yanked her out. He then reached across the front seat for the smaller female with a lacerated arm. Much blood covered the right arm from her elbow to her wrist. Two simultaneous events followed. First, the female on the driver's side of the Lexus bit the man who was holding the baseball bat. At that moment, a police car arrived.

The CCTV video then froze.

After viewing the video half a dozen times, Max invited Nate to review the tape once more. Nate asked, "So what can we deduce from the tape, Max?"

"First, someone tampered with the CCTV files. Secondly, we can be certain, although we do not have license plate numbers, that Miriam was driving her silver Lexus RX350, heading south on Lakeshore. It's also quite clear that the passenger is Minnie. Seconds before the collision, the video shows a black Suburban heading east at a higher than normal speed on a side road behind the school's soccer field. Given shots of the intersection prior to the missing portion, it does not appear that the Suburban stopped at the three-way intersection. Although Miriam appeared to swerve to avoid the collision, the Suburban T-boned the Lexus and hit the passenger side with enough force to ram it off the road."

"You're missing the major point," Nate said. "That missing portion of the video can lead us to Minnie, Miriam, and their kidnappers."

. . .

Out of respect for Finn's position, Max took him to the side and asked, "Okay, Finn, an outsider was given access to the CCTV tapes. Who?"

"Tex, you're asking me? I'm a low-level detective who can't even pull a weekend off if I beg."

"C'mon, Finn. You use that 'poor country boy' routine when it suits you. You know more than what you're saying."

"All I know is… if someone can manage that kind of influence, we're dealing with serious power. Way beyond our pay grade."

"Have you guys checked hospitals or clinics in the area?" Nate asked from the viewing room. "My daughter needs medical attention."

"Yes, we've checked... and we know Max has also been snooping around, calling area hospitals and clinics," Finn said. "Didn't you say the kid's grandmother is a physician?"

"That's true. If allowed, her grandmother could care for her," Max said. "That's a big question, though. Isn't it, Finn?"

. . .

That evening Nate and Max returned to Nate's home in Evanston. Abraham joined them later. Uncharacteristically quiet, each attacked a different chore. The mood was somber. Late into the night, Max and Nate checked in with Finn and called area hospitals and clinics. Without Nate knowing it, Max called the morgue. No information on the victims. No police reports of the black Suburban being sighted.

The four spent the night in Nate's home office. Exhausted, Miró fell asleep in Nate's favorite chair-and-a-half. Abraham walked into the den and made a few calls. He dozed off for a few hours. Aided by prodigious amounts of caffeine, Nate and Max worked through the night. Max searched the dark web, hoping to get an isolated discussion or images of the kidnapping. Nate called Horace Rosenberg at the Tribune to inquire about any possible clues unearthed during the day. Rosenberg had nothing.

While Nate was speaking to Rosie from the Tribune, Max made some fascinating discoveries. In the dark web, he found his own conversations with Nate and Miró replicated verbatim. When he reviewed dates, he determined that for at least the last five days, all their calls and communications, including emails, had been compromised. More interestingly, any recipients of their calls or communications were also tapped. It appeared the hackers were 'piggybacking' from their calls to people at the other end to capture a string of communications that grew exponentially.

"Nate, check this out. You need to see this," Max said. He stepped away from his laptop and showed their verbatim conversations splashed across cyberspace.

"Whoa! I had no idea that was possible. How many people have seen this, Max?" Nate asked.

"I truly have no idea, Nate. However, what I can say is that I will probably be able to identify the hackers."

"How long will it take?"

Max smiled. "I'm not certain, but these characters are not very sophisticated, probably kids. What I mean to say is that they do not cover their tracks very well. Nonetheless, I realize how disturbing this can be."

Before dawn, Max had traced the hacking to the Chicago metropolitan area. It appeared to originate from one laptop, but it could also involve more than one device. He immediately consulted with Nate.

"I'm sorry to say, we're all affected. We need to change all our internet fingerprints, passwords, account numbers, the works. It seems they've been tracking our steps—they knew our schedules, our patterns, and heard our private conversations. Oddly, they didn't seem to get into our financials or investment accounts, as far as I could determine."

"But you can't be sure," Nate was inquiring.

"It's best to check, Nate."

"Whose number did they crack first?" Nate asked.

"The first evidence I found was at 5:45 AM on Monday morning, Nate. It seems they broke in through your email account at your office. However, there's traces of their monitoring your activities shortly before Monday."

"You know if they're monitoring other calls or emails?" Nate asked.

"We're safe now, as far as I can tell. However, they seem to be monitoring Agent Edmunds and Rosie from the Tribune."

"Anyone we know doing this?" Nate asked.

"I traced it to some Hispanic name from Chicago," Max said. "I'll call Rosie."

"I'll warn Special Agent Edmunds. I'll wait until 9 AM, though," Nate said. "Though they work weekends, on Saturdays, he may come in later."

. . .

"Hello, Dr. Shelley. I apologize for not reaching out to you regarding our last conversation." Ram Edmunds had answered the 9 AM call, and he assumed that Nate was following up on their last visit. "I have not neglected to request dental records for the deceased found at the Orrington Hotel. It appears that our Washington DC headquarters has lost track of those records, but they've promised to get back to me as soon as possible."

"Oh, no worries, Agent Edmunds. I'm calling regarding a different matter. Very quickly, let me tell you that my daughter and mother-in-law, Dr. Miriam Epstein, have been kidnapped. I know this is outside your purview, and the local police is investigating. I still wanted to inform you."

"I'm truly sorry to hear it, Dr. Shelley."

"Also, I have some additional information. We have reason to believe that our family's phones and electronic communications have been hacked."

"That's odd," Edmunds said. "That's exactly what I heard from our headquarters in Washington DC. Apparently, they, too, have been compromised by a foreign government, and the reason for the disappearance of the dental records is an alleged hacking."

"I see."

"Forgive me if I sounded insensitive. Of course, your personal concern is warranted." Special Agent Ram Edmunds was clearly interested. "When and how did you discover this, Dr. Shelley?"

"My brother-in-law Max Kempball, who is also employed as our private investigator, made the discovery early this morning," Nate said. "Furthermore, he also suggested that I call you, since he believes that your communications may also be compromised, because of the hacking directed at us. I'm no technological whiz, and I don't understand how these things work, but he seems to be certain that was the case."

"If you don't mind," Edmunds said, "I will transfer this call to our techie in charge, because he will need a few more details from you. He'll simply ask for dates, individuals whose accounts were hacked, that kind of thing."

"I'll be glad to provide as much information as possible."

Evanston, IL · Monday, December 9, 2019

Early morning, Miró left for her university office. She kissed Nate goodbye and promised to return after an important meeting. Professor Epstein-Shelley had called a meeting of her faculty to elect the department's tenure committee. She reminded her colleagues of the grave importance of an ancient revered process respected by the fraternity of academia. Several junior members of the faculty eagerly nominated their tenured colleagues to gain favor with the most influential seniors. Their accolades bordered on excess, but everyone observed with decorum the young scholars' efforts for self-endearment. The theater in the dynamics of faculty meetings were remarkably similar in most academic settings, and Miró had learned the sophisticated games well.

Into the second hour of deliberations, Miró's executive assistant interrupted the meeting. Miró stared at her assistant, but trusting her judgment implicitly, she took the handwritten note from her. She read the photocopy of the note: "We're holding your mom and Minnie. Meet us at the main lobby of the Drake Hotel at exactly 5 PM. You and Nate come alone—we're watching."

Miró lost her concentration. She abruptly postponed the faculty meeting until 'first thing' in the morning. That meant to everyone 8 AM sharp. Miró rushed to her office and called Nate. She interrupted Nate's session with a patient, explaining it was an emergency.

"The note says to meet them at 5 PM at the Drake, Nate. And it also said they're watching us."

CHAPTER 17

Evanston – Chicago · December 9, 2019

THE FOUR FAMILY MEMBERS—Nate, Miró, Max, and Abraham—returned to Nate's home office.

"All I'm saying, Nate, is that I won't let you and my sister walk into that hotel alone." It was Max, treading lightly since Nate's outburst against him. "You may not trust my judgment completely, but I've been hired to do a job. And Dad wants the family protected."

"On the other hand, you can't guarantee my daughter's nor Miriam's safety either, can you?" Nate said. "The note to Miró clearly said, 'Come alone'."

"I understand completely, Nate. I simply think that it's unsafe to walk in there without protection."

An awkward silence ensued. The family was stunned and momentarily without an alternative plan.

"Okay, y'all, I made some discoveries during the night," Max said. "I've shared this with Nate, and he reported all of it to Agent Edmunds from the FBI. Our calls have been tapped and our electronic mail and social media accounts have been hacked. I've learned from the Israelis how to create a chuppah, or a tent of protection that I think works, because it allows me to speak on the phone without electronic eavesdropping. I'm back to secure communication. And, if you allow me, I can do the same for all of us."

"Hooray! How can that possibly help us right now, Max?" Nate's comment was dripping with sarcasm. "We've got a deadline, and it's coming up in three hours."

"Yes," Miró said. "Nate, we need to go."

"Unless this discovery sheds light on the most recent kidnapping, mi'jita," Abraham said. "Max is attempting to insulate us from additional intrusion from the culprits."

"Well, we now know someone scrambled our calls and the GPS on Miriam's and Minnie's phones," Max said. "They've been tracking all of us."

"Big Brother, that's great information, but it doesn't help ensure my Minnie's safety, or Mom's," Miró said.

Hands on his hips, Max turned and stepped away, raking his straight blond hair. As if muzzled, he pulled at his T-shirt's ribbed collar, turned back to Nate, and started to respond. He was unable to verbalize a response. He threw a right hook at an invisible punching bag above his head.

"How about Finn and his boys?" Abraham asked. "Shouldn't we ask for their help?"

"Abraham, I do not trust Finn, nor any of his bunch, for that matter." Max turned to Miró.

"Nor do I, Dad," Miró said.

"Those guys will be spotted from a mile away," Nate said.

Abraham told everyone to give him ten minutes. He retreated to his bedroom for prayer and guidance.

The wind outside seemed to pick up. A whistling sound seeped through the triple-paned windows and the snow was blowing horizontally across the property. The darkening skies suggested a storm was brewing.

For the next ten minutes, the three desperate family members brainstormed with tension building every moment. At mid-discussion, Nate's phone vibrated, announcing a call. He ignored it. Then it vibrated a second, and a third time. He had deliberately silenced his phone, not wanting to be interrupted.

Then, Max's phone rang. He picked up, "Yes? Sorry, but this is not a good time…"

"Congratulations, Mr. Kempball. You've temporarily stymied their eavesdropping—and mine. Do me a favor and tell your sister and brother-in-law not to show up. Call their bluff. Wait to see what they do." Without another word, the caller ended the call.

"Wait," Max said, "Please identify yourself."

The caller had killed the connection. Max repeated the message to all. "This dude, he complimented me for the secure link I've established, and he wants us to call the kidnappers' bluff and wait to see what they do."

"Yeah, right," Nate said in disgust.

"It did sound like the voice you've described," Max said.

"So, if the call was indeed from Tío, then it means he's probably involved," Nate said.

Max shook his head, took Nate's elbow, and stood facing him. "No, Nate, listen to me. Why would Tío demand a meeting with you at the Drake, then turn around and ask us to 'call their bluff'? It doesn't make sense."

"True." Nate bit his lip. He stopped pacing and sat.

"What doesn't make sense is to ignore the threatening note," Miró said. "Let's go, Nate."

"Hold on," Nate said. "Your brother has a point."

"Don't trust the caller, I tell you," Miró said. "We're playing with our daughter's life, Nate. If Tío has been orchestrating this from the beginning, then he's playing us. He may still be working for his boss, Diego Montemayor. I smell a huge rat."

Nate remained silent.

Now in tears, Miró threw up her hands. Almost to herself, she mumbled, "I cannot believe this is happening!"

A thunder clap temporarily caused the electricity to go out. "Great. That's all we need now—a power shortage," Max said.

"Consider this, my love," Nate said, "if this mystery caller is the same one that tipped me off about your whereabouts the day we found you at the hotel, shouldn't we believe him?"

"You tell me," Miró said. "I thought we agreed that the kidnapper was Diego's right-hand man, Tío."

As suddenly as the lights had gone out, they came back on.

Nate rose from his easy chair. He led Miró to the sofa and kneeled beside her. Taking her hand, Nate said, "Consider this. In all likelihood, Tío called me the day we found you. And, consistent with your description, he probably kidnapped you. However, I suspect that he's not the man who died at the Orrington Hotel."

"And the mysterious call to my dad," Miró said. "And, now the call to Max. I suppose you'll say it was probably Tío Dante."

"I'm not a betting man. But I do believe for some unexplainable reason Tío has been reaching out to us."

"Nate, have you forgotten that Tío was the right-hand man of Europe's most wanted criminal?"

"Exactly. Three years ago, however, Tío cooperated with Interpol and gave them Diego's whereabouts."

"But Interpol, my dear Sherlock, never found Diego Montemayor. What makes you think they're not working together?"

"It's true that Diego Montemayor went underground, then somehow managed to leave the Canary Islands... unscathed. But if he discovered Tío's betrayal, I'm certain that Tío is aware of it," Nate said. "Thus, Tío knows that he's a marked man... that he's a dead man."

"I can follow your logic, my dear husband. Explain to me, then, why Tío would come to this country for the sole purpose of kidnapping me—and possibly even Minnie and my mom?"

"Tío is aware of Diego Montemayor's resources and the extent of his power. If Tío knew that he was in his boss's crosshairs, then, as a last resort, he would seek to endear himself by regaining Diego's trust," Nate said. He almost pleaded with Miró, "Delivering you to his former boss would've put him back in the fold."

"If you're so brilliant, Surfer Sleuth, tell me who the dead man was, then," Miró said. She almost smiled. "I appreciate your efforts to solve this case, honey, but it's almost time to leave. We can't afford to miss the kidnappers' deadline."

"You're absolutely right. I don't have all the answers, but I know something about people's motivations... their behavior," Nate said.

"Dude, you make a lot of sense," Max said, who was recording their own conversation and taking copious notes. Raking his long hair, Max added, "But if the dead body found at the hotel—as claimed by the Feds—was Tío Dante, then this whole discussion is moot."

Before Nate and Miró departed, Abraham prayed over them. "May a mighty host of angels protect you, my children."

"So, the bottom line is that we can listen to the advice from my kidnapper... Or, show up at the Drake Hotel, knowing that we may not make it out of there alive. Is that about it?" Miró asked.

. . .

On their way to the Drake, Nate acknowledged the danger. He pleaded with Miró, "Can we, at least, notify Special Agent Edmunds of our 5:00 appointment?"

"Go ahead," Miró said.

Before he had a chance to call Edmunds, Nate received a call.

"Hello. Is this Dr. Nathaniel Shelley?"

"Yes, it is. Who's this?"

"I was certain you'd recognize my voice by now, Dr. Shelley. We've spoken twice before. You visited me at the E-LEVATE headquarters in Las Palmas... and, of course, I made a call to you the morning of September 22."

"Mr. Dante, I believe."

"Exactly. I won't waste your time, or mine, Dr. Shelley. As you know, your stepdaughter and mother-in-law are being held by some amateurs working for Diego Montemayor."

"I do not know who is holding them, Mr. Dante, but if you or your boss are involved, tell me what we can do to get them back, unharmed."

Tío Dante chuckled. "If I were involved, I would not be placing this call."

"They want my wife and me to meet with them at the Drake Hotel. They've threatened to kill them if we don't show up alone," Nate said.

"I know. Ignore them."

"That's easy for you to say, Mr. Dante. I can't gamble with my daughter's life... or her grandmother's," Nate said.

"They don't have any other leverage, Dr. Shelley. Call their bluff."

"Lives are at stake, Mr. Dante, my loved ones' lives," objected Nate.

"I know Diego Montemayor, Dr. Shelley. He will not allow the three of you to be touched, until..."

"Until what, Mr. Dante?"

"Until he himself has you in his clutches."

Again, the caller killed the call.

• • •

Nate called Agent Edmunds after speaking with Tío Dante. Nate said a silent prayer. *Lord, let Edmunds be there; let him answer the phone.* One ring and Edmunds picked up. As Nate began his explanation, Edmunds interrupted him. "Since our last conversation, Dr. Shelley, we've been monitoring your phone calls, expecting the kidnappers to make their move. We know who they are. Sit tight."

"We're ten minutes away from the Drake."

Edmunds was curt and direct. "Then drive directly to the Drake and park in the hotel's guest parking. Do not leave your car until I contact you. We have this under control. Please leave the rest to us, Dr. Shelley."

To their surprise, upon arrival at the top of the Magnificent Mile, two Chicago fire trucks and the two

Chicago Police bomb squad vehicles were blocking entrances to the hotel. Two officers who were redirecting traffic motioned to Miró's SUV to drive directly to the indoor parking. As they approached the parking area, Nate and Miró saw the five-member SWAT team, dressed in protective gear, entering the main lobby with weapons at the ready.

"Nate, what is going on?" Miró's voice trembled. "Did Edmunds tell you of a bomb scare? Minnie and my mom are in there!"

"Let's follow his instructions," Nate said. "My best hunch is that Edmunds called in a distraction to buy some time. He wanted the area secured before attempting to rescue Minnie and your mom. We can only put our trust in him... at this point."

For an agonizing eight minutes, Nate and Miró waited without any communication from Edmunds. Then the call came, "We've cleared the area, and there is no sign of your daughter or mother-in-law. We think they were being held in these premises, but we doubt they're still here. Trust us, Dr. Shelley. We think they're still alive, and we've got some excellent leads."

Miró took the cellular phone from her husband. "Agent Edmunds, what makes you think they're not still in the hotel?"

"We're in the process of checking every single room in the hotel, and we have some video footage of a white Suburban leaving the parking garage immediately after our arrival. We believe the kidnappers and your loved ones are in that vehicle," Edmunds said. "We're tracking them."

CHAPTER 18

Chicago – Mazatlán · December 10, 2019

"**B**oss, we're at the pool table. The prep shot is almost in place. The cue ball is all yours, over and out."

"Who the hell is this? Half-Pants, is that you?" Rodrigo laughed. "You clowns are hilarious. This is a secure line. My phones are safer than the FBI and CÍA put together, Half-Pants. Stop the cloak and dagger garbage. You guys watch too many gangster movies."

Silence at the other end. Finally, Mudo said, "Boss, we're in Chicago... still."

"I gathered that much, Mudo."

More silence at the other end of the call. Rodrigo heard a muffled voice say, "Pedro, tell him."

"'Tell him what,' Mudo? You tell me. What is it I need to know?" Rodrigo asked.

Rodrigo was lounging, sipping on a mango margarita that Estevan had prepared. It was an overcast sky that presumably would bring welcome rain to the compound.

Rodrigo's mood was tranquil, and he didn't want to hear bad news.

"Hold on, boys," Rodrigo said, "I'm in the middle of something."

Normally not a fan of frou-frou cocktails—which only *maricones* drink—Rodrigo was impressed by Estevan's beverage. He instructed Estevan to instead, "Use Patrón tequila, half the triple-sec, add a touch of mint, and never, under any circumstances, use a margarita glass."

"Also, serve it on the rocks in a large beer mug, garnished with a lime wedge," Rodrigo ordered Estevan. "Add salt, and we'll call the man's drink 'el caudillo'."

"Boss, are you still there?" Pedro Half-Pants asked. "We tapped the Shelleys' phones, and we're now able to intercept their emails. We can even scramble their calls. Thanks for teaching us all that."

"I'm still here."

"Boss, are you sure we can say all this over phone lines? I mean, if we can tap into their phones, can't the Feds do the same thing?"

"My little Half-Pants, trust me," Rodrigo said. "Our technology is light-years ahead of the American intelligence community, even ahead of most military operations."

"Okay, then I'll tell you that since the Shelleys contacted an FBI agent, we broke into that agent's phone line. We think he's the same one that hunted down our old boss, El Chato Gómez."

Not bothering to cover the mouthpiece, Rodrigo congratulated Estevan, "This one is a masterpiece. It will be my afternoon drink from now on—el caudillo." The boss took a few moments to return to the call. He noisily moved a piece of furniture on his flagstone patio.

"Now that you have completed your assignment in Chicago," Rodrigo said, "when can I expect you to proceed to the next steps? Are you ready to meet with me?"

"There's been a slight adjustment to our plan."

"I don't adjust my plans, Half-Pants," Rodrigo's voice was down to a whisper. "Vocalize, Pedro."

"What do you mean 'vocalize', boss?"

"I mean articulate, explain, speak up. What do you mean by 'adjustment to the plan'? I did not approve any adjustment to the plan." Rodrigo was ready to explode into one of his customary tirades.

"I know you wanted us to get rid of our target, but the collision did not... eliminate... her."

"Are you saying she survived the crash, you morons?"

"Yes, but we have her in our... custody," Pedro Half-Pants said.

"Where?" Rodrigo asked.

"We can demand a ransom," Mudo said. "Maybe we can even hold her as a hostage until you get here."

"We don't need a ransom, you ignoramus. Nor do I need to have a hostage. Why would I want a hostage?" Rodrigo asked.

"Well," Pedro said, "we can lure the ultimate goals—
you know, the ones you really want. She can still lead us to
your primary targets. You even told us this assignment was
just a prep for the real thing. Didn't you?"

"It did not mean that you could afford to botch this
assignment, Half-Pants." Rodrigo had tossed the beer mug,
breaking it against the enormous brick fireplace in his patio's
garden area.

"Another thing," Mudo added, "someone else was also
in the SUV."

"Dios mío," exclaimed an unbelieving Rodrigo, "estos
imbéciles serán mi ruina. What more can you possibly tell
me that will convince me to let you live?"

"We believe it's her granddaughter. She was also in the
same vehicle."

"Are they both alive?"

"Yes. We have them both. And, we've made sure that
no one, and I mean no one—not even our cops, the ones in
our payroll—know where they are," Pedro Half-Pants said.

"Also," Mudo said, "we're on the move. We think we're
being followed."

"By whom?"

"By the Feds."

"Of course," Rodrigo said, with exaggerated seriousness
in his voice. "I'm certain that I can depend on you to handle
this without any complications."

"If you don't mind my saying so, boss," Pedro said, "you
sounded very sarcastic when you said that."

Rodrigo ignored the complaint. "This is what I want you to do. Keep both alive. In fact, do not touch a hair on their bodies. Be courteous, be kind, be as nice as you can be. Treat them like royalty, without allowing them to communicate with anyone... until I get there."

"Are you traveling to Chicago?"

"I'll be there," Rodrigo said.

CHAPTER 19

Chicago, IL · December 11, 2019

AX WAS SURPRISED THAT he, not Nate, received the unexpected call from Finn informing him that Miriam and Minnie had been released by the kidnappers.

Max immediately drove to the pick-up point, an address close to Lincoln Park that he didn't recognize. Upon arrival, he saw his niece and Miriam standing outside an emergency clinic, shivering in the cold, but happy to see him approach. Minnie had run up to whisper to him that Miriam needed attention. She told him that her grandmother would refuse help, but that she had been unable to sleep throughout their captivity.

"You know, I was more concerned about Grandma than myself," Minnie said. "The only time she cried was when she saw my bleeding. But these two young dudes—the ones that hit our SUV—seemed like nice guys. They both have kids, and they told us they'd treat us like their own family."

"Well, don't believe a thing they tell you, Mouse. Those 'nice dudes' work for the most heartless criminals in the world, and I'm sure they've committed their share of crimes," Max said.

"Maybe, Uncle Max. But please, please stop calling me Minnie Mouse."

Miriam reassured Max, "… the only thing that I need to recuperate is some rest. I know that all of you were extremely worried about us, but after those young men forced us into their Suburban, they treated us with kid gloves."

"Are you pulling my leg, Miriam?"

"Seriously, Max. Very strangely, the local police arrived shortly after the car accident. Then they called in their report, but during that interim one of the officers received a call and immediately handed the phone to one of the twins, the one in the passenger seat named Pete or Pedro. By the time Pedro finished his call, the police car left. The police officer even left his cell phone with the twins."

"Strange," Max said. "So, the police never reappeared?"

"Not once," Minnie said. "This evening, Grandma even asked the twins why they weren't driving to the police station."

"How did they respond?" Max asked.

"From the beginning, they said we shouldn't ask any questions. After the collision, they soon got me the medical supplies I needed to take care of Minnie. Then they drove around for hours, probably not knowing what to do."

"Are you sure they didn't hurt you?" Max asked.

"Not once, Max. Minnie's injury was caused by the crash, of course. But other than being a little rough initially, their whole demeanor changed after they talked to a man they called Leo," Miriam said. "In fact, they put us up at the Drake. Great accommodations and more room service than we wanted. Of course, they took away our phones and disabled the hotel's TVs, phones, and internet. Other than that, they continued to provide all the medical supplies that I needed to take care of my granddaughter."

"So, did you know of the threatening message to Miró? They demanded a meeting with her and Nate at the hotel."

"We had no idea that they'd communicated with Mom, Uncle Max." Minnie was all smiles. "We just wondered how long they were going to keep us."

Miriam added, "The only time we feared for our safety was when the twins rushed upstairs at the hotel. They said Miró and Nate were supposed to meet with them, and instead the FBI and other law enforcement people showed up. I could tell that they were frightened."

"There was panic in their eyes, Uncle Max. They kept on talking about the 'Straight Arrow Edmunds' and his men appearing in the lobby instead of Mom and Dad."

"They rushed us out the service exit of the hotel and threw us back in a different Suburban," Miriam said. "I thought our troubles were about to start."

"Instead, Max, they dumped us at the emergency clinic where you picked us up," Minnie said. "Without a word, they just left us at the front entrance."

"We must count our blessings," Max said.

"Thank you for picking us up, Uncle Max. I'm so happy to see you."

"Minnie, I wish I could take the credit, but it's Special Agent Edmunds from the FBI that deserves your appreciation," Max said. "He protected your mom and dad and reassured us that the kidnappers would not harm you. He was right."

CHAPTER 20

Evanston, IL · December 23, 2019

N ATE SHELLEY WAS LIMITING his office hours to four, at times six, hours. Since that fateful Sunday in September, when Miró turned up at the Orrington Hotel, the entire Shelley/Epstein family had been reliving the Iberian nightmare. The only difference was that they were in Chicago. They were all facing suspicions from the legal authorities, each member of the family appeared to be in danger, and their enemy was faceless.

Now, with the holidays approaching, their emotional states were fragile, if not perilously shaken.

Nate arrived at his Jackson Street high-rise office to find an empty waiting area. Some of his patients had switched therapists, others had simply canceled appointments... repeatedly. Ms. Farnsworth's full-time schedule was reduced to thirty hours weekly, but Nate could not continue to keep her at a full salary for much longer. She offered to quit to help his practice. She even volunteered to take a cut in salary.

When he entered his inner office, Nate removed his overcoat. Before hanging it, he noticed an unusual item already on the coat rack, a gray fedora. He immediately walked out to Ms. Farnsworth to ask who'd been in his office. The question confused her.

"No one, of course, Dr. Shelley. Why?"

"There's a strange hat hanging on my coat rack," exclaimed Nate.

He dedicated the rest of the morning to filing the strange report with the building supervisor, the authorities, and later his own family.

At, 3:30 PM, Nate decided to call it a day. He took the train home.

. . .

As had become customary for Nate, he changed into his surfer sleuth garb immediately after getting home. Though tempted to take a glass of wine, he resisted the urge. His drinking had markedly increased from one or two glasses with his meal to three, sometimes four glasses before bedtime. He disliked his need for palliatives.

That afternoon, Max was occupying Nate's home office. It was Max's turn to pick up Minnie after piano lessons and drive her home. She was upstairs doing 'piano homework', and he was busily investigating the names and limited files that had been provided by Edmunds' colleagues.

Max had transformed Nate's home office into an elaborate communication center. He'd installed an indoor 'pergola' of sorts, which he called a 'chuppah', for shielding against wiretapping and compromised communications. Nate sat in the living room instead.

Within ten minutes after arrival, Nate's private cell line rang again. It was the same five-digit number that had appeared on his screen before their Drake Hotel scare.

"Tío Dante here, Dr. Shelley. I was responsible for your wife's kidnapping. And, I was also responsible for the death of the man found at the Orrington Hotel. It was self-defense."

Nate signaled to Max, asking if he should keep Tío on the line. "And you expect me to believe, Mr. Dante, that you were not responsible for the kidnapping of my daughter and her grandmother?"

"You can believe what you want, Dr. Shelley. However, Diego's amateurs are responsible for the present sloppiness." The line went dead.

. . .

After receiving the call from Tío, Nate asked if Max had traced the call.

"Although I was unsuccessful, the map on the screen tracked the call to a broad area that includes the Upper Peninsula and Door County, wherever that is. The caller was good. He took many precautions to ensure his information was scrambled."

Nate looked at Max. "We told you Tío is no dummy."

"Don't know where he is, but it looks like a God-forsaken place," Max said. "What exactly is the Upper Peninsula? And Door County?"

"It's Michigan's Upper Peninsula and Wisconsin's Door County, where many Chicagoans go for summer retreats."

"Summer up there must be nice, but you'd need to pay me to drive to that area in the winter. Help me understand this, Nate. Why would Tío Dante confess to you, admit to the kidnapping and the murder?"

"Correction, Max. He clearly said that he'd killed the person in self-defense."

"Okay, granted. Why come to you and not the authorities?" Max asked. "Though I've got some ideas of my own, I want to hear your take on this."

"I'm still processing this, Max," Nate said. "But I still believe that Tío is attempting to find someone he can trust to 'come in from the cold'. I believe he fears for his life. He's primarily afraid of his former boss, Diego Montemayor. But for some reason, he does not trust law enforcement in this country either."

"You lost me with the phrase, 'come in from the cold', Nate."

"Sorry, I was referring to le Carré's novel, *The Spy Who Came In from the Cold*, about a man who'd gone into seclusion for fear of losing his life to either his enemies or his own government."

"I see. That's a fascinating take," Max said. "Have you considered that Tío might be setting a trap for us?"

"Yes, from the beginning." Nate said. "I was the skeptic, remember? And you convinced me that if Tío was still working for Diego, his tipping us off made no sense. You were right."

"Nate, it occurs to me that we haven't made full use of our connections in the Canary Islands. Although I don't think I need to travel to Las Palmas to visit with Chief Inspector Sánchez, perhaps a telephone conference with him will shed some light on this mystery we're facing."

"Wow, brother-in-law," Nate said. "I didn't think you'd ever come around to my way of thinking."

"Okay, okay, Nate. Just don't gloat over every single victory!" Max laughed good-naturedly.

CHAPTER 21

Evanston, IL · December 23, 2019

N ATE WAS STILL WEARING his surfer sleuth outfit when Miró arrived late that evening. He'd added a thick cotton cardigan to the wardrobe, however. Though she needed some rest, Miró was happy to be reunited with her entire family—including Minnie and her mom, Miriam—in the Shelleys' den.

"I can see that Nate has summoned everyone to finally resolve this ongoing mystery," Miró said.

"I'll warm the leftovers for you, mi'jita," Miriam said. "I brought over a casserole that we all enjoyed."

"Thanks, Mom, but I had a salad late today, so I'm skipping dinner," Miró said.

"My love, I've been sharing with the family how fortunate we've been to find the needed support," Nate said. "Of course, I'm referring to Special Agent Edmunds."

Abraham came in from the kitchen, beaming with pride. "Mi'jita, I remembered how much you enjoyed Bellinis in the past, so I've picked up a new skill. Tell me if you approve."

Miró joined Nate at their love seat. She took her first sip, and smiled, "Yummy, Dad. Well done."

"Good," Abraham said. "When you came in, Nate was asking if we thought it was a good idea for him to return to the Canary Islands. He'd like to interview Chief Inspector Sánchez."

"I certainly hope he's not thinking of traveling there during our Christmas break. Regardless, I'm not sure that's a good idea. Nate is convinced he can trust Tío Dante, and I believe he's wanting to persuade me to go along."

"Tell us why you're opposed to picking Sánchez's brain, Miró?" Miriam asked.

"It seems to me, Mom, that Tío and Diego worked together for so long, that it's difficult to believe that their collaboration has ended. It's too suspicious."

"And, don't you think that Inspector Sánchez could shed some light into that relationship?" Miriam asked.

Miró was pensive. "Maybe."

"Wait a minute, Sis," Max said. "Didn't you also agree there had been a falling out between the two?"

"What I said," Miró said, "was that Tío Dante had gone to the authorities to provide information regarding Diego's whereabouts. He believed that Diego's wife was influencing Diego to make very poor choices."

"Exactly," Abraham said, "and don't you also believe that Diego discovered who betrayed him to the authorities? Tío himself bragged to Nate about their technological capabilities. Not only did they have presidents of nations wiretapped, but they also had them on their payrolls. They controlled politicians throughout the world, even those in our own country. Certainly, Diego must've known of every step taken by his trusted assistant, Tío himself."

"So you all believe that Diego Montemayor and Tío Dante are no longer working together?" Miró asked.

"That's just it, my love. We can't be certain. We can all agree on that," Nate said. "What I propose is that we try to find out what Inspector Sánchez knows. Perhaps his friend from Interpol can also provide information."

"I agree with Nate. If Tío foolishly betrayed Diego, you can be assured that Diego found out. He didn't get to his position by trusting traitors," Max said.

"Tell me, Dad," Miró asked. "Do you think it's a bad idea to send Nate to the Canaries?"

"Yes, mi'jita, I do. However, I agree with Nate that we should consult Inspector Sánchez. I'll add something else." Abraham paused. Nate could tell that his father-in-law was having a difficult time articulating his feelings.

After a long pause, Abraham added, "I feel useless, like I have no stakes in this." Though he was addressing Miró, Abraham's complaint was directed at his son-in-law, Nate. "Why don't you let me call Inspector Sánchez?" Not until then did Abraham turn to Nate.

"You must admit that back in the Canary Islands he and I developed a close relationship. Though he's a Spaniard, he and I forged a common bond. I understand him; he's from my generation. He's a wise old buzzard who's deliberate, brilliant, and philosophical. Besides, I think I may be able to contribute a quick fix or two to the present imbroglio facing our family."

"Okay, Abraham, you're right. Sánchez and you did hit it off nicely," Nate said. And, attempting to add some levity, Nate mused, "As I recall you and his buddy Bishop Gómez also got along well, especially during our wedding," Nate said.

"As I recall, his title is Archbishop, a significant thing in the Catholic hierarchy," Abraham said.

"The three of you spent a couple of hours during the wedding celebration drinking that cava."

"If I didn't know any better, the archbishop took more of a fancy to Miriam than me," Abraham said.

"I remember that well," Nate said. "And, although you never met Picard, the inspector's friend from Interpol, I believe you both communicated through Inspector Sánchez quite well."

"On more than one occasion, we were involved in conference calls with his friend Gabriel Picard from Interpol," Abraham said. "What about the rest of us? Would you agree that I should reestablish our communication with our Canary Islands connection... by phone?"

"I think it's better than traveling to the islands," Max said.

Looking at Nate and Miró, Abraham said, "So, should I call Inspector Sánchez tomorrow afternoon?"

"Of course, Dad," Nate and Miró answered in unison. Abraham beamed again, "I feel useful again."

. . .

"All warfare is based on deception."

Chief Inspector Eduardo Sánchez, from the Las Palmas Police Department, had answered Abraham Epstein's call with that statement. Then Abraham remembered that Sánchez was a fan of Sun Tzu.

"Inspector, I don't know if you remember me…"

"Of course, I do. So, listen to me…" There was a dramatic pause. "All warfare is based on deception."

For Abraham, the conversation was taking a bizarre, unexpected twist. "Inspector, the reason I'm calling is that I may need your help."

"And I have been expecting your call, Dr. Epstein. You have got my wholehearted cooperation."

Abraham was taken aback. This man, with whom he'd had zero communication since Miró's wedding in the Canaries three years ago, seemed to be picking up on a recent chat.

"But how could you possibly have known that I'd be calling, Chief Inspector?"

"I completely believe," Sánchez said, "that if you know your enemy and you know yourself, not only can you anticipate the future battles, but also know the results."

At this point, Abraham felt inadequate. "Inspector Sánchez, you're speaking in riddles, riddles that, I feel, should be perfectly obvious. However, they're far from understandable to me."

"That is just because you cannot imagine that I have a notion of your present difficulties and challenges, Dr. Epstein."

"How can you, Inspector? Then again, what is it you do know?"

"Mere generalities, my friend," Sánchez said, with a chuckle. "Let me explain. In my line of work, I do my best to subdue my enemy—the culprits—without fighting."

"But how can you possibly do that?" Abraham asked.

"I not always can, of course. But when I excel at my work, I attempt to break my enemy's resistance without fighting."

"Okay, I'm listening. But how does that relate to me or my family? More importantly, how does that relate to my present situation?"

"Well, Dr. Epstein..."

"Please call me Abraham."

"If you call me Eduardo, it is a deal, Abrám," Inspector Sánchez said. "I am attempting to explain that I learned as much as possible about my ahijada's husband, Diego Montemayor. When I learned that he had masterminded the murder of that poor American young lady, Penny Rhoads, and the kidnapping of your granddaughter here in the islands, I knew we were facing a formidable enemy. Then, it turned out he was responsible for those two other casualties."

"It was tragic how Yael, your ahijada, chose to end her own life," Abraham said.

"Yes, it was. I still wish I had been able to stop it," Sánchez said.

"Inspector—okay, I promised to call you Eduardo—there's quite a leap between those circumstances three years ago in the Canary Islands and what is happening here in Chicago with us."

Again, a barely audible chuckle from Sánchez prompted a statement. "If you are speaking of a conceptual leap, Abrám, think about it. It is not that far removed. Con su permiso, let us 'connect some dots', as you Americans put it."

"Okay."

"We knew even before you left the Canary Islands that Diego Montemayor was a major player in international crime—drugs, cyber-data, and human trafficking. We just did not know how big an involvement it was."

"You're about to tell, aren't you?" Abraham asked.

"Yes. His network is extensive. Although he's disappeared, we now believe his enterprise is worldwide. He's directing all activities from somewhere in the world."

"Does Interpol confirm it?"

"They can neither confirm nor deny it. Which means, claro que sí!"

"Help me, Eduardo. Connect some more dots," Abraham pleaded.

"A powerful criminal like Diego Montemayor does not like to be thwarted or outsmarted. Furthermore, he lost the love of his life, my goddaughter. And, to add insult to injury, his right-hand man, Tío Dante, betrayed him."

"I remember Diego had gone underground to escape the Spanish authorities, your forces, as well as Interpol's. It was Tío that gave us his whereabouts, no?"

"Yes, it was his closest associate, Tío Dante."

"So, did that weaken his dynasty?" Abraham asked.

"No, Abrám, as you recall, Diego was able to flee after going underground for several months. If anything, Diego Montemayor has resurfaced with greater resources and a firmer control of his organization. He's an astute businessman, make no mistake about it. He has expanded his cartel's reach. But"—another pregnant pause—"his greatest motivating force is no longer greed, money, or power."

"What is it then, Eduardo?"

"It is personal revenge, Abrám. Unfortunately, it is not revenge against me, Picard from Interpol, nor Tío, his right-hand man... not even his cartel competitors."

"So," Abraham asked, "if you're saying you know enough about your enemy that you can predict where his next battles will be, what, exactly, are you saying?"

"My message to you," Abraham's friend said, "is that his vengeance is directed squarely against your daughter Miró, Nate, and their daughter Minnie."

CHAPTER 22

Mazatlán – Chicago · December 16, 2019

"**P**EDRO, RESERVE THE PRINCESS Diana Suite at the Drake Hotel in Chicago... with an adjacent suite for Estevan. Make the reservations under the name Miguel Cervantes," Pedro's boss said. "We'll arrive at noon tomorrow."

"Boss, I think you should stay away from the Drake for now."

"Why?"

"Let's just say we had a bad experience the last time we were there," said Half-Pants.

"I don't want to know. Just reserve the best suite at the Trump International, or better still the Peninsula Chicago, which is owned by some of my Chinese friends."

"Are you flying a commercial flight, boss?"

"Why would I do that? No, of course not, I'll fly into the Executive Airport."

"Into the small Wheeling airport?"

"Yes, and I want you to pick me up," Rodrigo said.

Pedro Half-Pants could not believe it. Many times, he'd asked his boss to visit Chicago and he'd refused. "I thought you hated this country."

"I need to attend to urgent business, Half-Pants… and clean up your mess. I'll expect you and your brother to drive us around. Is that clear?"

"You'll need to show some ID at the hotel."

"I know that, you simpleton. I've got plenty of forms of identification. Now, get on it."

"One more thing. I think you'd be happy at the Trump International. I could get you a nice lake view."

"Just do what I told you." Before ending the call, Rodrigo added, "By the way, how's your face? Is it totally healed?"

"Oh, yeah, my wife thinks you made me more handsome. Thanks."

"Good. Listen, Half-Pants, I'm sorry that I lost my temper."

"No problem. We're good," Pedro said.

Rodrigo ended the call.

"You'll need to stand up to Rodrigo one day," said his brother, Macario.

"Mudo, just mind your own business."

"Pedro, are you going to tell Rodrigo what we found out?"

"You mean the crap we heard from the doc—what's his name, Abraham Epstein? We don't even know if the information is accurate. And, if it's true, how will it change things? If Rodrigo thinks that Tío is dead, what does it matter?"

"Of course it matters. If Tío turns up without you telling him, Rodrigo will blow a gasket," Macario said.

"Yeah, maybe you're right. I just don't want to be the one to tell the boss. You know, he can be so unpredictable."

. . .

Late the next evening, Rodrigo arrived at the Chicago Executive Airport. His pilot landed the Airbus A380 without much fanfare. Other than the pilot and his bodyguard Estevan, only a long-time office assistant accompanied their boss. She remained on the plane until Rodrigo and Estevan deplaned.

The large, white Suburban with tinted windows drove up to pick them up. The Rosales twins drove directly to the Peninsula Chicago. On the drive along Lakeshore, Rodrigo commented on the Chicago skyline and the view from the lakeside's undulating perspective.

"Not bad," he said. Estevan handed him his iPad. Rodrigo remained unusually quiet, reading multiple emails. Then, "Tell me, Half-Pants, what can you tell me about this FBI special agent?"

"We've tapped his phones and can intercept his emails," Pedro said proudly. "Mudo had him pegged from the beginning. He thinks that Edmunds will be trouble."

"Only if you'll allow him to be trouble, Mudo," Rodrigo said.

Without saying a word, Mudo turned and glared at Rodrigo.

Pedro Half-Pants said, "Boss, we're talking about an FBI agent."

"Tell me, have you read any news reports about any infectious diseases or any epidemics?"

"Not that we know of," Pedro Half-Pants said.

"Where can we get a decent evening meal?" Rodrigo asked.

"It's impossible to get a decent meal after 10 PM, or 2200 hours," Macario said. "At least, not for your tastes. But we can get good food in Little Village."

"Drive us there, then."

. . .

Rodrigo was not a fan of Mexican food. He picked at the greasy appetizers, and pulled away from the table. "Can't these people prepare a dish without using lard and cumin? How about their seafood? Is it decent?"

"Look, it's a Northern Mexican cuisine. Their style is not Iberian; it's consistent with the food from that area in Mexico," Macario said. "The seafood may not be as fresh as you like."

"So, you've tapped whose communications? Tell me more. By the way, order whatever you think I'll like. I can't make heads or tails of this menu," Rodrigo said.

Macario immediately summoned a waiter. He ordered for the four of them, and gave specific instructions for the preparation of each dish.

"Do you boys remember our conversation about 'prepping'? And do you remember what I specifically said?" Rodrigo asked.

Smiling, Pedro said, "You told us that it was a set-up for the kill shot, which is why we initially took the target to hold her as a hostage."

"No, Half-Pants, I specifically said I wanted her killed… not held as a hostage, not to demand a ransom, nor any other nonsense. I wanted her eliminated." As he whispered, Rodrigo leaned over the small table and took Pedro's face, squeezing his high cheekbones.

Averting Rodrigo's glare, Pedro's eyes pleaded in Macario's direction. Macario moved, as if to remove the vise-like grip on his brother's face. Estevan immediately reached inside his coat pocket. An unearthly guttural sound came from his mouth. Macario sat back down.

Still whispering, Rodrigo asked, "And, the woman's grandchild. How on earth did you manage to involve her?"

"We got lucky," said Half-Pants. "We got two—for the price of one, you might say."

Macario interjected, "Pedro, he's not complimenting us."

"Listen to Mudo, Pedro. No, I'm not complimenting you, you moron," Rodrigo said.

"Boss," the normally quiet twin said, "when we hit the woman's SUV, it was not with enough force to drive her into the lake. We didn't even topple the vehicle. We got to the SUV and found the two females inside."

"I thought you were monitoring their calls and their emails. You said you had schedules, routes, all relevant details," Rodrigo said. "What do you mean, you were surprised her granddaughter was with her?"

"Apparently," Mudo said, "there was a last-minute change in plans. Her uncle was supposed to pick her up from school."

"You idiots!" Rodrigo finally released his grip, leaving his finger marks on Pedro's face.

Looking down at his dinner, Pedro said, "The good thing is that we've taken care of the whole thing."

"I'm afraid to ask," Rodrigo said. "How did you take care of it? Where do you have them now?"

"You said to treat them kindly, courteously, to be nice," Pedro said. "So, we released them."

Mouth agape, Rodrigo, with a reddened face, looked at Estevan, then turned to Macario, the silent twin. As if begging for a different explanation, Rodrigo began to mouth something without forming a single word.

Estevan quickly got up, held Rodrigo's forearm, and shook his head. He mouthed an intelligible word, "Breathe." Only when Rodrigo took several deep breaths did Estevan release his hold.

The twins and Estevan took several bites of their food. Although Rodrigo's breathing was still agitated and his blood pressure probably high, he verbalized clearly, "I did tell both of you to treat the two females like royalty. I told you to treat them nicely, courteously, and kindly... *until* I got here." He held the twins in place with a venomous glare.

Pedro was about to respond, and Rodrigo raised his right forefinger to indicate he wanted silence. "I *did not* ask you to release them."

Again, Pedro opened his mouth, and Estevan extended his arms to hold the twins' forearms fast to the table, in the same fashion he had held his boss before. He shook his head very slowly.

Rodrigo rose from the table and demanded they return to the hotel. He, Estevan, and the twins left the restaurant in absolute silence.

CHAPTER 23

Chicago, IL · December 18, 2019

"**S**o, what you're saying is that I should tread deliberately," Rodrigo said. "Before eliminating these two obvious liabilities, we must first secure the information we need from the Rosales twins."

Rodrigo had learned to formulate his plans with Estevan's assistance. Though mute, Estevan was a valuable resource. He was astute, deeply loyal, and he had a good understanding of organizational dynamics. Through his written notes and some sign language, Estevan was remarkably articulate and clear-headed.

Nodding, the devoted companion and bodyguard handed Rodrigo his cognac. He added to his notepad,

'Contacts with Feds? Tío? FBI Agent Edmunds?'

"I'll get the info on the twins' access to the Feds… and find out about Edmunds. But your second point regarding Tío… Our own FBI contact at headquarters said the dead man found on September 22 at the Orrington Hotel was Tío Dante. Why do you think he's still alive?"

Estevan scribbled another note, 'Who hired assassin?'

"The Rosales twins, of course," Rodrigo said.

Estevan just shrugged his shoulders.

"I see what you're saying. If those imbeciles handled the job, can we be certain of anything?" Rodrigo put his drink down. He put his hands in his trouser pockets, and he walked toward the picture window. In his reverie, Rodrigo meditated on the obvious questions. *If the Epstein females have their descriptions, clearly, the twins have been identified. The key question is how much do the Feds—especially those not in our payroll—know about us? With the twins' communications now compromised, will their communications reveal the link to me, Rodrigo Díaz? Will my federal connections insulate me— and my real identity—from the damage already done... and for how long?*

CHAPTER 24

Chicago, IL · December 19-22, 2019

RODRIGO WAS BLESSED WITH a good education, an analytical mind, and a better than average business acumen. Yet, his empire had been built with the help of a close friend, a colleague, a confidante who had become the brother he'd never had. That trusted friend was now gone. He'd betrayed Rodrigo, turned him in to the legal authorities in Europe. For what? To this day, Rodrigo failed to understand the motivation behind the betrayal. Nonetheless, it had happened at the time when he needed a friend the most. Rodrigo had lost his wife in a gut-wrenching fire. He'd been forced to go into hiding from the authorities, and his most trusted friend had repaid him with treachery. Now, Rodrigo lived for one thing, and one thing only—his raison d'être had become revenge.

He'd been an only child raised by a single parent. Well, for all practical purposes, his mom had raised him without assistance. Though his mother had remarried when he was a teenager, she'd remained an independent woman who made most decisions regarding his upbringing. His stepfather, a Spaniard from Toledo, had never become part of his life.

Rodrigo married in his late thirties. He fell in love with his best friend's wife, and convinced her to forsake her marriage vows, a serious matter for a devoted Catholic. The marriage had been tumultuous in the early years, but it settled into a stable and respected union. The couple had become esteemed community leaders and generous philanthropists of numerous causes, especially those promoted by the Catholic diocese in the Canary Islands.

Eventually, Rodrigo's wife had become his soul mate, his friend, and the love of his life. She served as a sounding board. Because of the great respect for her husband, she preferred to be guided by him in most instances. Then, suddenly she died in a tragic fire, and an acrid, somber cloud darkened Rodrigo's tormented soul. He lived embittered, convinced that his only relief would arrive through a justified revenge that would calibrate the scales of divine justice.

Except for the loss of his wife, what Rodrigo missed the most was the counsel of his former friend and business associate, Tío Dante. However, Estevan Chengfu sometimes reminded him of Tío. Like Tío, Estevan was levelheaded and wise. He had the patience that Rodrigo lacked. Secretly, Rodrigo acknowledged his weaknesses. He was impulsive and sometimes reckless. He needed someone like Estevan to prevent him from making foolhardy decisions.

After a longer than normal after-dinner discussion, Estevan and Rodrigo had reached an agreement to remain in the U.S. for an extended period, despite the precarious situation involving his CIA and FBI protectors. Rodrigo's identity was still unknown to most government officials and the few who were aware of his identity were loyal—and well compensated—collaborators. Even those who knew of his reemergence in the underworld were unaware of his physical appearance. Few had seen his new face. No fingerprints, nor any other records, were on file anywhere. Other than the occasional CCTV images, which would've been collected inadvertently, there were no accounts of his existence. Since traveling to the U.S., he had shaved his head as an additional precaution.

Of course, staying in a Chicago hotel under an assumed name had its perils and limitations. Never having a desire to live in the U.S., Rodrigo had not, prior to this period, secured a safe house in the Chicago area. Although he kept safe flats in Washington DC and New York for business necessities, Chicago held no former interest. It was time to rectify the situation.

Having full power of attorney, Estevan Chengfu began an aggressive property hunt in Chicagoland for a safe house. Of course, Estevan visited several real estate agencies, primarily screening them for an agent that was knowledgeable, discreet, and familiar with interpreting sign language for the deaf and mute. His goal was to review some options during the weekend and to vacate the Chicago Peninsula suite by the end of the year.

After many protests from Rodrigo, Estevan had convinced him to forgo returning to the Mazatlán compound for the Christmas celebration. Estevan had the remarkable ability to make Rodrigo feel childish and foolish without uttering a single word. And, he could do it without robbing Rodrigo of maximum respect and dignity.

On the first day of his search for adequate properties, by 6 PM Estevan had sent photographs of five attractive and discreetly located safe houses in the North Shore area of Chicago. In Wilmette, he found two options which seemed logical and accessible to public transportation. In addition, a Northbrook possibility had served as a similar 'very private residence for a well-known CEO of a major corporation', per the real estate agent.

That evening, Rodrigo reviewed the various available properties, without being impressed by any of them. Estevan promised to resume the search early in the morning. Rodrigo asked Estevan to withhold sharing any information on his visits to the various properties until he had filtered and narrowed down his search.

Several urgent matters had surfaced which required Rodrigo's attention. Since he had funded Chinese laboratories that were experimenting with the development and containment of infectious diseases, he needed to deal directly with researchers who were having difficulty containing leaks of information regarding the exportation of 'contaminated packages'.

Estevan wrote on his notepad, 'Don't forget to contact Dr. Wu, regarding the impending trip to this country.'

"That won't happen until later," Rodrigo said. "You're right, though. He needs to prepare."

The following two days, Rodrigo spent much of his time speaking to friends in academia from Texas who had indiscreetly disclosed to news sources that they were assisting their Chinese counterparts in developing means of immunizing the public against viral outbreaks. Their collaboration with laboratories in rural provinces of China had piqued the interest of nosy reporters wanting to know if potential outbreaks could have occurred during the experimentation phase of their research. Rodrigo had been incensed at the obvious lack of discretion, given that the 'grants' had come from his private funds.

That week, by the time that Estevan returned from the real estate hunt, Rodrigo was moody and frustrated. For days, he'd been forced to order from the abominable kitchen of the hotel. Although the steak dishes had been adequate, they had been unimaginative and paired with some red wines from Argentina, which he'd spilled down the drain 'in hopes of not corroding the plumbing'.

Estevan signed slowly, knowing that his boss was frustrated. '*You need to visit some properties this coming week. I think you'll be pleased.*'

"Good. I need some good news. Where are these properties?" Rodrigo asked.

Estevan opted to write in his notepad, 'There are several, but my favorites are in Winnetka'.

"Where the devil is Winnetka?"

Again, Estevan signed very deliberately, '*It is by Lake Michigan. Very discreet.*'

"Just don't force me to spend an entire day looking at properties, and I'll be fine," Rodrigo said.

'*I want you to consider two,*' signed Estevan.

. . .

Rodrigo insisted that they drive their own vehicle to meet the realtor at the Elm Street District of Winnetka, although the realtor had offered to pick them up and give them a tour of the community. Disappointed, the young realtor agreed to meet them at a trendy coffee shop. He bought them coffee and croissants.

"The village of Winnetka is very proud of its recent accomplishment," the perfectly coiffed real estate agent said. He was a thin man with fine features and delicate, almost ballet-like movements. His smile was charming as he displayed copious notes, photos, and articles on his laptop, all regarding the city's efforts to restore the commercial area and open the community to more cyclists and pedestrians. The vast renovation of the central district was impressive and 'elegant', he said.

"We don't ride bicycles." Rodrigo addressed Estevan, complaining about this unnecessary feature.

Bruce Jones, the realtor, turned to Estevan in fear, as if asking to be rescued. Estevan was already signing to Rodrigo that he would explain his motives later. Then Estevan turned to Bruce to reassure him. He asked him to continue with his virtual tour of the Winnetka business district. Rodrigo was surprised to see that Bruce was an accomplished interpreter, since he had a sister who was deaf and mute.

Bruce then suggested that it would be helpful to leave Rodrigo's Land Rover parked in the central district of Winnetka, which would allow him to use the driving time to explain to Rodrigo more thoroughly the advantages of 'moving' to Winnetka. Rodrigo reluctantly agreed, but insisted that he could not take more than ninety minutes.

Again, Bruce gave Estevan a horrified look. Estevan merely patted Bruce on his forearm, and reassured him all was fine. Riding in Bruce's Mercedes permitted Estevan to pass on to Rodrigo a few written notes. Rodrigo read them and agreed that Estevan had a sensible notion of the location of their safe house.

As he drove, Bruce rattled off municipal statistics, including the high average income of residents, their high educational levels, and the vast interest in improving the aesthetic quality of the tranquil village. "Above all," he said, "it is safe, secure, and unhurried. People keep to themselves." He discussed the proximity of Lake Michigan and the pastoral quality of life in Winnetka. "Although public transportation is available, it is not a hub for commuters."

The first property that Bruce introduced to Rodrigo was Estevan's favorite. It was more of an estate, occupying a large and expansive property by the lake. Twelve-foot walls surrounded the estate. It had multiple garages, two tennis courts, and a covered swimming pool. Bruce reassured them the pool was heated and available during the entire year. Three separate two-story buildings surrounded an expansive circular driveway with an enormous weeping willow in the front. The estate had a total of ten bedrooms. Each building had a separate kitchen, and it appeared that several families could live there. The property was electronically secured, and the actual buildings were two-hundred yards from the main entrance. Of course, a separate cottage was included for the house staff.

Although Rodrigo had considered a much smaller property, he was impressed by the charm of the estate. He wondered to himself if Estevan was contemplating a longer stay in the U.S. And, if so, why?

Bruce felt more confident about Rodrigo's favorable reaction to the first option. He was almost apologetic about the second, 'tiny' alternative, as he described it. However, he soundly endorsed Estevan's taste, by saying that some of the best things 'come in smaller packages'. Indeed, the second property was much smaller, probably one-fourth the size of the first one. It, too, had a European charm. It was a two-story stone structure, with only three bedrooms, but ample front and backyards. The construction of the property was solid, sound and of high, durable quality. Rodrigo had envisioned something similar. However, he considered both alternatives with very different criteria. For a shorter stay in the Chicago area, the second alternative appeared to make more sense.

"Bruce, I will need the weekend to make a decision. I like both alternatives," Rodrigo said.

As he drove back to the center of town, Bruce proceeded to apologize for not meeting Rodrigo's deadline. Although he had tried his best, he had taken 'a smidge' more than two hours, but he hoped that Rodrigo would find it in his heart to 'forgive him'.

Estevan again reassured Bruce Jones. During the ride back to Chicago, Estevan signed several points regarding each property. Rodrigo was surprisingly agreeable, indicating a definite appreciation for each. Instead of driving directly to the Peninsula Hotel, Estevan maneuvered their Land Rover into the Hancock Building's circular garage. At this point, Rodrigo asked if Estevan wished to treat his boss to the sights of the Chicago skyline. Estevan's response suggested he was indeed treating his patrón to more than a view; he was buying dinner at the Signature Room on the 95th level.

Two hours later, Rodrigo seemed entirely satisfied, even impressed, by dinner, the impeccable service, and the more than adequate selection of wines. Although he had rudely dismissed two sommeliers who had offered help with their wine selections, preferring to select his own from the extensive list, Rodrigo softened the blow by smiling agreeably and thanking each with a generous cash gratuity.

"This is more like it, Estevan. Despite being distinctly American, it was better cuisine, and they certainly had a better selection of wines. I also commend the service. Good choice."

'*And, what do you think of the Chicago skyline?*' signed Estevan.

"Not bad at all," Rodrigo said. "I admit that this view of the Navy Pier is more impressive than my first eye-level impression. And the illuminated shoreline is unique."

'*I hope that you realize it may be home for longer than you anticipated,*' signed Estevan.

"Estevan, I have my own estimates, but I'm uncertain what you're planning."

. . .

The head waitperson rolled an impressive cart of delectable desserts to their table. Rodrigo waived the waiter away, but he asked for a large mug of cappuccino, plus a double Hennessy. Estevan ordered an espresso.

"Let's talk about the safe houses. Which one suits our needs best?" Rodrigo asked.

Estevan went into a lengthy signing explanation. Rodrigo gave up after a thirty-second attempt at deciphering. "Write it down, my friend. I don't want to work so hard this late in the evening," Rodrigo said.

The notepad came back with 'We need both safe houses.'

"Why in the world would I need two safe houses? I don't plan to move here!" Rodrigo said, as he sipped his Hennessy.

'That explanation will be lengthy. Let's wait until tomorrow.' Estevan smiled and included a generous tip for the wait staff.

PART THREE

CHAPTER 25

Evanston, IL ·
December 24, 2019 – January 8, 2020

S INCE ESTABLISHING CONTACT WITH Inspector Sánchez, Nate gave up the notion of traveling to Spain. However, the need to unveil the many mysteries that threatened his family's well-being survived. True, Minnie escaped serious injury, and Miriam was also unharmed. Though neither had endured suffering, a looming foreboding and an uneasiness infected the entire Shelley and Epstein households. No one participated fully in holiday reveling and celebration. Privately, each harbored a dread of the next horror that would befall a member of the family.

To break the gloom, Nate's Sonos home system played continuous Christmas carols. Early Christmas Eve, while Miró and Miriam finished their shopping, Nate called his brother-in-law. Noting Nate's agitation, Max drove to the Shelley residence.

Max arrived at Nate's and joined him for a glass of wine.

"Max, I've decided to meet with Tío Dante." Nate's own Bermejo sat untouched for twenty minutes. Max finished his first glass and moved on to a bottle of Negra Modelo.

Nate shared with Max that since the return of Minnie and her grandmother, Tío Dante had communicated with him on three occasions. Twice Nate received texts and once Tío had called after midnight. Still torn about those communications, Nate was reluctant to share with Miró several ideas that had crossed his mind. The more he withheld from Miró, the more conflicted he became.

On the one hand, he wanted total openness with his wife. But on the other hand, Miró failed to understand why maintaining communication with her kidnapper was either safe or well-advised.

"You're nuts, dude, and, my sister's right. This dude, he's dangerous and unpredictable. Let's get some help."

"Help from whom?" Nate asked. "We can't trust anyone. Besides, Tío will only talk to us."

"Given what I've learned about Diego Montemayor, and his long tentacles that crisscross the world, we may never hear from Tío again. This dude, he could die at any moment... or disappear. Let's go to Special Agent Edmunds and get those two to meet." Max took a swig.

"No, Max, if we want to resolve this mess, I need to meet directly with Tío. Can't you set up some cyber communication? You know, through the dark web, or something?"

"Look, dude, we know Tío is monitoring every move we make. We can assume he's tapped our phones, and he can intercept every online connection we make. Sending him a message would be easy."

"Then do it."

"Be careful what you wish for, Bro."

"You pinpointed his location to either Door County or the U.P. I can make a drive up there."

"No way, not by yourself. Let's compromise. Let's communicate by phone, Facetime, or some other video means."

"Max, I need to meet with him face to face. I'll know if he's lying." Nate took the first drink of his wine. "Hey, I'd forgotten. Miró prepared some assorted tapas. She left us some manchego cheese, olives, Iberian ham, and some delicious cheese-stuffed dates wrapped in bacon."

"Is that your subtle form of bribery?"

"Whatever works," Nate smiled.

.   .   .

Max attempted to convince Nate that meeting with Tío was foolhardy. He finally convinced Nate to, at least, share his plans with Miró. Nate waited until after the 26th of December to bounce 'a few ideas' off his beloved. His first attempt was met with total resistance.

"Nate, are you out of your mind? What makes you think you're invulnerable? Meeting, alone, with a known criminal is not only reckless, but it is absolutely thoughtless." Exasperated, Miró continued, "Have you not thought of me... and Minnie? Don't you think that we deserve some consideration? We need you, and so does the rest of the family."

After several conversations, Nate and Miró agreed to consult with the rest of the family, "...unless you've already done so," Miró added.

Nate confessed that he'd shared his thoughts with Max, 'only as a hypothetical' but not a serious plan. Nate then reassured his wife that he would not have decided anything like that without first consulting those closest to him.

That week, Nate and Miró spoke with Abraham, Miriam, and even Minnie. Nate's 'foolhardy plan', as Max described it, was fully laid out. They all listened carefully, skeptical of the possible outcomes, but open-minded enough to consider the potential advantages.

Privately, Nate had decided to set a deadline for himself. He was determined to make his final case to the family before the end of the year. Since the family had agreed to get together at Abraham's residence on New Year's Eve to watch the Alamo Bowl, featuring the University of Texas Longhorns against the University of Utah, Nate decided that the post-game festivities would grant him the best atmosphere for a 'fair and unbalanced' consideration of his case.

In his mind, although the Utes were favored to win, the Longhorns had an indomitable quarterback who could beat the odds. However, since he and Minnie were the only non-

Texans by birth, he egged on the rest of the family by claiming the 'impossible odds against UT'. He specifically targeted Max, who was a dyed-in-the-wool Orangeblood and lover of all things Texan. Though Nate was not a gambler, he made an exception, and challenged Max to a $100 bet, stating that the Utes, ranked #11 in the nation, would make mincemeat of the Texas defense. Max quickly agreed to the bet.

Nate announced on Sunday evening that he was planning to unveil a special dessert for the family on Tuesday, the night of the Alamo Bowl, and coincidentally New Year's Eve. Although he had not selected a specific dessert yet, he wanted as much goodwill as possible from his family. He felt guilty manipulating his family, but not enough to dissuade him from his strategy. *It's for a worthy cause*, he thought to himself.

Nate was certain that with the loss of his bet, he would have a sympathy vote or two from the family... a calculated bet, but a good one, he thought.

The night of the football game, Nate kept himself from cheering for the Longhorns. He criticized the University of Texas' coaching staff, their inability to make use of their talented quarterback and receivers' squad, and, generally, even criticized poor 'Bevo', the University of Texas mascot standing on the sidelines. Of course, as Nate secretly hoped, Sam Ehlinger, the star quarterback from Austin, threw for three touchdowns and more than 200 yards. Duvernay, the receiver headed for the professional ranks, snatched up almost 100 of those yards. And, Ingram, the Texas' running back, scampered for more than 100 yards. The score wasn't even close. Texas won with a convincing 38-10 score.

Feigning disappointment, Nate reluctantly handed over a crisp $100 bill to his brother-in-law, while the rest of the family whooped and yelled in glee. Pretending to wipe the egg off his face, he good-naturedly joined in toasting the University of Texas team with the prematurely opened bottle of champagne. Of course, Abraham's Dom Perignon was reserved for the midnight celebration.

Since the entire family would be celebrating until past midnight, Nate 'unveiled' his surprise dessert of mangomisu. It was a variation on tiramisu, including Grand Marnier, but with the addition of mangos and a raspberry sauce. Everyone enjoyed it, including Miriam who promised to learn the recipe. Then, at 11:30 that night, Nate raised the issue of his meeting with Tío. His opening was bold, direct, and on the mark.

"While Diego Montemayor is free, our family will not be able to rest. We'll never feel safe." He made certain not to sound overly impassioned. Instead, he had practiced a sedate, thoughtful, and calm delivery. He briefly glanced at Miró, then looked in Abraham's direction, again calculating that Abraham's opinion would sway most in the room.

"If I enlist Max to travel with me, at the first sign of danger, we'll bail out," Nate said. "I believe that among us, we can arrive at a plan with plenty of safeguards to ensure our safety."

Max was the first to attempt a response. Fortunately, Miró interrupted. "Dad, tell us what you think."

"I believe that Nate makes much sense. If there's a possibility of neutralizing Diego Montemayor, in my estimation the rest can be handled by Ram Edmunds and his team. And to be open about this, I believe that our friends at Interpol and our friend, the Chief Investigator in Las Palmas, would agree with Nate." Then Abraham added, "No one can assume that Tío can single-handedly bring down such a powerful criminal as Diego Montemayor, but if he truly can bring credible evidence to Special Agent Edmunds, I trust that he can shield us from further attacks."

There was a lasting silence, which signaled to Nate that each member of the family was reconsidering. Rather than putting up the issue for a vote, Nate cleverly diffused the tension of decision making. He changed the subject by inquiring what everyone thought of his dessert. The positive responses broke the ice and prepared everyone for the welcoming of the New Year.

As the ball dropped in Times Square, two bottles of Dom Perignon were uncorked and consumed, and every bit of the mangomisu disappeared. Max even downed the crumbs, claiming that he'd limited himself to only three servings.

At exactly 1:15 New Year's Day, Nate inquired of the family, "So, do I have your blessing to work on a safe plan for contacting and scheduling a meeting with our only hope, Tío Dante?"

"As long as I can ask that you join us all—as I'm asking the entire family to do—to petition God's blessing in this undertaking," Abraham Epstein said.

Nate and everyone else agreed. Given such an endorsement, Nate reserved the following day to assuaging his wife's worries and meeting with Max to draft a tentative plan for contacting Tío Dante.

. . .

The following Monday, January 6, Max initiated multiple emails and texts to Nate, repeating Nate's desire to meet with Tío Dante. Nate responded in like fashion.

Later the following day, Max removed the charade and texted Nate the following: "Nate, let's both agree that we are reaching out to Tío Dante. If you're intercepting this, Mr. Dante—and we're both certain you are—please contact us!"

One minute before midnight, Tío called Nate's cell phone directly. "I will be at the Country House Resort in Sister Bay. When you get to the front desk to register for your room, ask the clerk to direct you to the park bench that sits on the grassy knoll. I will wait for you there."

"Is there only one bench in that entire property?"

"It's the bench close to the trail leading to the water," Tío said. "At a distance, but within view of everyone."

"Will you be armed?"

Tío chuckled. "I could've shot you in September when you arrived at the Orrington Hotel accompanied by your brother-in-law. I was wearing the fedora."

"And, the fedora left in my inner office?"

"An extra one that I carry around... just to let you know someone was watching out for you."

"Hardly a reassuring thing to do, Mr. Dante."

"Ha. If you're concerned for your safety, I know that your brother-in-law will be watching. The bench is clearly visible from any room in the property. Max will be satisfied knowing that he can watch us from your accommodations." Tío chuckled hoarsely. In his raspy voice, he added, "Not only will his binoculars come in handy, but his unsophisticated audio surveillance equipment may work from that short distance."

"I cannot travel until this coming Saturday, Mr. Dante," Nate said.

"Saturday it is, then," responded an agreeable Tío.

"Anything else?" Nate asked.

"Dress warmly."

CHAPTER 26

Chicago, IL · December 23, 2019

RODRIGO LIMITED HIS CONTACT with the Rosales twins after their dinner at the Mexican restaurant. Consequently, Pedro and Macario Rosales began to inquire with the staff at the Mazatlán compound if Rodrigo and Estevan had returned to Mexico. When they learned that Rodrigo was still in Chicago, their curiosity turned to paranoia.

Pedro knew that his brother Macario was home helping his wife prepare the traditional holiday tamales. Pedro telephoned his brother before 8 in the morning, and he learned that Macario's entire family had been up since 4 AM. When Macario picked up the phone, he shared with Pedro that the preparation of tamales had become a family affair. Macario and his twin sons were helping their mom apply the masa on the corn husks, and Mom was working on the pork and venison filling. Ignoring the details, Pedro asked, "You think Rodrigo is planning to get rid of us? What do you think we should do?"

"I have an idea," Macario said. "We have an excuse to contact Estevan. Let's tell him that we've got a Christmas gift for the boss. Then we ask him if we can deliver it."

"What should we get him?" Pedro Half-Pants asked.

"Give him the solid gold revolver we had specially made for Dad before he passed," Macario said.

"Sometimes I think you're smarter than me, Bro," Pedro said. "That's a great idea... but what if he says Rodrigo doesn't want us to go near him?"

"Then we'll know we're in deep trouble," Macario said. "We'll ask Estevan what's up. He'll tell us."

Before noon, Macario used his laptop to send an encrypted message to Estevan. Within ten minutes, Estevan responded, using the voice transcription program developed especially for him by their Chinese colleagues.

Macario telephoned Pedro to give him the good news, explaining that, contrary to their worst fears, Rodrigo was intending to surprise the twins and their families with a special holiday trip. Estevan said that Rodrigo knew he'd behaved rashly the last time he saw the twins, but he was ready to make amends. Estevan had concluded, 'Believe me, it'll be a nice surprise.'

Totally confused, Pedro asked his brother, "What do you think Rodrigo is planning? Does that mean no partying after midnight mass on the 24th?"

Macario convinced Pedro they needed to cancel existing plans. "Furthermore," he told Pedro, "Estevan had a strange request. He wanted us to convince the owners of the

Nuevo Leon Restaurant to close for the day and let him take over the kitchen. He doesn't care how much it costs."

"He wants them to close the restaurant?"

"Yes. I've already handled it," Macario said. "It cost us twice as much as the gifts we bought for our families."

"Why did Estevan want the restaurant?"

"He wanted to prepare a special dish for Rodrigo. The restaurant manager has already gotten Estevan all the ingredients he wanted," Macario said.

"Will Estevan deliver the meal to Rodrigo at the hotel?" Pedro asked.

"No, I think he'll ask a realtor friend of theirs to drive Rodrigo to the restaurant. They'll have the restaurant to themselves," Macario said.

. . .

When Rodrigo entered the Mexican restaurant, he hardly recognized it as the same establishment he'd visited before. The night of his arrival in Chicago, the twins had treated Rodrigo and Estevan to a Mexican meal at the Nuevo Leon. Rodrigo had refused to eat.

Between Estevan and Bruce Jones, they transformed the restaurant. They selected a small dining room on the far corner and created a less garish, almost sedate, venue more to Rodrigo's liking. Bruce had personally removed some adornments and enlisted the help of an interior decorator to add a few tasteful accents, creating a quiet and somewhat elegant environment. Fresh flowers and wool rugs had been brought in temporarily to fashion a different motif. Bruce and the interior decorator had hurriedly hung drapes which had been chosen by Estevan. A few classical selections played in the background to complete the ambiance.

"What's on the menu, my friend?" Rodrigo asked.

Estevan was wearing a tuxedo, minus the jacket. He smiled and uncovered the dish at the center of the round table covered with a white linen tablecloth. If eyes could salivate, Rodrigo's eyes expressed a ravenous appetite that said, "I can't believe it!" Saucer-like, his eyes almost teared up. "I was afraid you'd serve me a Mexican dish. You've prepared my former wife's specialty."

'*First, however, we have an appetizer. Enjoy,*' Estevan said, in sign language.

Estevan had a note prepared. It said, 'I will challenge you to identify one ingredient that is primarily used by Mexican chefs. I've incorporated that ingredient into your appetizer.'

Rodrigo tasted the Chilean sea bass appetizer that had a nutty, sweet flavor unlike one he'd ever tasted. Rodrigo took multiple guesses to identify the secret ingredient, but failed each time.

"It tastes woody, earthy and somewhat nutty and smoky, yet it has a subtler taste than the French chanterelle mushrooms, and without the fruity odor. It's a fascinating taste, my friend. What is it?"

Estevan had prepared a written note stating, 'It's known as a Mexican truffle. The name is huitlacoche, but let's simply call it a truffle.' Estevan knew better than to describe the truffle's origins or its composition.

After a few bites of the appetizer, Rodrigo tasted the white wine. He recognized it as a rare find from Lanzarrote. Then the pièce de résistance—osso buco—was presented with exaggerated fanfare. Estevan sat at that point, joining his master. The slightly chilled Barolo was served, just as Rodrigo liked it.

"Ah, my favorite Gaja!" Rodrigo insisted that Estevan join him. Without hesitation, Estevan proceeded to take a separate serving which had been left at a buffet behind the table. The bottles of wine were also sitting on the elegant piece of furniture.

In a rapturous state, Rodrigo enjoyed his meal. Instead of darkening his mood, Bach's melancholic violin concerto for two violins gave Rodrigo amorous memories of his departed wife. It reminded him of her gifted culinary talents and how she had introduced him to countless delights. Enjoying his meal, Rodrigo almost forgot Yael was no longer with him, but instead waiting for him in paradise. Again, his eyes teared in joyous gratitude for having enjoyed her in this life.

Over dinner, Estevan proceeded to organize his note cards with bulleted explanations for his Christmas plans for the twins. As he prepared his written notes in order, he deliberately signed for Rodrigo, '*Over dinner, we should discuss the lengthy rationale for needing two safe houses instead of one.*'

. . .

"Absolutely not," complained Rodrigo. "It would be sacrilegious to discuss business as I enjoy osso buco. We'll consider rationales over dessert." Estevan understood. He was enjoying dinner also and was willing to delay the discussion.

As if taking delight in every bite, Rodrigo spoke of Yael, his deceased wife, with a fond melancholia. He especially recalled their holidays together, always entertaining guests who were never associated with his business. Often, the archbishop would be present, since Yael was an ardent sponsor of Catholic charities and social events. Although Estevan had met Yael once or twice, he had established a long-distance relationship with Rodrigo's business when Rodrigo lived in Europe. Estevan, however, had lived most of his life in the Chinese mainland and later in Central America. When Rodrigo relocated to Mexico, he recruited Estevan to be his aide and bodyguard. Estevan's role had evolved over the last two years, when he'd become more of a consigliere.

When Estevan served dessert, Rodrigo exclaimed, "Ah, crema Catalán. Well done, my friend."

'It's flan, Rodrigo. Although the recipe is like the Spanish version, this little Mexican-influenced dessert includes a bit of cognac. You'll enjoy it.'

Rodrigo tasted the flan with some skepticism. "Hmm, not bad at all. Does it have orange, or orange zest in it?"

'I added a bit of orange zest, yes,' signed Estevan. 'The cognac was also my touch.'

"Okay, Estevan, it's time to convince me why we need two safe houses."

Fortunately, Estevan had anticipated a lengthy discussion, so he had prepared several note cards to expedite the explanations. He had planned well. Estevan opened with the need to offer the Rosales families a Christmas holiday trip to the Mazatlán compound. Rodrigo's plane was already en route to Chicago. Anticipating Rodrigo's protests, Estevan outlined his rationale with his index cards.

"I'm not at all interested in rewarding the twins' ineptitude by regaling them with a trip to my hacienda," Rodrigo said.

'You must include their families, their wives and kids,' explained Estevan. *'While we purchase and settle in at the safe houses here in Chicago, you will treat them with a splendid Christmas vacation fit for royalty.'*

"Why on earth?"

Ignoring the question, Estevan continued with flash cards. 'Both families will enjoy Christmas in your estate and celebrate the arrival of the New Year in Mazatlán. I've ensured that your entire staff give them an extravagant reception and stay. We've planned for activities for the children as well as guided tours off the coast and the mountains for the adults.'

"Why?" Rodrigo asked, for a second time.

'On January 2, both families—minus the twins—will be flown back to the U.S. However, Pedro and Macario will remain behind at the compound. Upon the families' return, they will be your guests at the larger of the two safe houses in Winnetka.'

"Do you mean to tell me that they will live with me?" Rodrigo asked.

'There is plenty of room in the larger estate. Remember, you have three separate buildings, and you will have your privacy. I've already arranged for the kids to have their private tutors,' Estevan signed.

Before Estevan had an opportunity to serve the second bottle of Barolo, Rodrigo rose from the table and took the corkscrew to open the second bottle. The bottle was already breathing on the buffet behind them, and it was ready to serve. Estevan proceeded to elaborate on his meticulous plan.

Deliberately, with the visual aid of prepared note cards, Estevan explained, 'The families will remain at the safe house under strict supervision, for their safety, of course. The twins will remain in Mazatlán, until they're needed back in Chicago, probably until late January or early February. Upon their return, neither twin will be allowed to move in with their respective families. They will be separated from their families, and all communications will be controlled by you and me.'

Rodrigo surrendered his full attention to Estevan. He slowly sipped his Barolo.

'During the first few days, the twins will be allowed to return to their empty and respective family homes in Chicago, but by mid-February they will be moved to the second safe house in Winnetka, the smaller one, which will be more adequate for their needs.' Estevan disclosed his plan a layer at a time.

With much deliberation, Estevan paced his presentation to outline how at that point, once the twins were settled in their new safe house in Winnetka, Rodrigo would reveal his last assignment to the twins. Since their families would be safe under Rodrigo's own roof, the twins' full cooperation would be ensured.

"So, my friend, you are suggesting that the twins' families would be my hostages?" Rodrigo asked.

Estevan took his last sip of Barolo. He offered Rodrigo a snifter for his Hennessy. '*I prefer to call them,*' signed Estevan, '*your guests.*'

CHAPTER 27

Sister Bay, WI · January 11, 2020

THE FIRST THING THAT Nate noticed when they stopped for gas was Max's soaked cowboy boots. They'd crossed into Wisconsin and had hugged the eastern edge of the state to have a direct path to Door County. Not only was the blanket of snow on the ground heavier, it was wetter and colder. The snowfall had been so heavy when they got to Sheboygan that visibility was reduced to zero. They'd temporarily stopped until conditions improved.

Although Nate preferred to continue hugging the water's edge, and avoid fighting the Green Bay traffic, he realized it might be necessary to do some shopping. Bypassing the Green Bay metropolitan area would save them time, but more than likely the footwear needed for Max could require a change in plans. Fearing the answer to his question, he asked, "Max, did you pack your snow boots?"

Like a doe paralyzed by headlights, Max stared at Nate with an interrogating look, "Was I supposed to?"

"My fault. I should've checked with you first. You've managed without snow boots during our first snowfalls, but up in Door County, it'll be a necessity. Let's stop in Green Bay and get you a pair."

"I've been getting by wearing double socks and my cowboy boots, but if you think it'll be necessary, let's do it."

"Believe me, Brother, you'll appreciate the extra protection," Nate said.

The brief stop in Green Bay afforded them an opportunity to warm themselves with coffee, coffee, and more coffee. Max, in addition, stocked up on goodies for the road, just in case he had a munchies attack.

When they drove through Sturgeon Bay, Max exclaimed, "My toes, dude, I can no longer feel them. Can we stop while I change my socks and put on my new snow boots? I thought I'd only need them for walking in the snow. Now, I realize that the extra insulation is even necessary inside the car. My God, do people actually live here?"

Not thinking his question required an answer, Nate simply laughed.

Early afternoon, Max and Nate arrived in Sister Bay. They checked into the Country House Resort, which Max realized was a beautiful property lined with spruces, fir, and deciduous trees which, at the moment, looked uninspired and leafless.

"What a great place it must be in the summer, dude!"

Focused on checking into the property, Nate virtually ignored his brother-in-law, and asked the desk clerk if they had any messages. The cheerful young woman checked, and indeed found a brief note stating, "Meet you at the bench." It was signed "T.D."

"Max, would you mind if I ask you to take our bags to our rooms? I'd like to get on with our scheduled meeting."

"Dude, I'd feel better if I set myself up. I need to set up long-range sound equipment, cameras, and, you know, be properly armed in case there's a need." Max almost pleaded.

"Okay," Nate said, "I'll go up to my room. I'll set up my iPhone on record mode, and give you a little bit of time. I think Tío's waiting."

After fifteen minutes, Nate walked to the grassy knoll. Rather, he ambled to the knoll. The bitter cold froze his face and sharp needles stuck to his face on his way to greet Tío. The hairs in his nostrils froze on the way. Tío was sitting, smoking, legs crossed, reading *The Revolt of the Masses*.

"I see you're reading Ortega, Mr. Dante. Are you a fan?"

"Why, yes, I am," Tío said, as he put out his cigarette. "Very few Americans know about his writings. Are you familiar with him, Dr. Shelley?"

"I'm proud to say that I am," Nate said. "What do you think of his thesis in that particular piece?"

"Like Ortega," Tío said, "I'd like to think that I, too, celebrate excellence. Often misunderstood by critics—especially young critics nowadays—Ortega continues to be wrongly labeled an elitist, an oligarch."

"I'm glad to say we agree," Nate said.

Shutting his book closed, Tío uncrossed his legs and exhaled sharply. The vapor of his breath froze instantly. However, the nicotine stench of his breath hung in the air. "Look, I kidnapped your wife. I'll confess to that. But I truly did not intend to bring any harm to her. I had a different motivation."

"I'm listening, Mr. Dante."

"I knew I'd lost Diego's trust, so I wanted to give him what no one else could deliver: Miró."

"You'd regain his trust by kidnapping her? And you expect me to believe that Diego would not 'bring harm' to Miró?"

"Of course I'm not expecting you to believe such a thing. All I'm saying is that if any harm came to your wife, that it would not come through me."

"How virtuous."

"Look, I don't claim to be what I'm not. But when I realized that Diego was already tailing Miró more aggressively than I was, I got worried. I knew the man who was pursuing Miró."

"Who is he?"

"Let's just say that I had known him. He had approached me some time ago offering to help Diego's business."

"Where is he now, Tío?"

"Six feet underground. I killed him."

"Is he the man that was found dead at the hotel in bed with Miró?"

"He was an assassin; one of the best."

"How did you do it, Tío?"

"When I realized that he was a step ahead of me and that he'd been hired to kill me, I accelerated my plan and took Miró. I knew he'd come after us."

"Was he interested in kidnapping my wife?"

"Not initially, but he knew Diego wanted revenge against her… and you… and your daughter."

"So, you're telling me that you laid a trap, using Miró as bait? How in heaven's name can you claim that you had no intent to harm Miró?"

"I intercepted that assassin before he got to either of us. I used an umbrella, a lethal device he'd used in his line of work many times before."

"You used an umbrella to kill him?" Nate asked, almost chuckling. "And, you're telling me that he used an umbrella when he was hired to assassinate people?"

"It was one of many instruments he used."

"I see," Nate said. "So, this infamous assassin had many secret weapons. Where did he come up with such an assortment of gadgets?"

"Your own country developed those gadgets, as you call them," Tío said. "You see, this assassin was trained by the best. He was former FBI and CIA."

"Now, Mr. Dante, you're suggesting an assassin was hired by the U.S. federal government to kidnap and kill my wife."

"It's complicated, Dr. Shelley. This individual retired as a federal agent. After retirement, he freelanced and did work for major drug cartels. He also continued as an informant to the American intelligence community."

"He played both sides."

"You could say that."

"So, not only did you want to ingratiate yourself with your former boss by handing my wife over on a silver platter, but this other known killer also wanted her dead. Is that your story, Mr. Dante?"

"He had done work for Diego Montemayor many times before," Tío said.

"Ah, a match made in heaven," quipped Nate.

Tío broke out in genuine laughter. "In fact, there is probably much truth to that comment. If you'll give me enough time, we might get back to that important point."

"How did Diego establish this tie with an ex-federal agent, Mr. Dante?"

"When I ran E-LEVATE, I brought him to the table, so to speak. After several contracts, I learned that he was probably the most effective hit man that we'd ever employed. Diego, however, was always cautious. He did not like to get his hands dirty, so he preferred not to have direct contact with our... 'consultants', if you will. So, all of his communications came through me."

"So you knew this man well."

"Not intimately, but I knew how he worked. I knew his modus operandi."

"And you found him how, exactly? If you don't mind my asking."

"I asked around, always seeking the best specialists, Dr. Shelley. I considered discretion and precision to be primarily important. This individual fit our mold. I was actually very proud to have found him."

"A good headhunter, in other words. Forgive the unfortunate term, Mr. Dante."

Again, Tío laughed out loud. "You are genuinely funny, Dr. Shelley. Yes, I considered myself to be a good talent scout. However, I came to find out much later that I had been manipulated by this individual. He actually wanted me to find him."

"How so?"

"Well, I mentioned before that we could return to an important point. This may be an opportune time to do so. From the start, this individual had a special interest in Diego. He would ask about his family, his past, his likes and dislikes. He also seemed to know quite a bit about Diego's early history."

"Were you suspicious of his motivation?"

"Very suspicious, Dr. Shelley. Knowing his M.O., I thought he might be informing the Feds to set a trap for my boss. So, I watched him carefully."

"Was he informing the Feds?"

"To my surprise, not only was he informing certain offices in Washington DC, but those federal officials were cooperating to insulate Diego from any incriminating evidence."

"Like my daughter would say, Mr. Dante, this is where I get off. That is extremely difficult to swallow."

"It was doubly difficult for me, Dr. Shelley. However, I have no interest in persuading you. My purpose here is something entirely different."

. . .

Tío brought out a pewter monogrammed cigarette case and lit up. "Dr. Shelley, I would like you to present my case to your FBI contact, Special Agent Ram Edmunds. I would offer full information on Diego Montemayor in return for total immunity."

"Mr. Dante, why would I consider your request? You've confessed to me that you kidnapped my wife. You have said that you would've handed her over to your former boss, whose only intent is to kill the three of us. You put her life in danger when you used her as bait to allegedly defend yourself against a skilled assassin. Why would I honor your request?"

"Because you know that as long as Diego Montemayor remains free, you will not live in peace. That's why, Dr. Shelley."

"Why don't you approach the authorities yourself?"

"Agent Edmunds would not give me the time of day. On my own, I would not get an opportunity to present my case."

"Well, approach the FBI headquarters in DC, or someone else in the Justice Department."

Tío scoffed and commented, "Your intelligence comm-unity has been corrupted, Dr. Shelley. I should know. There are few I can trust."

"What could I offer that you could not?"

"An enormous amount of credibility. I'm not asking you to defend my actions, nor am I asking you to justify my behavior. All I ask is that you propose to Agent Edmunds a brief conference, so that I can confess to the kidnapping and admit to contributing to the death of a known assassin."

"That's a laugh, Mr. Dante. 'Contributing to his death'? Don't you mean that you murdered him?"

"I killed him in self-defense, Dr. Shelley. That is an important distinction."

"Don't forget you drugged my wife. She was unconscious for days!"

"I was cautious to use sedatives that would not have any lethal effects. I learned my craft well, because I learned from the very best, my former boss, who is a renowned botanist and biochemist."

"I don't care what you used. You kidnapped my wife, drugged her, and put her in great danger. And, now, as soon as they find out you're alive, you'll be charged with murder. And you have the gall to ask for my help?"

"Yes. I know it's difficult for you. But what I can offer can bring your family safety and security. While Diego Montemayor is alive and free, your family will never be safe. I will give you information that can bring Diego and his syndicate down… not to mention other powerful people in your country."

"And in return for that information you want to go scot-free?"

"I will confess to kidnapping, but the killing of Calabrese was self-defense."

"Was that the presumed assassin's name?"

"Yes."

"I'll need to think about it," Nate said.

"All I ask is that you intervene by speaking to your FBI contact. If not, you could approach the new Attorney General. The information that you and I can bring to them is invaluable. And the people they will convict will be of great interest."

"I thought you said the intelligence community was compromised."

"Most of them," Tío said. "Though I doubt the new appointees will be able to unscramble the roots of corruption, they're trying."

"What makes you think that the DOJ will listen to me?"

"They'll listen when you tell them you've got sensitive information regarding Diego Montemayor."

"Give me some time to consider your request," Nate said.

CHAPTER 28

Sister Bay – Chicago · January 13, 2020

NATE AND MAX DELAYED their departure from Door County due to heavy snowstorms nearing blizzard conditions. Weather advisories convinced them that any attempt at travel would be imprudent, and even Miró agreed.

"I'm just thankful that your meeting with Dante is over," Miró said. "Be careful on your drive back, honey."

Because the road from their lodging to the central registration area was barricaded due to impassable restrictions, Nate and Max walked approximately three hundred yards to the resort's restaurant. The main lobby was comfortable and the restaurant offered a bountiful breakfast buffet with a roaring fireplace that invited travelers to seek refuge, warmth, and comfort. The coffee was rich and the cherry-stuffed French toast and cherry pancakes were delicious. Max had two servings. For Nate, in addition to several mugs of coffee, Swedish limpa toast with cherry preserves completed his breakfast.

Late in the evening, the storms broke and the weather advisories were removed. Nate and Max decided to spend the night, and leave early the following morning.

Upon his return to Chicago, Nate called the DOJ's office in DC. He was unable to get an appointment with the new Attorney General. Since Tío had warned him not to trust others at the DOJ, Nate telephoned the local head of the FBI's field office.

"Agent Edmunds, I've got some information," Nate said. "I've met with the man who kidnapped my wife and killed the man at the hotel… the one found dead next to Miró."

"Hold on," Ram Edmunds said, "I will record this conversation. Do you mind?"

"'Course not, but first tell me if I've got your promise that you'll try to help."

"First, Dr. Shelley, you know that I'm trying to help you and your family. But—forgive me for being blunt—you must be out of your mind. When you meet face to face with someone of that ilk, you're risking your life. These people can't be trusted. They are many times more dangerous than the mob."

"I know. I know. But just listen to what I have to say."

It took Nate twenty minutes to explain how he'd traveled to Door County, met with the kidnapper, and interviewed him. He explained how he wanted to make a deal with the Feds. Furthermore, he also wanted Nate to approach the DOJ on his behalf.

"Since the DOJ will not give me the time of day, will you help us?" Nate asked.

"Absolutely not. Every Tom, Dick, and Harry nowadays wants to make a deal with the Feds. In the previous administration, every crook could make a deal if he incriminated the 'right people', but these are different times. At least in my office."

"Just listen to what I have to say."

"Who's this perp, anyway?"

"His name is Teodosio Dante, but he goes by Tío."

"Are you...?" Edmunds needed a moment to compose himself, and his voice rose two octaves higher when he was able to resume. His voice volume also rose considerably. "What the...?" Again, Edmunds stopped himself. "I'm sorry. I don't normally use profanity, but it almost slipped out my mouth. Do you realize he's wanted by every international law enforcement agency... worldwide? Tío Dante is linked to a notorious crime syndicate. He's high in their ranks."

Nate was so surprised by Ram's reaction that he failed to respond.

"Besides, he allegedly died at the Orrington Hotel. Are you telling me he's alive?"

"Yes, he is," Nate said.

"How do you know that you did not meet with an impostor, someone pretending to be Tío Dante?"

"Because I had met Mr. Dante two years ago in the Canary Islands," Nate said. "My wife and I went through very similar circumstances once before, I'm afraid."

"I've read about that in your files," said Special Agent Edmunds.

"Wait," the unnerved agent said, "not only are you saying that Dante is alive, but that he's in this country?"

"Yes, I'm telling you that I met with him in Door County at a secluded resort."

"What the devil is he doing there?"

"Well, Agent Edmunds, I believe he's hiding…"

"Hiding from whom?"

"From Diego Montemayor and from your agency, I suppose."

"Not us. We—at least, I—had no idea he was stateside."

"Holy Toledo! Are you implying that your own colleagues—other field offices—may be running a parallel investigation separate from yours?" Nate asked.

"I can't be sure."

"So now do I have your attention?"

"Of course you do. However, if Dante wants to make a deal, I cannot promise to help a fugitive of the law. If you say that he killed a man, I will not help him."

"Like I said, he thinks he's got valuable information that could put very important people behind bars."

"Sorry, Dr. Shelley, I can't make any promises."

"At least, promise me that you'll consider his request to talk to you," Nate said.

The conversation between Nate and Agent Edmunds appeared to reach a stalemate. Ram Edmunds firmly indicated that he would not help Tío Dante. Furthermore, he suggested that upon meeting him, Edmunds' men would be obligated to arrest the international fugitive. In his capacity as head of the Chicago field office, Special Agent Edmunds explained, he could only respond to such a request by saying that an immunity deal with Dante was out of the question.

In summation, Nate finally added, "I understand, Agent Edmunds. I told Tío that I was not optimistic. By the way, at the end of our meeting, Tío mentioned the name of the man he killed, whom he claimed was an assassin. It was 'Calabrese'. I think it was a slip."

"What did you say?"

"I don't think he intended to share the name with me," Nate said. "I think it was a slip of the tongue. He said the assassin's name was Italian, Calabrese."

"Okay, that's enough. This conversation has ended."

Nate was confused. He paused. At the other end, Edmunds continued.

"Sorry for sounding so abrupt, Dr. Shelley. I turned off our recording. We're off the record from here on."

Not knowing what to say, Nate simply waited.

"Are you certain that Tío identified the dead man as Calabrese?"

"Yes, I am."

"Not only was Calabrese a former FBI—and CIA—agent, but he was a close friend," Edmunds said. "We must continue our conversation, but I suggest that you visit my office. Or, perhaps we can meet somewhere, if driving to our offices on Roosevelt Road is inconvenient."

"Actually, my office is close by. I'll ask Miró to join me," Nate said.

. . .

Late that afternoon upon arrival, Nate and Miró were greeted warmly by several receptionists at the FBI's Chicago field office. Two assistants offered refreshments as they led the visitors to the large conference room occupied by Special Agent in Charge Ram Edmunds.

Nate and Miró were impressed when they walked into Ram's strategy room. Two walls were filled with photographs, maps, and interconnecting ribbons that led to a missing piece at the pinnacle of a pyramid. At the second level of the hierarchy appeared the pictures of Tío, a blurry picture of a tuxedoed individual at the head of a filled board room, and the photographs of two younger individuals. Tío's photograph was tagged by an interrogation mark.

"Welcome, Drs. Shelley—actually I should say, Dr. Shelley and Dr. Epstein-Shelley. I invited you to our offices primarily to reassure you of our commitment to this investigation. However, I still cannot promise you that I'll entertain Tío Dante's request." Ram Edmunds was standing next to the stringed pyramid.

Edmunds invited them to sit close by. "To my first point, I realize that you've had many reasons to doubt our law enforcement efforts. We hope to change your impression." Special Agent Ram Edmunds earnestly delivered an impassioned introduction to persuade Nate and Miró to trust his office and his investigation. He sat close by.

"First, Agent Edmunds, please dispense with formalities. Call me Nate, and this is my wife, Miró. Second, please realize that we are confident of your efforts to help our family. You've already been helpful, and you've earned our trust."

"Thank you, Nate. Please call me Ram; my friends do. I have a feeling we will have numerous conversations as this investigation evolves. So, a candid communication will be required. Please let me know if you need reassurance regarding other matters."

"Umm… Ram. I do have one little concern," Miró said. "How did you and former agent Calabrese become such good friends?"

"Fair question, Miró. Cal and I became very close in college. As freshmen, we were roommates and remained friends until we graduated. We ran around the same circle of friends, partied together, traveled together, and met each other's families. After graduation, we both joined the Bureau, and they put us through our master's program in Texas."

"But you seem to have taken different paths. Did Calabrese become involved in illicit affairs early on? And, more importantly, did you remain close, even after you realized Calabrese was helping the cartels?"

"I was not aware of Cal being involved with criminals early on. Nonetheless, from the start, Cal was the ambitious one. He aspired for promotions and authority, but the FBI did not satisfy his ambitions. But when he was aggressively recruited by the CIA, his fortunes changed. The promotions came quickly. Because he worked undercover, he became the government's plant in several sting operations."

"So, where did he go wrong?" Miró asked.

"Don't really know, but soon after he joined the CIA, he began to do quite well in the DC area... financially. He drove fancy cars, owned several condos, and lived in a mini-mansion."

"And you believe that he could not have afforded that much with government pay?"

"Let's say that it was too much, too soon. Even Cal's wardrobe was upgraded. So, I asked him directly, 'Cal, where's the wealth coming from?'"

"And?"

"He said his present wife, his third, came from money. I believe her name was Allison Saltzman. He cavalierly said, 'easy come, easy go.' Frankly, I wasn't convinced, because his third wife soon left him, but his prosperity continued."

"Yet, you continued your friendship?"

"Call it blind faith, call it being naïve, maybe even stupid," Ram Edmunds said, with a sheepish grin. "But yes, Miró, you know how sometimes things don't sound quite right, but you ignore that check in your heart. And, since you're close to that person, you give them the benefit of the doubt. Cal had many good qualities. He was intelligent, funny, skilled, articulate, and very, very disciplined in most things."

"Are you saying he was undisciplined in a few things... like what?" Miró asked.

"Booze and women. He was careless with both."

"Agent Edmunds, do you mind if we ask you an even more indelicate question?" Nate asked.

Ram Edmunds smiled. He reminded Nate that they were on a first-name basis. "Of course, ask away. I'm assuming this conversation will help our investigation along. And we need to be open with each other."

"When," Nate asked, "did you and Calabrese last work together?"

Special Agent Edmunds assumed a slightly more formal tone to explain that although he was entrusting Nate and Miró with sensitive information, some details would need to be withheld due to the nature of classified information that he was obligated to protect. By no means, he said, should Nate and Miró misinterpret his intentions. With that caveat, Ram Edmunds became almost extravagant in his openness. Had Edmunds been his patient, Nate would've jotted in his notebook, 'remarkable stream of consciousness... uninterrupted flow of information.'

For the next six or seven minutes, Ram Edmunds spoke uninterrupted. Nate and Miró remained quiet to keep from rousing Ram from his reverie, which he was fully verbalizing. It was one good friend reminiscing about the exploits of two buddies on the same side of the law, if only for one last episode.

Federal agents Ram Edmunds and Angelo Calabrese had collaborated in bringing down El Chato Gómez and his drug empire. Calabrese, in fact, had been the liaison between Ram and the Gómez cartel lieutenants, the twins who betrayed the drug lord Gómez and testified against him to make possible his conviction.

After Gómez's conviction and incarceration, the twins were given federal protection to ensure their safety from cartel hit men. Within months, however, they both disappeared from their safe houses located in Arizona. Federal officials had no explanation, but Ram thought the new cartel boss—a Spaniard—had 'freed' the twins and offered them jobs. The new cartel boss, Ram Edmunds said, was allegedly more ruthless and vicious than El Chato Gómez had ever been. Ram got most of his information from his friend Calabrese. Possibly, Ram said, Cal was already playing both sides of the law.

Soon after Gómez's conviction, Ram gathered his investigative team at the 'control headquarters', the conference room they were in. It became the strategic nexus of Ram's investigation of the new syndicate, the one taken over by an opportunistic Spaniard 'who seemed to be at the right place, at the right time'. This Spaniard, known only as Rodrigo, consolidated El Chato's Mexican cartel with his own formidable European drug and human trafficking syndicate. Soon after Rodrigo's arrival on the drug scene, a corporation named AXIOM appeared in this country as the center of the U.S. syndicate's activities.

The length of the 30'x 14'conference room was plastered with photographs, maps, and suspected U.S. political/corporate ties to the corporation. Pending indictments of powerful businessmen and government leaders were in sealed files accessible only to Special Agent Ram Edmunds.

Tentatively, Miró, still hesitant to break the flow of communication, asked, "Forgive my interruption, Ram, but when was El Chato convicted?"

"A year ago in February."

"So you collaborated with Calabrese up to February 2019?"

"Yes, I did. Calabrese even testified in El Chato's trial."

Nate noticed that Ram Edmunds was now standing. He had walked over to the wall filled with strategic connections of the main players in the cartel's hierarchy. As careful as Miró had been, Edmunds' reverie was broken.

"You probably noticed," Ram Edmunds said, "that it was not difficult to convince me that Tío was alive."

"Frankly, I had made mental notes in that regard," Nate said. "Though your own colleagues at the national headquarters made a public statement identifying the dead man at the Orrington Hotel as Tío Dante, you quickly believed that I'd met with him in Door County."

"Well, you did say that you'd met him before," Edmunds smiled. "But your instincts are correct, Dr…, I mean, Nate. I seriously doubted the agency's public announcement."

"Do you mind telling us why, Ram?" Miró asked.

"When I became interested in your kidnapping, several offices of law enforcement refused to provide the identity of the dead man found next to you. I first thought your kidnapping was part of an international sex trafficking operation, which

would demand tightly controlled information gathering...
especially if it was an ongoing investigation."

"Would that justify your local field office being left out
of the loop?" Miró asked.

"Not really, unless the Director himself was imposing
such secrecy," Edmunds said.

Nate and Miró waited.

"When local detective, Lionel Finn, informed me
that 'federal officials from Washington' had taken over the
investigation, my curiosity grew," Edmunds said. "So I called
the Department of Justice. They put me in touch with several
colleagues at CIA. In the early stages, CIA colleagues gave
me different names, each one described as a low-life, drug
pusher, or pimp. A peer of mine refused to divulge the name,
because it was classified as 'sensitive information that could
damage national security'. That simply did not satisfy me."

"We thought we were the only ones getting blocked at
every step," Miró said.

Edmunds smiled, explaining that after the first
conversation with Nate, he received a communication from
a friend at the FBI's DC headquarters telling him that his
superiors were calling it a 'screw-up in the bureaucratic chain
of command'. That same person called him a day later to
suggest that the federal medical examiner screwed up the
identity of the dead man. After his numerous inquiries,
the FBI Deputy Director's office called Edmunds. Deputy
Director Homely personally invited Edmunds to brief him
regarding 'the matter at hand'. In Homely's words, "The

boys merely wanted to shield Ram from the personal pain of knowing his former colleague and friend, Angelo Calabrese, had been viciously murdered in a married woman's hotel room."

"Are you serious?" Miró asked. "He truly phrased it like that?"

"Homely went on to say, 'You and your friend Angelo Calabrese were the ones responsible for bringing down the most powerful cartel boss in the world. El Chato Gómez would still be free if it were not for you and Cal. The agency will be eternally grateful, Ram'."

"Again, for fear of being indelicate," Nate said, "I hesitate to ask what you thought of that... puff of smoke."

"Ha," Edmunds said, "I did think someone was blowing smoke up my... nostrils. I left Homely's office with a sour taste in my mouth. 'Disingenuous' is the way I described the meeting to my wife."

"No wonder you did not seem overly surprised when I said Tío Dante was alive," Nate said.

"I'm still not certain why our offices are claiming Tío Dante is the dead man. More critically, I'm wondering if other colleagues are aware that Tío is alive and that he's in our country."

. . .

"I'm forgetting the second reason why I invited you here," Ram Edmunds said. "Of course, it was to discuss Tío Dante and his request for immunity. I must reiterate that immunity is out of the question. On the other hand, given the additional information you provided regarding former agent Calabrese, I would like to meet with Tío Dante, if he's still willing," Edmunds said.

"Although I cannot pretend to speak for Tío," Nate said, "I don't believe he expects to be completely absolved from wrongdoing. He explicitly told me he's willing to admit to kidnapping, but he claims that the killing of your friend and colleague, Agent Calabrese, was self-defense."

"That may be a tall order, but I'm willing to sit down to discuss details" Edmunds said. "I assume he would like to propose a meeting place, rather than meeting me in this federal office."

"He is proposing Door County."

"That would be out of the question. We will choose a more neutral site."

CHAPTER 29

Chicago, IL · January 17–31, 2020

P EDRO AND MACARIO ROSALES flew in Rodrigo's luxurious Airbus A380 private plane from Mazatlán to Chicago. Estevan arranged their return trip, and Lucas was assigned to escort them to their respective homes. Accompanying them was Dr. Ivo Wu, the physician that had performed plastic surgery on the brothers. They landed in Chicago's Executive Airport in Wheeling and quickly rode directly to their residences. Lucas apologized for his role as chaperone and driver, but explained he was only following the boss's orders. While he'd be living with Macario, Dr. Wu would temporarily move in with Pedro. Lucas also explained to the twins that Rodrigo insisted that the twins continue to be treated with maximum care and concern.

"Mates, you will have all meals delivered to you, but you will have limited access to the outside," Lucas said. "He wants me to reassure you that he's taking good care of your families."

"Not to seem ungrateful," Pedro said, "but we'd like to be with our families, dude. Where are they?"

Lucas explained that Rodrigo felt that the twins' families would be safer under his protection. Because the twins' identities had been compromised since the botched kidnapping, the authorities would stop at nothing to apprehend the twins. No telling how their families would be treated if captured by the Feds.

"You will see them as soon as Rodrigo thinks it's safe," Lucas said.

During the next three weeks, the twins were kept indoors. At first, both twins were permitted to see each other. They spent their time exercising together. Soon, the exercising stopped, and they both lost their appetites. They lost a significant amount of weight and fell into frequent bouts of depression. Pedro's natty attire soon deteriorated to gym shorts and T-shirts, while Macario rarely changed out of his sweat suits. Both went unshaven and became morose. Although Lucas Williams and Dr. Ivo Wu did their best to provide a healthy diet, the twins' preferred nutrition became chips and beer.

On the morning of January 31, Dr. Wu discovered Pedro unconscious, lying on the bathroom floor. He discovered an empty stash of depressants hidden behind the commode. Wu quickly went into action, and pumped his stomach. Pedro's color slowly returned to normal, but Wu had to use an IV to bring him back to life.

Upon hearing reports from Lucas, Estevan was alarmed. After all, they would need the Rosales twins to successfully complete one last assignment.

Before informing Rodrigo, Estevan personally visited Dr. Wu. Estevan inquired if he thought either twin again would attempt suicide. Wu informed Estevan that the depression was severe and that he could not ensure whether a second attempt would be made. Estevan wrote in his notepad, 'What do you recommend?'

"I recommend they be allowed to see their families," said Dr. Wu.

Immediately, Estevan informed his master. He underscored the need to sustain the twins' health, at least until their assignment was completed. However, he doubted that Rodrigo would permit the twins any contact with their families.

After much consideration, Rodrigo permitted the twins to enjoy videos of their children at play, and even had the twins' wives record video messages for them. Of course, all videos would be filtered and edited by Estevan. The families were instructed not to disclose their locations, but they were encouraged to share everyday activities and events. They were permitted to share information, if no negative requests or complaints were made. Foremost, it was critical that the twins knew their families were safe and healthy.

The videos turned out to be an effective solution. The twins' attitudes and well-being changed overnight. When they asked for daily video updates, Rodrigo willingly obliged. It became clear to Rodrigo that the twins were loving parents and devoted husbands. Their families were closely knit, a quality that he admired.

Because Rodrigo and Estevan were not ready to execute the details of an elaborate plan, they had to decide how to ensure the twins' safety. A change was needed, but what would be the ideal solution?

CHAPTER 30

Chicago, IL · January 21, 2020

ABRAHAM'S TEACHING ASSIGNMENT AT Northwestern's Feinberg School of Medicine included the supervision and training of medical interns and residents. Abraham also insisted on treating a limited number of patients in order to stay current in his practice. His work days began early four days a week.

The train ride from his home to downtown Chicago allowed Abraham enough time to plan his day and respond to urgent emails. The 1.6-mile walk from the N. Canal Street station to his clinic at the hospital also gave him a useful jump-start to his ten-thousand-step daily regimen. Nowadays, Abraham played little racquetball and almost zero tennis, which in the past had enabled him to remain at a healthy weight for his height and build. At exactly 7:30 his cell phone rang. It was Special Agent Ram Edmunds calling. As he waited for the traffic light to change at the intersection of Michigan Avenue and E. Huron Street, he answered the call.

"Dr. Epstein, I hope I'm catching you at a good time. This is Ram Edmunds."

"Good to hear from you. Just getting to work, Agent Edmunds. What can I do for you?"

"I'm hopeful you can assist me in this investigation regarding your family. As you know, I spoke with Nate and Miró, and since that conversation I've uncovered numerous fascinating details. I'm hopeful you can help us with tying up loose ends."

"I'll do my best. By all means."

"Per an official reversal from our DC headquarters, the dead man discovered at the Orrington Hotel on September 22 was a former patient of yours."

"Excuse me? The morning traffic is quite noisy. Did you say the dead man was a former patient?"

Ram Edmunds went on to explain that the Washington DC medical examiner recovered some medical records and rather thorough files on an Angelo Calabrese. Edmunds claimed Calabrese had listed Abraham as his personal care physician for a brief period during the years 2016 and 2017— for less than a year.

"That's odd," Abraham said. "I usually remember my patients. Unfortunately, the name does not sound familiar. I'll need to review my files."

"I would be personally grateful, Dr. Epstein," Edmunds said. "You've got my number. It's my cell; please call at any time."

As he walked into the hospital, Abraham asked his receptionist to retrieve the files for the former patient. She informed Abraham that he had two hospital residents waiting for their daily assignments.

Shortly after Abraham's session with his two young protégés, his receptionist handed Abraham the file on Angelo Calabrese. Indeed, Abraham had added Mr. Calabrese to his limited list of patients on the 11th of November, 2016. He performed the first physical exam, noting that the new patient was in superb physical and mental condition, given his age of seventy-one. Calabrese was 5'11", 210 pounds, and muscular. Of Italian descent, his complexion was medium-dark, and he had straight dark hair. The patient was a retired FBI and CIA agent; however, he still served as an occasional consultant to both agencies. Marital status was single, having been thrice divorced. Furthermore, the patient indicated he enjoyed deep-sea diving and flying private planes in his spare time. He freely offered to Abraham during his initial consultation that he was a sworn enemy of all-things-President Strong. Calabrese had aced his blood test and his stress test.

When he looked at the dates more carefully, Abraham identified the reason for his memory lapse. Since Abraham had taken a leave of absence to travel to the Canary Islands to help Miró during the Canarian nightmare of 2016, he had transferred his new patient to his Feinberg School of Medicine associate, Dr. Alan Soho. Abraham felt justified.

Although he'd attempted to communicate with Edmunds later in the day, Abraham was unsuccessful. After playing phone tag for two hours, Abraham gave up and returned home. On his train ride back home, he asked Max to pick him up at the Wilmette Station.

"Why so far?" Max asked. "Errands to run?"

"No, I need some time to bounce an idea off you," Abraham said.

Forty minutes later, Abraham boarded Max's new rental, a Grand Cherokee that he seemed to enjoy driving.

"Would you like to stop somewhere to ensure my undivided attention, Dad?"

Abraham smiled. He declined, but asked Max not to hurry getting home. "I believe the CIA or some other federal agency was involved in Miró's kidnapping."

"Please, Dad. This mystery is strange enough already without your adding to this bizarre scenario. Why in the world would the CIA want to kidnap her?"

"That's precisely why I want to have your undivided attention, Max. Before jumping to any conclusions, I want you to listen to my case," Abraham said.

"All I'm saying, Dad, is that I know your strategy. You overwhelm me with your vast knowledge, then you convince me to accept your wild ideas."

"That's unfair, Son. I've never pulled rank on you. If anything, I regret not being there enough to guide your steps during childhood."

"Dad, that's not what I'm referring to. I just..."

"I was a totally absent dad. I'm aware of that, Max."

"I know that Mom also had something to do with that."

"Olivia did the best she could as a single mom. She raised you successfully."

"Yep, and that's the way she preferred it," Max said. A long silence followed.

"So, can we go back to my theory? It relates to a former patient."

"A former patient—who was also CIA, I suppose—kidnapped Miró. Is that your new wild story?"

"I received a call from Special Agent Edmunds early this morning. And, he asked if the dead man found at the Orrington Hotel was a former patient of mine. I checked, and for a brief time, he was indeed my patient."

"Okay, Dad, I agree that is an unusual twist of events, but to connect this former patient to Miró's kidnapping is a very different matter."

"In addition to Special Agent Edmunds' call, I received a call from our friend from the Tribune, and he shared interesting details with which I was unfamiliar."

"Pray, tell me," Max said with exaggerated surprise in his voice.

"Our reporter friend has also found out the victim's name was Angelo Calabrese. He probably quizzed law enforcement officials."

"Rosie has been busy, eh?"

"Max, stop at the Starbucks. My treat."

It was good for Max to get some coffee and a snack to hold him over till dinner. Abraham asked for hot tea.

"On his first visit, when I saw this former patient, he reported bouts of anxiety regarding the nature of his work. I was tempted to recommend therapy with Nate. Glad I didn't."

"Dad, when was the last time you saw him?"

"I never saw him after the first visit. However, my colleagues saw him on several occasions. I just checked the patient's records, and it was five months ago that they saw him last. That's about three weeks before Miró went missing."

"Anything about his personal life that could help in this investigation?" Max asked.

"Son, I examine medical symptoms, not their personal lives. Of course, very personal information emerges often when discussing one's health."

"That's what I meant, Dad."

"Well, it was clear that he knew—or knows—the specific machinations of drug cartels."

"You hadn't shared that with me."

"He was on assignment to delve deep into powerful cartels, including the one that was recently brought down by the Feds. You know, the one masterminded by the guy who'd escaped several prisons, 'El Sapo,' or 'Japo'."

"You're kidding," exclaimed Max. "You mean 'El Chato' Gómez? That's a big profile. But isn't it unusual for a Fed to share that kind of information?"

"He spoke about it after it became public knowledge. The news was splashed across the media outlets. But yes, the case was a big one."

Max envisioned various scenarios. He thought, *If the dead man in Miró's room was not Tío, could it possibly be this former patient of my dad's?*

Abraham stood up, asked for a refill, paced the floor, and shook his head. "My patient resembled Tío physically. At first I couldn't remember him, perhaps because I thought he was inflating the importance of his work. But per my notes, my ex-patient was approximately the same height as Tío, and his Italian heritage gave him an olive complexion. Straight, dark hair."

"Certainly, we can find many six-foot men with straight black hair who have an olive complexion, Dad," Max complained.

"That's a fair point," Abraham said. "However, Nate is the only member of the family who spoke to Tío face to face, and he assured me that he remembered those prominent gold beauties. You've seen Tío's passport pictures. Even that photograph features those gold incisors front and center. Per my records, and my own memory, my patient did not have any gold teeth."

"And, your point is…?" Max asked.

"If the Feds cannot verify that the dead man had gold teeth, then we'll know the dead man was not Tío Dante."

"As the Feds have already concluded."

For the next twenty minutes, Max and Abraham reviewed the various details. They got back to the SUV, and drove around Skokie for a few minutes, mulling over and speculating different scenarios. Abraham stated the possible ties, and Max dedicated his time to dismissing each argument.

"Dad, I've got an idea. Instead of all this brainstorming, why don't we simply gather more information. Certainly, you cannot object to that. I'll investigate this patient's past, and you give the Interpol guy, or the Canary Islands' chief inspector, another call to see if they have any information on your new target, Calabrese?"

"Son, that's an excellent idea. Except that I've already called them."

. . .

"You're being melodramatic, Dad. What did you find out?"

"Not much," Abraham said. "Inspector Sánchez—from the Canary Islands, you remember—had no information on Calabrese, my absent patient. When he asked his Interpol friend Picard to search international files, all Picard said was that Calabrese had a 'healthy' file that listed a distinguished career with American intelligence agencies."

"There you are. No suspicions of nefarious activities. You satisfied?"

"Ahem... not so fast. Picard did say that the Russians have a separate file on him."

"Russians? I didn't think Russia cooperated with Interpol," Max said.

"Per Picard, Interpol's National Central Bureau is in Moscow. And the NCB's focus is organized crime and cybercrime."

"I learn something new every day. So, I have an idea you're about to drop a bombshell. I can tell by your smugness and the way you're stroking your goatee."

"Ha, you've been observing your old man, have you?"

"My training as a private investigator helps," Max said. "Please enlighten me."

"Well, Picard shared with us—through Inspector Sánchez, of course—that his men at the NCB in Moscow place the former CIA agent, Angelo Calabrese, in the center of an ongoing investigation of human and drug smuggling."

"As an investigator... or the investigated?"

"Until very recently," Abraham said, with a dramatic pause, "Calabrese appears in Interpol files both as an 'informant' and 'participant' in this large-scale investigation."

"What exactly does 'informant' and 'participant' mean? Did Picard explain?"

"Per Sánchez, Picard suggested only that Calabrese was under suspicion."

So, Calabrese may have played both sides, thought Max. *He misinformed the intelligence agencies, then turned around and engaged in the crimes.* Max went into deep thought, and Abraham realized that his son was now willing to consider his 'outlandish conspiracy theories' about Calabrese. In fact, Abraham could see that Max could be persuaded that the dead man found at the Orrington Hotel might be CIA.

However, Abraham himself still had trouble connecting the proverbial dots. As Max said, *Why would an ex-CIA agent kidnap my daughter Miró?*

"So, where does that leave us? Did Sánchez offer any ideas?"

"None, Max. Picard, however, has put out an All-Points-Bulletin—or whatever you law enforcement types call them."

"In Europe?" Max asked. "Don't they trust the conclusion of the American authorities?"

"No, they do not. Interpol is limiting its search to the American Midwest. Interpol wants to locate Angelo Calabrese—dead or alive—to assist in the international dragnet."

"Wow, if I didn't know any better, I'd say you're perfecting your law enforcement lingo. How'd you like to totally retire and join me in my practice?"

Max and his dad shared a laugh, but awkwardly agreed to bring Miró and Nate up to date on their new 'findings'.

"Let's wait another day, though," Max said.

Evanston, IL · Wednesday, January 22, 2020

The following day, Nate and Miró received the call from Abraham shortly after dinner.

Abraham had placed several calls to Inspector Sánchez, and he got a response on the third try. Sánchez returned the call from Brussels, where he was meeting with Gabriel Picard, the Secretary General of Interpol. Sánchez had picked Picard's brain and asked him to investigate Angelo Calabrese's birth records. Picard had not found any further data on Calabrese.

On the other hand, Teodosio Dante's birth records, his family history, military and work history were all there. He was a Spaniard, born in Sevilla, fifty-four years old, and had served in the special forces. Since he specialized in explosives, he was one of a handful of Spaniards to be deployed to Iraq during the Gulf War, assisting NATO forces. While there, Dante sustained injuries and received reconstructive facial and dental surgery. Dante's passport from 2007 showed a smiling Teodosio Dante sporting gold teeth.

Since such thorough information was available regarding Tío Dante, Abraham asked if Interpol had similar information on Tío's boss, Diego Montemayor. Surprisingly, for years Picard's researchers had scanned records throughout Europe but couldn't come up with any birth records for the drug lord.

"I can't believe that Interpol has all this information on Tío Dante but cannot find Diego Montemayor's birth records, his history, or his recent activities. Abraham, do you buy that?" Nate asked.

"Well, let me clarify. Interpol does have other information about Diego," Abraham said. "They have other life details, making his files quite extensive. They have his illegal activities, his many business ventures, his studies in botany, chemistry, and his expertise in the field. In fact, per files, his publications in botanical research had earned him a formidable reputation in academia."

"How far back does the information take them?" Nate asked.

"He first pops up as a student at the University of Salamanca. Nothing before that. There he was radicalized, or, at least, that's the assumption. He traveled north and became a Basque revolutionary, living underground several years. He has dual citizenship in Spain and the U.S., but there is no record of any travel or residency in the U.S."

"Don't you find that to be strange, Abraham?"

"Somewhat, although Sánchez didn't seem to think that was peculiar."

"What else?"

"Oddly enough, Sánchez stated that Diego's deceased mom was a Spanish citizen. She, however, was evidently born elsewhere. Also, there are ample records of Diego's marriage to Inspector Sánchez's goddaughter, Yael Vidaurri

Montemayor. Then, after his wife's death, Diego went underground and disappeared. No one knows where he is."

"Where did they get married, Dad?" Miró interjected.

"Hi, mi'jita! Diego and his wife Yael were married in the Canary Islands—in Las Palmas, in fact."

"Obviously, you're on speakerphone, Abraham. This is Nate again. When Sánchez stated that Diego's mom was born elsewhere, did you inquire about her birthplace?"

"Sánchez didn't specify, and I didn't ask," Abraham said.

"I'm surprised," Nate said. "You, a genealogy buff, with a wildly active imagination, certainly you must have some interest in that. Where was Diego's mom born? If her European birth records cannot be found, then determining her birthplace may give us a clue to Diego's origins."

"Excellent point, Nate."

"If you don't mind, I need to go. I'd like to call Inspector Sánchez again," Abraham said.

CHAPTER 31

Skokie, IL · Saturday, January 25, 2020

OR THE NEXT TWO days, Abraham was unable to
speak to Sánchez. His numerous messages were not
answered.

Abraham had not dwelled on Inspector Sánchez's
morbid warning. He especially kept it from Nate and Miró.
However, Abraham could not shake the chilling possibility
that Diego Montemayor was using his powerful influence to
eventually kill Miró, Minnie, and Nate. Guessing that their
principal nemesis was between forty-five and sixty years old,
Abraham secretly searched the various genealogical sites for
every Montemayor birth that could have occurred between
1960 and 1975. He only knew from Sánchez's accounts that
Diego was older than his wife, but how much older only
birth records could say.

On the third day, a Saturday, Abraham received a call
from Inspector Sánchez. The inspector confirmed that, from
his estimation, Diego was approximately fifty-five years old.
As for Diego's mom, Sánchez could only rely on her Spanish

citizenship records. Her name was Linda Montemayor, and she had obtained her citizenship when she moved in with a merchant from Toledo, Spain. It was unclear if she came from Central America, Mexico, or the U.S. The records were not digital nor legible. Although she lived with her common-law husband in Toledo until her death in 2003, she never adopted the husband's surname.

Abraham again called Nate and Miró to give them an update.

"Dad," Miró said, "doesn't Sánchez or Picard have a working hypothesis regarding Diego's birthplace, or his mom's, perhaps?"

"Yeah," Nate chimed in, "surely, these guys at Interpol have the resources to do better."

"I agree," Abraham said. "It appears that they simply decided to move on. Diego Montemayor's birth records don't seem to be of great interest to them. Obviously, they're more interested in his location, his trafficking, and his cartel's involvement. Since his wife's death, he has not been seen."

"There must be some threads there, though," Nate said.

"Well, the only threads may be unpleasant to hear. Though Sánchez hated to be the bearer of bad news, he said Interpol believed that Diego Montemayor was definitely alive but no longer in Europe."

"So, have they tracked him down?" Nate asked.

"They think he's living in Mexico or here in our country."

CHAPTER 32

Skokie, IL · Tuesday, January 28, 2020

BRAHAM LOUNGED IN HIS den by the fireplace, deep in thought. Since he'd taken a half-day, he was still in his slippers and robe. He drank his favorite French roast, which Abraham brewed from beans ordered from an online source. He'd slept miserably, tossing and turning in bed, pondering Sánchez's disinterest in Diego's origins, while wondering if Picard was truly unable to trace Linda Montemayor's lineage. He dialed Max's cell shortly before 7 AM.

"You're needed downstairs, Max. I'll brew some more coffee, and you can join me for breakfast."

"Now?"

"Yes, forget about tidying up. Brush your teeth and walk down in your PJs and robe."

"I do not own a robe."

"Okay, skip the robe."

Five minutes later, Max, in his sweats, shuffled to the oversized granite kitchen island. He pulled up a stool and flopped, slouched and beady-eyed. "I'm assuming you have some great revelations."

"No, the reason I want you here is that I'm thinking of traveling to your part of the world, Austin to be specific. And I want to hear what you think."

"Reason being?"

"While doing online research last night, something hit me," Abraham said.

"Yesterday, you said your online research was going nowhere."

Abraham smiled. "That was until I came up with a hunch during the night."

"Is the cardiac surgeon going with a hunch? The man that seeks persuasive evidence even before diagnosing and treating an ingrown toenail?"

"You'd be surprised how much I rely on my intuition when doing my work. Just ask Miró. She'll tell you how I drive her crazy with my 'unsubstantiated conclusions'."

"Well, as I hear it, your record is pretty solid right now. Previous hunches have proven right."

"That's all it is, Max—a feeling, a sneaking suspicion, an inkling, if you will. And I need to verify it."

"How about that coffee, Dad?"

Abraham apologized and served two fresh cups. He sat next to Max.

"Would you like to share any of it?" Max asked.

"It may be a shot in the dark, but last night while I was lying awake reviewing the information that Inspector

Sánchez and Picard gave us, I got up and did another search. I've spent days examining online records, and I realized that I was limiting myself to Linda's married name. What if Montemayor was Linda's maiden name?"

"Sorry, remind me again who 'Linda' is," Max said.

"I've been on this day and night, so I assume we all have these names memorized. Linda was the name of Diego Montemayor's mother."

"Go on."

"So, I was hitting a dead end at every turn."

"Not sure how that would matter, but you're the family history researcher," Max said. "It must be quite a hunch to make you fly across the country to Austin."

"Since I found several references to a Linda Montemayor in Travis County, Texas, I'm hopeful that some links can be made. And, Sánchez did say she was not European."

"What, you're thinking she was an immigrant?"

"Not necessarily. Sánchez said she was from Mexico, Central... or North America."

"Hmm."

"I will quickly find out if this intuition of mine is onto something. It shouldn't take long to find out—a couple of days at the most."

"Okay, let's assume that you identify Diego's mom. Why is that critical?" Max asked.

"I don't know if it'll be critical, but my instincts tell me that her identity will open other avenues of investigation— other clues—that will help us understand our enemy."

"Ah, that's it. The inspector from the Canary Islands, he shares this Lao Tzu or Sun Tzu nonsense, and now he's under your skin. This 'art of war' crapola about knowing your enemy is at the heart of your motivation."

"I suppose much of it does make sense to me," admitted Abraham. "Besides, Max, finding this additional information may help us in other ways."

"Name one."

"Look, if you're in disagreement, I'll find my own transportation to the airport. My genealogical research cannot hurt—that much I know," Abraham said.

"I didn't mean to upset you. Just know that I can find my way around Austin," Max said. "I could help you."

"I think you should stay here and take care of the family," Abraham said. "I'd feel better if you stick around to take care of them."

"You're right," Max said, "but remember that I know people there. If you need anything, give me a buzz."

"I will. Remember that Miriam also prefers to stay with her two favorite girls."

"Plus, you're the genealogy expert. I get it. I just thought I could be helpful to you. By the way, you've said you depend a lot on the Mormon archives; is there a temple in Austin?"

"No, the nearest Mormon temple is the one in San Antonio. Austin has several churches, but no temples. I'll begin with county and state records in Austin."

"If you need to travel to San Antonio, I also have a few contacts there," Max said. "For whatever it's worth, I believe the trip is a good idea. I'll watch the fort."

"Thank you, Son." Abraham looked away, but he prayerfully thanked God for the opportunity to restore much that had been lost between him and Max.

"I'll drive you to the airport. Midway or O'Hare?"

"I'm using my accumulated miles. Sorry, it'll have to be O'Hare."

"Just tell me when, Dad."

"I've made a reservation for an early flight tomorrow. We'll need to leave the house by 6 AM."

. . .

Upon arrival in Austin, Abraham was reminded of the Texas weather. Although it was late January, a balmy temperature greeted him. Abraham quickly shed his overcoat and rented a car. He drove through East Austin, where enormous urban development and gentrification was underway. Interstate 35 still sliced Austin into east and west. West Austin, where major real estate and commercial contracts were transacted, and East Austin, where green and eco-friendly businesses and independent foodie establishments flourished.

Like many tourists, Abraham attempted to straddle the great divide by selecting a hotel situated on the western side of the I-35 boundary.

Though his room was not ready at 11:00 when he arrived, the concierge at the Four Seasons invited him to have a light lunch at the Ciclo Restaurant, on the lower level of the hotel, which offered the best view of the Congress Bridge. The concierge recommended he return for drinks at 6:30 PM to witness the 'bat nocturnal exit' from the Congress Bridge underbelly. With raised eyebrows, she added that it was the largest urban bat colony in the world.

"And their nightly exit in search of dinner can be viewed from the hotel."

Her demeanor was serious, as if she were describing the Eighth Wonder of the World. Abraham smiled and thanked her, agreeing that he'd experienced it before, and it was, indeed, a 'remarkable sight'.

Since the poor concierge appeared to be genuinely disappointed, Abraham consoled her by asking whether she could secure a local map with directions to three sites in Austin: the Texas State Library and Archives Commission, the Family History Center, and the Texas State Genealogical Society. With renewed cheer, the concierge promptly left and returned with the three locations clearly identified on the map.

After consuming a filling brunch, Abraham summoned the concierge once more. "You know, I could also use some help finding the Travis County Courthouse and the nearest Mormon church."

Delighted to be of help, the young concierge left momentarily and returned within minutes with both additional locations marked clearly on the map.

"Also, please remember that the Horns basketball team plays TCU tonight at 7 PM, so, we expect most sports bars to be crowded, and traffic downtown will be impossible to maneuver. I will be glad to make any restaurant reservations." She wrote down her extension number as well as her name— Lucy Scholz—on the upper right-hand corner of the map.

Searches that afternoon produced few helpful details. A Linda Montemayor from Ben Bolt, Texas, had married an Austin boy by the name of Brian Canales in 1966. Another Linda Martin Montemayor got her driver's license in Buda, Texas, in the same year. A death certificate listed her as deceased five years later. Other unsuccessful searches followed.

Then, seven minutes after the closing hour of 5 PM, Abraham found a confusing entry in the archives. The embarrassed clerk apologetically approached Abraham and explained she needed to retrieve 'all archives' from 'clients' because it was past closing time.

"But you'll be able to return at 9 AM, Dr. Epstein."

Hardly responding, Abraham took an iPhone picture of the entry that intrigued him.

He returned early the following morning and waited for the doors to open at nine. The return visit clarified several matters. The second search disclosed that Linda M. Cruz, age nineteen, gave birth to a male child at St. David's Hospital in Austin, Texas. The birth was recorded on November 13, 1966. The father was listed as Angelo Calabrese. Furthermore, the child's name was recorded as Diego Raymundo Calabrese.

Oddly, the mother, 'Linda M.', had been married to a Juventino Cruz. She took on the legal name Linda M. Cruz. Abraham, however, was unable to find her maiden name.

Poor fit, Abraham thought. *But the name of the father, Angelo Calabrese, could that be a mere coincidence? Calabrese is not a common name in these parts. An out-of-wedlock birth? Could this be my former patient, Angelo Calabrese? Was my patient in Texas during the Sixties?*

At noon, Abraham texted Max and asked if he could get any of his buddies in the Austin PD to search for a Linda M. Cruz. Was there any police record in Austin of such an individual in the mid-Sixties? Max promised to get on it right away.

CHAPTER 33

MAX PICKED ABRAHAM UP at O'Hare. Just like he thought, it took a couple of days for his dad to verify his hunch. Once again, Abraham's 'intuition' led him to unlock the key to further investigations. His dad, of course, firmly believed it was divine guidance that led him to his findings.

"So, Dad," Max took Abraham's carry-on from his hands. He swiftly placed the bag in the trunk and nodded to the airport "officer", who was telling him his parking time limit was up. "How was your trip?"

"Excellent, Max."

Pulling out into the fast-moving exit lane of O'Hare, Max discovered he'd adopted Chicagoland's driving customs—aggressive and non-apologetic. "Yeah? Tell me more."

"Well, why don't we stop for one of those German pancakes from Walker Brothers and I'll tell you all about it?" Abraham said, with a glimmer in his eye.

"You're kidding, the brilliant heart surgeon, he recommends one of the worst possible culprits in the heart attack realm. Are you serious?"

"Well, Max, I just remember your epiphany when I introduced you to those babies," Abraham said.

"You called them apple pancakes. How was I to know that a single cake could feed three people? I didn't eat for the rest of the day."

"No one forced you to finish the whole thing, though. Let's stop at the Northbrook location."

Abraham knew better than to begin a conversation with Max before half the pancake was consumed. He checked his phone for messages; nothing there. When Max came up for air, Abraham asked, "Now will I be able to command half your concentration?"

"Funny, very funny." Max hailed their waitperson. "Even coffee tastes better with these things."

"My hunch was correct," Abraham said. "Aided by your police buddies' research into Linda's old parking violations—and my own confirmation through Travis County records—it turns out Linda Montemayor was legally named 'Linda M. Cruz' for a short while. Since she married a Juventino Cruz from Austin in the summer of '65, she took on that surname. Unfortunately for them, hubby joined the Air Force and was deployed to Vietnam shortly after the wedding—I believe it was in October of 1965."

"And the poor kid was killed."

Abraham nodded. "For the longest time, no one knew. The government officially declared him 'Missing in Action'. Along with ten Aussies after a battle north of Saigon, he disappeared. Don't quote me, but I believe it was the Battle of Ho Bo Woods," Abraham said, without certainty.

"I'd never heard of it. I'm no expert on the war, though."

"Shortly afterward, Linda Cruz legally reclaimed her maiden name. She became Linda Montemayor."

Abraham paused because Max was ordering his third cup of coffee. He looked well on his way to finishing the gigantic meal. "You know you could take that home and freeze it, Max."

"No way. Things never taste as good when reheated."

"Okay, can I continue?"

"Yes, didn't mean to interrupt you."

"So, we've got a setting where we have a recently married twenty-year-old woman whose husband has gone missing, living alone in Austin, Texas, during the wild and crazy mid-Sixties. Plus, although not students at UT Austin—as far as I could determine—the Cruz' lived close to campus on the corner of San Gabriel and 25th."

"Wow, that's just blocks away from the Drag and the West Campus," Max said. "Living there in the mid-Sixties—you're in the thick of sex, drugs, and rock and roll."

"Exactly," Abraham said. "Well, Linda found herself pregnant by someone other than hubby. Her husband was MIA. And the biological father did not appear to be present at the birth of the child. However, he is referenced in both hospital and county records."

"Okay. So, you think you've identified Diego Montemayor's mom? And, you're saying that Diego—Europe's most wanted criminal—may have been born in Austin, Texas? And, that he was illegitimate?"

"I believe so. I may not have absolute certainty, but I'm going with my findings," Abraham said.

"Wow, if that's true, we may be onto something. I can't see now how useful it can be, but that's a fascinating discovery."

"If you consider that 'fascinating', Max, wait till you hear the rest." Abraham took a sip of his tepid coffee, and paused dramatically.

"There's more?"

"Although the biological father was not present at the birth of the child, I told you that his name appeared in both hospital and county records." Abraham took another sip of coffee. "His name was Angelo Calabrese."

"Your former patient?"

"It appears that way. The age would be right," Abraham said.

"The same individual that Special Agent Edmunds says was found dead at the Orrington Hotel?"

"It appears that way," repeated Abraham. "Although early on Diego's mom retained the name of Linda M. Cruz, she named her child 'Diego Raymundo Calabrese', after the biological father."

"Why would she do that?" Max asked.

"I have no idea," Abraham said. "However, with a little more digging, I found out that Linda kept her husband's surname for a few months, but when her husband was declared dead, she adopted her maiden name as her legal name. At that time, she changed her child's legal name to Diego R. Montemayor."

"That must be the discovery of the century, Dr. Epstein. You've certainly made me a fan of genealogical research."

"Did your friends get any information regarding the nature of the parking violations or make of Linda Cruz's vehicle?"

"Nothing earth-shattering. Violations were all for 'time expiration' at the meters, and the vehicle was a '65 VW bus, you know, the 'hippie vans' that were so popular."

"Not too bad for a newly wedded couple," Abraham said.

"Hey, let's get home. Guess what time it is?"

"We also need to stop for some wine that I ordered."

CHAPTER 34

Chicago, IL · February 16, 2020

To TELL THE STORY of how Rodrigo learned with certainty of the dead man's identity, Estevan first had to explain how the corpse's identity had been suppressed and why a lie had been disseminated by U.S. federal agents. Although the lie may have favored the Rosales twins, they had not authored the fiction. Motivated primarily to save the intelligence network from admitting that one in their own ranks had participated in an attempted assassination and kidnapping, they instead fabricated the myth that the victim was a famous international criminal and not a former federal agent. So, it was Rodrigo's own FBI informants who had hidden the truth from Rodrigo and not the twins themselves.

Rodrigo, nonetheless, could not completely absolve the twins' participation in this fracas. Their incompetence reached colossal proportions. *However, Estevan was right. I had assigned those brainless halfwits to hire the hit man that would erase Dante from the map, and who ends up dead? The hit man, of course.* As unpalatable as it may be, he was partly to blame.

Rodrigo had just received a call from his DC contact at the DOJ. The news he received had been unsettling for many reasons. Not only did Rodrigo express his deep disappointment to the penitent FBI executive, who received five-figure monthly checks from Rodrigo's coffers, but he secretly began to doubt his own choice of associates. Staffing his managerial team had not been problematic when it was in the capable hands of his former executive vice president. Yet, since Rodrigo had assumed the role of selecting and assigning duties to his managers, he had repeatedly faced setbacks.

Rodrigo's FBI connection not only had admitted to falsely reporting information to the media, he had also confessed to the 'buying of time' for the correction of a grievous mistake.

"I was ashamed to tell you we'd messed up at the Bureau's headquarters. That's why we let your boys think Dante was dead. But don't worry, Tío's days are numbered. Now, we know where he is." Rodrigo's trusted FBI source was almost whining and begging for forgiveness.

"You've had your opportunities," Rodrigo said. "I'll take care of Tío Dante."

Rodrigo killed the brief conversation on his secured line to the DOJ. He was not happy. Nonetheless, he laughed without mirth. "Estevan, our Washington DC friends at DOJ inform me they can ensure our protection in this country for only a few more days. According to them, since Miriam and Minerva Epstein identified the Rosales twins, it's too risky to be seen with those two."

For the next two hours, Rodrigo and Estevan prioritized their next moves. They decided to summon the twins by text to the Botanic Gardens in Glencoe. "Tell them to meet us at the Keiunto Island within the Japanese Garden at 1400 hours," Rodrigo said. "That way, we'll be able to see whoever comes and goes from the tiny island."

· · ·

"Hell, boss, we're locals and we never knew these gardens even existed. How'd you find this place?" Pedro Rosales asked.

"You should get out more, boys," Rodrigo said. Estevan had set out three lawn chairs, and Rodrigo was seated opposite the two reserved for the twins. The approach to the small island was behind the twins, where Rodrigo could maintain a constant watch. Estevan, with his surveillance equipment, was his only sentry.

"We know where Tío Dante is, boss. I know we can get him now. We'll do it ourselves," Pedro Half-Pants said.

"No, Pedro, I asked you here to get information. I need two things from you. First, I want to know how you first got access to the FBI and the CIA. Secondly, I want to know how this Agent Edmunds fits into the picture. I cannot find him in our payroll; is he ours?" Rodrigo asked.

"It's complicated," Pedro said.

"Simplify it for me. I'm a simple man."

"My father knew a man, a homey from Chicago who worked with him in his business."

"You mean a mule, transporting and selling drugs?"

"Yeah, more or less. My dad sort of ran all sorts of contraband, you know, drugs, weapons, stolen goods. He also became a coyote, transporting immigrants to this country for a fee."

"Okay, so this homey hired your dad, or was he an associate?"

"Just a friend. They both worked on the same projects, but this guy was smarter than my dad, and he went to college. Even got a degree."

"Is this the guy that first paid you to hide drugs inside a car's gas tank?" Rodrigo asked.

"Yeah, that's the same dude. His name is—or was—Cal."

"This is not so complicated so far. Get on with it."

"This dude sort of went straight. He even became an FBI agent. Then, he became CIA."

"What are you waiting for, Half-Pants? You want prompting each step of the way? Spit it out," Rodrigo said.

"Well, my brother Macario and I believe you know this dude. That's why we're wondering why you keep on asking about someone you probably know quite well."

"You've said that before, and I don't know why," Rodrigo said. "I tend to lose my patience, so I advise you to keep going until I tell you to stop."

"Okay, okay, boss. This dude, Cal, comes back after many years and tells us he knows we're involved with El Chato Gómez, and that it's time to bail out."

Macario, the quiet twin that Rodrigo called Mudo, jumped in. "At that point, boss, like, we knew Cal was a Fed, but we didn't know if he was just trying to lay a trap for us. He wasn't. He said he and the Feds would protect us if we cooperated. He'd make sure our families would be safe from the cartels. If we testified against our boss, he'd give us federal protection."

"Yeah, but he added one more condition," Pedro said.

"Don't stop," Macario said. "The boss told you, Pedro, to go on till he tells you to stop."

Reassured, Pedro continued. "Cal said he'd help us if we cooperated—and, if we helped you—except he didn't give us a name, just a contact who ended up being Estevan. We needed to help you get all of El Chato's business holdings."

"You see," Macario said, "Cal knew we were El Chato's lieutenants."

"So, you're telling me this Cal, who was a federal agent, brought you to me?" Rodrigo asked.

"Not exactly. He got your former Vice President of Operations to hire him as a consultant. Cal did a few jobs for your former VP, and he won your organization's trust. It was your VP, working through Cal, that brought us to the table."

"I think I understand now," Rodrigo said. "The complicated part is that you did not have any direct contacts at the DOJ. It was this Cal who brought you the FBI and CIA contacts on a silver platter."

"You could say that," Macario said.

"But how did you know that Cal was not simply setting a trap for my organization to fall into the hands of the Feds?" Rodrigo asked.

"When Cal came to your side, you became, like, untouchable, Rodrigo. All the other cartel bosses fell, but your organization just grew. Funds from all directions came our way, and politicians came hat in hand offering favors in exchange for political donations for their foundations and PACS. They paved the way for dozens of new 'contracts'," Macario said.

"This other Special Agent Edmunds. Where does he fit in? You said that you'd tapped his phones and even broke into his electronic communications. Why are you two so interested in him?" Rodrigo asked.

"Cal worked with Special Agent Edmunds to bring down El Chato Gómez, Rodrigo. When Cal worked at the FBI—and it seems like even before—he was close to Ram Edmunds. I think they went to college together and became good friends."

"So, did Edmunds help Cal gain access to other dirty cops inside the intelligence community?" Rodrigo asked.

"No, no," Macario said. "This dude was like a 'straight arrow', that's what Cal called him. He hated dirty cops. He even tried to get Cal to give up any shady connections."

"And you're saying they remained friends?" Rodrigo asked.

"Yes, boss, as far as we know they remained friends. For some reason, Edmunds remained a friend of Cal's, thinking he would return to his senses."

"You're saying that they remained friends, though he knew Cal was a dirty cop?"

"Sure looks that way."

"Nah, this Edmunds must've been getting something on the side. Believe me, Half-Pants, everyone has a price." Rodrigo smirked. "So, why should I care about this agent Edmunds?"

"Because I think he is hot on our trail. Just like he hunted down El Chato, he's coming after us."

"You mental runts. I've got the most powerful organization in the world, and you're bringing me sob stories about Edmunds' threats?"

Rodrigo was situated at the summit of the tiny island's slope. He faced the only access to the area, and behind him tall junipers and cherry trees framed his seated throne. Behind the twins, freshly mown winter grass descended to the edge of the land where the man-made waterways undulated throughout the lush landscape. Like an oasis at the far north end of a barren wintry Chicagoland, the Botanic Garden served as a year-round land of Eden, a beautiful setting for family portraits.

For the first time, Estevan turned to look at Rodrigo. He slowly shook his head, offering a quick reminder to control his temper. Rodrigo nodded, looked down at the thick carpet of grass, took a deep breath, and counted to ten.

"One last thing," Rodrigo said. "You said that Cal is—
or was—the same individual who taught you how to hide
drugs inside a car's gas tank. Why the doubt? Why use the
past tense?"

"I'll explain," Macario said. "My brother and I
contracted Cal to take care of your former Vice President
of Operations, Tío Dante. If the dead man in that hotel was
not Tío, then…"

"Then what, Mudo?"

"Then," Mudo said, "we think the dead man may be
Cal, our guy."

The twins had just confirmed what Rodrigo had heard
earlier in the day from his FBI contact in Washington DC.
He was surrounded by ineptitude.

CHAPTER 35

FOR SEVERAL WEEKS, SPECIAL Agent in Charge Ram Edmunds had culled his task force and reduced it to known associates whom he trusted and screened. He reassigned any recent transfers, especially transfers from the Washington DC office, to ancillary positions that focused on domestic issues pertaining to white-collar crime and preliminary investigations. He debugged his strategy room once weekly, and at times more often. He deliberately left intact two cameras, which had been surreptitiously installed in a small conference room. They became useful, because he planted false conversations and presented information that circled back to his office as 'unsubstantiated leads,' which he continued to plant to amuse himself. Someone that was spying on him was being fed exactly what he wanted to plant.

Edmunds asked his team to help clarify a consistent pattern of cover-ups and misinformation propagated by various agencies of law enforcement, including high-level administrators in the intelligence community. He suspected not only his own FBI colleagues, but also other National Security Agency and CIA administrators who were regularly giving Ram Edmunds misleading and false information. The patterns were repeatedly followed. In his efforts to bring to justice major criminal networks, Ram was constantly challenged by his superiors, and at the same time blocked and impeded from apprehending suspects involved in human enslavement and prostitution. Worse, well-connected perpetrators of such crimes were being released from custody based on technical flaws and procedural errors.

FBI Regional Office Building, Chicago, IL · February 6, 2020

Nate and Miró decided to have a brief Facetime conference call with Ram Edmunds after Abraham's return from Austin. Although Abraham requested a little more time to allow him to verify some pieces of information, Miró convinced Nate that sharing even tentative findings with Ram could prove useful to Ram's own investigations. In addition, they would share Tío Dante's latest proposal.

Nate placed a call at 1:55 in the afternoon. "Hello, Agent Edmunds, Miró and I believe that a brief Facetime conversation with you may be in order, if you can spare the time."

"Please give me forty minutes, and I can call you back," Ram Edmunds said. True to his word, he called at exactly 2:40 PM.

"Although this call is also directly linked to Tío Dante's request to speak with you, there is another more pressing matter—to us, at least. This other matter may also be of great interest to you, Agent Edmunds."

"May I remind you, Nate, that we are on a first-name basis?" Edmunds said.

"Yes, I forget," Nate said. "Since you informed my father-in-law about the identity of the dead man at the Orrington Hotel, he's been researching that individual's past. He probably informed you that he met his former patient only once. Since Abraham took a leave of absence to help us through our Canary Island adventure, he transferred his patient Angelo Calabrese to an associate."

"Yes, he and I spoke, and he clarified all that," Edmunds said. "We have not revisited the matter, however."

"The reason he has not talked to you, Ram, is that my dad took a trip to Austin to examine some birth and marriage records," Miró said.

"Oh?"

"Yes, you're aware that my father-in-law is a cardiac surgeon who teaches at Northwestern School of Medicine," Nate said. "What you may not know is that he's also a genealogy buff. To pass the time, he enjoys doing genealogical research."

"That's right, Ram. Dad has reason to believe that Angelo Calabrese, his former patient, may have impregnated a young lady in Austin, Texas back in the mid-Sixties. You would've been college roommates at the time."

"That would be a young lady that Cal and I met while visiting mutual friends in Austin," Edmunds said. "We were students at Sam Houston University, and it was a short drive to Austin. Her name was Linda Cruz. We met her at a party, and he was quite smitten by her. Unfortunately, she was married. Like many young women at the time, she was a military wife whose husband had been drafted."

"So, Calabrese met this married woman at a party... did they have a one-night stand?" Miró asked.

"No, no. Cal and I ended up traveling to Austin almost every weekend for several months. The relationship became close, serious. Cal enjoyed her company. Like I said, he fell in love with her. She, too, seemed to genuinely care for him. We all became good friends."

"Didn't it bother Calabrese that she was married?"

"You know, as young adults, we were living in the moment. I think we all assumed—or hoped—things eventually would work out," Ram said. "Each of us who escaped the draft sought relief—and perhaps redemption— from the ugly reality of the times. You know, the daily TV reports of thousands of American kids dying every day in the rice paddies of Vietnam."

"And, was sex an escape?" Miró asked.

"Sex, drugs, and rock and roll," Ram said. "Those Vietnam years were destructive in many ways. Many casualties. Families suffered, relationships suffered, thus, the turmoil led to drug usage, illicit sex, and social rebellion."

"But you seemed to have gone through the Sixties unscathed," Miró said. Though she made a statement, her eyebrows implied a question.

"Ha. Though I had my problems, Cal called me a straight arrow. I enjoyed alcohol, but I refrained from drug usage. Believe it or not, I usually served as designated driver for most of our friends."

"Tell us a little bit about Linda Cruz, Ram," Nate said. "Did the relationship with Calabrese continue after the birth of their child?"

"Oh, no… she cut off the relationship with Cal halfway through the pregnancy. It became clear to her that Cal was not accepting responsibility for the child… nor their continued relationship. In fact, he wanted Linda to have an abortion, but she refused. At the time, abortion was still illegal and frowned upon by most."

"So, did you lose contact with Linda Cruz?" Miró asked.

"It was very sad. Cal did not want to have contact, but I continued to visit her," Ram said. "I may have developed feelings for her along the way. In fact, I was there at St. David's Hospital in Austin when their son was born. The child's first bunting blanket and teddy bear came from me, Uncle Ram. In my honor, Linda gave her child the middle name Ram, or Raymundo, per the birth certificate."

Nate pressed, uncertain if Ram Edmunds was familiar with Linda M. Cruz's life. "Did you stay in touch with her?"

"For a while. Shortly after giving birth to her baby, she learned her husband became one of the first casualties of the Vietnam War. She dropped her married name and legally adopted her maiden name."

"Then...?"

"Then, she dropped from the face of the earth," Ram said. "I tried locating her, but our Austin friends said she had moved abroad. Never heard from her again."

"Ram, do you happen to remember her maiden name?" Miró asked.

"Can't say I do... It was something like Montoya or Morelos... not sure," Ram said.

．． ．

"Ram," Miró used a deliberate pace, "Do you remember the given name of the child?"

"That I do. I remember quite well. I helped Linda consider various names, but I didn't think she'd use Cal's last name. For some reason, she chose the name Diego Calabrese. Like I said before, she chose my name, Raymundo, for her child's middle name... I felt honored. Diego R. Calabrese."

"What Nate is implying, Ram, is that my dad believes that Linda Cruz moved to Spain. It may sound far-fetched, but we want to know what you think. As you said, Linda Cruz dropped her married name and assumed her maiden surname. My dad is almost certain her maiden name was Montemayor."

"Yes, Miró, that's it! Her maiden name was not Montoya, but Montemayor," Ram said.

"Well, Ram, when Linda moved to Spain, she was known as Linda Montemayor. Though my father-in-law cannot be sure, he believes that Linda's son, Diego, also adopted his mom's last name and changed his legal name from Diego R. Calabrese to Diego R. Montemayor."

"And," Miró added, "Diego Montemayor not only became a renowned botanist and chemist in Spain, but he also became an international drug and human trafficker and cartel boss."

Ram Edmunds got up from the head of the conference table and walked to the large window facing W. Roosevelt Road. Hands in his pockets, he unbuttoned his suit vest and looked toward the Picasso sculpture that sat on his credenza. It was a replica of the Picasso in Chicago's Daley Plaza. He made a humorless laughing sound. "You're telling me that my college roommate may have fathered the most wanted criminal in the Western Hemisphere?"

"We believe so," Nate said.

"And, you're also suggesting that Cal knew of his son and his... criminal activities." Ram was begging for a response.

"You may be the best person to answer that, Ram," Miró said. "But we suspect that Calabrese discovered his son's whereabouts and helped him consolidate his organization's power base."

. . .

It took Ram Edmunds several minutes to regain his composure. Nate and Miró offered to call back later to finish the conversation, but Edmunds rebounded. He excused himself by walking to his conference room coffee station and serving himself a fresh cup of 'java'. Almost as if he were self-medicating, Edmunds took a large gulp and refilled his cup.

"We'll make this quick," Nate said. "Tío would like to Facetime you, and I'm quoting him, 'so that you can assess his sincerity'. Those were his exact words."

"What a character," Ram Edmunds said. "Tell him to call me tomorrow morning at 8:15. No Facetime, I prefer a simple voice call."

CHAPTER 36

FBI Regional Office Building,
Chicago, IL · February 7, 2020

R AM EDMUNDS' PHONE RANG at exactly 8:15 AM.
"I just released pictures of former President
Doug Winston aboard the Juliana Express,"
Tío said.

"You mean the ones published by the New York Post
today?" Ram asked.

"The same ones. I'll bring the originals to our meeting."

Ram signaled to his team that he wanted the call
traced. "I have not agreed to a meeting yet, Mr. Dante. And,
if I were to agree to a meeting, you would need to satisfy
certain requirements."

"Oh, I think you'll want to meet. I have much more
than incriminating photos, Agent Edmunds," Tío said.

"Such as...?"

"Correct me if I'm wrong, but you're combating
pedophilia, sex slavery, and human trafficking in your country,

right? And, of course, drug trafficking and the opioid epidemic are also high on your list... all correct?"

Ram Edmunds ignored the question. "Go on," he said.

"In your efforts, you've probably wondered how the 'Elevated Executives Programs' sponsored by AXIOM relate to cartel monies. They're connected, you know. You also want to unravel the AXIOM network, and if you do, you'll discover a two-headed dragon. If I can give you one head on a silver platter, you'll identify the other one."

"That's old news, Mr. Dante. Those cases are already in the courts. Your two-headed monster I know nothing about, but it sounds like nonsense. Besides, many of those accusations were debunked."

Tío guffawed. "Ah, yes, 'debunked', we suggested the use of that term to bring derision upon any accusation that got close to the truth. And you know how those pending prosecutions will not see the light of day or simply be dismissed on technicalities," Tío said.

"Don't be too certain, Mr. Dante. It is a new day in America," Ram said. "I have faith in our judicial system. In this case, I'd prefer to concentrate on the topics at hand—not so-called American corruption."

The long, raspy chuckle turned into a coughing spell. "Corruption," more coughing, "corruption runs deep in your country, Agent Edmunds. Sophisticated, concealed, protected by media empires, perhaps. But widespread and more profound than most Americans realize."

"I'll make one thing clear, though," Ram Edmunds said. "I'm not inclined to provide any immunity for wrongdoing on your part. Kidnapping and murder in our country carry consequences, serious ones."

"Except for a select few, am I right?" Tío asked.

"If some squeeze through the cracks, then shame on us," Ram said. "I'm committed to minimizing the damage."

"I believe that you are, Special Agent. I believe you are."

"So, do we have an understanding?"

"For the sake of clarity, what if I told you that I'm ready to accept the consequences for my wrongdoing?"

"Go on."

"I kidnapped Dr. Miró Epstein-Shelley. My personal motivation for that kidnapping is indefensible."

"Are you willing to testify to that?" Ram asked.

"Certainly. But I also want to be treated fairly for a killing that I committed in self-defense. Will I have your word that you will objectively examine evidence, evidence that I submit regarding your dead friend at the Orrington Hotel?"

"You only have my word that I will objectively look at whatever evidence you give me. I will not, and cannot, promise leniency nor immunity," Ram said.

Silence at the other end of the line.

"You, of course, must realize that if we meet face to face, you will be taken into custody. You will be treated fairly, but you will be turning yourself in," Edmunds said.

"That's good enough for me, Agent Edmunds," Tío said. "You know, years ago I spoke to Calabrese multiple times. In fact, he did some work for me—well, for Diego Montemayor through me—and I admired his... um, abilities. He brought your name up a few times, Agent Edmunds, always referring to you as a 'straight arrow'. I believe he respected your integrity."

"When you say that Cal did some work for you several years ago, what kind of work exactly?"

Tío chuckled again. "You are a deliberate man, Agent Edmunds. You're probably recording our conversation and attempting to trace my call. Undoubtedly, you're already building your case against me, which is something I expected."

Tío paused and politely excused himself while reaching for a tissue. He coughed loudly and seemed to expel some sputum.

"Take your time, Mr. Dante."

Tío continued, "I served as Diego's Executive Vice-President. In other words, I was his right-hand. Diego trusted me implicitly. To insulate Diego, I never allowed him to be even remotely close to any wrongdoing. If he wanted someone eliminated, I would call on professionals. When I identified Angelo Calabrese, I knew I had found one of the best. He was a skilled and experienced assassin."

Ram Edmunds took elaborate notes. Although he carefully scribbled comments throughout the call, he suspended note-taking when he heard his old friend Calabrese being described as an assassin.

"Will you describe how you killed Agent Angelo Calabrese?"

"You mean 'sometimes-agent Calabrese', don't you? Remember that he did work for both sides, Agent Edmunds."

"Well, will you, Mr. Dante?"

"I believe we're getting ahead of ourselves. Let's hold our face-to-face meeting and we can dedicate as much time as is necessary," Tío Dante said.

"I invite you to our offices here in downtown Chicago."

"Sorry," Tío Dante said. "I would like a more public site that can offer a semblance of neutrality, Special Agent Edmunds."

CHAPTER 37

MAX

Skokie, IL · February 7, 2020

Y DAD, I'VE WATCHED him conduct his genealogical research, and I've come to realize two things. I've got two distinct families. By that I mean that I, Max Kempball, have kept my early life away from Abraham and Miriam. There's little they know about my childhood or my grandparents on the Kempball side. It's not that they have no interest, it's that I've never offered any information.

Since they know nothing about the other half of my closely knit family, the Kempball side, I decided to share information. Although I can't be sure, I believe that even during their courtship at UT Austin, Dad and Mom shared little about my mom's family background. Knowing Mom, she withheld information from Dad. Perhaps seeing Abraham and Miriam share details about their families with Miró has made me jealous. I've got some stories about my Kempball family history, but I want that closeness with Abraham also. And, if they appear interested, I want Abraham and Miriam to know about my past.

"Dad, I've decided to break my silence," I announced over dinner.

"I didn't know you'd been silent, Max. I hadn't noticed," Abraham said.

"What I mean is that y'all know little about my Kempball part of the family. I'd like to change that."

"Well, thank you," Miriam said. "Sincerely, I feel honored."

Over the next few weeks, I shared my childhood experiences with Abraham and Miriam. To my surprise, even Miró and Nate expressed interest in learning about my history.

Without violating Mom's privacy, I shared some of my Kempball family memories. I even brought out photo albums and journals that Mom passed on to me which portrayed a young 'Livvie' Kempball who came from a hardy stock in southeast Texas, where the climate was semi-arid and vegetation was low to the ground and thorny. Though Mom grew up in a harsh environment, she seemed to grow up a well-adjusted and happy kid.

"I met your mom a few times," Miriam said, "and she was a beautiful woman. She passed on to you her wavy blonde hair, her refined features, and her remarkably lean and lithe strength."

"Yeah," I said, "folks who knew her said I favored her."

"I suppose growing up in that environment toughened her," Abraham said. "Funny, Max, but I never gave much thought to Olivia's past. It was the Sixties, and we lived in the moment. It's not an excuse, but..."

"Hey, I can understand, Dad."

From old photographs and newspaper clippings, I explained that Mom's parents owned an enormous spread of land, where scarce greenery could be found. Instead, like plants of the desert, an abundance of mesquite and huisache trees had learned to survive with little moisture. It was here where Mom had been born and raised. And, it was here in this brush range that I had spent many a summer.

"How I wish I'd been close to you back then," Abraham said, his vision obviously blurred by tears that filled his eyes.

I just squeezed his shoulder. I did not know how to verbalize that from here, deep in cattle and oil country, I had learned to unravel the intricate connections that life had woven into a rather prickly canvas. And that because of him, I'd become more curious about examining my past. Because my dad had stimulated my interest in family history, now I desperately sought to understand more deeply how my own life had been shaped by earlier experiences.

In the second week of February, I announced that I was making a pilgrimage to South Texas. Because I'd decided to move to Skokie to live with Abraham and Miriam, I wanted to bid a temporary goodbye to my Kempball grandparents.

Little did I know then that during my Texas visit, I'd take a momentous leap in my understanding of life and its serendipitous connections. Like a cattle rustler, I'd bring into my possession former truths that had not been mine. And, like Abraham in his many discoveries, I would wrestle out of the information some revelations that would bring into clear focus much of what I'd ignored in the past. With that critical decision to return to Texas, I allowed my memories to iron out the folds of priceless, hidden truths.

. . .

Growing up, I knew nothing about the Kempball's influence or wealth. Heck, as a kid I didn't know Grandfather Kempball, as in the land-owning Kempballs, was a well-known rancher and oil baron. As a child, visiting my grandparents was just enjoying life in the country. Visiting them later as a teenager, I simply enjoyed time far removed from Austin's rarefied cosmopolitan, left-wing pretentiousness. I couldn't wait to get away from that environment, and, frankly, I needed to get away from my overbearing feminist mom, who worshipped all things 'weird' and all things 'far-out' in the language of the Sixties.

Even back then I probably knew that much of Mom's joylessness came from a distant disappointment, the one probably caused by my dad Abraham. Once I asked Mom, "Did he leave you, I mean, did he leave you when he found out you were pregnant?"

She answered, "I wouldn't give Abraham the satisfaction. I knew he wasn't ready to get married; so, I told him it was someone else's, that someone else was the father. It hit him right where it hurt, his manhood." To this day, I can't understand that reasoning.

Three Rivers, TX · February 15, 2020

Driving at dusk from Austin to the Kempball Ranch near Three Rivers, I was reminded of a different cadence, you know, a different pulse and tempo. Even my heartbeat took on a slower rhythm. When I stopped for gas by the side of the road, I heard the familiar croaking and clucking of frogs that announced an adagio, as my band director called it, a musical slow-down. While filling the gas tank, I paid attention to the crickets' finale and realized that time had slowed down. The posted speed limit said seventy, but locals refused to accelerate to the 'breakneck velocity of outsiders' driving to the Gulf Coast or further south to Brownsville. Most of the road traffic moved at crawl speed through Seguin, Stockdale, and Karnes City.

With my ears sharpened, my vision duly noted a lingering burnt orange daylight illuminating the road for me as I approached Kenedy from Karnes City. It failed to bring into full perspective the beauty of the darkening landscape.

A rich and familiar aroma of wet weather—or 'petrichor', as my science professor insisted on calling it—told me rain had come after a prolonged dry spell. The earthy scent mixed with manure blew in through the air vents of the 4x4 rental. Strangely, the fragrance was not offensive.

In fact, driving southward toward Kenedy, the undulating terrain reminded me of many winter drives through the brush in Grandpappy's pickup before the break of dawn. He and I liked to sneak into the blind before the deer started flocking to the two feeders. The same smells, mixed with freshly percolated coffee in thermos containers, brought vivid images of an occasional doe, freezing in place at Sulphur Creek when the pickup's lights approached. I was so thankful at that moment for the wonderful childhood I experienced with my grandparents.

The smells and the sights took me straight back to those days. The rangeland extended for miles on either side of the road. The southeastern foothills, somewhat lower than the Texas Hill Country's, forced drivers entering this part of paradise to softly roll on the road, inspiring a melody of praise in my head. Other than the mournful lowing of cattle, a quietude—not unlike the silence of the first snowfalls in Evanston—stilled my emotions.

By the time I arrived at the unmarked gated entrance to the ranch, I had a smile on my face. I turned onto the familiar caliche road, drove for a mile and opened the second gate to approach Grandpappy's house. A hollow rattle, like someone running a stick along a fence, welcomed me. I remembered the caracaras that created the sound when disturbed. This Mexican eagle was welcoming me to the home of Eugene and Doris Kempball, my beloved grandparents.

Grandmother K was at the door accompanied by Bugsy, their faithful sheepdog. My grandmother threw her arms around me, kissed both cheeks, and brushed away imaginary dust off my shoulders. "Your grandfather's in the barn, doing God knows what. In the meantime, sit here and tell me all about Chicago." Grandmother waited until I obeyed. "Everyone okay?"

"Yeah, everyone's fine. We're staying healthy and safe." I must've had a silly grin on my face, because she had to walk over and pinch my face and tussle my hair, as she used to do when I was growing up. I sat in Grandpappy's favorite recliner. The nine-year-old sheepdog jumped on my lap, still thinking he was a puppy. As I started to remove my boots, Grandmother shuffled to the kitchen. "I suppose things are as good as can be expected, Grandma. Abraham wants me to stay there for a spell until the storms blow over."

From the kitchen, Grandmother K said, "Oh, my, it doesn't sound like things have settled." She walked back into the parlor, pineapple-upside-down cake in hand. "I prepared your favorite cake this afternoon, Max. I set out a second one to cool. Also, I'm brewing fresh coffee."

A gust of cold air blew in from the back door as Grandfather K came in and removed his canvas jacket. "Did I smell the pineapple cake, or is it the sweet aftershave of my grandson?" He walked in with a mouthful of cake and outstretched arms. "My favorite grandson—come here and let me give you a hug." Before the embrace, Grandfather K had to lick his fingers and wipe them on his jeans.

"I'm also your *only* grandson, Grandpappy."

"Then it makes you extra special, doesn't it?" Grandpappy's hair was turning silver. Finally, he was showing his age. Throughout my formative years, he'd been my only father figure, and his strong, virile presence seemed to be ageless and indestructible.

We spoke late into the night. I relaxed into an uneventful routine that soothed my nerves and calmed my soul. It was a peace that I only felt at church... occasionally. I thanked God for my grandparents and His many blessings.

The following day, chores for both my grandparents started early. By the time I joined them in the kitchen, Grandmother K was into her second cup of coffee. "You take yours black, Son?"

"Oh, no, Grandma. I need sweetener and cream in my coffee."

"I just checked the weather forecast," Grandpappy said. "Looks like this afternoon may be a good time to drive into Kenedy to have a late lunch at Bertha's Diner. We'll also pick up your favorite ice cream, Max."

"Grandpappy, you still spoil me as if I were your twelve-year-old grandson."

"Guilty as charged," he said. "Indulge this old man, will you?"

After the early afternoon catfish feast at Bertha's, we returned home for an afternoon nap. I was awakened by Bugsy's loud barking. He'd proudly returned to the back porch with a plump dove in his mouth. Although Bugsy had gently mouthed the bird into listless submission, the bird was still alive, and Grandpappy released it into the air. Favoring its left wing, the terrified bird flew directly to the nearest branch of an old mesquite tree.

Over sun-brewed tea on the back porch, I asked Grandpappy, "Remember when I asked you why Mom had never married?"

He stopped his rocking chair. "Can't say I do, Son."

"You answered that Mom was high-strung and bull-headed and that she was the most stubborn girl you'd ever seen. Of your three daughters, you said she was the brightest but the most obstinate of creatures. And, though you loved her dearly, she had caused you the most pain and worry."

"Yup, now I remember it well."

"'Grandpappy,' I asked you back then, 'why is Mommy so unhappy?'"

"What did I answer?"

"You said that for the life of you, you had no idea. You went on to say that my biological dad was a fine man, and that he loved Mom and would have done anything to please her. You didn't tell me he was alive, though. It was the first time I'd seen you cry, Grandpappy."

"Well, if it's worth anything, I still think that."

"It's good that you still think well of my dad," I said. "I came to tell you that I'm moving to Chicago. It may only be for a season, but my dad and his family need me up there. My half-sister Miró needs me. My niece, too."

Grandpappy smiled. As he sat on his rocking chair, he sipped on his tea and reached for my shoulder, just like he used to do when I would visit every summer. "You have my blessing, Max. And you know this here ranch will be yours someday. It will always be your home."

Grandpappy cleared his throat and turned to get a tissue. I knew that, in his old age, my Grandpappy Gene Kempball was becoming more sentimental. He was shedding some tears.

Just then, Grandmother K stepped out onto the porch to offer us more tea. We both declined, but I asked her to sit with us.

"Doris, Max was asking about his mom." Grandpappy invited her to join the conversation.

"Yep. I remember that summer well, Max." She smiled and sipped her chardonnay. "I also remember telling you a story about an Army buddy of your grandfather who did his portrait."

"I'd befriended him while I was stationed at Fort Bliss," Grandpappy said. "Your mom was just a little tyke. But if I'm not mistaken, she was so taken by the experience that she went on to investigate the artist's history. She repeated the story to you, and you turned around and wrote a paper on him as a college student."

"It was an article I wrote for The Daily Texan, the student newspaper at UT," I said. "But what does that have to do with Mom?"

"Well, Max," Grandmother K said, "when your mom met this artist, she claimed that this von Steiner fellow had his eyes on me. She admitted to us that she had eavesdropped on every conversation your grandfather and I had with Rudy von Steiner. I bet Livvie could still recite word for word all those conversations, which she considered 'creepy' and 'otherworldly'."

"Grandpappy, didn't Mom walk in on us, when you and I were having a conversation about her?" I asked. "Didn't Mom get upset with you, because she heard you call her bull-headed and stubborn?"

"Ha, so true. She stomped into the room and gave me a piece of her mind. It was also that night that she told me that von Steiner was a lecher and a creep, and that he wanted to bed your grandmother."

"Was that true, Grandpappy?"

"Maybe. I don't know. But I do know this. He sure was a good portrait artist, and, although Austrian, he sure hated Hitler and the Nazis."

"I know, Grandpappy. By the way, that same evening, it was Mom—not you two—that shared her recollection of the day von Steiner finished painting your portrait. She surprised even you, because she could remember that night so vividly."

. . .

The three of us sat on the back porch, sharing my mom's word-for-word account of the night that von Steiner completed my grandfather's—Sergeant Eugene Kempball's—portrait. We went late into the night remembering odd details about the self-proclaimed enemy of the Nazis, who later became a war hero.

"The last I heard of Rudy," Grandpappy said, "was in letters claiming that he married an Italian girl by the name of Sofia Calabrese, and that he'd become a father. For whatever reason, the child kept her last name. When he was recruited by a Brachmann or Brayman to join a secret operation by the name of the OSS, the letters stopped coming." Grandpappy laughed, "Knowing Rudy, it was another tall tale, like many others he'd shared throughout the years."

CHAPTER 38

MAX

Southeast TX · February 17, 2020

Perhaps it was Grandpappy's increasing sentimentality, or maybe it was my own fears that I would not see this land—or my grandparents—for a long time that made my departure more difficult than any other I'd experienced before. But the melody in my heart when I arrived now sounded more like a dirge. Driving away from Grandpappy's ranch, I noticed the weeds on the fields appeared less green, almost brown. The leafless trees seemed more brittle, and the wild hogs had destroyed more of the cactus along the caliche road. As I closed the outer gate by the highway, I waved goodbye, knowing my grandparents could not see me. I waved anyway.

A few miles out of town, I stopped at Hard-Eight BBQ. Although it was somewhat early for lunch, I felt a need to put down on paper—or maybe even better, record on my iPhone—some mental notes that I'd made during my stay. Stimulated by the first pint of sweetened tea, I stringed together a sequence of memories, and I carefully dictated my recollections on my recorder. I used my conversations with my grandparents to bring back nuggets I'd heard as a kid. Just like a necklace of asymmetrical-sized pearls, the smallest and least significant memories led to more sizable and noteworthy ones. As if someone had fired up synapses that I'd long neglected, subconsciously my cerebrum crafted random flashbacks into precious beads that came together in perfect order, like the unfolding of a Conan Doyle mystery.

Sitting at the restaurant, my reverie was trance-like. Instantly, I understood the source of Diego Montemayor's financial and political power. I must've acknowledged the gum-chewing waitress who served me a plateful of brisket, ribs, and sausage, because she responded with a cheerful, "Oh, you're welcome, Hon!"

Robotically, I took a baby-back and consumed the delightfully greasy piece of pork. Without chewing my next bite, I stopped as I traveled back in time to Mom's description of that fateful evening. It was when Grandpappy's portrait was completed.

. . .

"This recording is being made on my drive back to Austin from Three Rivers. It is Monday, February 17, 2020.

"I believe Mom had always been an aspiring playwright or dramatist. At least, she was certainly a dramatic storyteller. She used the present tense, always melodramatically quoted each speaker with simulated voices, each characterized differently. This recording is the closest that I can remember her account:

Rudy Steiner, ill at ease and fidgeting, devoured the fried chicken and asked for seconds. His thick German accent seemed to slur the word 'Yes' into a guttural 'Yah, yah'. He was a chain-smoker, so the words came out as a stage whisper, implying he was very, very pleased.

Although the El Paso heat inspired most locals to wear lightweight clothing, Rudy, during his off-hours, preferred his Army khakis, buttoning even his top shirt button. His collar was at least an inch too large, adding a constantly disheveled and ill-fitting look to his weekend attire.

Your grandmother thanked her guest, half-smiling with her patented and gleeful self-satisfied look of demure appreciation. "I'm glad you're enjoying my home cooking, Corporal von Steiner."

My dad echoed mom's sentiment and asked, "So, is it anything close to the Austrian cuisine you're used to, Rudy?"

Then, as I recall, Max, this creep ogled into Mom's eyes—your grandmother Doris's eyes—and held the stare for a few seconds. After pausing for a long, long while, he answered your grandfather.

"Your lovely wife's cooking is as good as my first love's mother. Several times I was invited to their table, when my fortunes were down. They knew I was poor, so they fed me to make up for my... how do you say... 'skipped meals'. I fell in love with her cooking and with her daughter. Unfortunately, the girl dropped me like a hot potato. So, to heal my soul, I joined the French Foreign Legion. I was only nineteen at the time."

Unaware of his friend's flirting, your grandfather said, "You never mentioned that before, Rudy. How long did you serve in the Foreign Legion?"

"Not long. After a few skirmishes in the Riff Wars in North Africa, I was ready to return home. So, I did."

"I don't understand," said your grandfather. "Wasn't your dad a high-ranking officer in the Austrian Army? Unless I'm mistaken, your family kept their wealth. So, you must've been well off, Rudy."

"It's true my parents gave me a great education in Germany," the creep said. "And, I developed my artistic talents at the Düsseldorf Art Academy."

Your grandfather seemed amused, since he later told me in private that half of Rudy's stories were tall tales.

The lecher then said, "All my life I've been... how do you say... a renegade? My teachers called me a 'misfit'."

All this time I was listening to the conversation from my bedroom, but your grandparents thought I was asleep. Later, much later, Max—probably after you were born—I realized the Austrian stranger, whom I knew to be a lecher and a creep, was recognized as a hero in the aftermath of World War II. This guy, who led a secretive one-man campaign against the Nazis, had enjoyed your grandmother's cooking in our kitchen before finishing your grandfather's portrait.

"I'm interrupting this recording to collect my thoughts and to finish my barbecue plate."

"How was it, Hon?" It was the gum-chewing waitperson. I found myself licking my thumb and forefinger before wiping my mouth with the third paper napkin.

"Delicious. As you can tell, I could easily finish a full rack of these ribs."

Agnes, per her name plate, blew a formidable bubble-gum sphere that could easily have been a winner in the county competition. With ease, she withdrew the perfect bubble into her mouth and exclaimed, "They're also my favorite." She slapped the check on the table and informed me to pay at the counter. "The one by the door."

. . .

I resumed the recording on my cell phone after a stop in Seguin, Texas:

"I will continue by using Mom's favorite form of narration. These are her words as I remember them."

Anyway, after flirting with your grandmother, the Austrian portrait artist, right in front of Daddy says, "Thank you, Mrs. K.; the meal was superb!" Then, he kissed your grandmother's hand. "Now, Sarge, let's dedicate two more hours to your last sitting. I need to remove the five o'clock shadow on your face. It's not becoming. I want your family to remember you in full military splendor. I want this portrait to become your posterity's heirloom."

And that's what I remember about that close encounter with the great Baron Rudolph Charles von Steiner. He finished that portrait, which now hangs in a military post's museum in San Antonio, Texas. This supposedly great war hero immortalized your grandfather. With the portrait of your grandpappy, he entwined his life with the history of our family in a 'serendipitous and fortuitous way', as Rudy would put it later.

"So, from my memory bank, those are the words of my mother, Olivia Kempball. Her disdain for Rudy von Steiner did not disappear. But her stories about this mysterious man motivated me to examine his peculiar history and trace his participation in the war."

. . .

During my drive to Austin, I formulated next steps for my investigation. I was tempted to call Nate. After some deliberation, I opted to examine my premises before presenting them to Mr. Analytical.

If I could describe my brother-in-law in one word it would be 'analytical'. Nate is the most thorough, the most inquisitive, and the most systematic thinker I've ever met. I've grown to admire my new best buddy—and brother-in-law—in a short period. If anything, Nate should've become the PI and not me.

Instead of calling Nate, I decided to reach out to Ram Edmunds. Since Abraham had received that first call from Ram, I had saved the number as a VIP contact. I quick-dialed him, expecting to leave a voicemail.

Ram answered his call after the second ring, "Hey, Max, what's new?"

"Special Agent Edmunds, so good to speak to you. How'd you know it was me? We've never talked."

"I've got you in my list of contacts. Your dad Abraham gave me all your numbers; he wants all of you protected by the good guys—that's what he said."

"Listen, I'm driving back to Austin after spending time with my grandfather in South Texas. I think I've got something."

"Shoot. And, please call me Ram. All my friends do."

"Thanks. Well, this may not amount to much, but I think my maternal grandfather may have known Calabrese's relative—his father or grandfather, maybe."

Long pause. Ram politely uttered something resembling, "Mm hmm." I quickly realized it meant, "So…?"

"Okay, Ram, I promise this is not merely a 'guess what?' The reason I'm sharing this matter is that Calabrese's relative may have been on the ground floor of the CIA's creation. He was a member of the original OSS."

I felt foolish. I could almost hear Ram chuckle a bit when he very patiently said, "Let's assume you're right, Max. How does that connection help us? The relative is probably dead by now, correct?"

"That's just it, Ram. My grandfather is not, and he knew him personally."

"And exactly what information could we mine from your grandfather's memory bank?"

"Ram, my grandfather mentioned that, in letters from von Steiner, he stated that a person by the name of Brachmann, or Brayman, recruited Calabrese's relative to join the OSS."

Again, another long pause. Ram Edmunds was courteous, but he pressed. "Tell me exactly what you're thinking, Max. I'm trying my best to accommodate your curiosity, and you seem to think that you've got something. What's your hunch?"

"You may think I'm crazy, Ram, but I really believe that Brachmann—or whatever his name was—recruited Calabrese's relative for a specific reason. And that reason was that Rudolph von Steiner, probably Calabrese's grandfather, was an artist plus a talented anti-Nazi crusader."

"Wait a minute, Max. You think Calabrese's grandfather was named von Steiner? The name sounds very German to me."

"That requires some explanation, Ram. But yes, it so happens that von Steiner, an Austrian, served with the American 168th Infantry which invaded Italy."

"The Red Bulls? Yeah, I know about them."

"Well, Calabrese's grandfather was a legendary force with the Red Bulls."

"And, you're saying he may have been legendary with the ladies, too?"

"Maybe," I said. "Although my grandfather would describe Rudy von Steiner as a gaunt, unimpressive-looking portrait artist, von Steiner may have been quite a ladies' man. I'm not sure my own grandfather took him very seriously."

"Okay, let's step back, Max. If your information is accurate, the question remains how that makes a bit of difference for our case. Even if we've traced Calabrese's relative to this artist-hero, why should we care?"

"Because the cache of art that was confiscated by the Nazis and recovered by the Allied forces after World War II provided the funding for the clandestine organization that Congress knew nothing about."

"How do you know so much about the formation of the OSS, Max?"

"C'mon, Ram, the internet has more information than you or I are capable of absorbing."

"You're right. With the vast amount of information available in the internet, I sometimes wonder why we need our alphabet agencies—FBI, CIA, NSA. There's hardly anything hidden anymore."

"The key word is 'hardly', isn't it?" I mused.

"Right you are, my friend," Ram said. "Max, are you serious about your family knowing von Steiner?"

"Per my grandfather, von Steiner was a pretty awkward-looking man at the time he met him."

"I'll be honest with you," Ram said, "the M.O. of our intelligence agencies continues to be one of self-sufficiency.

The only difference is that nowadays Congress makes generous appropriations, and the agencies continue their 'fundraising' in other creative ways. Their funds—maybe I should say, our funds—are astronomical."

"Now do you think that my reasoning is worth pursuing, Ram?"

"Let me ask you to keep on digging, Max," Ram said, "and, in the meantime, I'll look into this von Steiner character. It may be worth our while. I can't promise you more than that, though."

CHAPTER 39

Glencoe, IL · February 17, 2020

ODRIGO DISMISSED THE ROSALES twins by informing them that it was no longer safe for them to return to their respective homes. Their favored connections with federal and local law enforcement could only go so far, he informed them. After releasing Minerva Shelley and her grandmother, the twins' identity was announced to law enforcement agencies throughout the Midwest. With major news outlets beginning to broadcast their file photographs, Rodrigo could no longer guarantee their freedom.

"Did you think, boys, that treating your hostages like royalty would absolve you, would guarantee your immunity from the law?" Rodrigo asked. "Tell me what you were thinking."

"We can go abroad, boss. Can't you arrange that?" asked Half-Pants.

"No, I've got better plans. I can offer you a safe house here in Chicago that my associates have used in the past.

It's secure, and I will ensure your respective families' safety," Rodrigo said. "Estevan will make all the arrangements."

"Thank you, boss."

"I will also need you for one final assignment," Rodrigo said.

"What do you mean," asked Macario, the quiet brother.

"I'll explain everything," Rodrigo said, "once you're situated in our safe house."

. . .

A white Suburban was waiting for the twins at the Botanic Garden's parking lot. Lucas Williams, their favorite Aussie, was holding the sliding door open for them.

"I will take your cell phones now, if you don't mind. The boss does not want you being tracked, and he does not want you worrying about your vehicle, mates. One of the chums from the compound has already driven it off, and he will dispose of it."

"We're so glad to see you, Lucas. When did you get here?" Pedro said.

"Rodrigo had us flown here. Got here this morning."

They rode in silence for a few minutes, and Pedro asked, "Where's the safe house?"

"In Winnetka, mate. I've seen your digs... nice."

"Can we talk to our families?"

"No can do. Boss's orders." Lucas continued, "We'll take good care of them."

"Lucas, who else came with you?" Macario asked.

"A couple of chums from Mazatlán and Dr. Ivo Wu, your favorite plastic surgeon. You remember him, don't you?"

"Why is he here?" Macario asked.

"You tell me, mate."

"Hmm."

. . .

Back at his Peninsula suite, Estevan ordered Spanish tapas from Café Ibérico. Although the online order indicated a delivery delay of ninety minutes, Estevan offered a nice incentive to the delivery company for a quicker delivery. Rodrigo's delivery was made within thirty minutes.

"Sit with me, Estevan, and tell me what you think of my plan. I hope you tripled the orders of pintxos and montaditos."

Estevan was busy setting the table in the cavernous dining area. He served the wine and uncovered the various chafing dishes. With a theatrical flourish and a sweeping wave for the presentation, he led Rodrigo to the linen-covered dining table. Dishes of manchego cheese, queso de Burgos and queso mahón in addition to the various hams awaited Rodrigo and his new consiglieri at the table. The assortment of warm pintxos and montaditos in the chafing dishes emitted the Mediterranean aromas he so missed, and a seafood paella awaited in case the meal went into the night.

"First, tell me where my good friend Tío Dante might be found." Rodrigo bit into his first cheese-filled date, closed his eyes as if he were listening to his favorite sonata and exclaimed, "No, don't ruin this moment—no information yet. Let me enjoy this beautiful symphony of tastes." Rodrigo took a second and third bite, and proceeded to taste a manchego slice on some crostini topped with jamón Ibérico. "Not bad for an American imitation of decent food," Rodrigo said. "Estevan, do me a favor and make the bacon wrapping on those dates just a bit crispier. I don't want to taste the bacon fat." He took his first sip of wine and relished the aftertaste. "Very nice finish in the back of my palate, Estevan. Nice choice."

"Estoy listo," Rodrigo said, "ready for your briefing. Where's Tío?"

Estevan proceeded to sign a lengthy explanation, but Rodrigo could not follow. "Whoa, my signing skills aren't that good. Slow down. One concept at a time."

Instead of signing, Estevan stretched out his arms and brought his wrists together as if being handcuffed.

"Is he in custody?" Rodrigo asked.

Estevan then signed, '*Soon.*'

"Have you been a bad boy? Are you tapping Tío's phone? I didn't think we had the capabilities of breaking through Tío's layers of digital protection that he normally uses."

Rubbing his fingers on his chest, as if filing his fingernails, Estevan smiled as he took his first sip of the

Ribera del Duero's Tempranillo. Again, Estevan signed something that Rodrigo could not understand.

"What are you saying is fractured? Is the Dominio de Pingus bottle broken?"

Estevan resorted to mimicking again, and pretended to break an egg. Then he pointed to himself with pride.

"I got it," Rodrigo said. "You *cracked* the digital barriers that Tío concocted. Very good, my friend. Very good, indeed." As Rodrigo rose to examine the chafing dishes, he could not resist taking some paella along with an ample serving of tapas. "I was afraid you had broken the wine bottle."

Slowly, Estevan signed his next piece of information. '*He's planning to turn himself in to the Feds.*'

"That, my friend, will provide some challenges," Rodrigo said. "It'll simply make our stay in this gringolandia more interesting."

Though Estevan's signing was somewhat rapid, Rodrigo got the gist of his question. "I think you're asking if it's safe for me to stay in the U.S. a while longer. Per my connections in DC—as my American friends refer to their capital city— my new face is not recognizable to law enforcement agencies. Not even Interpol recognizes my most recent mug shots."

'*Good,*' Estevan signed. '*Dr. Wu did a good job.*'

"Yes, he completely reconstructed my facial structure, and made me look younger," Rodrigo said.

'*And, taller,*' Estevan signed. '*Wu added three inches to your height.*'

"Limb lengthening surgery is miraculous, Estevan. Although my recovery was longer than I expected, it's been worthwhile. Not even my competitors recognize me. I'm the new kid on the block."

Estevan rose from the table, and asked Rodrigo if he should clear it for dessert or a nightcap. Rodrigo told him to hold off, because he wanted another serving of paella... and another serving of the Tempranillo.

"I have a plan, Estevan. Tell me what you think of it." For the next forty minutes, Rodrigo explained logistics to his consiglieri. They would need the cooperation of his connections at the FBI in DC. They would need to 'plant' one of their own within the ranks of the agency. Although Estevan expressed reservations about that segment of the plan, he was convinced that, if limited to a few simple tasks for their 'plants', it could succeed. They both reviewed the scheduling of that phase of the plan thoroughly to their mutual satisfaction. Then, Estevan asked the most important question.

'*How?*' he asked.

"That's where I need your critical thinking the most," Rodrigo said. "We both know how I'll take care of my ultimate targets. That will be my incendiary masterpiece, my crowning glory. However, I need help with getting rid of Tío, now that we know he's going to be in federal custody."

'*Remember, boss, that Tío is an expert in explosives. He is capable of 'smelling' even the most sophisticated bomb.*'

"He's human, Estevan. I understand what you're saying, and it's true that he will detect most kinds of explosives. However, Ivo Wu and I have developed something new."

'Boss, remember that whatever explosive you use, must pass the test of the authorities' monitors. The suicide vests used by our Palestinian friends would never make it through the American federal authorities.'

"Of course, my friend. But Wu and I have developed the perfect so-called body cavity bombs," Rodrigo said.

Holding a full wine glass, Estevan rose as he shook his head from side to side. He repeatedly mouthed the word, 'No, no, no.' Still shaking his head, instead of signing, he decided to take his notepad and scribbled an objection.

'Complete disaster! Remember the previous failures? The Palestinians have only managed to create big holes in the ground. Complete disaster!'

"I knew you'd say that, Estevan. But I told you that Wu and I have worked on something better. Our terrorist friends had the wrong idea. You tell me why they failed."

'Bombs are too small. And, the Israelis and Americans can detect their magnetic fields. Plus, explosions come out of small holes.'

"Exactly," Rodrigo said. "Because the explosive gadgets were so small, the explosions could only destroy anything within a few feet. But the reason explosives were so weak is because the tiny bombs had to fit in small cavities, usually the bomber's rectum. And, like you say, many of our bombers were detected at airports. Monitors can detect the gadgets, even if they're rectally inserted."

'The explosions also go in the wrong direction!' Estevan added.

"Yes, I was getting to that," Rodrigo said. "Most of the attempted assassination failed because when detonated, the explosion was directed in a downward direction."

Nodding, Estevan set his wine glass down. He stretched out his arms toward the floor, palms outward, and mouthed the word, 'Therefore?'

"What if Dr. Wu can place the explosive device where it cannot be detected, higher up in the body?"

'Where?' Estevan hunched his shoulders.

"How about the stomach or the chest cavity? Wouldn't that allow us to use bigger explosives?" Rodrigo asked. "That could magnify the intensity—and the range—of the explosion."

An incredulous expression came over Estevan's face. Excitedly, he signed, '*Can he do that?*'

"He's been experimenting with animals. We think it can work."

'*Now, all you need is the perfect volunteer,*' Estevan signed.

"I've got a perfect candidate," Rodrigo said.

PART FOUR

CHAPTER 40

Winnetka, IL · February 17, 2020

"SINCE YOU WILL NOT have any other transportation, mates, the boss wanted you to be close to the Green Bay bike trail. He tells me it's a biker's paradise," Lucas said. "You'll be in the Hubbard's Woods area. And, like I told you, your digs will be bonza."

Macario looked at his brother, "Half the time, we don't know what you're saying, Lucas, but what do you mean 'our digs will be bonza'?"

"You know, your safe house, it's a ripsnorter—like saying it's 'dope' or 'Gucci' or 'cool'. No worries, mate, she'll be right."

Neither twin had cracked a smile since being picked up. However, Lucas' reassurance was welcomed. Though a short distance from Chicago, Winnetka was not familiar to the Rosales twins. They'd never had reason to frequent that part of the North Shore.

As they crossed the Elm Street business district, Lucas described Winnetka's support for safe bike routes to and from the village. As they approached the tree-lined Hubbard's Woods district, Lucas said, "Your place is close to Lloyd Park, and very close to the lake."

"Hey, dude, this place doesn't seem to have any brown faces. Is everyone white?" Pedro asked.

"I looked it up, mates. I'm afraid you're right. Primarily Caucasian and Asian and very well-educated. Ninety percent of the population has a college degree."

"Will that be a problem?" Macario asked.

"Only if you try to find a good place for Mexican food. Just keep to yourselves. Be polite, be quiet, and behave like model citizens. Smile a lot," their Aussie comrade said.

"Did the boss say anything about letting us see our kids, allowing us to play catch with them, take them out bike riding?" Macario asked.

"Yeah, or having our families over? No one knows us out here, anyway. We could stay away from people and stick to walks in the parks," Pedro said.

Lucas did not answer either question. He changed the subject instead. "The boss is making sure that your girls are getting dance lessons, and they're keeping up with their schoolwork and soccer activities. And, your twins, Macario, your two boys, they're into all sports—especially baseball."

It was clear that Rodrigo was not pleased with them, but the boss was providing safety for both families. Nonetheless, both twins worried about their loved ones. Although they still enjoyed their visits with family via recorded videos and the occasional audio file, they desperately missed their weekend gatherings, the barbecues, and the kids' competitive team sports. At least twice a week, the twins would send their respective spouses brief messages of endearment and love notes. Unbeknown to them, their children and spouses also suffered from extreme loneliness and bouts of depression.

Lucas drove into a large, circular driveway. When they approached the two-story stone structure that was sparsely but attractively landscaped, Lucas added, "By the way, Rodrigo wants you to keep the grounds mowed and well-kept. There's a shed in the back where you'll find more lawn equipment than you'll ever need. I trimmed everything for you, mowed the winter grass, and even fertilized what I could. From here on, it'll be your responsibility."

"Hold on, Lucas, aren't you coming in to show us the place?" Pedro asked.

"I don't think so. Go ahead and have a Captain Hook," Lucas said. "Sorry, mates, where I come from, to 'have a Captain Hook' means to have a look."

Pedro and Macario Rosales looked at each other and shrugged their shoulders. Before driving off, Lucas said, "You'll find the keys inside the fake rock next to the tulips."

As they entered the empty house, a musty smell greeted them. They walked through the foyer and into the living area. A white sheet covered two bulky items that sat in the middle of the wooden floor. The twins excitedly unveiled two brand-new Roadmaster, Granite Peak bikes, each with a yellow bow on the handle bars. A small card read 'For your enjoyment' in the familiar calligraphy.

As they explored their living quarters, their hiking boots made echoing sounds on the Brazilian cherry floors. Each twin claimed his bedroom. Pedro selected the one with the taller ceiling and stained-glass windows. Macario chose the bedroom with the built-in desk and floor-to-ceiling bookshelves. The room impressed him with a book collection that appeared to have all the classics, which he was hoping to read some day.

The chandeliers, sconces, as well as bathroom fixtures were wrought iron. When Macario, the aspiring chef, walked into the cavernous kitchen, he admired the stainless-steel appliances and the gas stove. "This Viking stuff is top-of-the-line, Pedro. If we can't find good Mexican restaurants, I'll be able to fix us all the good stuff we like. All we need is fresh ingredients, which I'm sure we can get close by."

"Hey, Macario," Pedro said, "come look at this backyard. It must be close to an acre, man. And, all those trees. We're going to have fun pruning them before spring gets here."

Macario took a few minutes to respond. He was busy exploring the rest of the house. "Don't forget, we'll also need to mow that baby," Macario said. "By the way, Pedro, the pantry is well-stocked. Whoever bought this stuff thought of our Latin tastes. They've got the spices, the right produce, and even some Mexican beers and meat stuff in the fridge. For sure, they weren't satisfying Rodrigo's tastes."

"One thing we forgot to do, Macario, was to ask Lucas how we'd communicate with the boss and the outside world. I feel lost without my cell phone."

"You need to go through the rest of the house, Pedro. The third bedroom has a control panel and equipment that enables us to communicate with Rodrigo. It's got a laptop with limited internet access."

"Can we call our kids?" Pedro asked.

"I already tried," Macario said.

"And?" Pedro was smiling, anticipating good news.

"Estevan intercepted my call."

"How could you tell it was Estevan?" Pedro asked.

"Because I received a computer-generated audio transcript of his text."

"What did it say?" Pedro asked.

Macario smiled, "His message said I was being a bad boy."

. . .

The twins settled for cold cuts, carrot sticks, cheese and crackers for their first meal at their new house. They ended with chips, salsa, and beer to satisfy their ravenous hunger.

"Now, Macario, show me what we have in this third bedroom. Is it used as an office of sorts?" Pedro asked.

"Probably. I don't really know. The bunk beds tell me Rodrigo's previous guests had kids... young ones," Macario said. "Spider-Man and Darth Vader sheets."

Loud static coming from the desk interrupted their conversation. Startled, Pedro turned to Macario, casting an interrogation, "Is someone listening to us?"

"Hello, boys," the voice coming from the laptop speakers said. "Wave to me," Rodrigo said.

"Where's the camera, Rodrigo?" Macario asked. "The laptop is shut."

"Look at the spine of Cervantes' classic on the desk," Rodrigo said.

Macario picked up the copy of *El ingenioso hidalgo don Quijote de la Mancha*. A tiny camera, embedded in the book's spine, perfectly fit in the final 'o' of the word 'hidalgo'.

"One more time, boys: Wave at me!"

Both twins obliged. "Rodrigo, is this the only way to communicate with you?" Macario asked.

"You'll soon find out, Mudo. At this point, I'm reassuring you that you've got a line to the outside world. Your families have been transferred to a safe house larger than yours. They're safe, well-fed, cared for, and, I believe, very, very happy."

"Can we speak to them?" Pedro asked.

"It is not a good idea, Half-Pants. Emotional states are fragile right now, and it takes time for kids to adjust. Both mamas are doing a wonderful job."

"We need to know if they're safe. Please let us hear it from them," Macario said.

"Am I detecting doubt? Are you doubting my word, Mudo?"

"They're my life, boss. I'll do anything to ensure they're safe."

"That's noble of you. Very admirable," Rodrigo said.

"Can you, at least, give us regular reports?" Macario asked, almost in tears. "I'll fully cooperate with anything you ask—if you can do that."

"Ha! I don't think you have a choice," Rodrigo said. "However, let me reassure you both, we want the best for your families. They truly are remarkable—truly remarkably beautiful—individuals."

"Will this be our only form of communication?" Macario asked. "Even if you don't allow them to speak, couldn't Pedro and I, at least, see them on screen?"

"That's not a good idea. Women and children, we must treat them with tenderness and care. They're fragile, delicate, weak. Entrust them to me," Rodrigo said.

"Boss, Macario's saying that you can ask us to do anything if you take care of our families," Pedro said. "I know we disappointed you, but don't punish them. We'll make it up to you."

"Boys, I will visit you from time to time. However, most of our communications will occur in this fashion," Rodrigo said. "And, just to satisfy your curiosity, it's fair to tell you that I've got multiple cameras in your safe house. And, every time you leave the house, a constant companion will be with you."

"Will that be Lucas?" Pedro asked.

"Ha! No, no, Half-Pants. Your constant companion will be a dedicated drone—an ever-present protector."

"It's not that we don't appreciate the protection," Macario said, "but, as nice as the accommodations are, we feel like prisoners. Why are you doing this?"

"Let's just say that I lost confidence in you two," Rodrigo said. "However, I will need you for another important job, like I said before."

"We'll make it up to you," Pedro said. "If we do well with the next job, can we come back to your good graces?"

"We'll see. We'll see."

February 25, 2020

To their surprise, Rodrigo regaled them with his presence early the following week. The Westminster chime of the doorbell woke Macario from his afternoon nap. He'd fallen asleep sitting on the solitary sofa in the living area. Rodrigo and Estevan were at the door, playing the role of welcoming neighbors.

"We wanted to welcome you to the neighborhood, boys," Rodrigo said. With a rarely seen smile, Estevan extended a steaming cherry pie to a speechless Pedro. "Aren't you going to invite us in?" Rodrigo asked.

"We thought you were staying at the Peninsula Chicago, boss. Have you moved close by?" Pedro asked.

"Hotel living is overrated, Half-Pants. We're staying in the neighborhood, just to keep an eye on you and to make sure you're safe. We're also greatly concerned about your respective families. Your lovely wives, by the way, are delightful. And your children must be your pride and joy."

Still standing in the foyer, Rodrigo asked again, "Are you planning to ask us in to visit for a moment?"

An embarrassed Macario rushed to the foyer and escorted Rodrigo and Estevan into the living area, where the solitary sofa stood. When Rodrigo extended his hand in greeting, Macario noticed the mini-flame shooter that was mounted on Rodrigo's bracelet. "I like your smart watch, boss."

"I've been practicing," Rodrigo said, "and it works like a charm."

"We apologize that we have only one sitting area. But of course, you probably know that."

"Estevan, tell the movers to first bring in the bar stools to sit around the kitchen island. After that, they can bring the other furniture in." Turning to the twins, Rodrigo said, "Hope you don't mind, boys, but I took the liberty to furnish your safe house, since the previous occupants were Asians who had no sense of Western décor. They were here for two years," Rodrigo said, "and, for some reason, they assumed that black lacquer furniture went well with this house."

Just then, Estevan walked out the door to summon the Mayflower employees to bring in the furnishings that

Rodrigo had selected. The boss asked for a slice of the pie, and Macario accommodated his request. He served four plates and offered to serve milk to wash it down. Rodrigo politely refused the milk, but he asked Estevan to open the two bottles of Gamay that he'd selected for the dessert pairing.

"We won't be staying long because you will have a full day tomorrow," Rodrigo said. "Early tomorrow, Estevan will be sending you a schedule for the day, but it may involve some additional exploration of the village. In the afternoon, I'll meet with you to provide some details for your next assignment."

"We're anxious to hear about our families," Pedro said. "Are they well? The kids were doing their schoolwork online. We used to help them. We miss them."

"Your two girls are fine, Pedro. Lucila, who incidentally looks exactly like your wife, may have a need for braces, or so she told me. As far as I'm concerned, her pearly-white teeth are perfectly fine, but she claims her bottom front teeth 'are crooked'. Her mom claims she's getting interested in boys. Anyway, I've got an appointment for your daughter with Chicago's best pediatric orthodontist. Incidentally, she's got Rosa María's smile."

"You've learned their names?" Pedro asked.

"I see them every day… and most nights, Half-Pants."

"And your son Marcos, Pedro, he's quite the athlete. I believe we've got a major-league baseball player in the making. His knowledge of the game is formidable. And, his batting shows much potential. I replaced the old infield glove he'd used for years, though. He seems to like it."

Pedro was silent. He turned to look at his brother.

"Can you tell me anything about my family?" Macario asked.

"I was forcing you to ask, Mudo. As you know, your wife Raquel is a bit rebellious. If I may add, she needs to be treated more firmly. She's been somewhat skeptical about my motives, and regardless of my assurances that you both are being cared for, she demands to talk to you."

"She's simply protective of her family, boss. She doesn't mean any disrespect," Macario said.

"Unfortunately, I had to take Raquel across my lap to spank her."

With little disguise in his voice or expression, Macario said, "I hope you're being funny, boss."

"No, I'm not being figurative. I literally had to spank her," Rodrigo said.

Enraged, Macario lunged at Rodrigo, but in one sweep of his elbow, Estevan struck Macario in the larynx and held his dessert fork to Macario's carotid artery.

"Boys, boys…" Rodrigo said. "Your families are in good hands. I'm protecting them as if they were mine. Well, in the meantime, I suppose they are. They're under my roof, not far from here, and I see them every day… and night, Macario."

"In fact, Mudo, you may be happy to learn that your twin boys—Pablo and Mateo—are as feisty as their father. They may be twelve, but they think they can talk back to their elders. I've had to discipline them a couple of times, but they're too old for spanking."

Holding his throat, Macario struggled to verbalize hoarsely, "You touch any of them, and I'll kill you, Rodrigo."

"Ha, it may be late for that," a grinning Rodrigo said. "After all, I've violated every one of your rules, and I'm still alive."

Macario made a move toward Rodrigo, but Estevan was quick to restrain him.

. . .

With a powerful left grip on Macario's corduroy collar, Estevan scribbled a quick note for both twins to read, 'Your patrón does not suffer fools gladly.'

Pedro was about to ask what that meant, but, with difficulty, his twin brother whispered in guttural sounds, "It means that Rodrigo has lost his patience with us."

"I'll explain what Estevan is telling you," Rodrigo said. "Both of you have failed me and jeopardized my enterprise from the moment you joined me. You have botched every assignment that I've given you."

Pedro pleaded, "We can make it up to you, boss. The only reason that Tío Dante is still alive is that we hired someone else to kill him. We should've done it ourselves."

"That's a laugh," Rodrigo said. "If Tío outsmarted the professional assassin you hired, he certainly would've erased you both from the face of the earth. You're no match for Tío... I should've known that from the start."

Still whispering with great effort, Macario said, "You may not appreciate the CIA and FBI connections we brought you... and you may not appreciate that we gave you El Chato Gómez, but if you kill us... we will take to our graves a secret that will haunt you for the rest of your life."

"What are you talking about, Mudo? You've outlasted your usefulness. I intend to make you pay for the damage you've caused. But, before I kill you, you will watch me torture every one of your loved ones, one by one." Rodrigo smiled, "I may enjoy myself with your wives first, before I..."

Regaining some strength in his voice, Macario added, "We knew your father... and the secret he kept from you."

"Macario," said his brother, "be quiet."

"You piece of garbage. My father died before I was born." The fury in Rodrigo's eyes was unmistakable. Estevan quickly moved in to restrain his boss.

"My father was a war hero," continued a half-standing Rodrigo. Estevan, still restraining him, sat him on the bar stool. "He died for an unworthy country in an unjust war waged against valiant youngsters in Vietnam fighting for their freedom. That's why I hate this country of yours, Macario. Your country killed my father."

"Your mother... and father... kept a secret from you," Macario said with a smirk on his face. "We know the secret, but if you kill us, you'll never know the truth about who you are."

"Let me go, Estevan, I'm about to finish these two right now." Rodrigo reached for his Sig Sauer, but Estevan held him firmly. Shaking his head, Estevan motioned for his boss to take several deep breaths.

Incredibly, Macario continued, "We believe that the Shelleys, as well as the Epsteins, also know the secret that was kept from you."

At this point, Estevan locked his boss's elbows behind his back. He led him out to their white Land Rover which was parked on the circular driveway. He removed the 9-mm from Rodrigo's hand and slipped it in the small of his back. He drove off before Rodrigo had an opportunity to object.

CHAPTER 41

MAX

Austin – Chicago · February 18, 2020

I WAITED FOR MY flight back to Chicago at the Austin-Bergstrom International Airport. I was full of anticipation and couldn't wait to share my newest revelations with Nate and Miró. So many connections were coming together for me. Old ties appeared to be unraveling before my eyes, or perhaps only my own imagination. I was uncertain which.

Abraham, he had invited the family for Sunday dinner which had become the new ritual. Miriam seemed to be back to normal, unaffected by the kidnapping. Though still healing from the lacerations on her left forearm, Minnie was also remarkably cheerful, unafraid, and full of confidence that the 'bad guys' would be brought to justice. I was thoroughly impressed by the resiliency of my dad's side of the family. In fact, I felt giddy about my return.

The flight attendant's voice came over the loudspeaker. He announced the boarding of the direct flight to Chicago O'Hare.

. . .

Rosie, the young Chicago Tribune reporter, had made it a habit to drop by unannounced. Sometimes the dude showed up during the week around dinnertime. After his second visit, Miriam automatically set an extra plate at the table. I suspected the bachelor reporter used as an excuse the 'series of articles' he was writing on Miró's kidnapping followed by the strange kidnapping of Minnie and her grandmother. Yes, his interest in the stories was genuine, but his appreciation of Miriam's cooking was even greater.

I couldn't fault Rosie's regard for Miriam's culinary talents. She'd become an extraordinary chef, and her attention to detail made her dishes five-star quality. Of course, this comes from a Texan who has not traveled much, except for a few ventures across the Mexican border and a little beyond.

The day that I returned from Austin, Rosie joined us for his dinner fix, Miriam's Thai chicken with green curry. I told him about my recordings regarding Rudy von Steiner, and he pounced on the account of my visit to Grandpappy's ranch. He asked to hear it after dinner, but I warned him the full recording lasted more than ninety minutes. Over a few glasses of Dad's Madeira, the four of us—Miriam, Abraham, Rosie, and I—listened to thirty or forty minutes of my recording. He then begged me to introduce him to Grandpappy and Grandma K for an interview. When Rosie asked me about my mom, I explained she was deceased.

For the next few weeks, Rosie poured himself into researching Grandpappy's Austrian friend. He asked to read my senior thesis, which expanded the research done for the newspaper article. He placed numerous calls to my grandparents in Three Rivers, and spent countless hours at the library. He suspended his investigation of a mysterious viral disease that appeared to be baffling scientists in Wuhan, China, because he felt this research into von Steiner's history could lead to 'enormous implications related to the sinister creation of the CIA and the American intelligence community'. "Besides," said Rosie, "the Health Organization of the World (H.O.W.) tells us that this communicable disease cannot be transmitted from human to human. Go figure."

Exactly ten days after my return from Austin, the first article related to the Austrian war hero appeared in the Chicago Tribune. It included much of the research that I'd conducted at the University of Texas, and, of course, he graciously credited me for my contributions, but he also uncovered many details that I'd missed. Somehow, Rosie had obtained government records stating that von Steiner lived in Berlin in his youth. Evidently, this was before the Nazi party established its power. And, because the budding artist sketched several cartoons that made fun of the ruthless party leaders, he was labeled a dissident by the Nazis.

"Once they assumed political power," said Rosie, "the Nazis sought to squelch free-thinking opposition throughout Europe, and von Steiner appeared on their blacklist."

In his article, Rosie explained that Rudy von Steiner lived his entire life as a hunted man, and he remained the Nazis' enemy throughout their reign. In turn, Rudy dedicated the rest of his life to the destruction of fascism throughout the world.

European sources documented that in 1938, the year that Hitler annexed Austria, Grandpappy's friend von Steiner came to the U.S. Following the attack on Pearl Harbor, von Steiner attempted to enlist in America, but he was declared to be 'medically unfit'. He found a way, however, to join the military and ended up with the U.S. War Department's 'artist corps'. Considering my family's conversations, it was at that time, while Grandpappy and von Steiner were stationed at Fort Bliss that they probably met.

From my conversations with Grandpappy, though sympathetic to von Steiner's cause, he chose to remain apolitical and, frankly, bemused—rather than motivated—by the tense, uneasy, and edgy Austrian with the thick accent. Grandpappy didn't realize what a hero von Steiner would become.

Rosie's article traced the Austrian's career after he left Fort Bliss and parted ways with Grandpappy. He uncovered government records which detailed von Steiner's adventures in Italy. Rosie confirmed the adventures with the Red Bulls in Italy and how he impregnated a young Italian woman by the name of Calabrese.

My initial suspicions were being confirmed at each step. Rosie's research was bringing up that name again—Calabrese. Wasn't that the name that appeared in the Austin birth records? The name discovered by Dad? The dates, however, did not, could not, match. Did it mean that Ram Edmunds' partner, Angelo Calabrese, was von Steiner's son? ... Plus being the man that sired Diego Montemayor?

And, by extension, Calabrese, the name carried by Ram Edmunds' partner, was somehow connected to me.

Yes, although von Steiner had married the woman named Calabrese, the offspring retained the name of the mother. Quoting an interview, in his article, Rosie stated that von Steiner hated his Austrian heritage so much that he would not allow his new wife or his offspring to assume a Teutonic surname. After his Italian adventures, von Steiner's history—Rosie cryptically explained—became quite vague, perhaps deliberately veiled by America's own clandestine and secretive agencies.

· · ·

The second article which appeared in the Sunday edition of the Tribune brought things together for me:

'U.S. Government files also revealed that, as part of the artist corps, von Steiner was assigned to the 34th Infantry—the Red Bulls—which invaded Italy.

Not content with merely depicting troop activities with his brush, he soon convinced his superiors to allow him to carry an M-1 rifle to defend himself while painting realistic front-line combat. From that vantage point, the Austrian managed to record enemy troop movements and positions in the battlefield.

Because of his language skills, von Steiner soon gained usefulness by interrogating German prisoners and providing intelligence. By 1943, he had become so valuable that he became an 'intelligence officer' of the 2nd Battalion, 168th Infantry Regiment. Von Steiner's valor and skills grew to legendary proportions. He led various patrols that turned the Allies' fortunes and secured numerous victories in the European front.

When he 'disappeared' from the 34th Infantry Division, he had two Silver Stars, two Purple Hearts, and a battlefield commission. His Red Bull compatriots learned, after the war, why von Steiner had 'disappeared'. He had been recruited to the Office of Strategic Services (OSS), America's first iteration of the Central Intelligence Agency.'

To me, it was clear that von Steiner was Diego Montemayor's grandfather. After many years of hearing stories of this misfit who had painted Grandpappy's portrait, I knew that the Kempballs are connected to Ram Edmunds' partner—the man who sired Diego Montemayor. A sobering realization that there is something to the 'six degrees of separation'.

Aided by my dad's influence to study family history and through Rosie's further research, I learned that the fabric of my own life was knitted into a universal blanket, one that implicated me in every evil deed ever committed. It's not that I felt responsible for Montemayor's actions; rather, I felt contaminated, stained somehow by knowing these unraveled threads touched me at the core. This unwelcomed illumination began as a clue, a suspicion, that led me to unlock the mystery of Diego Montemayor's evil power.

If von Steiner was indeed one of the original founders of the most clandestine operation in the world, could this be the reason that his son, Angelo Calabrese, was so well-protected by the CIA and FBI? Was he given a free pass because he came from CIA royalty? Worse still, was this the explanation for the immunity enjoyed by Calabrese's son, Diego? Was Diego Montemayor the seed of CIA royalty?

CHAPTER 42

Skokie, IL ·Sunday, February 23, 2020

THE SUNDAY MEAL THAT Max had been anticipating could not come soon enough. Max resisted calling Nate in the middle of the week. However, he spent hours each day preparing his delivery for 'Mr. Analytical'.

Sunday finally arrived, and Miriam's culinary masterpiece did not fail to impress. After the Spanish dish was consumed, Max—to the entire family's surprise—announced that he and Nate would probably skip dessert. He then turned to Nate and invited him to his upstairs man-cave, his private suite which had become his new home.

"That paella gets better and better every time I taste it," Max told Nate. "Don't tell Miriam, but since I first had it with you guys, I've tried the seafood paella at Ba-Ba-Reeba, and it, too, is terrific. However, my favorite paella is Miriam's."

"Are you feeling okay?" Nate asked. "It's the first time you skip dessert."

Max was relieved that the relationship with Nate was back to normal. "Yes, I'm fine. I'm just eager to share something with you." Since his outburst, Nate had come to Max and apologized. The two of them had shared a bottle of Bermejo and made amends. For Max, it was the closest he'd felt to a best friend. He had grown to respect Nate almost as much as his own dad.

"Dude, I need your help. Let's take a break from the NBA. It looks like the Wizards will win this game anyway."

"Whoa, Max. I thought you promised you'd adopt our Bulls, at least through your stay here in Chicagoland," Nate said. "Give 'em a chance. The game is still close."

Max ignored the question. "Have you read the Rosenfeld articles in the Tribune?"

"The ones regarding our family's misfortunes? I think Rosenfeld is crossing the line, Max. Frankly, I stopped reading after the first article on the Austrian artist. It seems to me that he's exploiting our situation, and your own history, to build a reputation for himself."

"Okay, Nate," Max said. "I want you to hear a recording I made coming back from my grandparents' ranch. I've got a hunch, and I can't seem to shake it."

"A hunch, eh? Max, you've been around Abraham too long. Has the conspiracy bug infected you also?" Nate laughed and followed Max into his study.

For more than an hour, the two men listened and relistened to Max's recording of his visit to the Kempball Ranch. As normally happens when recording on busy highways, the vehicle's wind noise affected the quality and the substance of the recording.

"Please explain, Max. Other than a fascinating connection with a Second World War hero, I'm not certain that I grasp the significance of von Steiner's relationship to our ongoing problems with cartels. What am I missing?" Nate asked.

"Okay, please follow my line of thinking. Although he's heard the recording, we'll bring in Abraham if you think his genealogical research can help us. But first, let's walk through this together." Max brought out the easel and dry board from his upstairs hall closet.

- As part of the artist corps, von Steiner was assigned to the 34th Infantry.
- The 34th Infantry invaded Italy.
- To paint realistic combat scenes, the Austrian requested assignment to the front lines.
- For self-defense, von Steiner was permitted to carry an M-1 rifle.
- From a front-line vantage point, he was able to record—on canvas, of course—enemy positions in the battlefield.
- Because of his language skills, he was asked to interrogate German prisoners.
- After his work with various patrols that secured victories in the European front, von Steiner disappeared from the 34th Infantry.
- Von Steiner's own colleagues at the 34th were unaware of his whereabouts.

- By 1943, now a war hero, von Steiner reappeared as an 'intelligence officer' of the 2nd Battalion, 168th Infantry Regiment.
- Rudy von Steiner was recruited by the Office of Strategic Services, the OSS.

Max made a dramatic pause as if he'd reached the punchline. Using his fingers, he raked his long blond hair. He looked straight at Nate, grinned, and waited for a response.

Nate had a vacuous smile on his face. "I'm afraid you need to spell this out for me, Max."

"Spell what out, dude? The Office of Strategic Services, the OSS, don't you know the significance?"

"Sorry, Max, I'm not much of a military historian."

"The OSS, Nate, was America's first version—or, as you would say, the first iteration—of the CIA, Central Intelligence Agency."

Long pause.

"Wow, Max, I can see where you're going with this. So, this von Steiner creep, as your mother called him, was in the inner circle of the CIA's creation. No wonder it caught your attention."

Max could tell that Nate was impressed but still unclear about the significance of these revelations.

"You mentioned earlier that everything had come together during this pilgrimage to South Texas. Explain to me," Nate said, "how this German, or Austrian, portrait artist, connected to your grandparents, is ultimately relevant to *our* predicament here."

"I may be reading way too much into this, but when von Steiner served in the 34ᵗʰ Infantry that invaded Italy, he was decorated so much that he became quite a legendary figure."

"That part I understand. He became a war hero," Nate said.

"In addition to becoming legendary with the Red Bulls," Max said, "he apparently also became legendary with the Italian ladies. Stories abound about this Austrian siring several illegitimate children, but he eventually married a local by the name of Sofia Calabrese."

"Voila, now, the story becomes interesting," Nate said. "I can see why you're excited."

Max went on, "The U.S. Army has records of only one child born to von Steiner and Sofia Calabrese, and his name was Angelo... Angelo," repeated Max, "as in Dad's former patient *and* ex-CIA agent. For some reason, von Steiner and Sofia Calabrese's offspring grew up using his mother's name, not von Steiner."

"Did von Steiner—Angelo's dad—return to the U.S.?"

"Records become sketchy after he was recruited by the OSS, but he reappeared in New Jersey after the war. His records became classified after that."

"We definitely need Abraham, Max. Let's bring him in."

CHAPTER 43

Winnetka, IL · February 26, 2020

The Mayflower movers were still bringing in the furniture that Rodrigo had selected for the safe house. The twins moved to the third bedroom where the laptop equipment awaited them. As Pedro began his protest, Macario asked him to be silent. He signaled to his brother that the 'walls have ears'.

"What do you mean, Macario?" the clueless Pedro Half-Pants asked.

Without answering, Macario led his brother to the bikes sitting in the garage. He instructed the movers to lock the doors behind them when they finished. Macario took the lead, and raced his twin brother to the nearby beach by Lake Michigan. Pedro gleefully obliged and pedaled for the next fifteen minutes, stopping at their favorite bench. The frigid air instantly caused Macario to quickly inform his brother, "Rodrigo's able to follow us with his prized drone, but the sound of the surf will drown out our conversation. Do you understand what I'm doing?"

"No," Pedro said, "you'll only make Rodrigo angrier by telling him we know about his parents."

"Think about it, it's the only chip we've got. If we can convince Rodrigo that his parents' secret is worth knowing, he may allow our families to live," Macario said.

"You think we can also save our skins?"

"Be realistic. Rodrigo's made up his mind. We're dead meat. The best we can hope for is that our kids will survive—and maybe, our wives."

"So, what's our next move?" Pedro asked.

"We wait until Rodrigo contacts us. If he tries to talk to us, it means he wants to hear our story," Macario said. "Remember when he told you that you had testicular fortitude? Well, now's the time to show it."

When the twins returned to the safe house, the moving van was gone. They entered the house, and the first thing they noticed was the lack of an echo. Thick, expensive Persian rugs had been placed throughout the house, and various Asian porcelain table lamps adorned the previously empty living room.

"Wow," Pedro said, "I could get used to this."

"Bro, our days are numbered. Now's not the time to get comfortable."

"What I kind of don't understand is why it would be so important for Rodrigo to know about his father," Pedro said.

Macario motioned to his brother to remember that Rodrigo's surveillance inside the house was complete. He could hear—and see—almost everything that went on.

With a voice volume that was louder than normal, Macario, walking into the kitchen to prepare dinner, spoke to Pedro from there, "Man, of course it matters. Rodrigo should know the identity of his dad. It can explain how his business benefited from his father, explain how he worked behind the scenes to protect Rodrigo, and clarify why he was protected by the federal government. Know what I mean?" Macario asked.

"What if Rodrigo finds out where we got our information?"

Macario rushed to the living room entrance, frantically waving both hands from side to side to tell Pedro not to divulge too much information. Then he added a universal slicing motion across his neck to clarify to his brother 'kill it'.

Then loudly, Macario said, "We should tell the boss all about the juicy parts regarding the FBI, dude. But first, we should give him some information regarding the old man, Miró's father." Again, he quietly signaled to his brother with his right finger vertically touching his mouth. "The Shelleys and Epsteins are getting close to the truth, but they don't know the whole story."

Pedro was getting more confused at every moment. His perplexed look told Macario that his brother still didn't understand his strategy. He resorted to Estevan's use of note writing. He quickly scribbled on a notepad, 'Don't say a thing. I'm feeding Rodrigo the info that we want him to get.'

With an exaggerated nod, Pedro said loudly, "I agree completely." Then he winked at his brother.

Macario finished his dinner preparation for them, opting for grilled cheese sandwiches. He opened two beers and turned on the 70" Samsung flat-screen mounted on the wall. He settled on a Mexican channel that was showing an old Cantinflas classic, *Ahí está el Detalle.*

. . .

Late that night, after Estevan's special dish of Solomillo al Whiskey, Rodrigo's mood improved. Estevan knew that the quick recipe of pork medallions, soaked in the garlicky whiskey sauce, always had a tranquilizing effect on his boss. Instead of joining Rodrigo for dinner, Estevan dedicated time to editing the evening's tapped information at the smaller safe house. He listened to the twins' recorded conversations, and although it was clear to him that Pedro and Macario were putting on a charade for Rodrigo's benefit, even if half-true, the so-called secret that Macario claimed to have could prove useful to Rodrigo. He decided to share an edited version with his boss after dinner.

Along with a cup of freshly brewed cappuccino, Estevan shared with Rodrigo the abridged version of the twins' late-night conversation. While reviewing the audio and video recordings on Estevan's laptop, Rodrigo asked for a second cup of cappuccino.

"I'm familiar with the heart surgeon, or, at least, I've learned enough about the man to know he's harmless,"

Rodrigo said. "I've got a complete file on him, and as I recall, he's quite a genealogist. Do you think that's where the twins got their information?"

Estevan shrugged. Then he signed a lengthy response.

"Estevan, it's too late for me to interpret such long messages. I think I got the gist of your response, though. Are you saying that the twins tapped the phones of all members of the Shelley and Epstein families? "

Nodding, Estevan added with simplified signing, '... *their phones and computers.*'

Slurping loudly, Rodrigo finished the last drops of the cappuccino. He remained silent.

'The twins said they <u>knew</u> your father. But they believe that Dr. Epstein traced the identity of your <u>mother</u>.' Estevan rapidly scribbled on a notepad an important clarification. He underscored the words 'knew' and 'mother'.

"Her identity? I knew my mom; I don't need a stranger's research to tell me who she was."

Estevan shook his head, then he signed very slowly and deliberately, '*What I should've said is that Dr. Epstein traced your birth, and he thinks he identified your biological father.*'

"What good is that information? My father died in Vietnam's fight for freedom as a young man. His last name was Cruz, but my mom kept her maiden name, Montemayor."

'*Well, Abraham Epstein thinks that your father was someone else,*' Estevan signed for his boss.

"Why the devil should I care what he thinks, Estevan?"

Estevan did not respond.

"My mother told me stories of being born in this country, but she took me to Spain early in life—I was two months old. She tried to convince me that since I was born in America, I was fortunate to claim dual citizenship."

Estevan signed, '*A lot of people would agree.*'

"First, these are not my people, my friend. Secondly, I've never had a desire to be a citizen of this abominable country."

Estevan wrote on his notepad, 'Would you like me to search for your birth records?'

"Gracias, Estevan, but my mother's last name was Montemayor, and she was briefly married to a Vietnam War hero by the name of Cruz. She remained single until she met her second husband in Spain. That's all I need to know."

Again, Estevan wrote on his notepad, 'Twins think that your biological father was responsible for the success of your international business and for the FBI's and CIA's protection.'

"Estevan, I own the CÍA and the American federales. And I worked hard for my business success. What do those birdbrains know?" Rodrigo said as he stared into the distance.

'*You should talk to the twins, boss,*' Estevan signed, as he took the cappuccino cup back to the kitchen.

"I said no." Rodrigo slammed the laptop shut.

CHAPTER 44

Winnetka, IL · February 27, 2020

R ODRIGO COULD NOT SLEEP. At three in the morning, he called out to Estevan, "Get those two morons here. I want to talk to them."

'*Boss,*' signed Estevan, '*it's best you not talk to them in person. You don't want to regret losing your temper.*'

"I just want to ask some questions. Without their cell phones, I can't Facetime them," Rodrigo said.

'*I can wake them. No worries. We'll force them to use their laptop equipment.*'

Pedro and Macario jumped out of bed as soon as the first fire alarm sounded. Then the smoke alarms started their chirping, which became annoyingly louder. Finally, the carbon monoxide trill went off. As Macario climbed on a side chair to disconnect the nearest smoke alarm, Pedro ran around the house trying to find the carbon monoxide box, which was installed on the wainscoting in the living room. Thankfully, the fire alarm did not sound again.

"Rise and shine," the cheerless, robotic voice from their laptop speakers said. Then, the same computerized voice message was repeated twice. Snapping the screen of the laptop open, Macario was greeted by Rodrigo's grin, the face of an insomniac in bad need of sleep.

"My birdbrained friends, let me tell you why I don't care who my biological father is. My safety is secured by powerful forces inside the U.S. intelligence community. In fact, because of my leverage, I'm untouchable in the Western world. El CÍA es mío... I own the CÍA."

Not able to contain himself, Macario spoke up. As soon as he opened his mouth, his brother looked at him with panic in his eyes. He knew his brother was about to reveal what they'd been forbidden to divulge.

"Rodrigo, do you know how you were able to access the upper levels of the CIA?"

"Tío Dante was my conduit, Mudo. He arranged meetings with my CÍA contacts. At one time, I foolishly thought you had helped Tío, but now I know better," Rodrigo said.

"What you don't know is that Tío gave you access to the CIA administration because of your biological father," Macario said.

"What the devil are you talking about?"

"Spare our lives—and our families' lives—and we'll reveal to you the secrets that have been kept from you," Macario said.

"Eres un hijo de…" At that point, Estevan came into view, looked at the camera, and signaled to the twins to give him some time. He quickly scribbled a note for Rodrigo. On camera, the twins saw Rodrigo take Estevan's notepad and hurl it at his face. Estevan did not flinch. His glare seemed to calm his boss slightly. Rodrigo appeared to push away from the desk, camera, and laptop connections.

Estevan held up a sign to the camera that read 'CHILL'.

Pedro and Macario waited for five minutes. Pedro got up to take two Tylenols, and Macario tapped his fingers on the desk. Finally, Rodrigo returned to the camera with a snifter, presumably filled with a double cognac.

"Okay, tell you what," Rodrigo said. "If you spill your guts—and I mean tell me everything you know—I'll consider your request. Frankly, I believe you're bluffing. I think you're making up stories."

Emboldened, Macario smiled, and shook his head. "Rodrigo, think about it. We've got everything to lose. Why should we give you any information without a firm commitment from you?"

"What are you saying, Mudo?"

"I'm saying we'll spill our guts if you spare our lives," Macario said.

"Out of the question," Rodrigo said. Estevan apparently handed Rodrigo a note off camera, because the boss turned, read something, and tapped his fingers on the crystal snifter.

"Give us some time to think about it, Rodrigo," Macario said.

"Hmm," Rodrigo smiled. "Apparently, I credited the wrong brother for having a certain kind of fortitude…"

A lengthy silence followed. Rodrigo paced the floor.

Finally, Rodrigo came back to the camera. "Okay, tell me what you know, and I will let your families live."

"Will you give us your word to take care of them, financially and in every other way… after we're gone?" Macario asked.

"Yes, you've got my word."

"Good. We have an understanding," a triumphant Macario said.

. . .

Pedro jumped into the conversation as soon as his brother allowed him. "Rodrigo, do you remember we told you about Cal, the person that worked with our dad, the one who first paid me for a job well done?"

"I do, indeed, Half-Pants," Rodrigo said. "You said he taught you to stash coca inside a gas tank… at the age of six, I believe."

"That's the one. We told you he became a cop, joined the FBI and later the CIA."

"Yeah, but he was dirty. He worked both sides," Rodrigo said.

"Exactly," Macario said. "He gave us the evidence we needed to feed it back to the cops when we took down our former boss, El Chato Gómez. That helped you take control of El Chato's business and…"

"Yes, yes, I know all that, Mudo. Go on," complained Rodrigo. "You also said that he had been responsible for your switching sides to my organization."

"Though he helped the Feds bring down El Chato's empire, he also helped you a lot," Pedro said.

"Didn't you call him a skilled assassin? And, didn't you hire him to take down Tío?"

"That's the one," Macario said. "We knew him as 'Cal', but his real name was Angelo Calabrese."

"Sounds pretty Italian to me," a smiling Rodrigo said.

"We found out that Cal was your real father, your biological father," Macario said.

"My father was a Hispanic Vietnam War casualty," Rodrigo said. "I told you that. His name was Cruz, but when he died, my mother took on her maiden name. She moved from Austin, Texas, and took me to Spain at the age of two months, and she remained there all her life. Her second husband was a Spaniard, not an Italian, and she kept her maiden name."

"That's why your legal name is Diego R. Montemayor," Macario said. "It's not Rodrigo Díaz—it's Diego R. Montemayor—the missing drug lord that escaped from Spain… and mysteriously disappeared. We know you went through facial reconstruction surgery, and you grew two or three inches from limb lengthening surgery performed by your doctors."

"Who in the devil's name told you that?"

"Your biological father. He tracked you down and kept up with you. You didn't know it, but he protected you all your life," Macario said. "He made us swear that we'd keep your secret."

"Your secret is safe with us," Pedro said.

"You're saying this Cal person, whatever his name is, knew about my former identity... and my surgeries?"

"He destroyed most of the information he had on you," Macario said.

"Why do you keep on insisting he's my biological father?"

Full of confidence, Macario continued. "As a federal agent he ensured that your mother's secret would be protected. Except for some municipal records that Dr. Epstein tracked down in Austin, he destroyed birth records and whatever historical records could tie you to him. That's why law enforcement agencies have very little data about your origins. In fact, not even you have all the facts."

"Spill your guts, Mudo. What are you saying?" Rodrigo asked.

"I'm saying that your mother and Angelo Calabrese fell in love, while her husband was still alive and fighting in Vietnam." Macario was silent for a minute.

"Do you want me to go on?" Macario asked. Getting no response, he continued, "Your mother got pregnant, and she initially named you Diego R. Calabrese. Soon, she changed her mind, changed her legal name from Linda Cruz to Linda Montemayor, and gave you her legal surname."

Rodrigo was silent for a long while. Then, he asked, "Didn't you say that Tío killed Calabrese?"

"The Feds have admitted that the dead person found at the hotel in Evanston was Angelo Calabrese and not Tío Dante. We think Tío ambushed Cal before he—Calabrese—had a chance to kill Tío."

Rodrigo appeared unmoved, but his hands began to tremble. He set his snifter down and, using his left hand, forced his clenched right one down to his lap. Almost to himself, Rodrigo asked, "Not only did Tío betray me, but he also murdered my father?"

Neither twin responded. On camera, they could see that Rodrigo rose from his desk chair and walked away. Estevan flashed a question in front of the camera: 'Can your claims be verified?'

Macario seemed to grow in confidence as he spoke. He explained to Estevan that Dr. Abraham Epstein had researched birth records in Austin, Texas. Not only did he discover that Rodrigo's mother changed her name from Cruz to Montemayor, he also verified birth records, where 'Diego Montemayor's' biological father was listed as Angelo Calabrese. The twins explained to Estevan that everything Cal had shared with them was confirmed by Dr. Abraham Epstein's genealogical hunt.

Estevan wrote, 'How do you know all this? How did you get this from Dr. Epstein?'

"We told you, Estevan. We tapped their phones and can intercept all communications," Macario said.

'Has Epstein shared this information with anyone else?' Estevan asked, on a scribbled note.

"Of course. The Shelleys know and they have also given their discoveries to Special Agent Ram Edmunds," Macario said. "But Edmunds was not aware of the connection between his buddy Calabrese and Diego Montemayor. The Shelleys revealed that connection to Edmunds."

The twins had to wait for Estevan to scribble a legible question, 'Do any of them know that Diego Montemayor and Rodrigo Díaz are one and the same person?'

"Not yet, Estevan," Macario said. "But I believe that Rodrigo needs to hear one more important fact."

"I didn't go far, Mudo, I'm listening," Rodrigo said off-camera. "What other nonsense do you want me to hear?"

"Angelo Calabrese's father—your grandfather—started the CIA," Macario said.

Rodrigo was immediately back in front of the camera. He remained standing. "You two must be delusional. Where do you come up with these stories?" he asked.

"We are certain all of this can be verified, Rodrigo. Miró Epstein's father collected the information, and, if you give us an opportunity, we can bring him to you." Macario's voice indicated that the request was being made without conviction. He knew that they would probably not leave the safe house alive.

Rodrigo broke out in laughter. "Mudo, you must be out of your mind if you think that I would entrust you with something like that."

"But boss," Pedro said, "you said that you had one more job for us."

"Half-Pants, I will visit you at 0800 hours tomorrow. I will outline the assignment then."

. . .

The twins were ready before 7 in the morning, expecting the normally punctual Rodrigo to be at their door on or before 8 AM. The doorbell rang at 10:20. A disheveled and unshaved Rodrigo entered the foyer, looking worse than he had at 3 AM. The dark bags under his eyes and his uncombed hair presented an image of a miserable man barely able to function. Without greeting the twins, he barked at Estevan, "Brew a strong cup of coffee—make it a French press."

Rodrigo walked straight to the kitchen counter to sit on the bar stool that he'd used the previous evening. He moved around the safe house as if he were intimately familiar with the furnishings. Almost to himself, he began an account of his fitful efforts at sleep.

"As you slept comfortably in your beds, a horrible vision came to me at night," Rodrigo said. "Rage gripped me... and fear. I shook with anger. An evil spirit grinned at me and swept across my face. This evil presence mocked me, exposing golden fangs that sent shivers up my spine. I couldn't see its shape, but it was a large form in front of me, saying—no, the spirit was cackling—'I came against you, I killed your father, and I will kill you, too.' I then cried out for help, and I woke up."

"It was just a nightmare," Pedro said. "We all have them."

Rodrigo tried to smile. He patted the seat next to him. "Sit here, Half-Pants. You and your brother will help me eliminate this one."

"Tell us how we can help." Pedro moved the stool a few feet away from Rodrigo and half sat.

"You, too, Mudo. Sit with us and drink some coffee."

"Thanks, boss, but I'm helping Estevan fill the coffee mugs."

"Mudo, I was not asking," Rodrigo said. "Sit."

Macario gave an apologetic look to Estevan, and approached his brother and Rodrigo sitting around the kitchen island. His own coffee mug in hand, he asked Rodrigo, "Do you have instructions for our next assignment?"

"Believe it or not, the two of you will be important to my cause. Both will play a critical role, and this time I will be supervising your every step."

"We're ready, boss," Pedro said eagerly. "We will make you proud of us. Just remember the deal you made with us."

"I don't want you interrupting, my little Half-Pants. And, by the way, I always keep my word."

"Okay, boss."

"This time you will succeed in your assignment. I'll make certain of that," Rodrigo said.

"You know who that rabid dog in my dream represents?" Rodrigo asked. Without waiting for an answer, he responded to his own question. "The beast had golden fangs. You know why? That beast was Tío Dante. And you, my friends, will avenge my father's death... and Tío's betrayal that occurred three years ago."

"We kept telling you to give us a chance to get him, boss, and you wouldn't listen," Pedro said.

"How do you want us to eliminate him, Rodrigo?" Macario asked.

"It may involve the three of us, my friends. I will be supervising your every move."

"If you think it's necessary," Pedro said, "but if you give us the plan we can do it on our own."

"I've lost my faith in you, Half-Pants. So, I'll be looking over your shoulders."

"Very well. What's the plan?" Macario asked.

"Do you remember our Palestinian friends and the other lunatics from Al-Qaeda? Remember when they asked for our help? You, Half-Pants, delivered the updated suicide vests?"

"Yes, the vests without explosives," Pedro said.

"Nobody said you delivered the explosives, Half-Pants. Do you remember how they became more demanding? And, do you remember why?"

"They wanted something that could get past the monitors, something they could hide from the authorities," Macario said. "Suicide vests were too easily detectable."

"That's right," Rodrigo said. "The technology changed. We had to improve, because the training for law enforcement became more sophisticated. So, we had to stay ahead of the game. Our friends from ISIS, and even the looney fringe from Asia, liked that we kept a step or two ahead of the technological advancements. We even developed the more recent explosives being used in Great Britain."

"Ah, yes," Pedro said. "Those crazies are now planting bombs inside suicide bombers' bodies."

"But they're not working, Rodrigo," Macario said. "Sure, the suicide bombers blew themselves up, but the explosions hardly damaged others. They only managed to create huge craters on the ground."

"Exactly, Mudo. Since the human body is mostly water, the explosive energy was mostly absorbed by the body." Rodrigo added, "And, since the explosives had to fit in someone's rectum, devices had to be tiny, a few ounces at most. Though they could hide the device, the explosions were released through the rectum, directing the explosion in a downward direction."

"Yep, the success of those implanted bombs was not great," Pedro said.

"Boys, you surprise me. You've been keeping up," Rodrigo said. "You've given me all the reasons why we needed to develop something better. That's why I'm working with Dr. Ivo Wu. Not only is he the world's best plastic surgeon and facial reconstruction expert, he's creative. I wanted to implant a larger bomb inside the body—pounds worth of explosives—in a larger body cavity. Now, he's done it."

"You mean in the abdomen?" Macario asked.

"Or the chest cavity," Rodrigo said.

"Does it work?"

"He's been experimenting with wildlife at the compound, where you met him. And, he's perfected the device," Rodrigo said. "The crazies from Yemen who have used it claim to have had success."

"They were shahids, Rodrigo, crazed fanatics who are willing to be martyred in the name of Allah," complained Macario.

"Where are we going to find a willing person?" asked a clueless Pedro.

"Pedro, he wants us to volunteer," Macario said.

"The explosion would be massive, boys, but you wouldn't feel a thing. You'd be obliterated instantaneously. One moment you'll be pressing the correct speed dial number on your phone, the next when it detonates, you'll be in heaven with your God. Of course, Half-Pants, you can always renege on your commitment," Rodrigo said. "But, if you want to save your families, this will be your last assignment... for you and your brother."

"Why do you need both of us, Rodrigo?" Macario asked. "I'll submit to the surgery."

"I'll need both of you, Mudo. We'll infiltrate the Feds and we'll take Tío into our custody. One of you will help me seize the target, the other one will be the *package*," Rodrigo said.

"You mean the suicide bomber," Macario said.

Rodrigo summoned Estevan, who was still standing by the coffee bar. "Bring me my lucky coin."

"What are you doing?" Pedro asked.

Rodrigo smiled. "We'll flip for this... to decide who undergoes the surgery."

CHAPTER 45

MAX

Skokie – Chicago · March 12, 2020

I'M WELL-READ AND WELL-EDUCATED. Not brilliant, mind you, but I can hold my own. I regret, though, not being able to travel more. Outside of Texas, I haven't traveled at all... until now. Oh, a couple of quick trips to the Texas border exposed me to the northern part of Mexico. I remember having great dinners 'across the river' at several venues along the border. Restaurants like La Cucaracha in Reynosa (across from McAllen, Texas) or The Cadillac Bar in Nuevo Cielo (across from Dearlo Heights in Texas) had superb Mexican cuisine. Of course, that's before the cartels moved into these Mexican communities and took over the news media and the local governments. Some crooks govern entire communities in Mexico. It's no longer safe to visit those places. At least that's an assessment coming from a gringo, as I would be labeled in those places.

For me, being in Chicagoland for a few months has exposed me to various regional cuisines. I've learned to appreciate Spanish food—completely unlike the Mexican food that I know. I've also learned to eat sushi, and Greek food, and oh, how I've learned to appreciate Italian. Yes, I love the deep-dish variety of pizzas, but the more elaborate Italian dishes have blown me away. I've put on some unnecessary weight around my middle, fourteen pounds to be exact.

I say all this to explain how I came to fall in love with—or be blown away by—osso buco. And, Tío Dante introduced me to the dish.

Perhaps, because the dude discovered my modest abilities with computers and cyber protection, or maybe it was simply convenient to find me online for a greater part of the day, Tío Dante began a daily chat with me during the latter part of February. The dude, he began by asking me if I knew the origin of the hysteria overtaking the country. When I responded by pointing to the Wuhan virology laboratories, I think he was impressed. I suppose, he'd assumed I'd be following the media's insane explanations about bats and wet markets.

Though he complimented me on being better informed than the average American citizen, he went on to credit his former boss for the funding of those research projects in China. At first I was skeptical. But he carefully and patiently outlined for me how Diego's plans had been put in place for several years.

"We've been—well, I suppose I should say—he's been helping several enemies of your country develop several types of weapons, including biological and germ warfare," Tío said, via a secure messaging function. "Max, these weapons are being developed as we speak, and they're being launched against your people."

Although now I realize how naïve I must've sounded, I asked him, "Mr. Dante, I thought the research projects in China were being developed to protect against infectious diseases. Aren't they considered immunology research labs?"

Tío simply brushed it off. "That's laughable," he texted. "Believe it or not, that's how we managed to redirect American university research monies to China. If we call this research 'preventive' in nature, our American scientists are all over it. Your top research institutions have sent your best researchers to help the Chinese Communist government develop weapons that will be used against your country."

"Aren't the Chinese interested in developing means of preventing the spread of infectious diseases?" I asked.

"Yes, of course, as a byproduct and for selfish reasons. But first, they must create the virus or the bacterial infection. So, obviously, the more difficult it is to protect against a certain viral strain, the more effective it becomes as a weapon."

After the first week, I asked, "Why do you want to reveal Diego's secrets now, Mr. Dante?"

"Because," Tío responded, "it is my only ticket to freedom or safety. Diego wants me dead. If I can convince your family and your justice system to protect me, then it's my only hope. Call it self-preservation, my friend."

I told Tío that I had many more questions. I suggested we meet for coffee. To my surprise, he agreed; however, he insisted on selecting the place and time for our meetings. In addition, he limited each meeting to less than one hour. So, I agreed.

Tío insisted on paying for coffee and refreshments each time we met. Contrary to my assumption, Tío was relaxed and at ease. He was forthright and assertive, but respectful. The first question that I asked when we met face to face was, "How did China get this viral weapon inside our borders?"

"That's a smart question, my friend. Your president, at the risk of being labeled a racist, imposed a ban on travel from China in January. By law, however, Chinese diplomats were excluded from this ban and allowed to travel to this country. They were the living weapons. Although most of those individuals were immunized for self-protection, they were carriers of the virus. In fact, the Chinese imposed a ban of travel from Wuhan residents to other parts of China, but they encouraged them to travel to other parts of the world."

"Go figure." Embarrassed to say it, but I learned quite a bit from Tío Dante. During a one-week period, I learned of such a twisted web of deception, that it gave me a deeper understanding of the widespread corruption that is being used to destroy this country. From a twisted mentality, I learned how easily our enemies fabricate myths for American consumption.

After three short visits at various coffee shops, I received a strange call. Tío Dante, he wanted to introduce me to osso buco, Diego Montemayor's favorite dish. Through the years, it had also become Tío's favorite. Tío asked to meet me at a small Chicago restaurant called Marco's, which per Tío, prepared the dish even better than the one prepared by Diego Montemayor's deceased wife.

"I'll be waiting for you at the door. I'll be the one wearing a gray fedora."

I agreed to meet him. When I arrived, he was waiting.

"I was afraid you wouldn't show," Tío said.

A man in a suit opened the door for us. We were then seated immediately. He rushed to a back office, and the owner of Marco's emerged, greeting Tío as if they were old friends. He summoned his best waitperson, and promised he would take care of us in a superb manner.

"Max, I want to talk to you about my former boss. Would you mind?"

"You called this meeting, Mr. Dante. The floor is yours," I said.

"Diego is a gourmand, my friend, a very refined man," Tío said. "He's also a brilliant man. Unfortunately, the love for his wife blinded him to the point where he became drunk with power. Although she led him to make poor business decisions, for a brief time I was able to influence Diego. It was enough to insulate him against his tendency to be reckless."

I noted that when Tío spoke of his former boss, his admiration showed. They must've enjoyed an uncommon bond.

"Your friendship must have been deep. Tell me, Mr. Dante…"

"Stop right there, Max. If we're going to share a meal, you need to call me Tío. All my friends do," Tío said, grinning to show me his trademark gold incisors.

"I didn't know you considered me a friend," I said.

This dude, Tío, just grinned one more time. "Do you enjoy Italian wines, Max?" Tío didn't wait for my answer. He hailed the owner who'd greeted us. "Bring us a bottle of Gaja's best Barolo."

After Tío allowed the wine to breathe a while, he raised a glass of the most delicious red wine that I'd ever tasted, and he toasted to his 'last day of freedom'. Downing his first glass quickly, he asked me to toast again, and he added, "Salud, amor, y pesetas!"

"What is that supposed to mean, Tío?"

"It means to your health, much love, and prosperity, my friend."

"No, no. I learned about that toast from my dad. What I'm asking is what you meant by your 'last day of freedom'?"

"I will turn myself in to Agent Edmunds tomorrow, and I want you to drive me there," Tío said.

Just like that I learned about this momentous step. After enjoying the osso buco, Tío ordered dessert. "You must have their tiramisu, Max. It is the best," Tío said. He ordered panna cotta for himself.

"So, you're willing to cooperate with the FBI, rather than attempt to return to your former life?" I asked the question, but Tío refused to answer. "Aren't you tempted to return to Diego's organization?"

"Ha. You don't know Diego as I do. When I learned that he'd sent Angelo Calabrese to kill me, I knew I could never return to the corporation, Max."

"When you face trial, I'm certain that Ram Edmunds will do his best to recommend leniency. Ram is an honorable man."

"Max, I doubt that I'll make it to trial. Diego's tentacles reach everywhere. Here, let's finish this bottle of Barolo. Cheers, as you say."

"Once you turn yourself in... Tío, you'll be in federal protection. I don't believe Diego Montemayor can harm you."

Tío grinned, but his eyes were sad. "If Diego wants to get to me, he will."

"By the way," I asked, "have you already spoken to Edmunds? Agreed on a time? The place, et cetera?"

"Don't worry. It's all taken care of," Tío said.

CHAPTER 46

MAX

Chicago, IL · March 13, 2020

I ARRIVED EARLY AT the West Jackson exit of the Chicago Union Station, where Tío asked me to meet him. He was wearing a trench coat and a fedora. He stood out among the crowd, since he carried a yellow umbrella. Without his large pewter belt buckle, I assumed Tío was adopting a new trademark.

"Good morning, Tío. Again, thank you for the awesome dinner last night. I can't remember having a better meal."

Tío Dante grinned. "Please drive me to the Marriott at the Medical District."

"I'll need an address, Tío. Around here, I depend on my GPS," I said.

Without hesitation, Tío patched me through to the earlier call he'd received from Ram Edmunds. The call had been recorded with the address and specific location of their meeting. Apparently, Tío had insisted in meeting at the courtyard of the hotel, an outside patio where they could sit in greater privacy. With the misty, cold weather, they would certainly not have many hotel guests joining them outside.

. . .

When we arrived at the Marriott, Special Agent Ram Edmunds was already situated at a wrought-iron table in the courtyard. He had not removed his topcoat, preferring to ward off the chill and the moisture. At the next table were two carafes and a large platter of what I presumed were pastries.

Tío was so distracted that, as I dropped him off, he barely thanked me. Though he bravely smiled, I detected fear in his eyes.

I proceeded to park across the street. I'd brought my long-range sound equipment in order to listen to the interrogation in real time. I also attempted to record it. I brought into focus my binoculars, which now revealed two federal agents who were sitting inside within view of the courtyard.

The courtyard was heavily treed. However, the branches were bare and soddened by the mist. As he approached Edmunds' table, Tío attempted to scout the surroundings. Before removing his topcoat, Tío placed his accordion container of assorted files and a large brown envelope on the table set up for the meeting. He hung the yellow umbrella on the back of his chair and left the fedora on his head.

As the two men sat for the formal deposition, I noticed from a distance that Edmunds did not offer a handshake. Agent Ram Edmunds took out his large fountain pen, and unscrewed the top. He laid it on the middle of the table. Without any pleasantries, he started. "To follow up with our telephone conversation, Mr. Dante, you indicated you were mixed up with the fabrication of conspiracy theories against the government, and so forth. Is that right?"

Tío coughed into his handkerchief. "My team messed with the right-wing 'Anonymous Cue' phenomenon."

"Let me get this straight," Ram Edmunds said, "you claim to be responsible for the right-wing conspiracy promoted by 'Anonymous Cue'?"

"I hope you are recording this, because I do not want to be misquoted," Tío Dante said.

"You can be certain that every word is being recorded, Mr. Dante."

Grinning, Tío said, "Unfortunately, I am aware of the poor quality of your federal government's surveillance equipment, Agent Edmunds. The products you've bought from China are inferior in today's marketplace. Most of it is faulty... and compromised. You're probably picking up the ambient noise around us. So, I recommend you bring out auxiliary microphones to guarantee maximum fidelity."

"Just proceed by answering my questions, Mr. Dante."

"Very well. Suit yourself." Tío crossed his legs, and attempted to light a cigarette. Ram Edmunds quickly stopped him, pointing to the prominent sign on the exterior wall informing hotel guests that the establishment was smoke free. The prohibition extended to the outside patio. Tío good-naturedly shrugged.

"What I initially stated—for the record—was not that at all. Neither I, nor Diego Montemayor, was responsible for the so-called right-wing conspiracy expounded by 'Anon Cue'. We only claim responsibility for its demise. What I stated in clear terms was that our enterprise ensured that statements made by individuals claiming to be that mysterious source— Anon Cue, or whatever—became laughable and discredited."

"And, how did you accomplish that?" Edmunds asked with a smile.

"Merely by exaggerating every one of his, or their, claims. When they referred to the presence of a 'deep state' that opposed POTUS and his supporters, we simply propagated an easily discreditable description of that 'deep state' being made up of 'Satan worshippers'."

"And, I repeat my question. How did you accomplish that?" Edmunds looked at his watch. Then, he looked away. "Did you invade their blog—take it over?"

"Yeah, our people started by spoofing their communications, then we completely compromised their blogs, websites, even emails." Tío Dante paused. He added, "Agent Edmunds, I get the impression that I'm boring you."

"In all honesty, I fail to see how your grandiose claims relate to the kidnapping or the murder that I'm investigating."

Tío had a coughing fit. Then, he said, "It's all connected, Agent Edmunds."

"Very well. Isn't it true that many who believe in such wild conspiracy theories are the same people who believe in the deep state?" complained Edmunds.

"Of course. That's the beauty, and the charming effectiveness, of the exaggerations. If we can get people who support the present administration to also believe in absurdly wild theories of powerful people who oppose their efforts, then the news media will take care of ridiculing those 'conspiracies'. We simply blow up their claims to ridiculous proportions. And, suddenly, the 'deep state' becomes a fantasy, a myth, which no one believes."

"Okay, what are you saying? You appear to be saying that the so-called deep state does exist, but that your job is to ridicule the notion so that the public will doubt its existence."

"Of course it exists. You may not call it what your president calls it—the deep state, or the swamp, or whatever else he comes up with. But in your work I'm certain you've realized that well-funded efforts control most policy decisions in this country," Tío said.

"And, are you also saying that you and your boss were funding these efforts?" Ram Edmunds asked. "Efforts which strengthened the deep state?"

"Not all of them, but a significant portion," Tío said.

"Correct me if I'm wrong, but you are hinting that your organization controls most of the media," Edmunds said.

"I will provide you evidence, rather than hint, to confirm my claims. The four major news organizations in this country are owned by us and three other... 'families', shall we say? But, that's one reason we create non-profit organizations to shield our efforts."

"Non-profit entities?" Edmunds asked.

"Of course. We're glad to protect the American and European public, Agent Edmunds." Tío grinned as he formed two quotation marks in the air, to underscore the word 'protect'. "A useful tool has been Journalism Matters, a non-profit that presumably ensures the accuracy of information shared through our news sources. When I left Diego's empire, I was promoting other such groups, such as Health Matters, Fair Voting Matters, this group-or-that-group 'Matters'. It seems to work." Tío laughed.

"And these groups helped you discredit the claims of the present administration, Strong's presidency?"

"All we do is accuse President Derek Strong and the White House of saying that all those who oppose them are Satanists and child molesters. The media does the rest," Tío said.

"Are you saying that Anonymous Cue never directly stated such a thing... that all who oppose POTUS are Satanists and pedophiles?"

"Initially, no," Tío said. "Later, even he, they—or whoever it may have included—bought the preposterous embellishments," Tío said.

"Okay," Ram stopped taking notes. He looked at Tío skeptically. "Maybe if I hear other so-called 'embellishments', Mr. Dante. You're not convincing me."

"Anon Cue uncovered much information that many of you in the intelligence community knew, but had either ignored or failed to pursue."

"Whoa there, Mr. Dante. Those are serious accusations against all federal agencies. Be precise. What sort of information?"

"I'm sorry if I offend your sensibilities, but for several years, your intelligence agencies, yours included, have known of various influential donors—people who donate to the campaigns of your Congressmen (and women) and your Executive Branch—who are engaged in child prostitution and trafficking."

"Do you have any names in mind?" Ram asked.

"For one, does Jeff Bernstein ring a bell?" Tío grinned. "Who do you think bumped him off?"

"We've determined that Jeffrey Bernstein committed suicide in a New York prison last August, Mr. Dante. Your claim won't fly."

"Believe what you want, but if you track your friend Calabrese's steps, you'll see his direct involvement in that so-called suicide."

Ram Edmunds fell silent. He changed his position in his wrought-iron chair, and he grabbed a pencil, tapping it rapidly on his legal pad.

Tío continued, "Legitimate reasons may exist for this inactivity on the part of law enforcement, but sources like Anon Cue exposed the truth. We simply stepped in and provided absurd overstatements to ridicule the accusations."

"And who benefited from that?" Ram Edmunds asked.

"For one, his associate and girlfriend, Elaine Sanborn, who was more responsible for child prostitution than he was." Tío cleared his throat. "Other... clients... also wanted Bernstein dead. While in custody, he was preparing to disclose information that would destroy many political careers."

"And who are those clients?" Edmunds asked.

"Like I said, well-known politicians and business associates whom we, um, support," Tío said.

"Do you mean to say that these politicians and influential businessmen are compromised?" Ram asked. "Or... involved in some way?"

"Either directly or indirectly, they're all complicit in accepting our bribes—er, I believe 'contributions' is a more delicate term."

"So, you're saying that through mere exaggeration you discredited information that could convict these corrupt politicians?" Ram asked.

"Yes, primarily through wild overstatements. For example, claiming to be Anon Cue, we stated that a 'Big Storm' was coming which would bring the eventual incarceration of major political figures in Guantánamo and other locations throughout the U.S. We even fabricated dates when these mass arrests would take place."

"And when these failed to happen," Ram said, "the whole Anon Cue phenomenon suffered a slow death."

"Exactly," Tío said.

"And how about the claims that most Hollywood actors are involved in sex trafficking, human enslavement, and even drug trafficking? Did that come from you?" Edmunds asked.

"Only the distortions. As we've learned, many in Hollywood—from producers to agents to actors—have been, and are still, involved. But all we need to do is to plant enough doubt in the minds of popular news agencies, and they run with it. The public then only hears about the preposterous hyperbole."

"So, now it's the followers of Anon Cue, and the ardent supporters of the present administration that have been labeled as deranged, dangerous terrorists, thanks to you and your boss, Diego Montemayor. Is that your claim?" Edmunds asked.

"Not even your poor-quality recorders will record me saying such a thing, Mr. Edmunds. What I stated was that we *made it possible* to discredit this movement to expose the deep state. Diego's organization has deep pockets. Very deep," Tío smiled.

CHAPTER 47

FTER DROPPING OFF Tío at the Marriott, Max parked across the street to have a view of the open courtyard. Ram Edmunds and Tío were seated next to a wrought-iron table ladened with pastries and a pot of coffee. Using the binoculars that he'd bought for the Door County stakeout, Max kept his distance so as not to attract attention.

Since Ram Edmunds was already seated when they arrived, initially Max was only aware of two other federal agents being present. He busily dictated notes to his trusted iPhone recorder. Concentrating on his surveillance, Max was surprised by the tapping on the driver's side window. A tallish, gangly person—dressed as only federal agents dress—smiled and asked Max to roll down his window. The agent was wearing a gray suit under his trench coat, and his ear bud was hanging from his left ear. Holding it against his ear, he held up his right index finger to ask for a moment. As Max waited, he noticed a peculiar twist to the typical agent's appearance. Max could tell that under his waterproof hat, this agent had shaved his head.

Presumably having gotten his remote instructions from the four black Suburban vans parked at the Marriott's curb, he courteously asked Max if he had a reason for casing the hotel building. Max indicated that he was trying to find accommodations and was considering the Marriott. When Max asked the agent for his identification, he amiably provided the information, and asked if Max could return the favor. Max then provided his driver's license. Still smiling, the friendly federal agent indicated that his supervisor, Agent Ram Edmunds, had Max on his safe list. However, he lamented having to ask Max to move on.

Max lied and stated that he was "fixing to leave anyway."

. . .

Max shuffled some papers to kill time. When he saw the agent return to the last of the four vans and enter the vehicle, he remained in his spot. Another agent, also sporting a shaved head, appeared to be at the driver's seat of the fourth van, and they both engaged in deep conversation.

Picking up his binoculars, Max could see that Ram Edmunds was about to take a break. Immediately, two agents came to stand guard by Tío's table.

Although the moisture in the air remained, the drizzle cleared and two solitary rays of sunshine peeked through the dissipating cloud cover. Thankfully, visibility was improving. Max drove out of his space and circled around the block to get closer to the hotel's courtyard. Finding no open spaces,

Max saw that the space he'd just vacated was still open. He decided to park there once again and take his chances with the federal agents.

With the aid of binoculars, Max could see that Ram Edmunds rejoined Tío. Again, Edmunds took out his fountain pen.

Loud static interrupted Max's long-range audio. Max adjusted his microphone. "Will you allow us to refocus, Mr. Dante?" Edmunds asked.

"Of course."

"What does all this so-called influence of our political system, business leaders, and entertainment industry have to do with the crimes that I'm investigating? How are the kidnappings of private citizens and the murder of a federal investigator related to this cartel kingpin you work for?"

"Mr. Edmunds, the cartel leader for whom I *used* to work, Diego Montemayor, not only has enormous power over your country's political system and economy, but he's also responsible for hiring the assassin, the renegade federal agent and your friend Angelo Calabrese. Furthermore, he's responsible for the kidnappings of the two Epstein women."

"By the Epstein women, Mr. Dante, I presume you mean Miró Epstein-Shelley's child Minerva Epstein-Shelley and Miriam Epstein. For the record, am I correct?"

"Yes, I stand corrected," Tío Dante stated.

"Will you please explain how these latter crimes would be so important to a cartel leader with such global influence, as you claim? These appear to be petty and insignificant crimes that pale in comparison to fixing presidential elections and human trafficking."

Tío Dante had another prolonged coughing spell. "To understand, you would need to know Diego Montemayor as I know him. Three years ago, Diego's wife, Yael, died in a hospital fire. Diego blames the American psychiatrist Dr. Nathaniel Shelley and his family for his wife's death. He will not rest until he avenges her death."

"It is well known that Diego Montemayor has disappeared," Edmunds said. "In fact, no one knows if he's still alive."

Mirthlessly, Tío laughed. "He may be working under an alias, Agent Edmunds. But he is in full control of his organization, and he is alive and well."

"Yet, you've previously stated that you were responsible for Dr. Miró Epstein-Shelley's kidnapping. You, Mr. Dante, not Diego Montemayor—I must warn you before you respond that your deposition can and will be held against you in a court of law, should the need arise."

"I'm aware of that," Tío stated. "And, yes I admit to kidnapping Miró Epstein. At the time, my plan was to ingratiate myself with my former boss. I was hoping to deliver her to Mr. Montemayor in Spain."

Ram Edmunds leaned closer to the fountain pen sitting in front of him. He articulated in practiced diction, "For the record, Mr. Theo Dante, better known as 'Tío' Dante, you are willing to plead guilty to the kidnapping of Dr. Miroslava Epstein-Shelley. Is that correct?"

A raspy chuckle from Tío, "Yes, I, Teodosio Dante, kidnapped Dr. Miró Epstein-Shelley." And, then in a whisper, he added, "Was that clear enough for your 'pen', Mr. Edmunds?"

Ram Edmunds ignored Tío's whispering. "And, isn't it also true, Mr. Dante, that on or about the 22nd of September, 2019, you killed federal investigator Angelo Calabrese in the room occupied by Dr. Epstein-Shelley at the Orrington Hotel?"

"I did kill retired federal agent Angelo Calabrese in self-defense. He had been hired by Diego Montemayor to kill me."

"Let the record stand that Tío Dante has admitted to killing Angelo Calabrese."

"…in self-defense," Tío Dante added.

"I suppose you have evidence to support your claim that your murder of Angelo Calabrese was in self-defense?"

"I disarmed Angelo Calabrese, and I used the weapon he intended to use against me, a dart gun concealed in an umbrella. I am certain that your local and state authorities could not determine cause of death. Isn't that correct, Mr. Edmunds?"

"In fact, the cause of death, per our Justice department, was cardiac arrest," Ram Edmunds said.

"Hilarious," Tío said, without a smile on his face, "so, Agent Edmunds, you cannot charge me with killing Calabrese—since the cause of death was a heart attack. You, therefore, cannot charge me with that crime. Is that right?"

"Not so fast. I want to hear your story."

"The reason the DOJ concocted the heart attack explanation," Tío said, "is that they were able to determine that the weapon used to kill Angelo Calabrese was a remarkable toy developed by the CIA years ago. It sounds like the DOJ won't—what's the American expression—'open that can of worms'?"

Ram Edmunds leaned back in his patio chair. "As outlandish as this sounds, Mr. Dante, I'll let you complete your statement. Go on."

"Surely, Mr. Edmunds, you can verify anything that I claim in this deposition. When the CIA was interested in developing a poison that could induce a heart attack, they attempted to find the best toxicologists, biochemists, and botanists in the world, preferably outside the U.S."

"Mr. Dante, I've been a federal agent for many years, and I have never heard of such a project. Nonetheless, go on."

"CIA Agent Angelo Calabrese identified a brilliant Spaniard, a botanist who was still a doctoral student, that became part of a small team of international scientists scattered throughout the globe. Although these scientists never met each other, their experimental results were remotely shared with the entire team." Tío made a dramatic pause, then said, "The person recommended by Calabrese... get this, was Diego Montemayor... and he became the first scientist to come up with the ideal solution."

"Okay. Tell us more." Edmunds got up to serve them both another cup of strong coffee from a carafe sitting on the adjacent metal table. "You stated Montemayor's drug was ideal. Why?"

"Diego's liquid poison could be produced as a frozen dart that completely disintegrates upon entering the target. The lethal poison enters the bloodstream, causing a heart attack. Because the poison denatures quickly, an autopsy cannot detect that the heart attack resulted from anything but natural causes."

"Forgive me, Mr. Dante, but I don't know the meaning of the word 'denatures'."

"I suppose working with Diego for such a long time," Tío said, "taught me a few scientific terms. I apologize. I believe it's a word that means a breaking down of a substance's natural properties. It was a brilliant way for the CIA to get away with murder... literally."

"So, you are telling me that Calabrese—or the CIA— had some sort of gun that could fire the frozen bullets containing the poison? Aren't you taking this directly from a popular spy movie?"

"No, the weapon was developed later, the same weapon I used to defend myself against my attacker at the Orrington Hotel. By the way, I left the weapon in plain sight."

"Mm hmm." Ram Edmunds made another note to have his team verify Tío's latest claim. "To help us trace the weapon, could you describe it?"

"When you review the creation of your own weapons, Mr. Edmunds, you'll find that Diego helped some ballistic experts develop a dart gun that could be incorporated into the webbing of an umbrella. When the umbrella is open, the dart gun can be fired without attracting attention." Tío smiled. "I brought a prototype with me." Tío took his yellow umbrella from the chair next to him and presented it to Ram Edmunds, just like a warrior would submit his sword to the victor—palms upward.

Edmunds took the umbrella. "Your stories get more fantastic by the minute. Forgive my skepticism."

"You might as well hear the rest of my story. Since the firing is completely silent, no one in a crowd can hear it, and the assassin can merely fold up the umbrella and walk away undetected. It may surprise you to learn, Mr. Edmunds, that many assassinations have been carried out by your federal colleagues in this fashion."

"If that is indeed true, I'm certain that every single case must have been justified. Your entire story will be carefully examined... each claim you've made."

"I hope you do, Agent Edmunds. I'm afraid we're merely scratching the surface," Tío said.

CHAPTER 48

"W<small>HEN YOU SAY WE'RE</small> scratching the surface," said Special Agent Ram Edmunds, "what are you implying?"

"I speak plainly, Agent Edmunds. I don't care about *implying* anything. I can tell you that your American State Department is aware of several much more lethal weapons that are being developed today... all funded by Diego's corporation."

"Of course. Our intelligence community is aware of many efforts against our country," Edmunds said. "Whether your boss is funding all of them is a different story."

"In my files—the ones I'm handing over—you will find various emails from federal officials based in China," Tío said. "One cable from two State Department officials warned your country of the Wuhan menace since 2018. The piece that I'm giving you is dated January 19, 2018. Other digital correspondence, calling the specific threat of coronaviruses, will pique your interest. These viral weapons, intended to bring the American economy to its knees, were developed and launched last November in the rural province in China.

It's a form of germ and viral warfare. We're now experiencing its effects."

"China, like many other countries—including Russia—is constantly developing such weapons."

"At least you will grant me that much, Mr. Edmunds," Tío said.

"Your cynicism is annoying, Mr. Dante."

"Please understand, China considers the revised trade deals that have emerged from the present American administration as an act of economic war," Tío said. "The Chinese Communist government simply retaliated by exporting an epidemic of colossal proportions. And, the pity is that your State Department could have prevented it."

"Neither the United States nor the other world powers would allow such a thing," Edmunds said. "How exactly does that incriminate Diego Montemayor?"

Tío shook his head. He said, "I admire your patriotism, Agent Edmunds. I'm telling you that Diego Montemayor's strategy of misinformation is enabling his political and business associates to benefit from the real enemy of the United States."

"China?"

"While Iran and Russia are not our friends, Diego Montemayor's funds are being funneled to the already incredibly wealthy Communist government of China. And the Chinese are developing powerful deadly weapons that will be used against your country."

"So, you're stating that man-made infectious diseases were developed as instruments of war against the U.S.?"

"That's exactly what I'm saying," Tío said, "though the American public has been lulled into thinking China is our friend, Diego's political and business associates are enriching themselves from China's secret war against the U.S."

"So now you're stating that Diego Montemayor is a Chinese agent, a rogue businessman or drug cartel leader in cahoots with the Chinese government?"

"Diego Montemayor is not anybody's agent. It is not that simple, Agent Edmunds."

"Explain then."

"No, Diego Montemayor is not a Chinese agent. If I can be less delicate, I will be plainspoken," Tío said. "For Diego to receive special favors from American politicians and corporate magnates, he buys them off... in different ways. Of course, he makes legal contributions to politicians' campaigns. Other 'donations' may go to their favorite foundations or their favorite philanthropic agencies. Corporate bosses will, at times, set up new start-up businesses, request 'help' with the acquisition of a newer-model Gulfstream, or Airbus."

"So these American politicians and corporate bosses are the ones supporting China. Is that your naïve claim?" Edmunds asked.

"Agent Edmunds, you surprise me. Why do you think so many American businesses opened plants in China? While some well-connected American businessmen were profiting from all those foreign plants, American politicians were supporting Congressional laws that promoted more favorable trade deals with your Chinese 'friends'. Unfortunately, your own Congressional representatives supported minimal tariffs for incoming Chinese products, while ignoring Chinese tariffs on American products that were astronomical. Yet, your politicians looked the other way, while China developed the most prosperous economy in the world."

"And I suppose you're implicating politicians from one political party, correct?"

Tío waved his hands, "Nah... Republicans, Democrats, Independents, they're all in it together, Mr. Edmunds. Greed is not partisan."

"Perhaps those American politicians merely wanted to level the playing field, Mr. Dante."

At hearing this, Tío Dante guffawed. Then he coughed into his handkerchief. "Now who is being naïve, Agent Edmunds? Our China-loving politicians were lining their pockets, while the Chinese economy prospered. And guess who was lining their pockets?"

"I suppose you'll answer your own question—Diego Montemayor?" Edmunds asked.

"Yes, Diego *and* the Chinese. The Communist government officials show even more gratitude to our politicians than Diego himself."

"When you talk of Diego's favors to our government and business leaders, you allude to mega expenses. I know you claim that Diego Montemayor has deep pockets, but the magnitude of his wealth cannot be that monumental," Ram Edmunds said.

"Diego Montemayor's line of business is very profitable." Tío Dante smiled.

. . .

Agent Edmunds rose from the table to stretch his legs. With his back to Tío, he asked, "Off the record, why are you doing this?"

Tío crossed his legs. "Before kidnapping Miró Epstein, I had to figure out who or what she cared for the most. It was not her husband, though she loves him deeply. I discovered by tapping her phone and listening to conversations that her daughter, Minerva, means the world to her."

"That's not unusual, Mr. Dante," Edmunds said.

Tío continued. "I then followed that child for three months. I learned where she attended school, what she enjoyed doing, and who her friends were. I also tapped her phone. And the more I learned about Minerva Epstein-Shelley, the more she reminded me of my daughter, who is now grown. When I left her mom, she was exactly Minerva's age—thirteen."

Agent Edmunds was now facing Tío. He stood still, not wishing to interrupt this ruthless killer.

"To get to Miró, I knew that I had to frighten her by bringing minor harm to Minerva—or Minnie, as she's called. But I couldn't do it. The closer I studied that child, the more endearing she became. I couldn't do it… she reminded me so much of my own daughter, María Luisa."

"So, you discovered your soft spot, Mr. Dante." Agent Edmunds was asking a question.

"You see, María Luisa is… what is the American expression for 'la niña de mis ojos'…the apple of my eye?"

After a long pause, Edmunds returned to the table. He cleared his throat. "We're back on the record now, Mr. Dante."

"Twice now, you've steered our conversation to generalities, to grand schemes supposedly concocted by Diego Montemayor. Yet, the principal reason that we met is to get information regarding the kidnapping of Miró Epstein and the killing of Agent Angelo Calabrese. Could we get back to the two central questions?" Special Agent Ram Edmunds was insisting rather than asking.

"I understand," Tío Dante said. "Ask away."

"Number one, did you kidnap Miró Epstein?" Ram Edmunds asked.

"Yes."

"Did you kill Angelo Calabrese?" Edmunds asked.

"Yes."

"As far as I'm concerned, this case is closed. We can take it from here." Ram Edmunds pushed away from his seat and stood up again.

. . .

"To use your own words, Agent Edmunds, not so fast. Unless you are willing to jeopardize your career, through this deposition you've also learned that, in addition to being a retired federal agent, Angelo Calabrese was a well-known assassin and connected to people involved in organized crime, like myself. Because you did not care to pursue that line of questioning, I will offer information that will reveal the fact that, following orders from Diego Montemayor, the now-celebrated Rosales twins hired Angelo Calabrese not only to kill me, but also to kidnap and deliver Nathaniel Shelley's family for execution."

"Go on. I'll let you finish. When you mention the Rosales twins, are you referring to the individuals Pedro and Macario Rosales, whose testimony led to the imprisonment of El Chato Gómez?"

"The same ones," Tío said.

"Per the press, El Chato Gómez is the biggest international drug dealer—or cartel kingpin—of our generation," Ram Edmunds said. "And the twins were his lieutenants."

"What does the press know, other than what we feed them? Diego has consolidated El Chato's organization with his own. His wealth and power are unmatched." Instinctively Tío reached for his cigarettes. He caught himself and slipped the pack back in his shirt pocket. "The reason that the Rosales twins betrayed El Chato was that Diego got to the twins... and their families. The twins are now Diego's lieutenants."

"In other words, they took your place in the organization?" Edmunds asked. "You probably have ill feelings toward them."

Tío gave Edmunds his customary smirk. "It'll be a long while before someone can replace me in that organization."

"Wait. Aren't the twins under federal protection—the witness protection program?" Edmunds asked, feigning ignorance.

"They were, until Diego came to their rescue. Let's say that he had help from a federal official that is high up in rank. He works in your nation's capital."

"You know, of course, that I'll need to verify that, too?"

"Please do. Don't take my word for it," Tío said. "You also need to know, Agent Edmunds, that I consider the Rosales twins inept and ignorant petty thieves. They are in a position way above their heads. You will soon discover that fact, and it will prove helpful in apprehending Diego Montemayor."

"You mentioned that the twins were charged with the responsibility of delivering Dr. Nathaniel Shelley's family to 'him'—to whom, exactly?"

"To Diego Montemayor personally. I know Diego. He wants Dr. Nathaniel Shelley, Dr. Miró Epstein-Shelley, and their daughter, Minerva Epstein."

"You said, per my notes, that Diego wanted the Shelley family to be delivered to him 'for execution'. Why not have them killed by his hired assassins? In Calabrese's absence, who will execute them?"

"Diego's wife was killed in a hospital fire in the Canary Islands," Tío said. "He blames Nathaniel Shelley and Miró, his wife, for her death. So, he will not rest until he personally burns—until he incinerates—the three members of that family alive."

"How do you know all this?" Edmunds asked.

"When Diego and I last spoke, Diego was still in hiding. He remained in Las Palmas, and he was hiding... underground literally. He placed complete trust in me. So, immediately after his wife died in the fire, he started working on the modification of an old World War II weapon, the flamethrower."

"But you've admitted you betrayed your boss." Edmunds said. His voice rose by two octaves, suggesting incredulity.

"Diego learned that much later," Tío said. "When I went to the authorities, I believed that Diego was following the wrong advice and that he had exposed himself—made himself vulnerable, that is—for his wife's crimes. I thought he was risking the entire corporation."

"Did you see yourself taking over?"

"Not in a million years. I thought Diego would return to his senses when I rescued him from jail. I already had a plan for his escape. But he was never caught."

"And, you mentioned—Las Palmas—is that in the Canary Islands?"

"Yes, it's the capital of the largest island in the archipelago," Tío explained.

"One last thing, you say that Diego went underground... literally. What did you mean?"

"Diego had constructed a large network of underground tunnels in the islands. It helped in various trafficking efforts, both drug and human trafficking. That's where he hid from the authorities, until he was able to travel to Mexico."

"And he began to develop a modified flamethrower down in the tunnels? You must understand, that's hard to believe."

"Agent Edmunds, Diego never does anything half-heartedly. When I say that he constructed a network of tunnels, I mean that this network was sophisticated and even offered a modest degree of comfort. His living quarters, for example, would compare favorably with a low-end Manhattan apartment. In addition, he also constructed an elaborate lab."

"And the flamethrower?"

"Those specifics I cannot describe. He spent a lot of time working on it. Diego only stated that he wanted a more portable, more efficient use of modern technology. I'm not certain what he meant."

"So, you're telling me, if given a chance, Diego Montemayor himself will execute Nathaniel Shelley, his wife, and his daughter—by burning them?"

"Incinerating them is a better term, Agent Edmunds."

. . .

Ram Edmunds started collecting his notes. He summoned the hotel staff to arrange for their departure. For the first time throughout the meeting with Tío Dante, Edmunds made eye contact with his two federal agents, who were sitting inside the lobby. Two waited outside, plus the three drivers present. He signaled to them they could now take Tío Dante into custody.

"While I ask my team to research your voluminous data, Mr. Dante, I will be filing your deposition."

Tío informed Ram Edmunds that he was only willing to deal directly with him or the new DOJ Attorney General. "I fear for my life, and the entire lot of the intelligence community is corrupt, Agent Edmunds. Believe me, I should know. More than half are on Diego's payroll, and the rest are rewarded with promotions by 'the swamp', as your president calls them."

"You won't need to worry, Mr. Dante. I oversee this investigation, and no one will bring you any harm."

"No offense, but you're incapable of ensuring my safety," Tío said.

Ram Edmunds looked away.

"What you need to realize," Tío said, "is that when I incriminate my ex-boss, Diego Montemayor, I will also bring down powerful members of your political and business establishment. Will you be ready to submit this information directly to the new Attorney General, without interference from your superiors?"

"Why is that so critical to you?" Edmunds asked.

Tío asked Edmunds if they could walk inside.

Blowing warmth into his cupped fists, Tío leaned closer to Edmunds. "They will stop at nothing, Agent Edmunds. Even you are expendable. Be careful."

Although Edmunds smiled, Tío knew he'd struck a chord. "I'll be sure to watch my steps, Mr. Dante."

A waiter arrived with the hotel's bill for the meeting. When he left, Tío handed over to Edmunds two files with multiple photographs, financial statements, and countless bank transactions that spanned at least eight to ten years. Oddly, in a thinner file, he also handed Ram Edmunds a plain brown envelope labeled 'For Nate and Miró Shelley. To be opened after my demise.'

"By the way, I thought the twins came to Diego's team after you left? How did you secure these photos and transcripts of their communications, Mr. Dante?"

For the first time during their meeting, Tío flashed a genuine smile. "I may have left the organization, Agent Edmunds, but I retained my skills. My equipment is still cutting edge, and my ability to tap even Diego's communications are intact."

CHAPTER 49

MAX

Chicago, IL · March 13, 2020

WHEN I HAD DRIVEN around the block only to return to my original spot, I noticed that sunshine was now penetrating the clouds, and the misty fog had completely lifted. The agents standing watch outside must have considered me harmless, because they left me alone. It was nearly noon when the agents seemed to move into position. As soon as the deposition was over, the two agents with shaved heads rushed into the hotel grounds to assist with Tío. No longer wearing trench coats, the two bald suits escorted Tío out of the hotel lobby. Though Tío did not appear to be handcuffed when he exited the courtyard, it seemed that he was wearing ankle restraints or ankle monitors. The taller, lankier agent took Tío by the arm, while the other shaved head seemed to pull Tío from his coat lapels.

A minute later, Ram Edmunds exited the lobby and walked alone in the opposite direction to his vehicle, a large black Chrysler 300. Edmunds' driver quickly pulled out into traffic. The suits hurriedly led, almost dragged, Tío to the third black Suburban. They shoved Tío in the back seat and signaled to the two government vans in front of them to drive on ahead. The lanky agent went to the driver's side of the third vehicle, apparently to give the driver last-minute instructions. Then, he and the other agent who had led Tío to the van, boarded the fourth and last Suburban in the caravan. They drove off in unison.

Without considering the flow of traffic, I'd foolishly parked in the wrong direction. As I attempted a turnaround, I realized that I had lost the motorcade. It appeared they were headed toward the major exchange of Interstate 290 and I-90. Attempting to catch up with the caravan, I sped through the first intersection. At the next one, a traffic light flashed red, and I screeched to a stop.

At the opposite corner, what appeared to be the fourth Suburban in the caravan was stopped by the curb. The motorcade of three vans raced ahead, but the fourth van had come to a stop. The bald, lanky agent got out of the van and looked in the direction of the speeding motorcade. Then, I noticed something shift in the agent's eyes. They narrowed, squinted almost, giving him a crazed, maniacal facial expression. Like a rabid dog snarling and salivating, he uttered something I could not hear. He held his cell phone, leaned forward, and used his forefinger as if to speed dial someone. Two seconds later, a blinding light up ahead, followed by a deafening boom, told me the man had detonated a massive bomb.

Instantly, the air was thick with smoke, and I could hear nothing but a ringing in my ears. I had instinctively ducked down, fearing that my windshield would not withstand the force of the explosion. I brought my head up to discover my vehicle's windshield was intact, but a wicked stench permeated the streets. As I scanned the scene, the first thing I noticed was the fourth Suburban charging in the opposite direction. The gangly agent and his driver were gone.

For the next few moments, I can only remember a slow-motion image of brick, stone, and body parts raining down from the sky. As the smoke cleared, I could see up ahead where the caravan had been, nothing but a smoking crater on the wide road. The traffic light for which I'd stopped had been blown off its mounting. Nothing moved, and the high-pitched ringing in my ears became louder.

Like other drivers stranded on the road, I left my vehicle and walked toward the scene of the explosion. Like speechless zombies, we slowly walked and brushed off the falling debris and the ash that was still heavy in the air around us.

As I walked, I remember checking myself for cuts or bruises on my face and limbs. I had no apparent wounds. Some of my fellow zombies approached others who'd been closer to the explosion and were on the ground. They helped them to their feet. A few were bleeding, and others resisted being moved.

I'm not certain why, but tears were streaming down my face. *They got to him*, I thought. The motorcade had been hit, and Tío had been right. Just as he thought, they'd gotten to him before he got to trial. I found the nearest intact curb and took a deep breath. *Do I need to see it?* Fighting an instinct to flee the area, I walked toward the sound of loud sirens approaching the scene. I was approximately ninety feet away from the crater.

To my astonishment, camera crews and TV cameras from CNBS were already there. A reporter was interviewing a young woman sitting on a curb, not far from the twisted metal and debris. Acrid smoke still rose from the asphalt where the major impact had occurred. The reporter beamed into the camera and described the woman on the curb as a young university student. As the reporter thrust the microphone at her, the woman, still in tears, attempted to speak. I got close enough to hear that she'd been struck 'by a flying body part.' She could not go on.

CHAPTER 50

Evanston, IL · March 13, 2020

L IKE MOST IN THE country, Minnie's school was undergoing much change, compliments of the COVID restrictions. Although the Ursuline Academy of Evanston prided itself on its personalized academic excellence for its all-female student body, reluctantly the board had accepted an adjustment in educational delivery methods. The news outlets were engaged in a full hysteria mode, announcing forecasts of millions of deaths in the continental U.S. alone. Thus, all teaching would be done online until further notice.

This imposed enormous sacrifices not only on educators but also on the students' parents, most who were professionals with busy schedules. Since Miriam had retired to dedicate more time to family, she took on the major portion of the supervision of Minnie's schoolwork from home. Miriam would arrive at the Shelley home at 7:30 AM and stay until 6:00 in the afternoon, when either of the Shelleys returned.

Max, on the other hand, had been busy but vague about his latest outings in the pursuit of information gathering. Since Miriam suspected that Max did not want to alarm the other members of the family regarding his present activities, she kept her suspicions to herself. On at least two occasions, she had overheard hushed cell phone conversations between Max and someone else with a name mysteriously sounding like 'Leo', 'Cleo', or—God forbid—Tío. She wondered, *If Max is speaking to Dante, why should he conceal it from his family? Is Max planning something careless, irrational, or worse?*

That morning, Max left before 7 AM, stating that he would be in the city most of the day. Again, he'd been uncharacteristically evasive and secretive.

Early that afternoon, Miriam received a frantic call from Max. He'd been trying to get a hold of Abraham but had been unsuccessful. Max informed Miriam of the downtown explosion and added that he thought Tío Dante had been killed.

"If you turn on the news, I'm sure they're reporting on it," he'd said.

Before Miriam had a chance to find the remote to the mounted TV in the den, the doorbell rang. A mysterious-looking stranger dressed in black was impatiently leaning on the annoying buzzer. "I'm coming; I'm coming."

Winnetka, IL · Two weeks prior to explosion

In addition to the purchase of the two safe houses in Winnetka, Estevan had been responsible for securing an unconventional toy for Rodrigo. While Rodrigo occupied most of his own time planning for his move against Tío in addition to the training of the slow-learning twins, Estevan traveled to Michigan to secure Rodrigo's gift to himself.

Since Christmas, Rodrigo had become interested in purchasing a commercial tour boat that was moored in South Harbor, Michigan. When Estevan asked for his motivation, Rodrigo only responded by saying that the boat would enable him to bring to closure a stage in his life.

Requesting Bruce Jones' assistance, Estevan traveled across Lake Michigan to South Harbor. Immediately, Estevan was impressed by Rodrigo's choice. Evidently, Rodrigo had discovered online a replica of a nineteenth-century sloop by the name of *Friends Good Will* that was for sale.

Though most sloops of the time averaged sixty feet in length, the *Friends Good Will* was larger. It was at least a hundred feet from bow to aft, and it mounted almost forty guns. The vessel had two large well-appointed cabins, with the aft master cabin having its own WC with shower compartment. It had large wardrobes and ample lockers and storage. The fore cabin, though smaller, was similarly appointed. The deck, or floor, from bow to aft was done in teak, but there was an impressive raised deck saloon which was, of course, covered. Its special deck was done entirely in fine mahogany.

A tall bar complemented the bow side of the deck saloon. The bar, however, had dual fronts which allowed those inside the covered compartment to access beverages as well as those on the exterior foredeck, which took up almost a third of the entire vessel. The open foredeck could easily serve as a sizable dance floor. The massive single mast, measuring three and a half feet in diameter, dominated the center of the outer bar, which served to separate the bar into port and starboard bars, each accommodating five bar stools.

From the present owners, Estevan learned of the ship's famous history. Through the skilled interpretation of his new friend Bruce Jones, he learned that during the War of 1812 the British navy had unlawfully confiscated the American merchant ship which gave the replica its namesake. However, the following year U.S. Commodore Oliver Perry recaptured the ship and quickly reported to his superiors, "We have met the enemy and they are ours."

Estevan read the bronze plaque which quoted Commodore Perry's famous dispatch, and he understood. The small sailing warship with a single mast—a charming sloop—would serve as the theatre where Rodrigo would complete his final act of revenge against the Shelleys.

Knowing Rodrigo's motivation, Estevan completed the purchase on the spot. He had the vessel's cover removed for winter repairs and maintenance. The complete up-rigging was performed within six days, and he had the boat transferred to Belmont Harbor on the northwestern side of an inlet of Lincoln Park in Chicago.

When Estevan gave Rodrigo the good news, Rodrigo wanted to see it immediately. He was forced to wait until it was docked, and ten days later, he set foot in his galleon, as he preferred to call it. The boat came complete with period attire. Even Commodore Perry's uniform was hanging next to the main, and only, mast. By the time he and Estevan left, he had renamed his ship *The Black Pearl*, after the legendary, but fictitious, Spanish galleon.

Estevan signed, '*Why* Black Pearl?'

"Because," Rodrigo said, "black pearls are symbols of hope for wounded hearts."

Winnetka, IL · March 13, 2020

Rodrigo had awakened at 0400 hours. It was still dark in Winnetka, but he joyfully prepared his own coffee without awakening Estevan. Feeling completely invigorated, he walked the grounds of his magnificent safe house complex. The other two large buildings housing the twins' individual families were still dark.

He walked the full length of the oval track that he'd constructed and covered with synthetic rubber over an asphalt base. Macario's twin boys enjoyed their morning jogs before their tutor arrived for daily schoolwork. Though Rodrigo walked briskly, he balanced his coffee mug without spilling a single drop. That's what tai chi had done to hone his equilibrium.

Fully energized, Rodrigo celebrated the arrival of March 13. He had meticulously planned for this day. It would commemorate thirty-nine months since his wife Yael had died in that disastrous hospital fire. But instead of it being a day of mourning, it would be a day of celebration. His day had arrived. It would be the day he would avenge his best friend's betrayal, as well as his wife's death. His best and final day in America would be his swan song, his final performance as Rodrigo Díaz, and his return to his beloved Europe where he would triumphantly return as Diego Montemayor.

CHAPTER 51

MAX

March 13, 2020 · Hours after explosion

HOURS LATER, I TELEPHONED Abraham to describe the explosion and Tío's ambush, but he'd heard the CNBS breaking story. When he was having lunch in his downtown office, Abraham said a TV newscast reported that a federal prisoner, 'Theo' Dante, had perished in an explosion. Per reports, medical personnel were examining DNA evidence that was splattered all over the blast's vicinity, but it could take days to determine victims' identities. Law enforcement officials could only confirm that the caravan that was transporting the federal prisoner also included seven federal agents. Oddly, of the four government vans in the motorcade, they could only identify the twisted and melted metal of three federal vehicles. They could not account for the fourth van.

"I assume CNBS has not made the connection," Abraham said. "But that was Miró's kidnapper."

"Yes, I was there," I said. "Well, I was close by, I should say. I'd driven Tío to his deposition with Ram Edmunds."

"You had done what, Max?" Abraham asked.

"I didn't want to worry you and Miriam, Dad."

"I had no idea you'd gotten to know Tío."

"Like I said..."

"You may not know this," Abraham said, "but Rosenfeld called after the CNBS report to tell me about some curious details. It appears the Feds believe that the two agents in the fourth van of the motorcade are also missing. Of course, they believe the driver of Tío's vehicle was killed, as well as the other four agents in vehicles #1 and #2. However, they can't find traces of the fourth van, or its occupants."

"Dad, what are you saying?"

"Rosenfeld believes that Tío's van was targeted. There is conclusive evidence that Tío died in the explosion, but, per hospital personnel, there is very little evidence anyone else was in his van."

"Hmm." I then added, "Yeah, I clearly saw two agents escorting Tío to the back seat of the third black Suburban, but they got into a fourth van in the motorcade. It's logical to assume someone was in the driver's seat of the third Suburban."

"Plus, no one can account for those two other agents..."

Again, in disbelief, I said, "How's that possible?"

"You tell me, Son. You're the PI."

I attempted to contact Ram Edmunds, but it was impossible. I drove directly to the FBI office building and left messages on his desk. Of course, I had little hope that the head of the Chicago field office could make time to reach me.

Later that afternoon, I walked into a bar and ordered a beer and a burger. However, I'd lost my appetite. In fact, I was nauseated, and even the normally appetizing aromas seemed repugnant. Reluctantly, I left my food and drink and drove to the Chicago Tribune office building.

Doubting that I'd find Rosie at his desk, I walked into the news pit anyway. The workaholic rushed over to greet me. His caffeine breath suggested he'd be wired for many more hours.

"How do you feel about today's events, Max?"

"I'm saddened. I can't say the world lost a model citizen, but..."

"It can be confusing. But, in the end, we all want the guilty to be brought to justice. I do have a feeling, however, that this man's testimony would've brought down extremely powerful people in our country," he said.

"If there's any truth to Tío's stories, this country's political system is steeped in corruption, Rosie."

He adjusted his thick glasses on the bridge of his nose. "Sadly, I see it every day, and half of it I cannot report."

"Listen, can I pick your brain for a minute?" I asked.

"I'm trying to finish this piece. It'll be a huge feature..."

"It'll only take a minute," I insisted.

"Okay, have a seat." Rosenfeld had to remove piled notes from the seat he offered me. He just turned to a corner of his desk and dumped the stack there.

I remained standing. "What's your theory on the missing FBI agents?"

"I was about to ask you the same thing. But my gut tells me that they were dirty cops... I can't print that, though. I have nothing to go on."

"And, you think they were responsible for the bomb?"

"Max, do you know something I don't? Because there is no evidence of a bomb. My sources tell me the Feds are still speculating—a drone, perhaps some sophisticated electronics, but they're not sure it was a bomb."

"I can't be certain. But I was there, a block and a half away from the explosion. I drove Tío to his meeting with Ram Edmunds. When I followed the Feds' motorcade, I was detained at a traffic light. Then—please don't quote me on this—I think I saw the fourth van of the Feds' caravan idling across the street. An agent... the one that had tapped on my window when he thought I was casing the hotel where the deposition was taking place... he stepped out of the van with a cell phone in his hand. When he pressed a single key, the explosion went off..."

"Holy communion. Are you sure?"

"No, I'm telling you, Rosie, I'm not certain about anything. With the explosion, I think I went into temporary shock. It's all blurry... I can remember sketchy details. For a while, I couldn't hear anything, just a ringing in my ears. It lasted about ten minutes. With the black smoke and the ash falling from above, I'm not sure I could see clearly either. Several buildings, they were damaged and pieces of concrete and brick were still falling from the sky, and... I'm sure I saw flying body parts when I stumbled to the scene of the explosion. I had to shake ash from my hair and clothing."

"You're sure, though, that you heard an explosion, right?" Rosenfeld asked.

"Of course, I'm certain of that."

"And, the man you saw across the street, are you sure it was the same federal agent you'd seen earlier?" Rosenfeld asked.

I paused. I had to admit that I wasn't certain. I told Rosie that I'd driven around aimlessly, not knowing what to make of what I'd seen. I told him I'd stopped for a beer and walked for an hour. After returning from the walk, I'd forgotten where I'd parked. I told him how I'd wept, not fully understanding why. So, I was trying to make sense of things.

"Nothing makes sense to me, Rosie."

"Full disclosure. I've recorded part of our conversation," Rosenfeld said.

I repeated that I didn't care and that nothing made sense.

"When you said you thought some dirty cops transported Tío, you think they killed him?" I asked.

"More than likely, but who knows?" Rosenfeld said. "Just my gut instinct."

CHAPTER 52

March 13, 2020 · Day of the explosion

AFTER THE EXPLOSION, MACARIO raced to the rendezvous point where he and Rodrigo would abandon the government Suburban and pick up a different vehicle. It was a rental from Acme's Ugly Duckling company that specialized in renting older-model panel vans. Estevan had recommended a less conspicuous, nondescript cargo vehicle that would attract less attention.

By the time they transferred vehicles, Macario was weeping. Rodrigo grabbed Macario's suit jacket and pinned him against the dirty side of the van.

"Listen to me, Mudo, I will not have you behaving like a woman. Man up, and comply with your side of the bargain. We still have work to do before the federales figure out what happened."

Macario wiped his eyes and opened the front door. Before his boss came around the side to climb onto the passenger seat, Macario found a box cutter on the front seat, which he slipped into his back trouser pocket. He used the vehicle key to crank the engine, but he needed to repeat the action twice before the engine started.

As Rodrigo adjusted his seat belt, Macario said, "You didn't see how Pedro suffered after the surgery. You told him his recovery would last a day or two, but it took several days, and I took care of him. He was in excruciating pain for five days. The scar on his chest was eight inches long and it almost got infected. He said it even hurt to breathe. I had to change his bandages twice a day... and now, he's..."

"Look, his body was obliterated instantaneously. He never felt a thing."

"That's a lie. When the blast happened, my own insides felt as if I was on fire. I had to gasp for air, and it hurt. I think I felt what Pedro felt..." Again, tears rolled down Macario's face.

Undoing his seat belt, Rodrigo grabbed Macario by the neck and slapped him across the face, twice. "If you want me to keep my side of the bargain—if you want your family to survive this—you better stop your whining and pray that the final part of the plan succeeds."

Macario turned to look at Rodrigo, and he was certain that he couldn't hide the rage he felt toward his boss. He averted his eyes to hide his feelings from him. Macario wiped his tears, and he asked, "Should I drive to Lincoln Park?"

"Of course, Mudo, we've gone over this plan a million times. I activated the second phase of the plan, once we confirmed that the detonation of your... the detonation of the bomb was successful."

"So, right now Estevan is…"

Impatiently, Rodrigo interrupted, "As we speak, Estevan is breaking into the Shelley home. He is taking Minnie hostage. And since we know that Max was outside the Marriott during Tío's interrogation, we can be certain that Miriam Epstein is taking care of her granddaughter. Estevan will deliver Minnie to us."

"What will he do with the grandmother?"

"Don't you worry about Miriam Epstein. Estevan will take care of her." Rodrigo smiled.

"So, explain to me again what our police contact will do?"

"Keep your eyes on the road, Macario. You're following too close behind that SUV. The last thing we want is a fender-bender."

"Okay, okay. Tell me how Detective Finn will help," Macario asked.

Rodrigo rolled his eyes. "It's his job to bring to us the good Dr. Nathaniel Shelley and his wife Professor Miró Epstein-Shelley."

"Yeah," Macario said, "but how will he do that? It could get messy, you know."

"Don't you worry your scrambled brain, Mudo," laughed Rodrigo, "everything will go according to plan."

Chicago, IL · March 13, 2020

Although the news reports had not come in, the explosion had occurred merely minutes before. The slight tremors and the sound of the blast had been heard for many miles, but few in the CNA Center, where Nate's office was located, had felt a thing.

Emily Farnsworth came into Nate's office and told him he had an urgent call. Learning that Nate could take the call, she patched it through.

"This is Detective Finn, Dr. Shelley. I would not disturb your workday if I did not think this is important."

"Go ahead, Detective. What is it?" Nate said.

"I hesitate to say too much on an unsecured line, but I believe that you and your wife should come meet me in my office so that I can provide details. What I can say is that we've recovered the missing CCTV footage."

"You mean the part of the video that was missing when my daughter and mother-in-law were kidnapped?"

"Exactly. And, frankly, I'm worried for your family's safety. The missing recording reveals the identity of the twins' handler."

"Well, we know the twins are still at large. Don't we need to start there, Detective?" Nate asked. "And, what do you mean by the word 'handler'?"

"In my line of work, the handler is the manager of a perp, you know, the one who pulls their strings," Finn said.

"Anyway, if we can identify their handler, we can get to the twins."

"At this point, we believe we have a pretty good idea who the man behind all this might be," Nate said.

"Believe me, the rest of the CCTV recording clearly tells us... And it's not who you think it is," Finn said. "Please meet me here in my office, Dr. Shelley." Finn ended the call.

Rushing out, he announced to Ms. Farnsworth that he needed to meet with Detective Finn in his office. Since Nate had been scheduled for several meetings in two different places in the central business district, he'd driven his own car rather than taking the train. He picked up Miró at her university office and together they drove to Detective Finn's office on Ridge Avenue in Evanston.

As they arrived, Finn was waiting at the front door. He hurriedly led them down the front steps of the building to his car.

"I thought you wanted us to see the missing video, Detective," Nate asked.

"Got it right here. You can both view it on my laptop while we drive to the spot where you, Professor Epstein-Shelley, were held for several days while you were unconscious." Finn opened the back door of his police car and asked them both to sit in the back seat. He explained they could watch the missing video together.

. . .

The drive to Lincoln Park took thirty minutes. The entire way, Miró and Nate had a difficult time viewing the prized video that Finn had promised. First, Finn claimed to have difficulty sharing his password; then, he feigned downloading the wrong copy. Finally, Finn simply said, "Well, we're almost there anyway. It's best that you see it with your own eyes."

Nate and Miró looked at each other. "Detective, could you tell us where exactly we're going?"

"I told you, Dr. Shelley, we're headed to the place where your wife was held when she was kidnapped. The place itself will provide all the answers you need."

When they entered Lincoln Park, Finn drove a short distance and parked haphazardly against a barricade at the end of the access road. In silence, he led them up a dusty footpath lined with umbrella pines. The wet and cold afternoon wind caused the larger pine branches to sway away from the lakeshore.

Past the footpath, Finn directed them into a mowed patch of grass. He pointed to a waist-level sign at the end of the lawn, which announced that they were approaching Belmont Harbor, one of the largest on Lake Michigan. The crushed red granite track led to a drawbridge welcoming people to *The Black Pearl*, a single-masted ship of approximately 100-foot length.

Walking onto the track, the sound of Finn's steps on the crushed granite scared a colony of gulls that had been looking for bread crumbs. They seemed to fly off in formation. Although there was no one within sight, when the three climbed onto the deck of the ship, they could hear two voices on board. A male voice was asking, "What is he saying?"

The response was, "That he took care of the grandmother."

As they climbed the drawbridge, Detective Finn took Miró by the elbow. When they reached the deck, Finn tightened his grip and led the Shelleys to the bow, or front, of the vessel. Walking past the wall of the raised deck saloon, they turned the corner and saw the spacious open area. The foredeck took up almost a third of the sloop's length.

As they turned the corner, Nate turned to Finn with the realization that they'd been lured into a trap. Miró froze.

"Welcome onboard!" an animated Rodrigo said, "…and to my production."

Twenty feet in front of them, on the opposite side of the deck, the starboard side, atop a makeshift stage sat Minnie, who was gagged and tied to a chair. Macario, the young man with a shaved head wearing a rumpled, dusty suit was holding a gun to her head. On the stage, next to her was an empty chair.

"Dr. Shelley and Professor Epstein-Shelley, I am Rodrigo, your host. I should thank my good friend, Detective Finn, for transporting you to my seafaring vessel, *The Black Pearl*. As you can tell, I have prepared a small stage for you at the far end of the starboard deck."

Rodrigo was standing between the recent arrivals on board and the stage. To Nate, Miró, and Finn's left was an extensive bar covered in mahogany and accentuated in the middle by the ship's mast. On one side of the bar, nearest the threesome stood a man dressed in black, who stood ramrod straight and perfectly still.

Rodrigo continued with his introductions. "The man standing over your daughter is Macario, and he is my assistant. The man standing by the…"

Suddenly, Miró broke free from Finn's grip, and ran to her daughter. Running past a surprised Rodrigo, she approached Minnie and instantly removed the cloth stuffed into Minnie's mouth. Ignoring the man holding the gun to Minnie's head, she knelt in front of her daughter and asked, "Baby, have they hurt you?" The man whom Rodrigo called Macario didn't make a move.

"Mom," Minnie whispered, "they've got Grandma at home. That man standing by the bar… the Asian… took Grandma down to the basement." Minnie looked at Estevan. "After coming onboard, using nothing but sign language, he told the other bald person behind me that he took care of her. What's that mean?"

"I don't know," Miró said. "Did they hurt you?"

Minnie just shook her head. Glancing up toward Macario, she said, "I think he's one of the two who kidnapped me and Grandma."

Smiling, Rodrigo tried to regain control. "Before being rudely interrupted, I was about to introduce my executive assistant, who is standing by the bar on the near side of the mast. His name is Estevan."

Rodrigo, who also wore a rumpled, dusty gray suit, appeared to be unarmed. He smiled graciously. "You have a smart child there, Professor. She was quick to recognize Macario, although he didn't have a shaved head back then." He approached Miró from behind and politely motioned for her to rise from her kneeling position and return to her husband's side at the opposite side of the foredeck.

"Allow me to set the stage, and I want you to have the best view. So, I want you standing exactly twenty feet away," Rodrigo said. "Allow me to introduce my supporting cast. As we stand here, facing the stage, the four of us— Detective Finn, you, your husband, and yours truly—we have front-row seats. As I said before, when we face your daughter, who is center stage, we have on our left, and by the bar, my trusted assistant Estevan. He is holding a gun to his side. Of course, in most stage productions, weapons are harmless. In our case, weapons that you see are definitely loaded and quite lethal."

"Release my daughter, Rodrigo," Nate said.

"Why are you doing this?" Miró asked.

Ignoring their questions, Rodrigo continued. "I believe that your daughter has already identified the young man standing by her side on the stage. As you know, that would be Macario... also armed."

Miró asked, "And, you, what role will you play?"

"Well, I'm the star of the show, and although I should need no introduction, in your country I am known as Rodrigo."

"Why are you doing this?" Miró asked again.

"I'm not finished. You, of course, have already met Detective Finn, who is temporarily here in the front-row. However, he doesn't know it, but he's got a small, but important, role in the show itself."

Finn seemed to narrow his eyes and looked in the direction of Estevan. Then he gave an inquisitive look at Rodrigo.

At this point, Estevan caught Rodrigo's eye. He tapped his watch twice.

"I do not have much time, so we must start the performance," Rodrigo said. He commanded Estevan to make the next move with a nod of his head.

Without warning and with an outstretched right arm, Estevan moved swiftly toward Finn. The detective snapped his head in the direction of Rodrigo, "What is he doing?" Holding his gun to Finn's head, Estevan grabbed Finn by the arm, but Finn shook free.

"I wouldn't do that, if I were you," Rodrigo said. "I suggest you do what you're being told."

Estevan shoved Finn, took the detective's gun from his holster, and forced him to walk up the stage. There, without any further objection from Finn, he motioned to the detective to take the empty chair next to Minnie.

"No," Rodrigo said, "Move the chair at least eight feet away from the girl."

"My name is Minerva, or Minnie, not 'the girl'," Minnie said.

Rodrigo smiled and turned to the Shelleys, "Smart and with spunk, eh?"

A frightened Finn remained standing by the empty chair. His expression had changed from curiosity to terror.

While Estevan was pointing the gun at Finn, Rodrigo added, "Now sit, Finn."

"Boss, wh... what are you doing?" Finn pleaded.

Ignoring Finn, Rodrigo instructed Macario to take from the floor of the stage the same cloth that Miró had taken out of Minnie's mouth.

"Now, stuff it in Finn's mouth," Rodrigo said.

After slipping his gun in his waistband, Estevan proceeded to strap Finn to the chair.

"Your turn, Macario," Rodrigo said. "Take this beautiful couple next to me and walk them over to the mast. Then tie them."

As Macario slowly descended from the stage, he came forward toward Nate and Miró. Nate, ever the student of human behavior, noticed Macario's momentary glance toward Rodrigo. To Nate, it was an unmistakable look of hatred. *Could it be that Macario is Rodrigo's weak link?*

After finishing with Finn's triple layer of thick rope, Estevan again took his gun and stepped off the stage. Macario, in turn, took the rope hanging on a hook and tied Miró to the mast. Macario was about to gag her, but Rodrigo stopped him.

"There's no need for that," Rodrigo said. Then, addressing both Shelleys, he said, "Though you will no longer be front-row center, consider it the opera box of the theater. You will be slightly to the side of the center stage but closer to it."

From the stage, Minnie noticed that her mom had immediately started to strain to free herself from the ropes. She saw how her efforts immediately chafed both her hands and her ankles. Suddenly, her mom stopped her wriggling and writhing because Estevan gave her a menacing look, and he slowly shook his head.

Still at gunpoint, Nate stood perfectly still. Macario took the rope and proceeded to use less rope for Nate. He only used two layers of rope. *Did he run out of rope, or was that intentional?* Nate thought to himself. Macario forced Nate's arms behind the mast without making eye contact. Nate then felt Macario place a flat, thin metal object the size of a pencil between his middle and index fingers. He carefully held the object in place with the folds of the second layer of rope. While Macario remained standing to Nate's right, he faced straight ahead toward the stage. Estevan stood next to Miró on the other side of the mast.

"I suppose you would say you have an even better view," Rodrigo said. Still smiling, he added, "I'd like to give you a demonstration of what my plan for you is—one, by one." Chuckling, he added, "A rehearsal, you might say."

Although he was not standing on the platform where Finn and Minnie were tied, Rodrigo had moved to within ten feet in front of the platform. He was merely five feet away from Nate and Miró, who were now to the side.

Rodrigo extended his left arm and pointed toward the four members of his audience—the Shelleys as well as Macario and Estevan. He held a magician's wand on his left hand and pointed it like a bayonet. Then, theatrically, he extended his right arm toward the platform where Finn and Minnie were seated. "Now, pretend that I am at the center of the clock and my wand is pointing toward the 9 on the face of the clock. My right hand will be pointing to the 12. You, my dear audience, will be tempted to concentrate on the wand, but the magic will occur at 1200 hours, where you see the actors on the platform."

Rodrigo had created his own theater stage. He was, indeed, standing front and center, and if the makeshift theater had had its own lighting, the spotlight would have been on him.

"Do you remember how you killed my wife?" Rodrigo asked.

"If you're referring to Yael Montemayor's death three years ago, you must be the husband. You must be Diego Montemayor," Nate said. "But you are mistaken. Your wife started that fire on her own. She set the hospital and herself on fire, rather than face prosecution. We were not responsible."

"My wife had no reason to commit suicide."

Suddenly, as if in a trance, Diego—aka Rodrigo—assumed the dramatic pose of a master illusionist. Grabbing the black cape of Commodore Perry, which was hanging on the mast next to Miró, he clipped it to his suit coat lapels and extended both arms in the direction of Detective Finn on the platform. It was as if he intended for Finn to take a bow. Then, Rodrigo stood front and center and extended his wand to the audience. Like a madman, he splayed his right hand and fingers outward toward the stage, as if performing a magical act. From the inside of his wrist, a tiny aperture in the thick leather bracelet opened and out of it emanated a single laser beam which instantaneously seared a gruesome, dark crevice and a smoldering flame in Finn's torso. The flame rapidly expanded upward as his gurgled screams penetrated the air. They were louder than Minnie's cries.

Oddly, although Finn was seated on a wooden chair, the laser-like flame burned his body with hardly a singe on the chair itself. The laser-like flame was surgical in its precision.

Macario remembered the sound that he and his brother had heard when they first witnessed Rodrigo's diabolical weapon in action. As he was incinerated, the detective's flesh made the same frying sound that an insect makes when it's electrocuted by a zapper. The sound galvanized the air and the foul smell of burning flesh nauseated him.

"Allow me to apologize," Rodrigo said to his captivated, but terrorized audience. "It happened so quickly that I suspect you failed to appreciate the process. Let me explain. Normally, when someone dies in a fire, the most common cause of death is either the extreme heat or asphyxiation from the smoke produced. With the use of my device, I've made certain that the victim will die in the most painful way possible. As you could tell from Detective Finn, there was little smoke. Mr.

Finn was fully aware of his skin tearing away from the rest of his body. And, he was certainly aware of his own fat and muscles inside of him sizzling and shrinking. Even his internal organs shrank from the extreme heat. As you can tell from his skeleton, the bones closer to his abdomen burned at a higher intensity because of the ample fat in his gut. The bones of his extremities, however, are darker because they burned at a lower intensity. I guarantee that he felt it all."

Macario silently wept. He could now appreciate the indescribable agony his brother Pedro had endured. He also knew he could not watch the thirteen-year-old be incinerated in the same way.

During Rodrigo's diatribe, Nate had discovered that the metal object Macario had placed behind his back and between two layers of rope was a box cutter. He used it to start cutting through the thick layers of rope. Suddenly, he felt a warmth flowing down his forearms behind him and realized that his own blood was trickling down his trousers and onto the deck. He'd cut himself in his desperate efforts. *You need to distract Rodrigo,* Nate told himself. *Direct his attention to your face. Show fear, beg for mercy.*

"For the love of God, please spare us," Nate pleaded. "Please have mercy on us, Diego," he cried again.

It was at that moment that Miró realized her daughter was in a panic. She had never seen Minnie in such a state. When she looked at her on the stage, she noticed the puddle that had formed under her chair. Minnie had lost control of her bladder.

"Oh, no, Dr. Shelley. This is for *my* own entertainment. I've been planning this for more than three years," the crazed man in the cape said.

Then Miró understood the thing that Minnie had observed from her vantage point. Her daughter had noticed that Nate also had a puddle beneath him, but it was his own bleeding that was staining the deck. Then, from the corner of her eye, she noticed a movement from Estevan who was next to her.

Fortunately, Estevan was catching Rodrigo's eye, and tapping on his watch more forcefully.

"Ah, yes," Rodrigo said, "my consiglieri tells me I don't have much time. All right, we shall do this in an organized manner. Your daughter Minerva will be the first to go. Being the gentleman that I am, I will then proceed to you, Madam Epstein-Shelley. Then, after you've witnessed your loved ones perish, Dr. Shelley, you will be the final act of my performance."

As Rodrigo assumed his theatrical stance and extended his right arm toward Minnie, his fingers began to slowly flay upward.

Macario remembered that the splaying of Rodrigo's fingers would activate the tiny aperture which would release the laser-like flame. If he was going to make a move, it would need to be now. In one single motion, he took his own gun and stuck it in the small of his back. He then leapt toward Rodrigo.

Estevan was not quick enough. He reached toward him, but Macario was already airborne. Arms outstretched,

Macario's body flew in front of Rodrigo as he activated the aperture to his wrist gadget. The lethal beam had been released, and it struck Macario's chest.

Nate would later describe how his vision was blurred when he saw a body leaping in front of him toward Rodrigo. Miró could only comment on the horrible frying sound of burning flesh, because her eyes had been shut in prayerful sorrow. On her part, Minnie simply said she never opened her eyes. She was afraid to open them only to discover that she would be in heaven with God.

Not knowing whether he would witness his daughter in agony, Nate, who was still immobilized by the rope, only saw Macario's pile of charred bones two feet in front of Rodrigo. He also saw the steam emanating from the burning flesh and smoldering bones on the floor.

Rodrigo held his left forearm, apparently hurt. His screams indicated he was in extreme pain. Evidently, the ricocheting beam of fire not only incinerated Macario Rosales, but must have been reflected onto Rodrigo's forearm, giving him second-degree burns. The heat also destroyed Rodrigo's gadget.

Not noticing the blood at Nate's feet, Estevan rushed to his boss's aid. He did not hesitate to attend to Rodrigo's burned arm. An unearthly howl penetrated the air. It was Rodrigo's reaction to Estevan's removal of the melting bracelet from his forearm. His torched epidermis was peeling off his forearm.

Within minutes, Estevan virtually pulled his boss away from *The Black Pearl*. Bolting from the scene, the production director and his assistant left the theater for the rest of the cast to fend for themselves.

CHAPTER 53

MAX

Skokie, IL · Day of the explosion

L ATE THAT EVENING, I drove—no, I meandered—
to my temporary home in Skokie. Driving along
Lakeshore Drive, I questioned my thoughts. I
drove up the North Shore as far as Lake Forest and back
to Skokie. Random and unrelated ideas invaded my focus.
A profound confusion filled my head. Other than Rosie,
I had not spoken to anyone for the rest of the day. I had
not listened to news reports, nor did I intend to. I was
hopeful that I wouldn't face Dad and Miriam for a replay
of the day's events. Not only was I confused, I felt wearied,
drained, and empty—emotionally and physically exhausted.
I had no energy to reexamine the many details and possible
motivations of people involved. Though exhausted, I knew
I wouldn't be able to sleep.

My mind wandered to random and disjointed
thoughts... the possibility of my overstaying my welcome in

Dad's home. I'd been at my dad's for almost five months. Though gracious, I wondered if Miriam's smiles at the breakfast table were becoming cool... Was it more logical to find an apartment in Evanston, since I spent so much time at my Evanston church and at Nate's and Miró's?

Was I getting too comfortable with Dad's hospitality? After the first forty days in Chicagoland, Miriam had suggested that I quit paying rent for my Austin apartment. My dad agreed. They provided a bedroom upstairs that was more like a small suite. I had my own bathroom and even a 'kitchenette' as Miriam called it. Although I didn't have a stove, I did have a small fridge, a microwave, and enough small appliances to prepare a gourmet meal. I'd transported my own flat-screen TV from Austin, so I made use of the loft upstairs to allow us all some privacy when needed. But Miriam was such a great cook that I seldom prepared my own meals. Other than heating leftovers from restaurants I'd visited, the three of us usually enjoyed our family meals together.

On the other hand, since Miriam hired weekly help from a housekeeper that took care of laundry and basic household cleaning, I had offered to pay for her salary... Was I trying to feel justified? After all, Dad and Miriam had refused any monetary help.

When I arrived, Dad's home was empty. No cars in the garage. I looked for messages at the kitchen counter. Nothing. The small message chalkboard hanging on the mudroom wall was also clean. I immediately text messaged my dad, "Where are you?"

I waited for his response upstairs and stayed up going over the day's events. At my desk, I reviewed the written and audio-recorded notes that I'd taken after leaving Rosie's office. The secondhand desk that I'd bought from my pastor at the Evanston Vineyard Christian Church dominated my living space. It's where I conducted my research. Well-used, the wooden desk not only served to hold my laptop and electronic equipment, but it served as my dining table when I had my private dinners. Had I grown complacent and spoiled? Maybe too comfortable and too spoiled. Had I become one of those middle-aged sons who've returned home to mooch off his parents?

I fell into a twilight sleep, and I suddenly awoke two hours later. Too exhausted to write in my notebook, I voice-recorded several questions:

1. Who detonated the explosion that killed Tío?
2. Why?
3. Who were the federal agents that took Tío into custody after Ram Edmunds' interview/deposition?
4. Where are the two missing agents?
5. How about the driver of Tío's van?
6. Is Ram Edmunds complicit?
7. Where are Dad and Miriam?

After falling asleep, I awoke before dawn, and I realized my iPhone recorder was still on. I turned it off and quickly dozed off.

Within a few moments, as if awakened by an alarm, I jumped up from bed. Dad had not responded to my message. *Where is he? Where are they? It's not like them to be out this late.*

Without putting my shoes on, I immediately went through the entire house, almost certain that I'd find it empty. As I walked by the mudroom again, I realized the door to the basement was ajar. I turned on the overhead light bulb at the landing, without bothering to turn on the fluorescent light of the unfinished basement. I hurried downstairs. There I discovered an empty chair and a filthy rag that had been used for oil changes... and additional stains that appeared to be darker and fresher. Two zip ties that had been cut were also on the floor. Then the blood stains that led to the staircase became visible against the burnished concrete flooring of the basement. In a rush, I returned upstairs for my cell phone and dialed Dad's number.

He answered the phone after two unsuccessful tries. "They got to my Miriam, Son. She's gone." I asked countless questions, but Dad was unable to answer any of them. He only knew she'd been shot with a 9-mm gun at short range. He said he'd been walking the grounds of the North Shore Hospital in Skokie.

I drove there immediately in my Cherokee Jeep, and before getting to the hospital's parking garage, I identified him walking down Gross Point Road. I don't think he knew where he was. I got out and asked him to get in the SUV. Unable to say anything, Abraham just gave me an empty look and sobbed.

CHAPTER 54

Corsica, France · Late March, 2020

THE EVENING OF MARCH 13, Estevan and Rodrigo hurriedly left Chicago and drove to Mexico City. Although Rodrigo had initially intended to use his private plane to leave the country, he had correctly assumed that all airports—especially private ones—would be closely monitored by authorities after a major attack on federal vehicles. Before leaving Chicago's metropolitan area, Estevan stopped to buy medical supplies—acetaminophen, Telfa pads, Polysporin, and petroleum jelly. Both men abandoned the rented panel van at the Richard Daley Park off Stevenson Expressway and transferred over to Rodrigo's Land Rover. On the drive south, they listened to multiple news reports of the 'calamitous explosions' in Chicago which had taken 'countless lives', including the lives of at least four or five federal agents.

'Don't you think by now they would have traces of Pedro's body?' Estevan asked, via handwritten note.

"That was a massive explosion, and his body was immediately obliterated. They may never find traces of his body," Rodrigo said.

Stopping only to fill up, change Rodrigo's bandages, and eat on the run, both men arrived in Mexico City two days later. They abandoned the Land Rover at the airport and took the next commercial flight to Rome. From there, Estevan flew to Berlin and Rodrigo to Frankfurt. The plan was to allow Rodrigo maximum opportunity to rest, while Estevan made his way to join him at a local gasthaus in Frankfurt.

Before leaving, however, Estevan realized they needed to supplement their wardrobes. COVID masks had become obligatory in most of Europe. He left an ample supply with his boss.

Unfortunately, though Rodrigo rented a small room in Frankfurt, he was unable to get any rest. Sleepless, he shaved and waited for Estevan to arrive. Satisfied they were not being followed, they both proceeded with the original plan to make their way to the southern tip of France by separate routes.

Taking every precaution, they traveled a circuitous route to their destination. Each man rented a vehicle and drove different routes to Geneva. Arriving in Switzerland a day before Estevan, Rodrigo flew commercially to Madrid and back to Paris.

In the meantime, Estevan flew directly to Marseilles to prepare for Rodrigo's arrival. He immediately traveled to the safe house in Corsica to prepare the staff and do last-minute training of personnel who would be attending to Rodrigo. He supervised their preparations but dedicated the rest of his time to the monitoring of federal investigations related to the Chicago bombing. He especially surveilled the work of Special Agent Edmunds, who seemed to be informed of Rodrigo's modus operandi. At any sign of danger to his boss, he would modify Rodrigo's travel schedule and his subsequent escape.

Arriving at Orly Airport at half past ten on Saturday the 21st of March, Rodrigo took a cab to the Gare de Lyon at 1400 hours and took the high-speed-rail (TGV) to Marseilles. He had only been able to catnap fifteen minutes at a time since he left Chicago. On his train ride to Marseilles, however, he napped for two full hours. Unfortunately, he was awakened by a nightmare in which a vicious snarling dog dropped an opened letter at his feet. Startled, he awoke without knowing the content of the letter.

For the next hour and a half, he tested his laptop's secure connection to Estevan. Satisfied with the results, he signed off and permitted himself the simple pleasure of admiring the colors of the French countryside—the sapphires, reddish browns, and deep yellows. The blurs that flashed by reminded him of his home on the cliffs of Las Palmas.

When he arrived in Marseilles, the bald, lanky stranger strolled the streets of the city's central district, traversing streets in both directions, using techniques he'd developed throughout the years to ensure he was not being watched.

Convinced he was not being followed, he stopped for dinner at Une Table au Sud where he ordered the large prawns, or the langoustine, accompanied by a bottle of rich Pouilly-Fumé. It was the first meal he'd enjoyed since leaving his safe house in Winnetka. After dinner, Rodrigo purchased first-class accommodations at the ferry terminal for the overnight crossing to Corsica.

The ferry arrived before dawn. When he, along with the other passengers, filed off the ferry, it was unusually breezy and cold. He stopped at the nearest open bar to warm himself with a cup of strong coffee.

The half-opened windows of the bar welcomed Rodrigo with a smell of lavender which filled the air. Rodrigo drank the first cup and asked for a second order with whatever pastry was available. Taking the first bite, Rodrigo realized the croissant was stale. Disappointed, Rodrigo connected with Estevan, 'Can you arrange for transportation?'

Almost immediately, the encrypted response read, 'Stay put. I'll dispatch a car to pick you up.'

Three cups of espresso later, an older man, driving an even older Fiat Chrysler Jeep, picked him up. He wore a classic Irish cap, which had become popular in certain parts of Italy. They drove along the coast of the island, but headed inland after a few minutes. The roads were lined with olive groves and pine. As they climbed the mountains, Rodrigo could smell the same lavender fragrance.

Prompting some conversation from the subdued driver, Rodrigo asked "Is the smell of lavender always in the air?"

The driver responded, "Yes."

Rodrigo waited for more explanation. After several moments, he asked, "Where does it come from?"

"The macchia," he said. As he eyed him from the rearview mirror, the driver noticed Rodrigo was still clueless. "The macchia is the brush, the dense growth of evergreen shrubs like rosemary, lavender, and God knows what else. It covers the countryside of the entire island."

Although Rodrigo owned the safe house which he would occupy for the next few weeks, he'd never been there. Several colleagues or clients, including well-known American politicians, had occupied the property many, many times. As they approached the town of Bonifacio on the southern tip of the island, the driver turned onto a short road and entered a gate which led to a winding road up an incline.

The ancient and majestic limestone buildings were roofed with red tiles. His driver stopped at the largest building, which had large stone steps leading up to the main entrance.

"You act as if you've never seen it," the driver said, "but they told me you owned it."

"You're right. I've never been here," Rodrigo said. Acting every bit as impressed as the average tourist, Rodrigo grinned as he climbed the steps and entered his temporary residence. He walked into the airy foyer with travertine flooring and heavy oak furniture.

As he trailed behind, carrying the two pieces of luggage, the malnourished driver stopped to ask for further instructions from Rodrigo.

"Just leave the bags there," Rodrigo said. "I should know this, but do you work for me, or were you simply hired to drive me?"

"I only drove you. I've been paid... and I wouldn't work for you. I don't like you."

"What makes you say that?" Rodrigo asked, curious rather than bothered.

"I don't know how you make your money, but you have a dishonest face." Without anything else, the driver put his cap back on, turned around and left.

. . .

The stubble on his head reminded Rodrigo that he had not applied a razor to his scalp since leaving Chicago. Though back home he got a daily shave from Estevan, Rodrigo had only facially shaved twice while on the road. He had a three-day beard, and he felt unkempt and unclean. His grimy look, however, enabled him to pass for a typical European traveler.

Rodrigo found his bedroom and proceeded to bathe and groom himself at leisure. He found his liquor cabinet and served himself a brandy to cut the chill in the air. Taking his first sip, he walked to the large kitchen. Though his fridge was well-stocked, he wondered if he was supposed to fend for himself. No one seemed to be present.

He took out his laptop, and used the secure connection to Estevan. 'Where's my 'Corsican Estevan'? Don't I have a staff here?'

Less than a minute passed, then Estevan responded, 'Where are you?'

'What do you mean, where am I? I arrived over an hour ago. No one greeted me,' Rodrigo wrote.

Again, Estevan asked, 'Where are you?'

'I am sitting alone at my dining room table, drinking a mediocre brandy. But there is no one else here.'

An encrypted message came back. 'You may be sitting at a dining room table, but it is not yours. The brandy is not yours either, Rodrigo.' A few moments passed. Then, 'Did you enter through electronic gates guarded by two men?'

'We entered through a gate, but it was not electronic. No guards either.'

'Ha, ha, ha!'

'It's not a laughing matter.'

'Sit tight. Chicho will come get you.'

Less than five minutes later, a uniformed driver was knocking at the door.

Rodrigo opened the door, drink in hand. The driver grinned, and said "Il padrone, eh? I'm Chicho. Follow me."

"Wait," Rodrigo said, "all my things are here."

"Don't worry. I'll get your things later. Come, you've got more than enough things—that are yours—at the main house."

Two miles down the road, as they approached the main electronically controlled entrance, two guards waved at them. They were armed, but relaxed. Their smile was genuine.

From Chicho's vehicle Rodrigo could see his splendorous complex—or was it a single structure—constructed in a U-shaped plan. It was a stone structure, seemingly pink granite. It was atop a taller and steep hill. Mouth agape, he exited the vehicle. The front door was open and he could see from the outside that there was full permeability between the inside and the back gardens. Indoors, Rodrigo could see overlapping arches and stairways. The porches seemed to be as wide as the outside gardens.

"Padrone, you didn't go far enough," said Chicho. "Beyond the gardens, you'll find the Mediterranean Sea."

"So, who owns that first house?"

"Some time ago, you sold that first house to an English couple that visits only during the summer. The house is usually empty. No view, no charm. But la dimora, your palazzo, is to die for." Chicho kissed his fingertips and tossed them up in the air.

"You mean I raided someone else's liquor cabinet, and bathed in someone else's tub?" asked an amused Rodrigo.

"Sì, you did," said Chicho.

As they entered the marble entrance, Alessandro and Federico greeted them. While Chicho stood at the entrance, Alessandro, smiling good-naturedly, said, "I heard you stopped to greet the neighbors. I'm Alessandro, your bodyguard and valet."

Extending his hand, Federico added, "Since you've met Chicho and Alessandro, allow me to introduce myself. I am Federico, and I hope to become your favorite chef. Estevan has already shared with me your favorite recipes. In addition, although I cannot compete with your extensive knowledge of wines, I attained the level of master sommelier at the Association de la Sommellerie Internationale. From time to time, I will, if you allow, recommend a wine for your approval."

"So, it will take two of you to make up for Estevan's role, eh?" Rodrigo asked.

"It appears that way," said Federico.

As if on cue, Estevan entered the room. He looked refreshed and clean-shaven. He wore his favorite linen clothing. Using sign language, he asked, *'How's your burn progressing?'*

"It's well. I change my bandages often," Rodrigo said.

'I've been setting up our electronic communications,' Estevan explained. *'You will be pleased with our control room.'*

"If you will allow me this brief interruption," Alessandro said, "Federico and I will leave you to more important business to be discussed with Estevan. Allow us to give you a short tour of your palazzo."

Both men started by pointing to the extensive collection of Spanish and French Impressionist paintings. The Picasso, Miró, and Cézanne works dominated the public areas.

Federico led Rodrigo to the floor-to-ceiling windows in the great room. "When you entered," said Federico, as he pointed to the fence, "you probably noticed the outwardly aimed security cameras surrounding your formidable steel fence. It was what you... and Estevan... requested before your arrival."

As he walked toward the front entrance, Rodrigo peered outside and pointed to the Baroque fountain decorated with the bronze face of a Roman god. "Whose face greeted me when I arrived?" Rodrigo asked.

"Estevan also wanted the bronze decoration on the fountain added before your arrival," said Federico. "It's Vulcan, the Roman god of fire."

"And the Roman statue of Pluto in your marbled entrance hall was also Estevan's request," Alessandro added. "As you probably know, he's the Roman god of the underworld."

"Hmm," Rodrigo said. "Nice touch, my friend." He turned to Estevan, who was standing by a large Italian tapestry that led to the gallery filled with Greek and Roman statuary. Most were antiquities of museum quality.

After a brief peek into the gallery, Alessandro guided them upstairs to a formal drawing room, which had a grand piano, a bar, and a small library. Comfortable Mediterranean furniture adorned the center of the large airy room. As he walked toward a set of floor-to-ceiling French doors, Rodrigo noticed that Alessandro was preparing him for another visual delight. In a sweeping motion, he opened the French doors and stepped aside.

Rodrigo stepped out onto the palazzo's magnificent rooftop terrace. The enormous terrace overlooked his expansive gardens. Beyond his manicured gardens, a red-granite cliff descended in a precipice that led to pink-tinged sandy beaches a mile below. There, away from the zenith upon which his estate was located, the aquamarine-blue waters of the Mediterranean Sea completed the palazzo's canvas in all its splendor.

Numerous gas heaters burned the chill from the sea breeze. Rodrigo stood there soaking in the setting of the Mediterranean sun, mesmerized by its beauty.

Estevan eventually invited him back to the drawing room. On his way to see his downstairs master bedroom, an extensive library captured Rodrigo's attention. Newer copies of the botanical and biochemical reference books, which he'd left behind in Las Palmas were stacked on the shelves. Estevan had ordered wisely. An anteroom to the bedroom contained his cache of electronic communication. He noticed that several screens fed into the main computer.

Federico added that they could leave the tour of the wine cellar for a later time, but Rodrigo insisted in descending downstairs. Estevan remained in the 'control room' to respond to emails. Down in the cellar, Rodrigo picked up the first dozen bottles, and texted Estevan on the secure connection, 'Tell me again why you had not insisted on my visit to Corsica earlier?'

The response came immediately, 'I did on several occasions. Each time you told me you had too much work to do.'

Indeed, his palazzo was far more impressive than the previous house he'd first entered. It even made the Winnetka safe houses look like second-class accommodations. Rodrigo was pleased.

CHAPTER 55

Skokie, IL · April 3, 2020

"**I** KNOW THAT I'M calling at an ungodly hour, Dr. Shelley, and I beg for your forgiveness. However, I just received a call from Picard at Interpol," said Inspector Sánchez. "I must offer my condolences for the loss of your mother-in-law, Miriam. I know how much she meant to you."

"Thank you, Inspector. I appreciate your condolences. And, you're not calling at an inopportune time. I haven't been sleeping much lately," Nate said.

It was 5:15 in the morning, Chicago time. Nate had been tossing and turning in bed since 2:30 AM, and he couldn't go back to sleep. Truth be told, he welcomed Inspector Sánchez's call to save him from his latest bout with insomnia.

"I hope that I'm not using bad judgment, but Picard shared additional information regarding your entire family's dreadful experiences during the last three weeks. He tells me that you're all under federal protection," Sánchez said.

"I believe that I have additional information that you may consider important, but please let me know if I lack prudence in overloading you with extraneous matters," the inspector said.

"Please go ahead, Inspector. No apologies required."

"Our conversation may require that you have at least one cup of your favorite caffeinated beverage. I'll be glad to wait," said soon-to-be-retired Inspector Eduardo Sánchez. "It's almost noon here in Las Palmas, and I've had four cups myself."

"I'm walking to my kitchen, and I'll set my Keurig to the strongest level. No need to wait. We can chat as I prepare my French roast."

The inspector proceeded at the caffeinated pace that suited his alertness. He explained that Diego Montemayor had reappeared in Europe on or around March 17.

"This may sound remarkable, but I did not recognize photographs of the man they identified as Diego Montemayor. He looked nothing like my goddaughter's former husband," Sánchez said.

As Nate took his first sip of coffee, he said, "Forgive me for interrupting, Inspector, but FBI Special Agent Ram Edmunds from the Chicago regional office believes that Diego went through extensive facial reconstruction and limb lengthening surgeries. The man that accosted us is younger, taller, and extremely dissimilar to the FBI's file photos."

"I'm glad you are confirming what Director Picard is saying. Interpol acquired a computer program from Israel that deciphered the mystery man's identity. And, now, Picard has information regarding a person of interest arriving in Europe at the Frankfurt airport. Though he flew in via Mexico City, Interpol believes that this man had been in the U.S. for a short time."

"Any information on his departure date from the U.S.?" Nate asked.

"Interpol believes that Diego left North America on March 15 or 16, 2020."

"On March 13, Tío Dante died in an explosion here in Chicago," Nate said. "It's also the day that my mother-in-law was slayed, and the day that he attempted to kill the three of us."

The lack of verbal follow-up from Inspector Sánchez suggested to Nate that he was already familiar with the Shelleys' misfortunes in the U.S. However, it appeared that Sánchez was uncharacteristically uncertain how to proceed. Sánchez helpfully explained that Interpol had discovered that Diego, under an alias, had amassed an even greater criminal network than he'd possessed before. Evidently, Diego now controlled more than eighty percent of the world's drug trade, as well as most of the world's illicit human and weapons trafficking. Known in cartel circles only as 'Rodrigo', international law enforcement experts had assumed he was European, but no one had certainty. Without any trace of a previous identity, historical record, or past... the new kingpin had suddenly appeared from out of nowhere. No intelligence agency—not the Israeli's, not Interpol, nor the Americans—had had a clue.

Nate listened politely, but he had learned from Ram Edmunds much of what Sánchez was describing.

"If I can impose on you for a while longer," the inspector said, with his typical Spanish courtesy. "Picard needs your help. He's using me as a conduit, because he believes your lines are compromised by... American agents. Though he believes this conversation is tapped, he is depending on what he calls 'plausible deniability'."

"Interesting that Picard would need my help," Nate said. "Somewhat flattering."

"You don't need to provide an answer, but he'd like you to consider whether you trust Special Agent Ram Edmunds." Without additional conversation, Inspector Sánchez simply said, "Have a blessed day, Dr. Shelley." He disconnected the call.

CHAPTER 56

Skokie, IL · April 8, 2020

I F MAX HAD PREVIOUSLY been impressed with the resiliency of the Epstein and Shelley households, he was overwhelmed by the courage and strength that he witnessed after the death of Miriam Epstein. The members of the family, of course, experienced the grief in various ways. Ironically, though, each in his private mourning turned to Abraham, who arguably would have had the greatest need for sympathy. Yet, it was Abraham's spiritual solace that he found in God that allowed him to comfort and guide each member of the family to stability. Even Nate, who admitted to having a shaky spiritual foundation and who described his condition as being shipwrecked, seemed to find his spiritual footing that allowed him to walk on solid ground. Max, too, had been affected, but he found his own place by edifying and honoring each member of the family as he battled through the sorrow.

The Shelleys—Nate, Miró, and Minnie—rang the doorbell. Abraham called out, "Come in; the door's unlocked."

Minnie pranced in and rushed to her grandfather's side for a hug. She did a perfect pirouette, and posed as if she were being photographed. Then, she stepped into the kitchen.

"My, my, Minerva." Max turned from the osso buco dish he was preparing for their family dinner. "Each day you look more and more mature. What a great outfit, and a matching face mask to go with it. That's you, Minnie, chic and safe!"

"Thank you, Uncle Max. I think you've become my biggest fan," Minnie said.

"I don't know about that. From what I hear," Max said with a smile, "those boys at Notre Dame High School are viciously competing for your attention. You've got some devoted fans!"

"Oh, Max, please..."

Abraham chimed in from the hallway, "Yes, Liam and Calvin are the heartthrobs at the top of the list, Max."

"Stop your teasing, Grandpa! Maybe we should start talking about A-r-a-b-e-l-l-a, a certain staff member at a certain Evanston church?"

"Oh, pray tell us, Minnie," Abraham said. Then he turned to Max, "Is there a certain love interest in the horizon, Max?"

"Okay, okay, let's call it a truce, Minnie Mouse," Max said.

"You know how I hate that name, Uncle Max."

"Truce, I promise. Truce," Max said.

Minnie and her mom had mail-ordered a reddish-tan corduroy jacket from 12th Tribe, that went perfectly over her black tank top and faded jeans. It matched Minnie's hair color.

Although Minnie and her mom enjoyed their shopping at the outdoor mall, COVID-19 had ended their monthly outings.

"I've got to take a photo of you sporting your new outfit," Abraham said, already approaching, camera in hand, to do just that.

"First, one of you," Abraham said, as he motioned for Minnie to pose by 'O'ahu', what Max had nicknamed the huge granite kitchen island. Abraham took five different poses. "Now, a couple more with your uncle at the stove."

"Grandpa, my hair's a mess," Minnie said.

"Mi'jita, you are never 'a mess'. You're the most beautiful thirteen-year-old on this planet," Abraham said, without a trace of doubt in his voice.

Nate walked into the kitchen. He took off his light jacket, and revealed his flowered beach shirt and light Dockers. Nate warmly greeted Max and Abraham. He placed two bottles of Bermejo Seco in the wine fridge

"Oh," Abraham asked, "are we in character, Nate?"

"Excuse me?"

"Isn't that you in 'sleuth mode'?"

"Oh, that," Nate said. "I've changed into my beach attire after work almost every day for the last two months. I am definitely in sleuth mode, as you call it."

Meanwhile, Miró was detained at the entry foyer, taking a call from one of her colleagues at work. An assistant professor, who was up for tenure, had decided to call her—his department chair—at least twice a week to update Miró on his 'unbelievable' accomplishments. At least three of his articles would soon be published in three major journals. As she walked toward her dad's living room, Miró, responded, "Thank you for keeping me abreast, Milton. Listen, I'm in the middle of something. But do take care. Have a great weekend."

Nate asked Max, "So, you're taking over chef duties at the Epstein household, eh? You trying out the recipe for osso buco that you had at Marco's?"

"No, after enjoying that meal with Tío Dante, I found Miriam's recipe for the dish. The recipe sounds like it may be even better than the one at Marco's. Y'all be the judges."

Abraham added, "Max claims it's all in honor of our sometimes-friend, Tío Dante."

Since the risotto was done, Max left the veal braising for a minute. He joined everyone in the living room. Abraham had opened one of two bottles of Barolo that he'd bought for the occasion. As Max walked in, Nate seemed to have the floor. He stood by the fireplace and faced everyone.

"I will open by saying that I had a fascinating conversation with our friend, Chief Inspector Sánchez from the Canaries. While visiting with his friend, Gabriel Picard, Sánchez discovered critical information that will concern all of us. I've had a couple of short conversations with him since then."

"Just to make sure, is that the dude from Interpol?" Max asked.

"Yes, Picard is the Deputy Secretary General of Interpol, based in Brussels," Abraham said.

Nate continued. "Picard believes Diego Montemayor left the Western Hemisphere and may be on his way back to Spain, or at least somewhere in Europe. Although he flew out of Mexico City, Interpol believes that Montemayor had been in the U.S."

"Do the dates coincide?" Max asked. "When do they think Diego was in the U.S.?"

"Though Interpol cannot pinpoint the dates, they believe that on or about March 14, Diego Montemayor traveled from the U.S. to Mexico City. He then took a commercial flight to Rome or directly to Frankfurt."

Miró asked, "So, does it sound like he might be anywhere in Europe?"

"Right. Despite undergoing several facial surgeries, Montemayor was identified by airport security cameras in Western Europe, the last being Germany," Nate said. "Since he set foot in Europe, he's been in different locations, sometimes two or three in a single day."

"It seems to me," Abraham said, "that Picard would have sufficient influence on our intelligence community to coordinate with Ram Edmunds' office."

"That's just it," Nate said. "Picard and our new Attorney General are in communication. Picard, however, cannot communicate directly with the Chicago field office of the FBI."

Max had to return to the kitchen to check on the veal. Miró followed him and asked her brother if he needed assistance. She returned to the living room with another bottle of Barolo. After refilling everyone's glass, except Minnie's, she threw up her arms and said, "So, that's charming. Our own Attorney General will not permit Interpol to have access to the Chicago field office of the FBI?"

"The interference is not coming from our Attorney General," Nate said. "Someone in the FBI's Washington DC office is blocking that communication."

"We must be in serious trouble if our own Department of Justice cannot penetrate that web of secrecy," Abraham said. "What on earth is going on?"

"I don't know, but I intend to find out," Nate said.

Tapping the Waterford goblet with a silver spoon, Max summoned all to the dining room. As they all ambled over toward the inviting aromas, Abraham reminded them, "I'm invoking my patriarchal authority here, so there will be no political nor law enforcement discussion at the table... until we finish with dinner and dessert. Let us pray."

. . .

Max apologized for not having the time to prepare dessert. Instead, at the last minute, he'd run to the neighborhood deli and purchased some ready-made cannolis.

"Like always, everything was delicious." Abraham was about to say that it was as good as Miriam's, but he stopped himself.

"Miriam's recipe is even better than the one used at Marco's Restaurant," Max said. "Her recipe is more citrusy."

"That's because she always doubled the amount of lemon zest in the gremolata. You approve?" Miró asked.

"Yum," Minnie said. "Abuelita was the best cook in the world."

Abraham had left the table and was going through his ritualistic handwashing of everything before starting the electric dishwasher. From the kitchen, he interrupted Minnie with a loud, "Ahem... Minerva."

"Oh, what I meant was that Grandmother *and* Mom *and* Uncle Max are the best cooks in the world!"

With a broad smile, Miró acknowledged the correction. "Thank you, Minnie."

While Abraham warmed two snifters, Max ran to the kitchen for one last cannoli.

Abraham was finishing preparing the cognacs when Max walked into the kitchen. Caught in the act of sneaking one last cannoli from the pastry basket, Max said, "Y'all, I always follow Clemenza's advice. 'Leave the gun; take the cannoli'."

Taking Max aside, Nate whispered, "Would you like to travel to DC tomorrow?"

"Sure, Nate. What's up?"

"I've set up a meeting at the FBI headquarters in DC. I need to find out what's going on, because at this moment I still fear for our lives," Nate said, biting his lower lip. He quickly took the stool by the kitchen island. As he sat, he added, "I've kept it from the rest of the family, Max, but this time, I feel completely exposed. Not only are we facing the danger of a ruthless criminal—who's still out there—but federal law enforcement appears to protect him. Who's protecting us?"

"Okay, break it up, you two," Abraham walked in with two snifters. "Here's a little Hennessy for your digestion. Quit all this secrecy, and join us in the living room."

Nate and Max followed Abraham into the living area. Minnie was in the far corner playing a soft rendition of *If I Fell* on the piano.

Miró spoke up. "I believe it's time for you to set up a meeting with Ram Edmunds. I know he's still overwhelmed with this whole mess, but I think he can now make the time to see us."

"The media has brutally attacked him for losing a man who was in his custody," Abraham said. "I can't blame him for being overwhelmed. He still can't account for his two missing federal agents."

"That's another matter that I learned yesterday," Nate said. "I finally spoke to Ram, and he floored me with this one... The men—three special agents who are missing—had just been assigned by the DC office for one specific purpose. Ram says one of the three agents assigned by the DC office was driving the principal van carrying Tío—the one that was targeted by the bomb. But he can't account for the two other agents, or the van they were driving."

"And, why were three agents assigned by DC?" Miró asked.

Nate's right eye twitched. "Edmunds told me his superiors from DC specifically directed him to use the assigned agents to take Tío into custody after the deposition. Evidently, they were going to deliver Tío back to Washington DC."

"Honey, I don't like it. Who are these people protecting?" Miró asked.

"Listen, everyone, when we've done all we can do, we then pray," Abraham said. "We pray."

"Agreed," Nate said. "But, in addition to praying, Max and I must attempt *to do* a few more things. We've got a long day ahead of us. Come on, Miró and Minnie. I'll share some things on the way home."

. . .

Driving home, Nate explained that he and Max were traveling to the nation's capital to meet with the FBI's deputy director. After briefly complaining, Miró finally agreed that some information gathering was in order.

The following morning Nate and Max arrived at Reagan National Airport. After checking into the Willard, they took a cab to the FBI headquarters.

Surprisingly, the Deputy Director of the FBI, Jacoby Homely had agreed to a meeting. Though the appointment was set for 2:30, a stern-looking administrative assistant summoned Nate in at 3:15. When Max got up to join him, she asked, "Are you joining Dr. Shelley?"

"Yes, I am," said Max.

"Your name, please."

While Max identified himself, Nate informed the young assistant that he had specifically provided information regarding Mr. Kempball. The officious young lady ignored Nate.

A pompous presence, Homely walked into his own office from a side door. Not only was he taller than Nate, he towered over Max. "When you set the appointment, Dr. Shelley, you indicated that you wanted to discuss the events that led to the Chicago explosion. It was an unusual request. Frankly, the only reason that I agreed to meet you was to extend a common courtesy. In addition, I also learned that the deceased international criminal had been involved in your wife's kidnapping."

"We appreciate your time, Director Homely. Let me explain my deep concerns…"

"You must understand, Dr. Shelley," Homely was obviously used to interrupting people mid-sentence. He proceeded as if he were delivering a lecture to college freshmen. "You must understand that the work of our national headquarters is to provide operational support for our field offices, like the one in Chicago. Because we were dealing with a known international criminal, I assigned three of our best agents from our local office to take custody of this dangerous man, Theo Dante."

"Did Special Agent Edmunds request help?" Nate asked.

"It was my call. Frankly, it does not surprise me that such a terrorist action was taken against Dante and our agents. Many criminals wanted him dead—competing drug lords, betrayed business partners, and God knows who else. All these people are dangerous. Ruthless. And, they will stop at nothing to silence their enemies. Unfortunately, not only was this animal's life lost, but the law enforcement community lost seven heroic federal agents."

Max chimed in, "Director Homely, your own field office in Chicago, as well as other authorities, can confirm that only five federal agents, including the driver of the Suburban transporting the prisoner, perished in the explosion. Two agents are still missing."

"The sheer force of these explosives can be beyond anyone's imagination, Mr. Kempball. I hear that you're an amateur detective of sorts, are you not?" Homely asked.

"Golly, ah'm just a Texas boy raised with an inquisitive mind, Director. No telling what I'll ask next."

Nate suppressed a smile. Ignoring Max, Deputy Director Homely turned to Nate to complete his homily. Nate, however, interrupted. "When you mention explosives, the authorities also questioned the origin of the blast. They have not publicly reported what kind of attack it may have been. Has your office determined the nature of the explosion? Was it a bomb?"

"Much cannot be disclosed to the public, Dr. Shelley. I'm certain that you understand the delicacy of our work."

At that point, the Deputy Director's young administrative assistant knocked on the door, opened it ajar, and tapped her watch.

"As I stated, these horrific attacks—these explosions— can detonate with such force, that everything within a three-block radius is pulverized. More importantly, our FBI headquarters can neither confirm nor deny that two of our special agents are deceased. Right now, this whole case is a matter of national security." Homely stood from behind his desk, indicating the meeting was over.

"Before we're dismissed," Nate said, "could you answer one more question?"

"I'd be glad to if the law and the Constitution will permit me," Homely said.

"As you know, several months ago, my wife Dr. Miró Epstein-Shelley was kidnapped. When she reappeared, a dead man was found by her side. The Chicago field office reported the dead man was a former federal agent. But your office has failed to confirm this. Can you explain why?"

"First, I'm saddened by the ordeal your family must have endured. As for the identity of the dead man, Dr. Shelley, this is the first I hear of this. It's an ongoing investigation, and it's always better not to report premature findings. I do promise to check on this. Should I confirm anything, I'll let you know."

"I'm sure you will," Nate said. "Thank you for your time, Director."

Nate noticed that Max was using a bow-legged stroll as he came out of the office complex. "What are you doing, Max?" he whispered.

"Ah just like to give people the impression that I just got off mah horse."

. . .

"You ever been to the Round Robin, Max?"

"What is it?"

Nate was hailing a cab. "It's the bar at the Willard, and I intend to have a mint julep... several of them, in fact. Please join me."

It was mid-afternoon and traffic in the capital was lighter than usual. When they arrived at the Willard, the doorman greeted both by name. Nate led Max directly to the circular oak bar. "This, my dear brother-in-law, is the Round Robin."

"Quite impressive," Max responded. "I bet more than a few deals have been made here."

An hour later, Nate was about to finish his second drink. "Are the juleps prepared to your liking?"

"Since I'm a man from the South, you probably assumed I was familiar with mint juleps, but before today I'd never tasted one," said Max. "I thoroughly approve."

"Let's have a second one, Max, and a third."

"This one will be your third. Go easy, Nate. I have a feeling these things pack a punch."

"Okay, Max, help me out. I've got countless questions, but the one that jumps out at me is why Diego Montemayor— or, whatever his new name might be—is still being protected by the Deputy Director of the FBI?"

"Nate, I know that we've put Dad's genealogical research on the back burner. However, let's review what he learned."

Over the next two hours, Nate and Max discussed specific pieces of information that Abraham Epstein had uncovered. All the details led to the same inevitable conclusion: Diego Montemayor's grandfather was CIA royalty. Because Rudy von Steiner was involved in the original formation of one of the most secretive organizations in the world, his descendants enjoyed broad-based immunity at all costs. Powerful dark forces inside the governing bodies of this country would ensure Diego's—aka, Rodrigo's— protection.

"One last thing before we leave DC, Max." For the next two hours, Nate described in detail the conversation he had with Inspector Sánchez.

"When he spoke of Diego going into hiding somewhere in Europe, he knew of Diego's ability to go underground. Sánchez said it would be like looking for a needle in a haystack."

Max laughed, "He certainly did escape from them last time."

"Sánchez also mentioned how Picard believed that 'American agents' were tapping all my communications, Max. In addition, he wanted to know if I trusted Ram Edmunds."

"It's obvious that Interpol knows we have some bad apples in our intelligence networks, but why would he doubt Edmunds?"

"I don't know," Nate said. "However, later that day, I got a call from Ram. He'd just spoken to Sánchez, and again, Inspector Sánchez was relaying a message from Gabriel Picard. Ram asked me if I knew anything about 'profiling'. Apparently, Picard wants to know if I'd be interested in doing some work for Interpol. They need a profiler that can pinpoint where Diego, or Rodrigo, might be."

"Nate, Sánchez said it. It would be like finding a needle in a haystack. I'm certain that Interpol has plenty of profilers in their vast network."

Nate was silent.

"You're not thinking of taking him up on the offer, are you?" Max asked.

"I'm seriously considering returning to Europe to help Interpol locate our family's nemesis," Nate said.

CHAPTER 57

Chicago, IL · April 13, 2020

OVID MASK IN PLACE, Nate Shelley caught the 7:50 Red Line train to Chicago. Although he read most of his news reports online, a feature article with a Horace Rosenfeld byline on the second page of the Chicago Tribune caught his attention. Putting on his protective vinyl gloves, he picked up the newspaper that had been left behind by a fellow passenger. The article stated that twenty-six members of Congress had been indicted for multiple federal crimes, including bribery, racketeering, and child endangerment. The article went on to name other prominent members of the technological community—identified by Rosenfeld as five prominent companies called the FAANG stocks—which were being investigated for treason and for divulging top-secret information that threatened the national security.

Upon Nate's arrival at his office on Jackson Street, Ms. Farnsworth greeted him with a fresh set of files. His patient list was returning to normal, and she reminded him of his first appointment at 9 AM.

Nate removed his mask as he sat at his desk. He picked up the phone, and he dialed Rosenfeld's number. "That was an impressive bit of investigative reporting, young man. Were these twenty-six members of Congress indicted simultaneously?"

"Dr. Shelley…"

"Oh, come on, Rosie, you can call me Nate."

"Okay, Nate, this whole thing is much bigger than what I can share over the phone. It is a monumental case that involves an incredible number of people. Many big names will be implicated."

"Rosie, are you saying there will be more politicians… national figures who might be indicted?"

"I'm certain of it," Rosenfeld said.

Emily Farnsworth knocked and entered Nate's office. She left a note on his desk, "I've got Agent Edmunds on the line."

"Rosie," Nate said, "I've got to take another call. We'll talk later."

Corsica, France · Late March, 2020

That first night in his palazzo, Rodrigo slept soundly. He woke up the following morning at 1000 hours and summoned Federico. Within ten minutes, a pot of French-press Italian roast was brought in by a uniformed brunette, who greeted him with a cheerful, "Buongiorno". She leaned over to serve his coffee, exposing a modest amount of cleavage, then quickly averted her eyes and left the room.

Still barefoot, cup in hand, Rodrigo decided to walk the grounds outside his bedroom. A rounded, freshly mown turf ended fifty yards beyond his French doors. It was bordered with tall Italian pines. The evergreens framed the same glorious scenery that he'd viewed from above just hours before. The skies were a cerulean blue with a few thin, wispy clouds in the horizon. The clouds were the color of snow in the distance.

As Rodrigo took his first sip of coffee, Estevan, also barefoot, joined him. He was wearing the loose black linen clothing that he normally used for his tai chi workouts. Slowly and deliberately, he signed for Rodrigo, *'Do not interrupt your breathing... breathe deeply and naturally... but now focus your attention on your bodily sensations.'*

"Not a bad idea, my friend. Since leaving Chicago, I have been away from our qigong. Perhaps that is the reason that I've been unable to relax the mind."

With a smile, Estevan nodded. He modeled the 'energy work' familiar to Rodrigo by dedicating two or three minutes to gentle breathing and slowly added a sequence of movements which emphasized a straight spine, abdominal breathing, and some *tuishou*, or the pushing of hands. By now, Rodrigo had placed his coffee mug on a nearby birdbath and joined Estevan in the slow, small circular movements.

After ten minutes, Rodrigo addressed Estevan as he went through his range of motions through his center of gravity, "Let's add 'white crane spreads its wings'."

Estevan shook his head without missing a beat.

"Don't you think I'm ready?" Rodrigo asked.

Again, Estevan shook his head.

Rodrigo proceeded anyway and, as he attempted the move, he rotated his forearm and screamed out in pain. Estevan turned toward the French doors, and, with a nod of his head, summoned the uniformed brunette. She rushed out with fresh bandages and petroleum jelly to attend to Rodrigo's healing forearm. Still bright pink, Rodrigo's skin was healing well, but his range of motion was limited. Estevan signed for Rodrigo, '*You need to heed my warnings.*'

Rodrigo acknowledged his mistake. Smiling widely, he asked the young Italian beauty, "Could you bring me a cup of fresh coffee?"

"Sì," is all she said. She turned and walked away. Within minutes she was back, bearing a steaming cup of the rich brew.

Though Estevan had returned to his 'control center', the anteroom to Rodrigo's bedroom, Rodrigo extended his regimen of deep, gentle breathing. He continued his stroll on the soft carpeting of grass, but when he stopped between the tallest pines, he gasped. Scanning the horizon, he breathed the fresh air and once again took in the view of the Mediterranean. It brought tears to his eyes. *If only Yael were here to enjoy it with me.*

Chicago, IL · April 13, 2020

After ending his call with Rosie, Nate answered Ram Edmunds' call. "Sorry to keep you waiting, Agent Edmunds."

"Every time we talk, Nate, I need to remind you we're on a first-name basis. Now, once and for all, stop calling me Agent Edmunds."

"Sorry, it's force of habit, but I promise not to forget from now on," Nate said with a smile. "Do you have any updates, Ram?"

"Two, actually. The first update is one that I could not share with you previously. As we learned, Detective Finn was in cahoots with Rodrigo, or Diego I should say. Although I suspected him from early on, I could not share that information with you since I had no proof."

"Hmm," Nate said. "What tipped you off?"

"I don't know if you remember seeing a yellow umbrella in Miró's hotel room at the Orrington."

"I do, as a matter of fact. It was standing on a corner when we showed up," Nate said.

"When Finn told me that 'the Feds' had taken over the investigation, I visited the Evanston PD, flashed my FBI badge, and asked to see the evidence from the case. Well, when I reviewed the evidence locker, since Finn was the evidence custodian, he'd checked out an umbrella claiming it had to go to the crime lab. That umbrella never made it to the lab nor was it returned to the evidence storage."

"So, if he removed it, how did you learn of its existence?" Nate asked.

"First, I knew that it was listed in the original booking form which itemizes every item taken from a crime scene. Secondly, Tío Dante mentioned it in his deposition. When Tío was killed, it confirmed my suspicion that Finn was somehow connected."

"From the start, we got a runaround from him, but we attributed his delays to incompetence," Nate said. "If we'd known..."

"Which brings me to the second update," Edmunds said. "We finally determined what killed Tío Dante. It was not a drone attack, as many of us suspected, nor was it a car bomb."

"What was it, then?"

"It was a BCB, Nate."

"A what? I've never heard of a BCB."

"It's a body cavity bomb. This type of weapon has been used recently by jihadists. It's an explosive device that is surgically implanted in the body of a suicide attacker, usually a religious fanatic. We can safely say that the driver of Tío's van was the suicide bomber."

"That's unbelievable. Why hadn't we heard?" Nate asked.

"That's just it. My superiors are directing me not to disclose our findings. They fear that absolute certainty has not been established."

"What unadulterated hogwash," Nate said.

"I agree. Although such an explosion kills the suicidal bomber by obliterating him instantaneously, the DNA is splattered in all directions. And, the driver's DNA, as well as Tío's, was identified."

"So, help me understand, Ram. How did you determine that it was a BCB?"

"We determined that Diego Montemayor, using an alias, had developed such explosives for the jihadists in Yemen. The surgeon used by Diego turned himself in, and he's singing like a canary," Edmunds said.

"And he identified the poor soul on whom he performed the operation?"

"This Dr. Wu, the surgeon, doesn't think the man was a volunteer... nor a martyr. It was one of Diego's lieutenants, a Chicago man by the name of Pedro Rosales. Wu thinks Diego forced him to submit to the bomb's implantation... in his chest cavity."

"Ah, one of the twins who kidnapped my daughter and mother-in-law," Nate said.

"That's exactly right."

"Well, you'll have to join us all for dinner soon, Ram, because I doubt that I have the stomach to share all this with my family," Nate said.

"That sounds good," Edmunds said. "Anyway, I still need to deliver something to you and Miró."

Corsica, France · April 6, 2020

Rodrigo had returned to his regular morning routine. Led by Estevan, Rodrigo now, more wisely, resumed his regimen by limiting it to qigong, which involves coordinated movement, breathing and awareness primarily for health and meditation. In qigong, the flow of qi is held at a certain point for a moment to aid the opening and cleansing of the body's channels of energy. Gradually, Estevan introduced tai chi, in which the flow of qi, or life energy, is continuous, which allows the development of greater power for use in combat.

Following early morning sessions, Rodrigo had resumed his normal diet of a healthy breakfast accompanied with plenty of rich Italian coffee. The recovery from his second-degree burns had been remarkable, especially since resuming a more normal schedule. He had become very fond of his Corsican assistants, including Isabella, the young brunette who was trying her best to learn English, which Rodrigo found himself using more regularly.

"I believe it is time that we inform the staff that my real name is Diego Montemayor, not Rodrigo," Diego said. "Do you think we can trust them?"

'*Of course,*' Estevan signed. '*They are fully devoted to you, Diego.*'

"Let's do it. After we inform all of them, I want to sit down with you in order to come up with our revised plan for the Shelleys. I cannot tolerate my last failure, nor do I want to delay its reversal. Do you understand?"

'Before developing the plan, tell me what to do with the twins' families,' Estevan said, using his notepad.

"Give them the deeds to the Winnetka properties and deposit the amount that I mentioned to you earlier," Diego said.

'*The deposit has been made. It will take care of their needs and the kids' education,*' Estevan said by signing. '*Do you want to set up a trust for the kids?*'

"Go ahead... and give *The Black Pearl* to a museum," Diego said. "Also, for dinner, tell Federico to prepare some veal scaloppini with plenty of lemon and sesame. Please join me for dinner, so that we can come up with some general ideas for our final plan for the Shelleys."

Before dinner, Rodrigo summoned Estevan so that he could pick out a bottle of wine for dinner. Although Estevan suggested that Federico was perfectly capable of pairing the wine, Rodrigo insisted that Estevan make the choice.

That night, Estevan surprised Diego with a couple of American pinot noirs from Willamette Valley. *'I found two cases in your cellar,'* Estevan signed. *'Although you haven't tasted it before, you'll be pleased.'*

Diego was pleasantly surprised, and Federico, after skeptically trying a bottle on his own, agreed that it was a perfect choice for his scaloppini. He complimented Estevan on his choice.

Diego informed Federico that he and Estevan would be having their cognacs in the control room that was becoming Diego's favorite office space. Though small, the anteroom served the convenient purpose of allowing Diego to call it a night after the drudgery of his administrative chores, then walk a few steps to his bedroom.

Late into the night, after brainstorming with Estevan and settling on three alternative plans, Rodrigo dismissed Estevan. He summoned Federico to ask him for a final glass of Hennessy. Federico asked Isabella to deliver the cognac. After setting the glass on his nightstand, she asked in her best English, "Will that be all?" With a wide smile, Diego dismissed her and said, "Buonanotte."

Unlike previous evenings, Diego slept fitfully. It was past two in the morning when the vision which had awakened him on the train to Marseilles, interrupted Diego's slumber.

The same snarling cur that had visited him in his dream growled more menacingly than before. His brief respite was shattered abruptly as Diego witnessed in slow motion not the snarling cur but Alessandro rushing to his bedside to deliver a message that had arrived in Estevan's digital mailbox. Was Diego awake, or was he dreaming?

Diego jumped out of bed. He was not dreaming. Alessandro was delivering the message received in Estevan's mailbox, but meant for Diego. He read on the laptop's screen a message from his only handler—a man he'd spoken to only once before.

The encrypted message simply read, 'Gachupín, I got you home safely. Now, let's part ways.'

Evanston, IL · April 14, 2020

When Nate arrived at his Evanston home that evening, Miró was waiting. She greeted him with a plain brown envelope that had been personally delivered by Ram Edmunds. The front of the envelope read, 'To Nathaniel and Miró Shelley—to be opened after my demise.'

"What did Ram say?" Nate asked.

"He said that he opened the packet a day after Tío was assassinated."

"But it looks sealed," Nate had an inquisitive look.

"He said that when he opened the larger packet, he discovered an envelope within the larger one. He said he also found instructions from Tío, which he followed. Tío wished for the inside envelope to be delivered to us unopened. So, I wanted us both to open it together," Miró said.

Nate and Miró found a brief note from Tío Dante. In the note, he asked them to forgive him for kidnapping Miró. Then in a scribbled addendum he informed them of the identity of Diego Montemayor's 'handler', the living protector of the drug kingpin—a name recognized by every person in the civilized world.

Shaken, Nate and Miró sat in their living room, speechless. Neither one said a thing. However, at that point, Nate's mind was made up. He would accept Picard's offer and join Interpol in Europe as a profiler. Unable, or unwilling, to fathom the depth of corruption in her world, Miró simply broke down in tears.

THE END